A DEADLY CONNECTION

Suddenly Ryan was suffocating. He grabbed the clipping and the slip with the phone number and dashed across the apartment. He tugged open the sliding glass door by the fireplace, walked onto the tiny wooden deck, and breathed in the thick air.

Finally, when he was steady again, he walked back inside and picked up the cordless phone. He punched in the phone number and waited for the circuits to turn over.

The phone rang twice, three times, four.

Hang up! This is crazy! Hang up!

Then it was too late. A crisp, anonymous female voice said, "Good morning, may I help you?"

No business name, no organization, just *Good morning, may I help you.*

Ryan cleared his throat. "Ah . . ."

"May I help you?"

"Department thirty," Ryan said.

"One moment."

Hang up!

But he couldn't. He looked at his mother's handwriting from seven years ago and he couldn't.

DEPARTMENT
THIRTY

DAVID KENT

POCKET **STAR** BOOKS
New York London Toronto Sydney Singapore

An *Original* Publication of POCKET BOOKS

A Pocket Star Book published by
POCKET BOOKS, a division of Simon & Schuster, Inc.
1230 Avenue of the Americas, New York, NY 10020

ISBN: 0-7434-6998-4

First Pocket Books printing July 2003

10 9 8 7 6 5 4 3 2 1

For information regarding special discounts for bulk purchases, please contact Simon & Schuster Special Sales at 1-800-456-6798 or business@simonandschuster.com

Designed by Melissa Isriprashad

Cover art by Jae Song

Printed in the U.S.A.

For Martha,
my best friend, wife,
and my breath when I had none.

ACKNOWLEDGMENTS

The following provided research assistance, for which I am deeply appreciative: Deputy United States Marshal Beth Wetmore, for her insights on federal law enforcement in general and the U.S. Marshals Service and Witness Security in particular; Darrell Tracker, attorney and expert on little-known aspects of governmental operations; John George, Ph.D., retired professor of political science at the University of Central Oklahoma, whose book *American Extremists*, co-authored with Laird Wilcox, was helpful in understanding the nature of extreme political movements; Lane Whitesell, chemist, chef, musicologist, educator, radio announcer, and book lover, for the crash course in nuclear physics; Larry Flenner of the United States Postal Service, for helping me understand the way mail is moved.

Of course, any errors of fact, and any liberties I may have taken, belong solely to me, not to these individuals or agencies.

I must also express my deepest gratitude to Mike Miller, Sami Nepa, Dave Stanton, and Judy Tillinghast. Their weekly comments, suggestions, encouragement, and occasional out-right insults were more valuable than I am able to put into words. Nancy Moore and Jane Solomon offered additional feedback, and Liza Dawson helped bring this story several steps closer to being ready for publication.

To my friends from the radio business, I love and value all of you and your friendship of many years. To my NWCC family, especially The Next Generation and Ryan Pfeiffer, thank you for helping to guide me back to where I needed to be.

A writer today cannot build a career without a good literary agent. You would not be holding this book if not for the efforts of my astounding agent, John Talbot. He took a chance on an unpublished, unknown writer from Middle America and helped shape this work. Then he saw the project through with style, professionalism, and good humor. Look carefully—you'll see his fingerprints lurking about in these pages.

My editor at Pocket Books, Kevin Smith, is that rarest of individuals—he is both easygoing and a thorough professional. He took this story to the next level and even answered my almost daily phone calls and e-mails with class and patience. It has been a joy to work with him.

Also at Pocket, I would like to thank Sarah Wright, who oversaw the actual production of this book; and copyeditor Carly Sommerstein, who did an amazing job of, among other things, making sure I didn't contradict myself. These people made this into a much better book than it would otherwise have been.

To my parents and sister, I offer my gratitude for depth of perspective and for letting me use the family typewriter whenever I wanted. I am grateful to the Watson family for support of many kinds as well. To Martha, Ben, Will, and Sam, thank you for not giving up. You are all I could have hoped for and more, and I thank God every day that we are a family.

David Kent
Oklahoma City, Oklahoma

DEPARTMENT
THIRTY

PROLOGUE

RYAN ELDER KNEW SOMETHING WAS WRONG THE MINUTE he stepped off the plane and saw his mother standing in the terminal.

She hated anything to do with flying and avoided airports with a childlike fear. This was Ryan's third year away at college and she'd never once come to the airport to see him off, nor to pick him up. That task always fell to his father.

Until now.

It was the day before Thanksgiving, the busiest travel day of the year, and people were elbowing their way quickly through Oklahoma City's Will Rogers World Airport. Even the name of the airport made his mother nervous—Ryan wished he had a dollar for every time she'd pointed out the folly in having an airport named after a man who'd died in a plane crash.

Ryan clutched his carry-on and folded his coat over his arm. Why is she here? he asked himself, then shrugged his way into the main corridor of the terminal.

"Tell me," he said.

"Tell you what?" his mother said, a little too quickly.

He looked down at her, nearly a foot shorter, with her fine, handsome Slavic face: the olive complexion, the still raven black hair, the cobalt eyes. Anna Elder was a tiny woman and her frame looked as insubstantial as melting snow, with the exception of her hands. Those hands, with their long tapering fingers and nails groomed with exceptional care. Ryan noticed the fingers of her left hand were manipulating the air at her side, as if searching for just the right notes on an imaginary violin.

But her eyes were everywhere—on the terminal floor,

the windows, the signs overhead. Everywhere but on Ryan.

"You two aren't very subtle," Ryan said. "Did someone die?"

"If someone died, don't you think we'd tell you?" Frank Elder said, taking Ryan's carry-on.

His father and he were the same height and build—six-three and slender—and had the same face, thirty-five years apart: smooth and symmetrical, ruled by a long, sharp nose. The hair and eyes were the same too, light brown on both counts. The only differences were the creases on Frank Elder's face and the fact that his brown hair was quickly surrendering to the gray, though Ryan had lately begun to discover a few gray threads of his own.

Frank clasped Ryan's shoulder for a moment—a strange, uncharacteristic gesture—as they moved through the airport. God, he looks old, Ryan thought.

"Well, you're not telling me a damn thing, so I don't know," Ryan said.

The eyes—all over the place. Looking for something? Ryan wondered.

"Are you sure—" he said.

Anna sighed. "A mother wants to see her son come into town." She shrugged, though it looked more to Ryan like she was trying to hunch into herself. "It's time I got over this silly thing with airports, yes?"

Her accent had thickened. Most of the time, little of her native Czech language could be heard in her voice—only general American dialect, with a dollop of an Oklahoma drawl. But when she was worried or angry, the Czech asserted itself with a fury.

They threaded their way out the front door of the terminal into Oklahoma November: fifty degrees, gray skies, and wind, always the wind. When Ryan had left L.A. that morning, it had been sunny and twenty degrees warmer. He shivered and tugged down the sleeves of his UCLA sweatshirt.

"Aliens," Ryan said suddenly.

His parents both stopped and looked at him.

"Remember *Invasion of the Body Snatchers*, where the aliens took over people's bodies but you couldn't tell just by look-ing at them? I'm thinking that's what's happened to you two."

"Ryan—" Frank said.

"Or try this one—it's something in the water. Some of those big hog farms up in the Panhandle dumped a bunch of sludge in the river and it came right downstream, got into the water supply, and presto! The Elders turn into two dif-ferent people!"

Ryan grinned at them, then his face froze. Neither of them laughed. They didn't even smile.

Throughout the half-hour drive home, his parents sat as still and quiet as mourners at a funeral in an unfamiliar church. They didn't talk about Ryan's classes or his father's job or his mother's students. They watched street signs and listened to muted classical music on the car radio, until his father pulled the car into their unobtrusive subdivision on an unobtrusive street in the suburb of Edmond.

As they got out of the car, Ryan looked at his mother. She was ghostly pale, disconcerting on someone with her com-plexion.

"For God's sake, you two," he said. "Talk to me. This is crazy. First Mom shows up at the airport for the first time in recorded history and now no one will say anything. If you're trying to get my attention, you've certainly got it. Just tell me what's up."

His mother took his arm at the front door of the house. A gust of wind kicked up, swirling leaves at their feet. A bird called somewhere over the back fence. Ryan and Anna both looked toward the sound. They shared an extraordinary sense of hearing.

"Grackle," Ryan said.

"Just one," Anna said. "He's been around for a few days. But just the one."

Ryan shook his head. "Too weird. Have you started the goulash?" His mother's authentic Czech goulash was a Thanks-giving Eve tradition.

Anna waited, her head cocked as if she were waiting for

the grackle to call again. "Can you believe it?" she said. "A single grackle in November."

Ryan turned toward her. Her eyes were focused up and away from him, as if he weren't there, as if she were seeing something other than gray autumn sky and the ordinary roof of their ordinary house. Frank, standing a few steps away, was statuelike.

Almost unconsciously, Ryan began digging at the cuticle of his left thumb with his index finger. The back of his neck started to feel hot.

These are not my parents, he thought with startling clarity.

"Mom? Mom, did you hear me? Are you—"

"Anna," his father said, almost whispering.

Anna turned her head slowly, first to Frank, then to Ryan. "Goulash."

"Remember?" Ryan said.

Anna stared at him, empty-eyed. Ryan took her hand and squeezed.

"I wonder where that grackle went," his mother said, then untwined her hand from his.

"Mom—"

Anna shook her head and blinked several times. When she looked at Ryan again, her eyes were more alive, some of the old animation coming back to her face. "Oh . . . the goulash. You know, you won't believe this, Ryan, but I ran out of paprika. Maybe you could run to the store and get some. Frank, give him some money. Take my car."

"What? But I—"

Then his father was shoving a twenty-dollar bill at him, his father who was so tight fisted that he never carried cash. "I'll take your bag in," Frank said.

"Go on," Anna said. "If you want to help me make it when you get back, we'll get started."

"Okay." He took the coat from his father, still in a haze of confusion. "Maybe when I get back, we can start all over again and you can tell me what this is all about."

Frank flinched as if he'd been poked in the ribs with a sharp knife.

Ryan raised the garage door and unlocked his mother's car, a no-nonsense black Taurus, three years old. He climbed in and started the engine, then felt a tapping on the glass.

He rolled down the window and his mother leaned in. He caught her scent, soap and shampoo and the vaguest bit of the White Shoulders she always wore. It was the smell of *her*, ever since he was a small child. For a moment he was ten years old instead of twenty.

She leaned over him and whispered, "Remember these eyes."

"What?" Ryan said. "What are you talking about? Mom?"

His mother pulled slowly away from him. Ryan's head swiveled as if it were being pulled along a track. He met her eyes, so utterly deep and so blue, striking under the black hair. He held her gaze for a long, silent moment, until he knew she wasn't going to say anything else.

Ryan backed the car out of the garage and into the street.

He drove down Santa Fe Avenue to Danforth Road, wading through one-lane traffic. At Danforth, he turned left and passed what seemed like acres of construction equipment on both sides. Bulldozers, earth movers, cranes—now all quiet, lined up like dinosaur carcasses. Orange and white markers closed off parts of the street. Mounds of brick-red Oklahoma earth rose phoenixlike from the ground. He'd never thought he would miss that red clay, but now that he'd been away from it, he found that he did.

Fifteen minutes later, standing in line with a tiny container of gourmet paprika in his hand, he heard a thump, then another, then another. Heads turned toward the door of the supermarket.

"Explosion," said the elderly man behind him. "That's what that was."

Ryan paid for the paprika, got his change, and ran to the parking lot. People were gathering into little groups, pointing west. Back toward Santa Fe Avenue, a mile away.

Tendrils of thick black smoke thundered into the gray sky, then were sucked into the clouds. He thought he saw flames.

Sirens sounded from far away. Horns honked. He heard a single shout.

A slow, stinging burn started in Ryan's stomach. His hands began to shake. He dropped the car keys twice before getting his mother's car onto the road. He was halfway to Santa Fe when the traffic began to back up. Now he could see the flames, close to the road, the smoke drifting like a homeless person across the orange and white construction markers.

Traffic came to a standstill. He got out of the car, still clutching the white plastic grocery sack with the paprika. The driver of the pickup truck ahead of him was also standing in the road.

"What happened?" Ryan said.

The man pushed his Edmond Memorial H.S. cap back on his head. "Someone plowed into one of those bulldozers sitting there by the side of the road. Then, boom! Must have hit a gas tank."

Ryan began to run along Danforth. Six cars farther down, he began to feel the heat from the fire. Three more cars and he saw the police blockade, half a dozen officers in the street, two fire units, an ambulance.

"What happened?" he asked an officer.

"Get back to your car, young man," the officer said.

"But I—"

"You'll be safer in your car. Go on, now."

Ryan shouldered past him.

"Hey!" the cop yelled.

Ryan broke into a run again. Now the fire was making him sweat. Gasoline filled the air, along with the smell of burning meat.

He slipped and fell into a puddle of water by the shoulder of the road. He could see it: the hulking remains of a car, its nose smashed into a bulldozer, the flames consuming both and spreading to the other construction equipment. Even the red mound of earth he'd noticed before was on fire.

Then, voices. A man's, high-pitched, excited: " . . . and I

came out of the 7-Eleven, and they'd pulled out, pointed northbound, then they sort of angled the car, and . . . and they never stopped. Just floored it, and . . ."

Ryan stepped closer. He recognized the voice. *There!* On the far side of the intersection, talking to a knot of police officers, was Dean Yorkton, his parents' nearest neighbor. He was some sort of an engineer, a pudgy, aging bachelor. Ryan remembered he had gadgets all around his house. Ryan moved closer. Yorkton was looking around wildly— then his eyes found Ryan. He pointed. His hand went to his mouth.

The officers started toward Ryan. First at a walk, then a jog.

"No," Ryan said.

He heard Yorkton's voice, talking to someone else: "They never slowed down, took that bump and just plowed straight ahead. I'd just come out of the 7-Eleven. I just don't know . . . I talked to them both just this morning. . . ."

The officers were nearly upon him. Thirty yards, twenty.

Ryan spun away, back toward the fire.

"Ryan Elder!"

He ignored the voice and stepped back toward the flames.

"Wait a minute, son! Don't go there. . . ."

He jogged around the side of the fire, until he was staring at the back of the car. A firefighter in full protective gear grabbed his arm. "Get back!" he shouted through his face mask.

Ryan wrenched his arm free, skittering around the other side. He felt his face blistering.

He heard Dean Yorkton's voice, farther away, but as clear to Ryan as if it had come through Bose stereo speakers: " . . . just looked crazy, I tell you. Eerie, weird . . ."

Ryan chewed on his knuckles. The flames were working their way slowly toward the rear of the car. He blinked, his eyes stinging. He caught a flash of color: there, on the bumper, was the bright blue-and-yellow sticker, just beginning to melt: ASSOCIATED MUTUAL INSURANCE—SERVICE AND INTEGRITY!

His father's company.

Ryan ran around the burning car until he was even with the passenger door. The footsteps behind him intensified, more in number and faster than before.

"Ryan Elder!"

His hair felt singed. So did his mind. His heart thrummed in his ears.

He opened his eyes wide and finally saw the two charred husks in the front seats of Frank Elder's car.

Ryan screamed as the two firefighters and two police officers tackled him around the waist and began to drag him away from the fire. He screamed until he swallowed smoke and his lungs began to feel as though they too were on fire.

He barely noticed the oxygen mask when they slipped it over his face. He didn't hear their questions. He didn't notice Dean Yorkton putting his arm around him. He didn't even notice his friend Jeff Majors, also home from college for Thanksgiving, running toward him half an hour later.

He saw, smelled, tasted, felt nothing but the smoke. He finally leaned against the side of the ambulance, realizing his hand ached. He looked down and saw why. He was still clutching the grocery sack with the tiny container of paprika in it. Spice for a meal that would never happen.

Ryan put his head between his legs and vomited.

At the police station, his senses gave out one at a time, all except his hearing, that exquisite sense he'd inherited from his mother. He caught snippets of several conversations:

". . . ruled as a suicide . . ."

". . . no other living family . . ."

". . . he can sleep at our house . . ."

". . . acting strangely . . ."

". . . waited until the boy came home from college to do it . . ."

". . . such good people. You just never. . . ."

There was a crush of people—police, fire department

investigators, his friend Jeff, Jeff's father, and Frank Elder's old friend and attorney Jack Coleridge, a man Ryan had known all his life. People touched his shoulder, people gave him Styrofoam cups of water, an EMT took his vital signs. Someone mumbled something about shock. "No shit," someone else mumbled.

An hour passed. Then two and three and four. He answered a few questions. Finally Jack Coleridge steered him outside. It was already dark, the air was cold, and the wind had decided to be brutal. Coleridge shook his hand and said in a shaky voice that he'd take care of everything.

Ryan was suddenly, acutely aware of two things: the fragrance of White Shoulders as his mother had leaned in the window of the Taurus back in the garage; and the words she'd whispered in his ear before he drove off to buy paprika. *Remember these eyes*, she'd said.

Then Jeff Majors was at his side, saying something about spending the night at his house. Ryan couldn't think anymore, and he let Jeff lead him through the cold wind toward his car.

SEVEN YEARS LATER

1

RYAN MOVED IN FOR THE KILL.

He leaned in so close he could inhale the man's breath. It smelled like he'd eaten peppers for breakfast. And now there was another smell—fear. The man had been caught and he knew it.

The January sun was full and warm and it felt wrong. Wrong that it should already be sixty degrees at nine in the morning in mid-January. But then, Ryan had spent seven years living in places like Maryland, Vermont, Ohio, and Wyoming, places that had winters. Here on Florida's Gulf Coast, it was perpetually spring, a shock to his system after these last few years. All his winter clothes were still packed away in boxes. Then again, he reminded himself, so was most of the rest of his life as well.

His prey was standing on a street corner in front of the Pensacola Chamber of Commerce building. The waters of Pensacola Bay lapped at the shore, a few hundred yards from the other side of the Gulf Beach Highway. He heard the water at the point where it made landfall and he tasted the air: wet and thick, like a washcloth that hadn't been properly wrung out.

Ryan looked around him—the morning rush traffic had abated and Pensacola was settling into the daytime rhythms of any medium-size city. To his left was one TV crew, from across the bay in Mobile. To his right were a couple of print journalists, one from the daily paper and one from the student paper at the university. But it was Ryan's show—Ryan's story—and all of them knew it.

"So where did the money go?" he asked. He inched the

microphone a little closer to the man's face and checked the batteries in the cassette recorder.

The man rubbed a finger under his nose. His name was Kirk Stillman and he was in his late forties, tan and lean, wearing a green golf shirt and khakis. His eyes matched his shirt and they never looked at Ryan, instead watching the video camera the whole time.

"I don't understand the question," he said.

"It's very clear," Ryan said. "The highway project was completed three months ago. Your office sent out a press release about how it came in ahead of schedule and under budget. Half a million dollars under budget. That's a pretty good savings—"

"Damn straight it is." Stillman smiled for the camera and nodded. "We work hard."

"I'm sure you do. But state law says that when a contractor using state-appropriated funds completes the project under budget, the excess is returned to the Department of Transportation within sixty days. The department says they haven't received a dime from you. Where's the half-million dollars?"

Stillman brushed his nose again, then again. "Look, if we could just turn off the cameras and the tape recorders, we can work this out."

"No, sir, this is an on-the-record interview," Ryan said. "You said that at the beginning and we have your consent on tape."

Stillman reddened, his tan deepening. "Look, I don't have to justify—"

"I'm sorry, but you do, sir. Your company is a contractor to the state, and that means the taxpayers of Florida paid for this project. Just answer the question. Where is that money?"

Stillman put a hand in his pocket, jingling keys. He whistled a couple of tuneless notes under his breath. Finally he met Ryan's eyes. "What did you say your name was, son?"

"Ryan Elder, WPSC Radio."

"Okay, Ryan Elder, WPSC Radio. You haven't been in town very long, have you?"

"I don't see what that has to do with—"

"You see, if you understood a little bit more about our community, you just might—"

"Condone fraud? Corruption? Graft? I don't think so, Mr. Stillman."

Stillman took a step forward. Ryan held his ground, keeping the microphone close. Stillman batted it away. "Get that goddamn thing out of my face!" He turned to the TV crew. "You! Turn that off."

Ryan pushed the microphone up again. "Didn't you recently take an extended trip to Europe, Mr. Stillman? Didn't you spend some time in Switzerland? Your travel agent's records show—"

"This is over!" Stillman shouted. "I've had it! I don't have to put up with this bullshit!" The man turned on his heel and stalked off down the street.

When he was out of view, the TV reporter, a slim, handsome black man a few years older than Ryan, said, "Whoa, Elder. You stuck it to him."

Ryan watched the direction Stillman had gone. "Yeah, well, he deserved to be stuck." He turned off his tape recorder and headed for his car.

The rush of bringing in a big story was still working on him and he had to check his speed several times on the drive back to the station. His heart thrumming, Tori Amos on the stereo, he tapped out a steady rhythm against the steering wheel with his pen. He hoped the editing room was available immediately. He was already thinking about how to frame the story. Should he open with his own introduction or go straight to Stillman's evasiveness?

Even after working steadily in the field for seven years, Ryan was still amazed at radio news's power to excite him. In fact, it was damn near the *only* thing that could excite him. Radio didn't have to rely on the same crutches that television and print journalism did. TV had its videotape and print had the capacity for rereading, but radio—the challenge was to tell the story using sound alone. He would use his voice,

Stillman's voice, and the "natural" sounds in the background, nothing more or less than that. It was just Ryan, the sounds he could create, and the audience, with nothing standing between them but their own senses.

After all the interviews were over, the sound bites gathered, then Ryan would go alone into an editing room to create the story, to mold it into an entity all its own, to communicate both fact and feeling to his listeners. That solitary time, that listening to all the threads of the story as they came together, was even more of an emotional high than getting into the faces of people like Kirk Stillman. And the intensity of the concentration, getting every element of the production just right, kept his mind from wandering into its own dark, solitary places.

The perfect environment for me, Ryan thought, as he pulled into the parking lot of WPSC, in a long, low building near the Pensacola Naval Air Station.

At the front of the building, a mountain of a man stood in the doorway, blocking him. Earl Penders was the general manager of the station, a former linebacker and local sports hero. He was in his fifties, with flesh to spare, wore ill-fitting suits, and always talked too loud, but he was a chamber of commerce regular and favorite luncheon speaker with local civic groups.

"You're back early," he said, his voice booming halfway across the parking lot.

"It didn't take long," Ryan said. "Stillman's so crooked he should run for Congress. It's going to be one hell of a story, Earl."

Penders leaned against the doorway, making no move to step aside. "Say, Ryan, remember when you came on board here, you told me how glad you were this was a locally owned station, not part of some big conglomerate?"

"Sure, I remember."

"You know Mr. Turner, don't you? Joseph Turner, who owns one half of the station?"

"I met him at the Christmas party, Earl. What's this about?"

"Mr. Turner has a sister, Elizabeth. Fine woman, contributes a lot of money to charity in the city. They named a whole wing of the hospital after her. You remember, the children's cancer center."

"And?"

"Well, Liz Turner is one of these very modern, independent women. Never took her husband's last name, you know."

Ryan's eyes widened.

"Yup. She's married to Kirk Stillman. Stillman called his wife, she called her brother, and he called me."

"You're joking," Ryan said. "That's so . . . so small-town."

"We're a small town at heart. Most cities are, come to think of it. You'll get a month's severance pay." Penders stepped aside and bent over, wheezing. He picked up a cardboard box and handed it to Ryan. "We took the liberty of cleaning out your desk."

"But the story. You can't just kill this story! It's half a million dollars, Earl. Doesn't that mean anything to you?"

"Doesn't matter. The story's dead. Embalm it, say a prayer over it, and bury it. And let me give you a little advice, Ryan. You're a smart kid with great instincts. Learn a little judgment and you'll go far in this business."

Ryan dropped the cardboard box on the concrete. The thud was as loud as a gunshot to him. "Don't do this, Earl. Come on, show some backbone."

Penders shifted his bulk in the doorway. "Got plenty of backbone, kid. I've also got five kids to feed and a business to run. Now give me your key and your recorder."

"You bastard, you can't do this!"

Penders's jowls shook. "Yes, I can. Now turn over the station property and get out of here before I call the cops and have them arrest your sorry ass for trespassing."

White with rage, Ryan took out his ring of keys, pulled one off, and put it in Penders's meaty hand. He very slowly unhooked the portable tape recorder from his belt, took a couple of steps back, cocked his arm, and flung the lightweight tape machine at the building. It shattered against the S in the WPSC sign and the pieces crumbled to the ground like matchsticks.

"Take it out of my last check," Ryan said, turned around, and walked to his car.

As Ryan pulled his five-year-old Toyota Corolla onto the Gulf Beach Highway and pointed it east, back toward the heart of Pensacola, a dark blue Ford Escort with a rental sticker on the window pulled in behind him and followed, staying a careful three car lengths behind. It accelerated when Ryan did, slowed when he slowed, and when Ryan signaled to exit near his apartment complex, the Escort did the same. Ryan didn't notice.

2

FIRED AGAIN, RYAN THOUGHT AS HE CLIMBED THE STEPS to his apartment.

It was in a sprawling complex near the bay, but just far enough away that there was no view. It had been built in the eighties and was populated mostly by transitory military personnel from the naval base and young single professionals who couldn't yet afford to purchase a home.

At the top of the wrought-iron stairway, he fumbled out his key and peeked into his mailbox, one in a line of six on the second-story landing. He pulled out a wad that included bills, magazines, and the usual junk. He hadn't checked the mail in three days, so it had piled up. He tucked the mail under his chin and, holding the cardboard box from WPSC under his other arm, unlocked his apartment door.

Inside, he dumped the box on the floor, crossed to the dining area, and threw the collected mail onto the glass-topped table. The kitchen was tiled, with all the standard apartment amenities—almond-colored refrigerator and dishwasher, faux wood cabinetry, fluorescent lighting. Ryan opened the refrigerator and said, "Shit."

He'd slept at the radio station again last night, only com-

ing home long enough to shower and dress before the interview with Kirk Stillman. He'd forgotten to buy groceries and
the only things in the refrigerator were three cans of Pepsi,
one already open, a package of American cheese, half a jar of
extra-hot salsa, and a pizza box holding two pieces of
Domino's pepperoni/sausage/jalapeño.

Ryan took one of the Pepsis and slammed the door.
"Shit," he said again, and went back to the dining room.

Fired again.

The last time had been in Dayton, Ohio, seven months
ago. He'd called the radio station's news director a stupid
prick to his face and told him he didn't have the slightest
notion of news judgment. Before that it had been Montpe-
lier, Vermont, low ratings combined with his "bad attitude."
In Laramie, Wyoming, it was budget cuts. Prior to that he'd
been in the tiny town of Frostburg, Maryland, the only job
from which he hadn't been fired. He'd been a one-person
news department there, the first real job he had after . . .

After Oklahoma. Ten days after his parents' funeral, he
notified UCLA he wouldn't be coming back, straightened out
the estate with his father's attorney, Jack Coleridge, and drove
east as the sun set behind him.

Now he'd have to get together his résumé and his tapes
again and start looking for work, thanks to crooks like Kirk
Stillman and idiots like Earl Penders. He downed half the
Pepsi and banged it on the table. A little sloshed out of the
can, dripped off the table, and onto Ryan's pants.

He jerked his knee against the bottom of the table, which
only spilled more of the drink and sent his mail flying.
"Dammit," he muttered, then threw the Pepsi halfway across
the room, where it bounced off the brick of the fireplace he'd
never used.

Let them take it out of my deposit, he thought, as he bent
and started to pick up the scattered mail: phone bill, electric
bill, *Newsweek*, *U.S. News and World Report*, three credit card
applications, and a booklet of pizza coupons.

He picked up the magazines and a sliver of white fell out
onto the floor. He picked it up, holding it by one corner, a

single business-size envelope with a green strip attached to the right side.

A certified letter.

What the hell?

The envelope was battered, with what looked like a dirty footprint squarely across the face of it. The lower right corner was bent backward. A variety of postal stamps covered the front and back: *Not at This Address; Return to Sender; Undeliverable; Sender Not Known.* He saw three postmarks: Oklahoma City, Los Angeles, Oklahoma City again. There was no return address.

The address was on a typed yellow label that had been slapped haphazardly on the envelope. It was curled upward, giving it a slightly sneering, sinister look. Ryan pulled it off. Underneath was another yellow label with his Ohio address. He peeled that one away and felt his heart sink like a stone into his gut.

The original address, the one this letter had first been intended for, was his dorm room at UCLA.

The handwriting was his mother's.

Across the street from the apartment complex, the Whispering Man sat in his rental car in the parking lot of a strip mall and watched the complex's entrance. He rolled down his window and gulped the salty air. He wasn't accustomed to it and the mere act of breathing it made a lump rise in his throat.

Patience, he told himself. He had a hunch his business in Florida would be finished quickly. The son of Frank and Anna Elder would be leaving soon, and the Whispering Man thought he knew where he would be going.

And then the man's questions would be answered. He would know what was in the letter. The boy would tell him. Ryan Elder would *beg* to tell him, and then he would finish the business he'd started a long time ago.

He could wait a little longer. He didn't mind. The Whispering Man was good at waiting.

• • •

Ryan was in a bubble, as if a sheath of plastic had enveloped him. Nothing existed outside it. Nothing existed at all, except for the letter. Not the Pepsi can whose contents were soaking into his carpet across the apartment, not the traffic outside, not Pensacola Bay or WPSC or crooked Kirk Stillman and his wife or spineless Earl Penders. There was only this sliver of white paper in his hand.

There was no question that the handwriting belonged to Anna Elder. He'd thought it odd, even as a child, that such clunky, blocky writing came from those beautiful, artistic hands that made such exquisite music. But they could never write worth a damn. *Oh, well,* Anna would laugh in those days. *These hands were made for playing Mozart and Dvorak and Paganini, not for scribbling.*

Ryan didn't tremble, didn't swallow convulsively, didn't stamp his feet. He simply sat and looked at the letter. He could barely make out the original postmark, but it was there. He held it up to the light of the fake chandelier above the dining room table.

It had been mailed the day before. . . .

The day before he came home for Thanksgiving. The day before the world exploded and everything in it changed.

Ryan let the letter flit down to the tabletop. He saw instantly what had happened. His mother had mailed this to his dorm in Los Angeles, but he'd never gone back there. When it arrived back in Oklahoma, the sender was dead and Ryan was gone from there too. So it had been working its way through the postal system for seven years. He hadn't stayed in any one place too long during that time, grinding through small- and medium-market radio stations, and sometimes forgetting to fill out change-of-address cards when he moved to a new city.

And here it was, on the day he'd been fired from another job.

He picked it up again and ran his hand along the ridge of the envelope's flap. There wasn't much inside, maybe a sheet or two. He held it up to the light again—it looked like newspaper inside.

He took the letter into the kitchen, popped open the lid of the trash can, and stood there. Ryan tightened his grip on the edge of the letter. He squeezed his eyes closed, then opened them wide. He finally ripped open the envelope and shook two pieces of paper onto the kitchen counter. He let the envelope flutter to the floor.

One thing was certain—this was no suicide note.

He was right about the newspaper, though. It was a clipping from the Oklahoma City daily newspaper, no date visible. The article was a review of a performance by the Oklahoma City Philharmonic.

Ryan wrinkled his nose as if he'd smelled sour milk. What was this all about?

He turned the clipping over. The back of it was advertising, part of an ad for a furniture store, part of one for a car dealer. No, it had been deliberately cut out for the orchestra review. Ryan read through it. There was nothing the least bit unusual, no penciled messages on the edge, no highlighted words or phrases. Just a positive review of the hometown orchestra.

He thought of standing in the airport, of his mother saying, *Tell you what?*

But the day before that, she'd mailed him this newspaper clipping.

Ryan's head started to throb as he put the clipping back on the kitchen counter. The second slip of paper was smaller, a tiny rectangular strip folded and then carefully torn from a sheet of standard white copy paper, the kind bought in five hundred-page reams at any office supply store. Medium thickness. White. Ordinary.

Ryan turned it over. Written on it in his mother's blocky hand was a phone number. Area code 405, then the seven-digit number. Beneath the number was scrawled *Department 30.*

He ran his hands over the printing, as if he could absorb some of his mother's essence through the black ink. For a moment he was back in the garage, with its aromas of motor oil and lumber and the heavy, sweet smell of Oklahoma wind through the open door. Then his mother, with her scent of White Shoulders, was leaning toward him through the open car window. . . .

And then he was even further back, lying face down on his bed at home, doing his best not to cry. Because he was seventeen and seventeen-year-old boys don't cry. The room mocked him—the UCLA pennant, the CD collection with its racks of U2 and Pearl Jam and Michael Hedges, the autographed photo—*To Ryan, I know I'll be hearing your voice again*—of his radio idol, NPR's Bob Edwards. None of it mattered anymore. And there was a knocking, a steady tap on the bedroom door.

Go away, Mom. I want to be alone.

Like it or not, I'm coming in, Ryan.

His mother was in the room, that fragrance trailing her wherever she went. She sat on the edge of the bed and said nothing until Ryan said, "I'm not going, Mom. Forget UCLA. I'm staying here. Allison said that if I stay in Oklahoma and go to OU or OSU or even Central, that it's okay. She won't—"

"Ryan."

He looked up at her. Behind her, on the wall, Bob Edwards stared at him expectantly.

"Ryan, all you've ever wanted is to be in radio news. UCLA has the program you want, you've been accepted. You have to follow your heart—"

"My heart? My *heart*? Oh, that's cute, Mom, thanks a whole lot. Allison dumped me. Just because I want to do something different than everyone else, she dumped me! I thought she understood—" Crying for real now, he flopped back onto the bed. "I thought she understood."

"I know," his mother said. "But you're going to have to make a choice. You can't expect others to be true to you if you're not true to yourself. And maybe Allison's the one with the problem." The Czech in her accent snapped down hard. "Nothing I say, or anyone says, will make you feel better, or even different, right now. You'll hurt for Allison for a long time. But you can at least hurt on your own terms."

Hurt on your own terms. At the time Ryan had thought that

was one of the stupidest things anyone had ever said. Later, he thought it was one of the wisest. This from a woman who'd sent him to the store for paprika so she could blow herself up. But she'd been right. He did hurt for a long time, well after he'd left Oklahoma for UCLA, but Allison McDermott eventually became a dim high school memory. Still, that was before seven years ago, before he was always angry, back when he was someone else, someone Ryan wished he could find again. He occasionally dreamed of Allison and of his mother, and they sort of melded into each other, like some high-tech TV commercial morphing their faces into one. But in the dreams, his mother became the one who'd dumped him, and it was Allison burning to death beside his father.

Now here he was, in a strange city in Florida, a city that meant nothing to him, out of a job, with a letter from the woman who'd told him to hurt on his own terms.

He turned it over and over in his mind, rolling it around like a gambler palms dice. His mother, reaching out from the grave. Except she had been a day away from the bizarre double suicide when she put this clipping and this phone number into an envelope and presumably drove to the post office and asked to send it certified mail. Maybe she and the clerk had chatted. Maybe the clerk had asked who his mother knew in California. *Oh, that's my son*, his mother might have said. *He goes to UCLA, you know. He's a junior, majoring in broadcast journalism. All he's ever wanted is to be on the radio.* Maybe the clerk would have smiled.

Suddenly Ryan was suffocating. He grabbed the clipping and the slip with the phone number and dashed across the apartment. He stepped into a puddle of Pepsi and tugged open the sliding glass door by the fireplace. He walked onto the tiny wooden deck and breathed in the thick air. He made himself breathe deeply for five minutes, glancing out across the parking lot.

Finally, when he was steady again, he walked back inside and picked up the cordless phone. He folded the newspaper clipping and slipped it into his shirt pocket. Then he punched in the phone number and waited for the circuits to turn over.

The phone rang twice, three times, four.

Hang up! This is crazy! Hang up! he thought.

Then it was too late. A crisp, anonymous female voice said, "Good morning, may I help you?"

No business name, no organization, just "good morning, may I help you." Ryan stiffened.

"May I help you?" the voice said again.

Ryan cleared his throat. "Ah . . ."

"May I help you?"

"Department Thirty," Ryan said.

"One moment."

Hang up!, his whole body was screaming.

But he couldn't. He looked at his mother's handwriting from seven years ago and he couldn't. *Hurt on your own terms*, she'd said.

"Department Thirty, Art Dorian," said a man's voice in his ear, considerably more animated than the woman who had answered the call.

Ryan's heart pounded. Who was this? What was his mother trying to tell him?

"Ah . . ."

"Speak up, please."

Ryan's throat felt as if shards of glass had been poured down it. "Ah . . . my name is Ryan Elder, and I—"

The voice brightened. "Well, Ryan Elder. What do you know about that? Well, son, I've been wondering if you'd ever call. Ryan Elder. Well, I'll be—"

Ryan stared at the phone in disbelief. "Who are you?"

"Name's Dorian, Art Dorian. I'd given up thinking that you'd ever call, Ryan. Where are you? Are you here in Oklahoma City?"

"No . . . ah, no. Florida. I'm in Pensacola, Florida. Look, who are you? What do you do? I got this number—"

"Whoa, wait a minute. I can answer most of your questions, but I sure don't want to do it on the phone. As to who I am—well, Ryan, let's just say your tax dollars pay my salary, okay? We'll leave it at that for now. Are you coming to Oklahoma?"

"No, I . . ." Ryan stopped. He had nothing to hold him in Pensacola, thanks to Stillman and Penders. Still, he hadn't been back to Oklahoma since he drove away from it seven years ago. He shook his head, feeling as though fog had seeped in from the bay and shrouded him. "You . . . you work for the government?"

"I do. Look, Ryan, why don't you come on back out to Oklahoma for a few days? I bet it's been a good while since you've been here." Dorian cleared his throat into the phone. "Ryan Elder. I don't believe it. You were a baby the last time I saw you. Even then, you looked just like your dad."

Ryan caught sight of his reflection in the sliding glass door. He still looked like his father, except the last few years Ryan had worn a beard. It had grown in surprisingly thick. The gray bothered him, though. He had more gray than any other twenty-seven-year-old he knew. He had more gray than his father had had when he died.

"So you knew my family."

"Yes, son, I did," Dorian said. His tone turned sad. "Knew them well. And I know you've been through a lot, but like I said, I have some answers you've probably been looking for. Let's meet."

"Where? In Oklahoma City?"

Dorian seemed to think for a moment. "No," he said finally. "Let's meet in Cheyenne. You know, your dad's hometown, out in western Oklahoma. You know that little store right at the main crossroads—"

"I've never been there," Ryan said. "My dad never took me there."

"Oh. Well, ah . . . I guess maybe he wouldn't have, after all. Considering—"

"He always said he wasn't happy there, especially after his parents were killed in the fire. I used to ask him about it when I was a kid. He never wanted to go there."

"Look, Ryan, you'll understand it all pretty soon." He reeled off a set of directions to get from Oklahoma City to the tiny town of Cheyenne, Oklahoma. "Today's Tuesday. We'll meet, say, on Friday at noon. How's that? That should give you time to get out here."

"Look," Ryan said. "I don't know who you are, but . . . what's this about? I have this letter—"

"Ryan," Dorian said, "there are some things you have to know."

"About my parents' death?"

"Their death, their life . . . and you. It's mainly about you."

The Whispering Man took his fourth cup of convenience store coffee back to the rented Escort and sat, his muscles cramping. The surveillance had been numbingly boring, but then, most surveillance was. The only moment of excitement had come when the son of Frank and Anna Elder had stepped onto his little apartment balcony facing the street. The man had instinctively slid down in his seat, although he was sure the kid couldn't see him from that distance. Still, one couldn't be too careful. He had come too far to lose it all now.

At one minute past noon, the Whispering Man sat up straight in his seat. The boy was coming down the apartment steps, a battered dark green backpack slung over his shoulder and a duffel bag in one hand.

He watched as Elder tossed the duffel and backpack into his Toyota. The boy drove to the apartment complex office, went in, and emerged fifteen minutes later. Probably making arrangements for his mail to be picked up.

Elder got back into his little car, hesitated for a moment at the mouth of the parking lot, then made a right turn. West. The Whispering Man followed, again three car lengths back. He followed onto the highway, always keeping a discreet distance. After Elder passed the airport without slowing, the man nodded to himself. He was going to drive to Oklahoma, not fly. That made his job easier.

He exited the highway, turned his rental car around, and drove back to Pensacola Regional Airport. He returned the car, then hurried into the terminal and found the first available flight that would connect to Oklahoma City. It would take Ryan Elder anywhere from twenty-four to thirty-six hours to make the drive, depending on how hard he pushed himself. The Whispering Man would be there in less than six hours. The timing was perfect.

"Got you," he whispered.

3

THE FEDERAL COURTHOUSE BUILDING IN OKLAHOMA City is not an imposing structure. It does not impress the visitor with the pomp and power of the United States judiciary. There are no statues of Lady Justice with her scales, no carvings of the profound words of former Supreme Court justices. More institutional than awe-inspiring, and except for the metal detector just inside the main entrance, it could be any downtown office building in any good-size American city.

From a small corner office on the second floor—barely larger than a janitor's closet, with only one desk, a phone, computer, and filing cabinet—Art Dorian sat and looked out the window across Northwest Fourth Street. *That* was what was impressive, the Oklahoma City National Memorial, with its giant carved "walls of time" at either end of the space once occupied by the Alfred P. Murrah Federal Building. In the center were the reflecting pool and 168 empty chairs, one for each person killed in the bombing.

Dorian sat and looked, lost in thought. He'd believed they should have saved the millions it took to construct the new memorial and left "the fence" with its homemade adornments and testimonies affixed to it. But then, they hadn't asked him. They couldn't have, because officially, Art Dorian wasn't there. Officially, this little corner office with the excellent view was vacant, although still under lease to another federal agency, whose "real" offices were down the hall. Department Thirty didn't even have a direct phone line. Its calls came through that other agency, then were routed to him here.

Art Dorian *was* the Oklahoma City office of Department Thirty and had been for many years, although he was occasionally gone for long stretches. He'd grown up in Boston and had gone to Cheyenne, Oklahoma to meet Frank and Anna Elder in the summer of 1976. The department was in its infancy then, and he was already managing two other cases in Oklahoma and Kansas. So he convinced D.C. to let him establish a permanent "regional" office in Oklahoma City. It was out of the way and the location would let him easily follow the Elders and his other cases.

Ryan Elder, after all this time. He'd sincerely doubted that he would ever hear from the boy. Dorian couldn't have sought him out, although there were times he'd thought of it over the last seven years. No, that would be too flagrant a violation of protocol. Things had changed drastically when Frank and Anna Elder's car plowed into that construction equipment in Edmond. That had changed the rules. The game was still going on, but Dorian's part in it had been forever altered. His part had turned to a waiting game—waiting to be contacted by Ryan Elder. He just hadn't thought it would take so long.

But why now?

He was considering that question when there was a light tap on the door. "Yes?" he said, although he knew who it was. Only one person ever visited him here.

Deputy United States Marshal Faith Kelly poked her head into the room. "I've been knocking for several minutes. Where were you?"

"Ah, Faith, my dear. In another world." Dorian wondered what Faith Kelly saw in him: a skinny man in his late fifties, thinking of retirement from this madness, his only vanities being his carefully groomed toothbrush mustache and his wardrobe. Art Dorian was one of the dying breed of men who didn't feel comfortable in public unless he was wearing a necktie. He'd heard one of the young bucks in Kelly's office call him "natty." It had been meant as a joke, of course, but Dorian liked it. It was such an old-fashioned word that it fit perfectly.

Kelly was the daughter Dorian had never had time to have. In her twenties, less than a year out of the Federal Law Enforcement Academy in Glencoe, Georgia, she was attractive, intelligent, ambitious yet cautious. That she'd opted to go into the good old boy atmosphere of the United States Marshals Service instead of the more sexually integrated FBI or DEA spoke volumes about the young woman. She was going to prove herself, in her own way.

"What does Chief Deputy Clarke think about you sneaking off down here to talk to an old fossil like me?" Dorian said.

Kelly laughed, a pleasant sound. Her hair was the color of brick, her eyes were winter seawater. Her teeth were white and straight, her cheekbones high and just a tad too sharp. Her looks, Dorian thought, were probably not in her favor. The fact was, their mutual colleagues in federal law enforcement tended not to take pretty women as seriously as they did those who were less attractive. Kelly, of course, was out to prove them wrong. She was not what their colleagues would call a "ball-buster," but could handle a situation so quietly and so deftly that it would be done before anyone knew it. And the people who counted would notice *that*.

"Since they've rotated me into Community Relations duty for six months, he thinks I'm doing a good job if I'm out of the office," Kelly said. "Out relating to the community or something." She sat heavily into the chair across from Dorian.

Dorian smiled. "Come, Faith, you're no good at hiding things. What's on your mind?"

Kelly shook her head. "You've figured me out. You see through me, just like that." She snapped her fingers.

Dorian shrugged.

"It's been a . . . well, a tough week. I talked to my parents again last night. I just can't deal with them, especially my father. He was on me about Mikael again."

"Ah." Dorian steepled his fingers.

Kelly shifted on the chair and lowered her voice to a mocking parody of her father's. " 'Faith, he's twelve years older than you are, and how many years has the guy been in graduate school? Studying philosophy—Jesus please us, what the hell do you do with a degree in philosophy? He's not Irish—with a name like Mikael LeFlore, what is that, some kind of French? He's not even Catholic. You're supposed to be smart, so why can't you get it through your head . . .' " She looked up and saw Dorian staring at her. "I'm sorry, Art," she said in her regular voice. "That was uncalled for. All my father's constant harping gets to me."

"But how do *you* feel?"

A curious look crossed Kelly's attractive face. "What, about Mikael? Why do you ask?"

Dorian leaned back in his chair. "I've made a lifetime out of advising people what to do. I've been told I'm good at it. And my dear, it has always seemed to me that this relationship is more about antagonizing your father than it is about you and Mikael."

Kelly waited a moment, then smiled. "You're right, as usual. What's strange about the conversation last night is that I couldn't get a word in edgewise."

"From what you've told me about your father, that doesn't sound strange at all."

"No, the strange part is that I didn't get a chance to tell him that I broke it off with Mikael earlier in the week. And by the time he'd finished ranting, I didn't even want to tell him. It would be almost like . . . I don't know, like conceding defeat. Like saying, 'You're right, Dad. I'm completely brainless. Thank you, sir, may I have another?' "

Dorian smiled again. "Faith, the best piece of advice I can give you is to stop trying both to irritate your father and prove yourself to him at the same time. Choose one or the other, but don't do both." He leaned forward again. "And the breakup?"

Kelly fidgeted. "You've already said it. In a nutshell, Mikael was everything Dad would hate and I made a point of flaunting Mikael at him. The earring, the trust fund, the philosophy degree . . . all guaranteed to drive Captain Joe Kelly out of his mind. But you know what? Deeper down, under all that, Mikael was the same as my father. He wanted to dictate what I eat, when I sleep, where I go. To him, my career is just an amusing little diversion. I think part of the reason he wanted to date me was the novelty of being with a woman who carries a gun for a living." She met Dorian's eyes. "You won't believe how it ended."

Dorian raised his eyebrows.

"Mikael was always wanting to have breakfast together. He wanted to come over to my house and whip up these elaborate breakfasts, six-course meals. I usually just like toast and coffee in the morning. But no, he thought he was proving how sensitive he was or something by making me a big breakfast. So he came over and made these beautiful omelets, food that's so . . . so pretty you don't want to eat it for fear you'll mess it up. And we sat down and he started talking about 'the next chapter' of our lives, and how he was looking at some private college in Massachusetts for his first teaching job, and how much we'd love it there and it would be so interesting to tell his colleagues about what I used to do for a living. *Used* to do. Well, that did it. I've worked my tail off all this time and I've barely started my job, and he's talking about what I *used* to do. It just went from there."

"And?" Dorian said. "I have a feeling this is building to a big finish."

Kelly smiled, a little shyly. She tapped her nails against each other. "He started quoting Emerson and Nietzsche at me, and finally I got up and . . ."

Dorian leaned forward even farther.

"I picked up the plate with this beautiful omelet on it . . ."

Dorian began to smile.

"And I said, 'Mikael, I'm sorry to interrupt, but I have to tell you something.' He sat there with this look on his face, wondering what I could possibly have to say, and I said, 'I hate omelets.' And I threw it at him."

They both burst out laughing.

After a moment, Dorian waggled his finger at her and said, "Faith, Faith. What a waste of good eggs."

Kelly cracked up again. "I know. He just sat there with eggs and cheese and ham and peppers all over his shirt. . . ." She devolved into a fit of laughter.

Dorian chuckled. Kelly's laughter was a wonderful sound, full of promise and energy and raw youth. "And you never got around to telling your father all this."

"No." Kelly shook her head. "And I had even meant to, until he started his rant. He's just such a jerk sometimes—make that most of the time. He's always playing cop, always being Captain Kelly, even with me. I wish—"

She stopped, and Dorian knew what she'd been about to say: I wish my father was more like you, Art.

No, you don't, Dorian thought, remembering Ryan Elder.

He saw the embarrassed flush on her face, saw the young woman reposition herself on the seat again. "Enough about my crazy life," she finally said. "What are you working on?"

"Oh, you know," Dorian said. She always asked and he never answered and they both understood. Department Thirty didn't share information with anyone. He talked with her in general terms about the work, but never specific cases. In all these years he'd never discussed a single detail about a single case with anyone outside the department.

"No, I don't know, and that's why I always ask." Kelly laughed again, then turned pensive. "You seemed preoccupied when I came in and that *is* unusual for you. But in perfect Art Dorian style, you shifted the conversation around to what's going on with me."

"I guess it's just as well I'm about ready to retire, since I'm getting rather transparent myself these days." He swiveled his chair back around to the window facing the street and the memorial. The tourists were already swirling around it like the wind of an Oklahoma thunderstorm. "I got a call from the past this morning, Faith."

He remembered being right here in this little room, seven years ago, and the phone was ringing. The first thing he'd heard was the man's voice saying, *It's over, Art.*

He'd begged them not to do anything crazy, to let him work it out. The next day, before he could get to them, he'd read in the newspaper about the bizarre car crash at the construction site in Edmond.

It's over, Art.

"Art?" Kelly said to his back.

He swiveled back around. "I'm going to give you some advice, Faith. We're in the law enforcement business, but you know something? The law is there to protect *people,* and if we lose sight of the people we're supposed to be serving, the rest of it doesn't matter a whit. Maybe that's what people like your father have trouble with. If it's not about the people, then it's all just bureaucratic blather."

"What are you talking about?"

Dorian shook his head, running a finger along his mustache. "Nothing. I made a mistake a long time ago. It was very early in the department's history and I had a tiny lapse of judgment that led to . . ." To what? Can't discuss details, old man. You know the rules.

"What?"

Dorian almost said Ryan Elder, then realized what a disaster it would be if he spoke the name aloud. Almost as big a lapse of judgment as the first one, all those years ago. He was getting old and Dorian thought he might see about starting the retirement paperwork earlier than he'd anticipated. He'd do it next week. After Cheyenne. After Ryan Elder.

"Faith, could you excuse me, please?"

Kelly nodded at him but kept her counsel. "All right," she said, and went out, quietly closing the door. Dorian heard her heels echoing off the floor in the hallway.

Dorian watched the door for a long time, then went to his old three-drawer filing cabinet. It was black, but splotched with gray where the finish was peeling. It was the same cabinet that had been here since he'd moved into the office. He unlocked the top drawer. It was not full—there were only a handful of files. The same material was on the computer, of course, but Dorian preferred the feel of the paper in his hands. He thought he absorbed more information, more of the *essence* of the information, through that rough paper than he ever did through any cold computer screen. He found the file he wanted, sat down, and began to read.

An hour later, awash in the past, Art Dorian put the file aside and unlocked the lower left drawer of his desk. The government-issue nine-millimeter Sig Sauer was there, carefully stowed in its government-issue holster. Dorian rarely carried it, since most of his work was here in the office, more often than not on the telephone. He thought it had been at least three years since the last time he'd strapped it on.

He turned the gun over in his hands, checking his ammunition supply. Another good thing about Department Thirty—he didn't have to go through all the paperwork to sign out a weapon and ammunition. He simply got what he needed and the department reimbursed him.

He ran his hand along the Sig Sauer, then laid it carefully on the desk next to the open file. It occurred to him that he was much more comfortable with the paper than he was with the weapon. But he would take the weapon to Cheyenne, not the paper. He hoped he wouldn't need it.

4

RYAN STOPPED ONLY ONCE, SOMEWHERE IN TEXAS, A little north of Houston. He slept for four hours in an interstate motel, then awoke disoriented, betrayed by his ears. He ran barefoot into the parking lot, swearing he'd heard a single call of a grackle. Thinking of his mother, cocking her ear toward the sky: *Can you believe it? A single grackle in November.*

He checked out of the motel, drove to the all-night truck stop next door, and ordered the high-cholesterol special: chicken-fried steak, mashed potatoes, white milk gravy, biscuits, fried okra. He almost allowed himself a smile—he'd been living for seven years in places where people thought chicken-fried steak was an agricultural experiment in crossbreeding beef and poultry.

When the food arrived, he sat for a moment as it steamed in front of him. The waitress asked him if everything was all right. She finally gave up and walked away when he didn't answer after the third time. Ryan couldn't remember the last time he'd shared a meal with someone. *Really, really* shared a meal. Oh, he'd had fast-food lunches with coworkers, but those didn't count.

He looked down at the chicken-fried steak, gravy running in little rivers all over the plate. Too many meals alone, too much utter bullshit rolling around in him like some great unexplored wilderness. He grabbed the pepper shaker and, almost by rote, started sprinkling until the food was covered.

"Like pepper, honey?" the waitress drawled.

Ryan looked up at her. The waitress was in her fifties, tired-looking, with raven hair from a bottle and the kind of drawl he hadn't heard in a long time.

Ryan swallowed. Was she talking to him? What had she asked? Pepper, that's right, pepper. He cleared his throat. "I always feel like I'm eating hospital food if I don't add something to it," he finally said.

The waitress laughed throatily, a laugh full of cigarettes and late nights. "Hospital food. That's pretty good, honey. Well, you enjoy your chicken fry, now."

He sectioned off a bite of meat, lifted it to his mouth, and put it down again.

He pushed the plate of food away, reached into his pocket, and pulled out the newspaper clipping, the review of the Oklahoma City Philharmonic. *Exquisite phrasing and sensitivity . . . energetic rendition . . . Beethoven . . . Smetana . . . Tchaikovsky . . . fortunate to have such a fine orchestra in a city our size . . .*

There was nothing, just words on a page sent to him by a dead woman.

The anger tried to rise, but then Ryan felt an overwhelming sense that he needed to hurry. He called the waitress over.

"Everything okay, honey?"

"I'm sorry, I've got to get back on the road. Could you box this up for me?"

She shrugged. "I suppose, but the gravy's not so good when it's cold."

"I'll risk it."

She returned with a polyurethane container, gravy leaking out the sides. Ryan gave her a ten-dollar bill and told her to keep the change, then left the noise and light of the truck stop. Before pulling the Toyota back onto the interstate, he backtracked half a mile to an overpass. As he'd come down the exit ramp earlier, he'd noticed a grouping of large cardboard boxes, overturned shopping carts, and tattered bedsheets set back from the highway.

He slowed at the corner, opened the car door, and heard movement among the boxes—quiet, furtive, the sound of people accustomed to living unseen by the world. He took the polyurethane container, placed it silently on the ground, and retreated to the warmth of the Toyota. As he turned back toward the interstate, he looked in his mirror and saw a shadowy shape appear next to the stark white of the container, then melt back into the cardboard darkness.

Sorry I couldn't do more, he thought as he merged onto the highway heading north. I'm homeless too. I may have a place to sleep at night that's not a box, and I don't have to stand on street corners to collect quarters from surly drivers, but I'm still homeless. You probably wouldn't understand that, but that's what I am. I have no place in this world.

Then the Toyota was humming along at seventy-five miles an hour in the late-night traffic and, for a little while, Ryan wasn't angry anymore.

He crossed the Red River on Interstate 35 at just past five o'clock in the morning, with dawn a red crayon line in the east. He made Oklahoma City at 7:15, grinding through rush hour. Some things never changed—even though he'd been gone for seven years, the city's highways were still masses of construction. The detours had just moved from one place to another.

He felt himself being pulled along like a dog on a leash. Centennial Expressway north, past the Oklahoma Health

Center complex and the state capitol with its working oil wells in the parking lot, past industrial centers and warehouses and more construction. Then he came into Edmond and it struck him that the suburb had grown even more, if that was possible.

Broadway, Danforth Road, Santa Fe Avenue. The corner where his father's car had exploded was now a shopping center. A right turn, then a left. In the cold gray light of winter morning, he stopped the Toyota in front of the house.

His house. The house of his childhood, his adolescence, his *life*.

Strangely, it looked smaller. Just an ordinary wood-and-brick suburban home with a two-car garage and a plank fence enclosing the backyard. All the other houses in the subdivision, built by the same contractor, were variations on the theme.

Ryan sat in the street, the car idling, the heater on. He'd realized it was cold somewhere around the time he crossed the Oklahoma state line. He looked at the house. A real estate sign was staked into the ground by the curb.

He got out of the car as if he were dreamwalking and the wind hit him full in the face. Freezing reality struck him. You can't dream in a strong Oklahoma wind, he thought. While Oklahoma didn't get as cold as, say, Ohio or Vermont, everyone here understood wind chill factor. He grabbed his coat, a bomber-style jacket emblazoned with the logo of the radio station where he'd worked in Dayton. Walking around the car to the curb, he touched the top of the real estate sign.

"This is a nice neighborhood," said a voice.

Ryan almost jumped. For a moment he'd forgotten the possibility that other people could exist here. He half turned. In the next driveway over, an Hispanic-looking woman, a few years older than he, was strapping three boys into a Voyager minivan. At least Edmond's not as lily-white as it used to be, he thought, then it occurred to him that the driveway where the woman stood had been Dean Yorkton's. His neighbor growing up, the man who'd come out of the 7-Eleven and seen his parents crash through the intersection.

The woman smiled pleasantly at him. "It's especially nice for the kids," she said. "And the prices here are a little better than some places in Edmond."

Ryan took a few steps toward her, his breath fogging around him. She slid the minivan's side door closed. "Wasn't this Mr. Yorkton's house?"

The woman's smile disappeared. "Yes, it was. But we've lived here for over six years. Did you know him?"

Ryan took another couple of steps. One of the boys, as fair as the woman was dark, knocked on the window of the van. "A little. Did he move?"

"I have to go," the woman said.

"Wait. I was . . . he was a friend of our family. I'd like to visit him. Do you know where he went?"

The woman gave a glance over her shoulder and used both hands to make a "wait a minute" gesture at the boys. She crossed to where Ryan stood, took his arm, and steered him back toward his own car. "He died. The realtor told us. We got the house at auction. He didn't have a will and didn't have any family."

"What happened to him?" Ryan thought of Yorkton's fleshy face, the way it always seemed red. "Heart attack?"

"No. He was murdered."

Ryan stared at her. Across the driveway, the blond boy was tapping on the window. It sounded as loud as gunshots to Ryan.

"The poor man was on vacation, no less," the woman said. "First vacation he'd had in years. That's what our realtor said. Someone just walked up to him, demanded his wallet, and shot him when he didn't hand it over fast enough."

Ryan looked up. He heard the wind in the trees behind the house . . . *his house*. But there was no single grackle calling out longingly, singing out a warning of things to come. Just the wind and a little boy tapping his finger on the glass of a van.

"When did all this happen?" Ryan finally said.

"Well, we bought the house at auction . . . let's see, it'll be seven years this summer. They said it happened in March of that year."

Four months after his parents, he thought.

Coincidences happen, he argued with himself. Lack of sleep and the newspaper clipping in his pocket had his mind working overtime, searching for . . . what? Ryan shook his head and the little boy kept tapping the window.

"I have to go," the woman said. "But this *is* a nice neighborhood, if you're interested in that house." She started back across to her own driveway.

"Where was he?" Ryan called after her.

"What?"

"Mr. Yorkton. When he was killed. You said he was on vacation. Where was he?"

The woman paused with her hand on the driver's door of her van. "It's very sad. He was walking alongside the Lincoln Memorial. He was in Washington, D.C."

5

As Ryan drove away from his house Dean Yorkton, the Lincoln Memorial, Department Thirty, and November grackles wrestled for space in his mind. He thought of birthday parties, trips to Lake Arcadia, high school teachers, and football games. All the mundane things and ordinary people which sew together the fabric of a life.

There were only two people in this entire city he felt he could call on. His old friend Jeff Majors, at whose house he'd spent the night after his parents' death, had gone to med school back east and had returned to Oklahoma City to do his internship at Memorial Community Hospital. And there was his father's friend and attorney Jack Coleridge, who had been a presence in Ryan's life as far back as he could remember.

He stopped at a convenience store and used a pay phone to call Memorial Community, known locally as MemCom. After being transferred three times, he was told Dr. Majors would be in surgery all day. Ryan hung up slowly, then steered the Toyota back toward downtown Edmond, turning south on Broadway. Like many upscale suburbs, it had a downtown of sorts, which it touted as "historic." Downtown Edmond was about three blocks square, with the hub along Broadway.

In the middle of a block was a small brick storefront with an oval glass-paned window. Scrolled in cursive white lettering was *T. Jackson Coleridge, Attorney and Counselor at Law.* Ryan parked in front of a restaurant, walked half the block, and entered the office. A small bell tinkled overhead.

He'd come here with his father many times, to this small, quiet place, with its mahogany paneling and plush leather chairs and the smell of Coleridge's pipe tobacco. There was an antique banjo clock on one wall whose works had fascinated Ryan. Likewise the law library, with the thickest books he had ever seen. In his youth, a tiny woman named Mrs. Carr had presided over the outer office, shooting stern looks at Ryan whenever he dared to move from one of the leather chairs.

"Just a minute, I'm coming," said a voice from within.

A second later Jack Coleridge came around the corner. He was still every bit the aristocrat, Ryan thought. Though shorter than Ryan, he had an almost military bearing which made him seem larger. He was still trim. Coleridge had been a couple of years younger than Frank Elder, so that would make him around sixty now, but his body was that of a man twenty years younger. His face was likewise lean and sharp, the face smooth under close-cropped hair now completely silver. Only the eyes were indistinct, a pale, clouded blue. Ryan remembered that even when those eyes were fixed directly on a person, they seemed to be peering somewhere else as well. He imagined the effect as quite disconcerting to courtroom opponents. Coleridge had spent ten years in the Oklahoma state legislature and more than a few political foes had weathered that strange gaze as well.

"May I help you?" Coleridge said, with no flicker of recognition. The accent was that of a New England prep-school graduate who'd been in the Southwest for many years.

"Well, Mr. Coleridge," Ryan said, "I guess I look a little different than the last time you saw me."

Jack Coleridge studied Ryan, then reached out to steady himself against the mahogany-paneled wall. "Well, I'll be damned," he said very softly. "Is that really you, Ryan?"

Ryan smiled.

"You're the last person I expected to see walking in this office today," Coleridge said. "I guess the khakis should have given you away. You're the only man in America under the age of thirty who chooses to wear something other than blue jeans, when they actually have a choice. I seem to recall you were teased a bit for that in school. But for heaven's sake, why did you feel the need to grow a beard?"

"Same thing as the khakis, I guess. Just my rebellious nature."

Coleridge waved a hand. "Bah. You were never rebellious. Come in here and sit down." He led the way into his private office. Photos, plaques, and commendations covered the dark wood-paneled walls: pictures with the governor on Coleridge's legislative retirement; a lifetime community service award from the city of Edmond; a framed letter to the editor, praising his many civic projects; a large photo of an older man Ryan had always assumed was one of Coleridge's many influential clients; and many smaller pictures of assorted dignitaries.

But no family pictures. Ryan's father had once told him that Coleridge's wife died very young, even before he'd moved to Oklahoma. He'd never remarried and there were no children. The law and public service were Coleridge's family.

Ryan shook his hand. The grip, while firm, wasn't as crushing as he remembered. Ryan wasn't sure whether that reflected more on Coleridge or himself. "How've you been, Mr. Coleridge?"

The attorney lowered himself into the chair behind his massive desk with its neat stacks of papers and journals. He waved the hand again. "We're both adults, Ryan. Call me Jack."

Ryan thought for a moment. "My dad would never have stood for that."

Coleridge steepled his fingers in front of his face. "Your father's not here, now is he?" He shrugged. "I'm sort of semiretired now. Had a mild heart attack two years ago. Even the governor called me up and told me I'd better quit before I ran myself into the ground." A wry smile. "That's the only time I ever let *this* governor tell me anything."

"Where's Mrs. Carr?"

"She finally gave it up, rest her soul. Six months ago. I think she died to get away from me. I haven't replaced her, since no one could, and being semiretired I don't really need a secretary anyway. I usually spend three or four hours a day here at the office, answering correspondence, returning phone calls. Then I play golf. I do what old men do."

"You don't look old."

"Bah. What brings you to town?"

"I . . ." He almost reached into his pocket for the newspaper clipping and the paper with Department Thirty's phone number on it. But he pulled his hand back. Until he knew what the man named Art Dorian was all about, what good would it do? "I'm between jobs again and—"

Coleridge sighed. "You're between jobs a lot, son. Ohio didn't agree with you?"

"Florida. I lost the Ohio job last summer. I'd been in Pensacola, Florida, the last few months. Sorry I didn't let you know where I was. Say, I drove by the house this morning. I noticed it's for sale again."

"I saw that too, not long ago. That family that bought it from the estate lived there a few years, then they had a few more children and outgrew it."

"How long's it been vacant?"

"Oh, seven or eight months. You're not thinking . . ."

"Oh no. God, no. I just . . . say, Mr. Coleridge—"

"Jack."

"Jack. Did you know our neighbor, Mr. Yorkton? Dean Yorkton."

Coleridge peered at him through the cloudy eyes. "He was

the one who was there that day, wasn't he?" He didn't need to say what day he meant.

Ryan nodded. "He lived next door to us most of the time I was a kid. He was some kind of engineer. Sort of a stuffy old bachelor."

"Watch what you say about stuffy old bachelors. No, I didn't really know him, except for the police station that day. Why?"

"I don't know. I met the woman who lives in his house this morning. She said he was killed just a few months after my parents died. On vacation in Washington."

"Killed?"

"Shot by a mugger. That's very bizarre, don't you think?"

Coleridge swiveled halfway around in his chair. "It's odd, I grant you. That probably didn't do much for real estate values in your neighborhood."

Ryan raised his eyebrows.

"Don't get indignant," Coleridge said quickly. His voice turned quiet. "We all deal with loss in different ways. I become sarcastic. You, I take it, change jobs and move to a new state."

Ryan shook his head. "Dad always said you could cut right to the heart of anything. I lose my temper, I blow up at the wrong people. I'm sorry."

"Sorry? Don't apologize to me, Ryan."

"It's just . . . I guess I don't know why I'm here. I've been sort of . . . I don't know, wandering around in a fog for a while now. I'm not really connected to anything." He bowed his head. "Or anyone. I'm looking for . . . something. Something about the folks."

Coleridge sighed again. He took a pipe from a rack on the edge of the desk, filled it with tobacco from a pouch in his drawer, and brought it to life. He sucked on it once, then pointed it at Ryan. "No one smokes pipes anymore. The backlash against smoking has even carried over to pipe tobacco." He looked thoughtfully across the desk. "What do you want, Ryan? You know as much, or more, than I do."

"I don't know what I want." He sniffed the aroma of the

tobacco, a special blend he'd never smelled anywhere else. He thought for a moment about what Dorian had said about the town of Cheyenne. "What do you know about Dad's hometown? All he would ever tell me was that his parents died in a fire the summer after he graduated from high school and he didn't feel there was anything for him there, so he left and joined the marines."

"That's about all I know," Coleridge said through a cloud of blue smoke. "As for the fire, all Frank ever told me was that he had gone into Elk City with some friends and when he got back that night, the house was gone. He left the next week and never went back." Coleridge reclined in his chair. "Very much like you did, Ryan."

Ryan shook his head, fatigue settling on him like a crown. He'd heard the story so many times, how Frank Elder had joined the U.S. Marines and was stationed in Berlin in the late sixties, during the height of the cold war. He'd later been posted to the U.S. consulate as a guard, and was on duty late one night when a petite woman with black hair and cobalt eyes swept in the gates from a thunderstorm, looked up at the tall young marine, and said, "Asylum."

The woman was Anna Malikova, considered one of the world's most promising young violinists. She'd left the Prague Conservatory with only her violin, a little money, and the clothes on her back, a few steps ahead of the Czech secret police, who, in league with the KGB, were going through one of their periodic crackdowns on creative artists and performers. She'd ridden by train to East Berlin, where she hid from the Stasi for nearly a month before finding a dissident who would smuggle her across the border. It had taken every bit of money she had.

Within a month, Anna Malikova was in the United States. Captivated by the woman who'd come in from the rain, Frank Elder requested a transfer back stateside. He caught up with her playing in a string quartet in California, and as soon as she finished playing Beethoven, he took her out for coffee in an all-night cafe near Camp Pendleton. Anna Malikova knew only that his was the first face she had seen in the

West, in freedom, and it had been burned into her, the calm brown eyes, the lanky frame, the slow drawl. Six months later they were married. Two years later a son was born, Frank Elder finished his hitch in the marines, and they moved to his home state of Oklahoma.

"Tell me again how you met them," Ryan said.

Coleridge stared at him uncertainly. "I'll ask you again, Ryan. What are you looking for? It would help if I knew."

"I told you I don't know, dammit!" Ryan shouted, then slumped in the seat and scrubbed both hands across his beard. "I'm sorry."

Coleridge sat back and pulled on his pipe. "Your mother's spirit. I never saw it much before. You were always so quiet and well-mannered, like Frank. But you are your mother's son after all. I met your father shortly after I moved to Oklahoma. Those were oil boom days here, and like thousands of other young men, I came to make money. I started putting together oil and gas leases and did quite well, but I didn't like being in a big corporate firm. I'd had enough of that in the East. I walked out and opened this office. Frank was my first client. The marines owed him some back pay and he was having a devil of a time getting it. I filed some papers and it just went from there."

Ryan looked up. To his own surprise, his cheeks were slick. "Why . . . why would a father never take his only son to his hometown, especially if it's only a couple of hours away? I mean, with my mother, I understood. Her home was half a world away and she'd escaped an oppressive regime. But—"

"Don't be too hard on your father," Coleridge said. "Cheyenne held nothing for him. He told me that over and over. He had nothing against the town or the people, but there was just nothing there for him."

"But I don't have any roots. I feel like I have no heritage. He could have at least shown me the spot where the house stood."

"Ryan, you're not listening. It's much like people who are unhappy in high school. Why on earth would they go back to a class reunion? Your father didn't—"

"He could have shown me the graves of my grandparents, shown me where he went to school, the places he knew. My friend Jeff and his family used to drive four hours one way every Memorial Day to visit the graves of his grandparents."

"And as a child, do you think you would have cared about such things?"

Ryan sat back. What was he doing? He was spinning out of control. That letter he'd opened Tuesday morning had sliced a razor-sharp cut through the thin veneer of his life. More than just a vague newspaper clipping and a phone number had slid out of that envelope.

Ryan ran his hands over his face again, scratching at his beard. "I'm sorry—"

"Stop saying you're sorry, Ryan." Coleridge gently put his pipe in an ashtray.

"It's just that . . . I drove nearly straight through from Pensacola and I guess I'm running on empty."

The attorney tapped the bowl of the pipe against the edge of the ashtray. "Come home with me. I'll have Mrs. Hennigh make some stew and cornbread and you can get some sleep in the guest room."

Ryan nodded numbly. Coleridge's cook/housekeeper was legendary for her stew and he needed rest before tomorrow. Before Cheyenne and the man named Dorian. "Could you find out anything about Dean Yorkton?"

"Are you trying to hire me?"

"Haven't you been on retainer to the estate this whole time? Just see what you can find out about his murder."

"I will, Ryan. But you have to understand, since neither of us knows what you hope to find—"

Ryan nodded. "Keep the expectations low. I understand. Just make a few phone calls. See what's there."

"If anything."

"Yes, if anything."

"You're also stubborn," Coleridge said. "A quality I believe you inherited from both parents. Come on, let's go have some stew." He stood up and led Ryan out onto the sidewalk. Ryan watched while he locked the office.

A wind gust came up, making Coleridge curse under his breath. In that wind, Ryan felt as if something else had just tumbled out of the envelope. "I'm an only child of two only children," he said suddenly.

Coleridge turned to look at him.

"How common is that in America?" Ryan said. "Or anywhere else, for that matter?"

At the moment Ryan sat down to a steaming bowl of stew with homemade cornbread in Jack Coleridge's dining room, another man was unlocking the door to a small motel room two and a half hours to the northwest.

In the brown, rolling, nearly treeless landscape of far western Oklahoma, a few miles from the eastern edge of the Texas Panhandle, Art Dorian had finally returned to Cheyenne. The small frontier town with the wide streets sat in an area most Oklahomans referred to as "out there." What trees there were tended to clumps every mile or so. Cattle clustered around them. Mostly there was brown January grass and the horizon.

The little motel, the only one in town, sat at the north end of Cheyenne. Dorian had stayed here when he came to this town before, so long ago. He'd even managed to get the same room, number 207. He wondered how many people would remember the number of the motel room in which they'd spent a single night many years ago. But then, Dorian thought, it was a bit like an old married couple returning to the place where they'd spent their honeymoon.

Dorian tossed his small overnight bag onto the bed. The room smelled a little stale, but otherwise seemed clean. After he'd closed and locked the door behind him, he took off his jacket and hung it neatly in the alcove beside the bathroom. Then he removed his holster and placed it on the nightstand.

Madness, he thought. I'm too old for this.

He sat on the bed, still fully clothed except for his jacket. He hadn't even loosened his tie. He doubted he would sleep much, but he needed the room. He needed to be here a full day before he met Ryan Elder, just as he had checked in a full day early when he met the boy's parents.

Twenty-four hours and it would be over. Then Dorian could retire with a clear conscience.

Twenty-four hours and Ryan Elder would know what Dorian had known for all these years.

6

RYAN DROVE SLOWLY NORTH ON U.S. 283, CUTTING AN arrow's path through the countryside and trying to visualize Frank Elder in this harsh place. It was difficult, but it did give him a little perspective on his father's nature. The vast empty sky, the openness of the land, could drive a person inward. Even though towns were scattered like marbles along the road, he'd encountered fewer than half a dozen other cars since he'd left the interstate.

Nearly noon, the January sun was high and bright. Ryan noticed a strange feature of the few trees clumped close to the road: most of them had a pronounced northward bent from being buffeted by prevailing southerly winds. Today, though, the wind howled out of Kansas from the north, as if trying to bend the trees back into shape. Ryan shook his head at the surrealistic quality of it all. He hadn't known what to expect from his father's country, but this wasn't it.

He'd slept in Coleridge's guest room for nearly twelve hours, then awoke to Mrs. Hennigh's homemade biscuits. Thanking her quietly, he slipped out of the house while Coleridge went to his office to make some phone calls. Ryan had been just as glad—he hadn't been prepared to talk more to Coleridge. His entire being was focused on this meeting, on discovering his father's homeland.

He slowed into Cheyenne, and as he approached the town's main crossroads, he remembered Dorian's directions. On the southeast corner at the intersection was a low wooden building with the words BLACK KETTLE MUSEUM across the front. A single car sat in the parking lot, a man standing beside it.

Ryan pulled the Toyota into the lot. The car was dark blue, midsize, an innocuous GM model. He got out, zipped up his jacket, and looked at the man. Dorian was like a cactus at the North Pole, he looked so out of place: small, neat, self-possessed, in a black pinstriped suit and elegant tie, with his graying hair and wispy mustache. He looked like someone's stereotype of an accountant or a male librarian.

Ryan nodded across the car to him, keeping his distance. "What's all this Black Kettle business? I saw another sign a few miles back."

The little man folded his hands together as if praying. "Don't you know your Oklahoma history?"

"Not really. My history teacher in high school was a coach. Mostly he diagrammed football plays on the board and occasionally read a chunk out of the textbook."

Dorian smiled thinly. "Black Kettle was a chief of the Cheyenne people. They had their camp near here." He unclasped his hands. "Hello, Ryan. You look like your father. Minus the beard, of course."

Ryan came around the car. "I wish people would stop telling me I look like my father. My father's dead."

Dorian nodded. "Thank you for coming."

"Did I have a choice?"

"A choice? Why, certainly you have a choice. That's what this is all about, in a way. Choices."

A wind gust rose and fell. Ryan hugged himself. He came within a few feet of Dorian. A dusty pickup truck went by on the highway. He thought he saw the driver stare at the two men in the parking lot. Ryan cleared his throat. "If you're with the government, how about some ID?"

Dorian smiled again, the same thin-lipped expression as before. He spread his hands. "You're going to have to trust me, Ryan."

"Trust you. Now forgive me, Mr. Dorian, but I don't feel very trusting right now. I've just come halfway across the country to a place I've never seen before, because of a letter that should have reached me seven years ago. You say you're with the government, but you won't produce any ID. You won't tell me what department you're with and you say to trust you. If I were working on a story and someone fed me that, I'd think it was the biggest load of bullshit I'd ever heard."

"Let's go for a drive," Dorian responded.

Ryan folded his arms against the wind. A truck clattered by on the street pulling an empty livestock trailer. "I'm not going anywhere with you. Tell me what you have to say and let's be done with it."

Dorian cleared his throat. "Ryan, you're making this difficult."

"I've been told I'm a difficult person."

"You've come a long way. What's two more miles?"

Ryan waited.

Dorian stared up at him. Ryan's light brown eyes were not intense—no one would ever call them piercing. But they were steady, not looking away much. Dorian lowered his voice. "I want to show you something."

"I bet you do," Ryan said, then wondered why he was doing his hard-ass reporter routine with this man. It made no difference at this point. "What is it?"

"A place that meant a great deal to your father." Ryan's expression softened a tiny bit. "It isn't far. In fact, it's the first place I ever met your parents . . . and you." The planes of Ryan's face shifted, like a river changing course. Dorian plunged ahead. "Oh, yes. You were a baby, around six months old. I remember your mother had dressed you in a little blue one-piece suit with an antique car stitched on it, over the left breast. You were very quiet, you slept most of the time. But when you did wake up, you were upset at first, then I recall your mother put her hand over your hand and that was all it took. You calmed right down, just at the touch of your mother's hand."

Ryan's mother's hands. He thought of how he'd sat at her knee and listened to her play, eyes closed, her entire body matching the rhythm of the violin. And then there was the little blue jumper. His mother had carefully folded it and put it away in a cedar chest at the foot of Ryan's bed. He'd last seen it when he went through the house seven years ago. He tossed it into a box for the Salvation Army and it was hauled away, part of his life that could no longer be explained or understood.

"Where?" Ryan said.

Dorian nodded. "You drive."

Ryan's eyes narrowed again. "Nothing about this—any of it—makes sense, Dorian. You realize that, don't you?"

"Yes." Dorian shivered in the wind. "I realize that. More than you know."

At Dorian's direction, Ryan drove the Toyota west on State Highway 47 from the crossroads. The small business district was gone in less than a minute and they crossed a bridge over a tiny stream that a sign announced as Sergeant Major Creek. A mile into the countryside, Dorian instructed him to turn on a side road. A brown-and-white sign pointed to the Battle of the Washita Historic Site.

"What's this about?" Ryan said.

Dorian said nothing. To the side of the road was a low brown building with federal government insignias. "Black Kettle National Grassland," Ryan read. "A national grassland? You must be kidding. I've heard of national parks, national forests, but a national grassland?"

Dorian frowned at the window. "Don't belittle it, Ryan. In the history of the southern plains, this is an important area."

Ryan watched the brown countryside roll past. "Well, they got one part right. There's nothing but grass out here."

One more mile and another sign pointed to a gravel parking lot. It was empty. Just like the rest of this country, Ryan thought, again having trouble imagining his father growing up here. He parked and the two men got out of the car. To their left was a large, round open-sided structure with a brown shingled roof supported by steel beams, which in turn were planted in concrete.

"An observation deck," Dorian said, anticipating Ryan's question.

"Observation of what?" Ryan said.

"Come over here."

They walked around to the rear of the raised concrete circle. A rectangular granite historical marker confronted them. THE BATTLE OF THE WASHITA read the caption. Ryan scanned the few sentences beneath the legend. In November 1868, army troops under the command of George Armstrong Custer had attacked a village of Cheyenne people led by Black Kettle. Black Kettle, a peaceful chief, had promised the army his group would not conduct raids into Kansas. He'd kept his word, but a few of the men in his party, without his knowledge, had indeed raided white settlements to the north. Before dawn on a snowy November morning, with the entire Cheyenne village still sleeping, Custer's men swept down from behind a ridge a mile or so away and massacred most of the population while they slept.

Ryan held his breath. After reading the marker, his eyes swept up. He didn't notice Dorian watching him intently. A few yards beyond the marker was a wooden fence and beyond that was only grassland. He shaded his eyes against the winter sun. Ahead and far to the left he saw the ridge where Custer's troops must have hidden. He thought of a community of people, asleep in the predawn, not knowing that death was coming from that ridge. Just like himself, stepping off a plane for Thanksgiving, not knowing what awaited him. He thought of the blood, white and Cheyenne, soaking this ground.

"Did your father talk to you about this place?" Dorian asked.

"No. He never mentioned it, not even once."

"Oh." Dorian seemed temporarily at a loss for words. "Well, then. Perhaps . . . perhaps he had such intense feelings about it that he couldn't talk about it."

Ryan shook his head. He had a strange sort of feeling, the sense of something building up, like water behind a cracking dam. "Frank Elder wasn't one for talking about feelings."

Dorian shrugged. "This place can have a strong effect on people. It's so . . . so stark, so unforgiving."

"Unforgiving. That's a good word for it." Ryan turned slowly to face the shorter man. "Tell me what this is all about." He reached into his pocket, took out the newspaper clipping, and handed it to Dorian without speaking.

Dorian read it, then read it again. "What is this?"

"You tell me."

"I don't know. Did it come in the same letter?"

"Exactly. The same letter with your phone number in it. And you don't know what it means?"

Dorian's brow furrowed. "No, I don't." He handed it back to Ryan. "But I suspect you do. Or at least you will."

"You're talking in circles, Dorian."

The little man smiled. "That's part of my job. Let's walk. I think better when I walk."

They went through the low wooden gate, past a sign that read simply TRAILS, with an arrow. The path was perhaps four feet wide, and on either side of it, the grassland stretched away.

"The river's that way," Dorian said, gesturing back to the east. "The Washita. It's not much, as rivers go, but it serves for this part of the country. The Cheyenne people made it their home."

Ryan stopped, listening.

"What?" Dorian said, three steps ahead of him.

"Nothing." Ryan shook his head. "Thought I heard something. I have my mother's sense of hearing and sometimes it plays tricks on me."

Dorian smiled again and it seemed almost nostalgic. "Your father asked me to take this same walk. He and I walked along here side by side, although it was summer, just about dusk and still hot, at least ninety degrees. Your mother stayed a few steps behind us. She was carrying you and she kept switching you from one side to the other. And I remember your father said, 'Can you feel it? This ground is full of blood.' I'll remember that as long as I live."

It seemed strange—Ryan had thought something very

similar just a few minutes ago, looking out over the plain. "Why were you here?" he said finally, the dam breaking. "Why did my father bring you here? And while we're at it— *who are you?*"

They'd walked a good distance from the parking lot, closer to the ridge now than to the observation deck. "It's so cold," Dorian said.

Ryan clenched and unclenched his fist. "Stop playing these fucking games with me, Dorian. I want to know what this is all about." Suddenly Ryan stopped walking and cocked his head. "We're not alone."

"What?" Dorian whipped around to face him.

"There's someone else out here."

Dorian scanned the horizon. "I don't see anyone."

"Don't look. *Listen!*" Ryan strained to capture the sound again, like a butterfly in a net. *There!* Above them, a human sound, someone moving . . . moving ever so slightly. Not footsteps, but definitely human.

"Where?" Dorian whispered.

"The ridge. From up on the ridge. There it is again!" Moving, moving . . . and then something nonhuman. Metal. Metal scraping the hard earth.

"Not now," Dorian said under his breath, then his hand was in the holster, unsnapping it and getting a grip on the gun. He hadn't fired at anything that wasn't on a target range in over twenty years. He'd spent all these years driving a desk, making phone calls, doing paperwork. Other people— *younger* people—drew their guns.

What have I done? Dorian thought.

The Whispering Man sighted through the scope of the assault rifle, keeping the target in clear focus. It was an unexpected prize—he hadn't expected Ryan Elder to meet Art Dorian in the museum parking lot in Cheyenne. He hadn't known what to expect, but nothing was ruled out. Not anymore.

Dorian was part of the reason everything had happened the way it did. It was Dorian's doing that had made him change his plans, that had made him wait so long. The Whispering Man hadn't seen him in years, but Dorian's face was branded on his memory as if with an iron. He was the same, with his little mustache, all gray now, and the impeccable dress, even standing in the middle of acres and acres of grass. Now, to have him standing there, only a hundred yards or so away . . . it was too good to be true.

Had Dorian told the boy anything yet? It was impossible to know what they had talked about in the car. And the boy had stood for a long time at the historical marker, gazing out across the plain. He was too far away to read the expression on Ryan Elder's face, but perhaps it was shock, disbelief, anger, maybe even fear.

Yes, the Whispering Man thought. He nodded to himself, altering his position slightly so he could better see them on the trail below. Yes. Ryan Elder's work was soon to begin. The work the Whispering Man had awaited for so long—for Ryan Elder's entire life, in fact.

For a moment, he caught the tip of a memory, just a tiny corner in his mind: a young boy, six or seven years old, gazing up at his impossibly tall father, a godlike figure. And the boy was asking over and over, *Why, Daddy, why? Please tell me why. Why, Daddy, why? I want to know.*

The Whispering Man shook his head, driving the memory back where it belonged, and nudged his finger onto the trigger.

"Go back to the car," Dorian said.

"What?"

"Throw up your hands like you're angry with me, curse a little bit more—loudly, if you please—then turn around and walk back to the car."

Ryan took a step toward the man. "Well, the part about being angry is no lie. But are you out of your mind?"

Dorian brought the automatic out into full view, pointed at the ground. "No, I'm trying to save your life, Ryan."

Ryan's eyes settled on the gun. "You're a fucking lunatic." He grabbed Dorian's other arm. Dorian twisted away from him, then swung his arm around and shoved Ryan in the chest. It wasn't a hard blow, but Ryan wasn't ready for it, and he tumbled backward off the trail.

He heard Dorian's footsteps moving away. "Dorian! Dammit, Dorian . . . !"

Ryan raised his head. Dorian was running down the trail and the gun was no longer pointed at the ground. He veered off the trail, lumbering through the dead January grass, starting to work his way around the ridge. For a crazy moment, Ryan thought of Custer and Black Kettle. He raised himself up and stepped back onto the trail.

Dorian had stopped, as if indecisive. He took one more step.

Ryan started to sprint. He'd gone ten yards when he heard the shot.

He instantly left the trail and rolled into the grass, arms over his head, pure instinct. Conscious thought was gone. When he raised his head again, he couldn't see Dorian. A scrabbling reached his ears. Damned hearing, he thought. It was so acute he couldn't tell how far away sounds were. Things from half a mile away sounded like they were breathing down his neck.

He stumbled through the grass toward the place where Dorian had been. Closer, closer . . .

Then he saw the dark shape against the earth. Dorian's expensive suit. Ten more feet.

Crimson on the white shirt. Dorian tried to roll over. Blood dripped out of him. Blood on the earth, Ryan thought.

"Oh my God," he whispered.

He reached the man. His chest had exploded. Blood was everywhere, down the man's back, in his pants. His chest cavity was torn open.

Ryan's stomach felt like it had been pumped full of hot tar. He slid down in the grass next to Dorian. He put out a hand, then jerked it back. So much blood . . .

Dorian was alive. He was still breathing, his eyes half-focused on the ridge. Then he slowly turned his head toward Ryan. Blood at the corners of his mouth. Dying right before Ryan's eyes.

"Jesus," Ryan said. "Look, Dorian, I'll call . . ."

Dorian moved his head from side to side, a herky-jerky motion, like the old silent films. He raised a hand, squeezed Ryan's forearm. His face was paper white.

His lips moved. His eyes darted back and forth, beckoning Ryan down. Ryan put his ear next to Dorian's mouth. Dorian's breathing was as loud as thunder. The older man's lips moved again.

"What?" Ryan said. From somewhere else, more scrabbling. Movement, movement . . . what direction? Ryan wanted to scream, but there was no scream in him.

Dorian's mouth, moving again. Finally the words came, clear as rain in Ryan's ears.

"Adam and Eve," Dorian said.

His eyes rolled back in his head and his chest heaved once more, then stopped.

Ryan scrambled backward as if he'd been burned. Then he slowly crept forward again. He felt Dorian's wrist, though he didn't know why. It was what happened in the movies when someone died, so he felt he should at least try.

After a moment, clear-eyed realism struck Ryan like another blow to the chest: Someone had murdered Dorian. And was that same someone waiting to send another bullet into Ryan? More muffled sounds, somewhere. Were they farther away? He couldn't tell, his ears toying with him again.

Ryan quickly went through the dead man's pockets. No coins, one set of car keys, what looked like a motel room key. No wallet, no credit cards, no notes on what he was going to tell Ryan. *Nothing!*

Ryan's eyes came to rest on the automatic in Dorian's hand.

The Whispering Man slid halfway down the ridge, then climbed up again. He had to see. He'd been waiting too long.

The shot had been true, and if Art Dorian wasn't dead, he soon would be. The boy was kneeling next to the body.

Why, Daddy, why?

I'll show you why, the Whispering Man thought, and

smiled. He was going to give Ryan Elder another push in the right direction, just to make sure he got the message. He raised the rifle again.

Target, Ryan thought. I'm a target out here.

He wrenched the gun from Dorian's dead fingers and jammed it into his jacket. He rose into a crouch and a shot exploded three feet from him.

He screamed wordlessly into the wind and began to run in a straight line back toward the parking lot.

The next shot came even closer. Ryan saw the indentation it made in the ground.

Blood on the earth.

He began to zigzag, moving toward the parking lot. No one knew they were coming here. Ryan hadn't known himself until he'd met Dorian in Cheyenne. No one could have known—unless they'd been followed. That meant the assassin knew where the car was.

A thought dripped down Ryan's mind: Who were they following? Dorian or me?

He zagged away from his course, crossed the trail, and started bearing away from the parking lot. East. A little bit north. Which way was the highway? He would have to run into it sooner or later.

But then what?

Survival. At this point, that was all there was.

He heard noises in the grass, but couldn't look back.

He felt Dorian's gun in his pocket, then thought of the dead man in the grass, now far behind him.

Adam and Eve, Dorian had said.

What was that? Thinking of Genesis as he lay dying. What did it mean?

He went down a slight rise, lost his footing, and tumbled end over end. He popped back up, oblivious to pain in his foot, making sure he still had the gun.

Water. Somewhere ahead, he heard water. The Washita River, Dorian had said. Ryan crashed through the grass toward the sound and whatever lay beyond.

7

CASSANDRA CHAMBERS WAS THINKING OF CHOPIN. EVEN out here, driving a dusty pickup truck down an empty stretch of highway with the Elk City country music station blaring away, she couldn't drown it out. The music of Chopin—one of the impromptus this time—was all she could hear, all she could feel.

Now, forever more, Chopin was wrapped up in her mind with a little Hispanic boy named Guillermo, five years old with with beautiful brown skin and wide dark eyes. On Friday mornings Cass made the drive from her home near Cheyenne to the elementary school in Elk City, where she worked as a teacher's assistant in a preschool class for developmentally delayed and disabled children. She brought her little portable CD player and had the kids listen to music—autistic kids, those with Down's syndrome and cerebral palsy, those who were just slow in learning.

The teacher, an old high school friend of Cass's, had called her nearly two years ago, when she heard Cass had moved back to Oklahoma, and asked her to come and put together a sort of music therapy for her students. Even though she knew next to nothing about working with children, Cass tried it, and before too long both she and the kids looked forward to Friday mornings. For her, it was the only time of the week, other than grocery shopping, when she was able to leave the house.

Guillermo was one of the autistic ones and spent most of his time running back and forth, stamping his feet, and dropping handfuls of pens and pencils on the floor, into boxes, into the sink that stood in the corner of the room. But when Chopin came on the CD player during music time, he stopped, his hand full of pens, and gently set them down on the table. Then he would walk to the speakers and stand quietly, his eyes on the stereo as if searching for the pianist inside the little silver box. When Chopin would end and music by another composer—Beethoven, Mozart, Brahms, it didn't matter—came on, Guillermo would wave his arms and run off in search of his pens.

Although the day was cold and the wind brutal, Cass rolled down the window of the truck, hoping the air would clear Chopin and Guillermo out of her head. The closer she came to home, the more she had to refocus her thinking, to slip back into her other role, to leave the rest of the world behind. She barely registered when she left the Cheyenne city limits and was completely oblivious to the Washita River bridge. She drove by rote. She knew the country as well as she knew Chopin.

For a moment she had an image of herself a few years ago, long hair pulled back, wearing a flowing designer evening gown and her mother's string of pearls, flexing her fingers, waiting the last few minutes before she made the entrance for which she'd trained her entire life. Chopin, sweet Chopin.

Cass Chambers snorted. Here and now: her ash-blonde hair was cut short and haphazardly, almost like a boy's. Her clothes were earth-stained Levi's that had once been blue, a baggy dark green sweatshirt, and a down-filled sleeveless vest. Instead of six-inch Italian heels, she wore brown lace-up hiking boots that were scuffed from battling the hard ground. And her fingers, God, her *fingers*. . . .

She turned the country radio station a little louder. Anyone passing her going south on 283 would have been able to hear it clearly. But still Chopin filled her senses, which was part of the reason she didn't see the dripping wet man run into the middle of the empty highway.

Cass didn't scream. She'd screamed herself out long ago. She'd screamed out her surprise, her shock, even her fear, until all those things were no longer part of her. So she simply clamped both hands on the wheel and jerked the truck hard right to avoid hitting the man. The truck left the highway and rattled up the embankment on the east side. There was a thud and Cass didn't know if she'd missed the man or not.

She brought the truck to a stop halfway up the embankment, a few feet shy of a barbed wire fence and thirty feet from the road. Cass breathed out very slowly, the only outward sign that anything unusual had happened. Then she calmly took her hands off the wheel, unsnapped her seat belt, and as was her custom, jammed her left hand in the pocket of her vest, reaching across her body with her right hand to open the truck door.

She saw the skid marks first, a hard, black arc on the gray pavement. Then she saw the man, ten feet farther along, lying in the "bar ditch," a depression just off the shoulder of the road before the rise of the embankment. Cass studied the angle of the skid marks and the place where the man was lying, then decided she hadn't hit him after all.

She sighed and started deliberately down toward the man.

A deer in the headlights.

Except for the fact that it was broad daylight and Ryan was hardly a deer, that was what came to mind. He'd had no thought except to put as much distance as possible between himself and whatever—*whoever*—was back there. At some point it registered with him that he wasn't being pursued, but he'd plowed forward, splashing across the muddy shallows of the Washita River, tripping on a rock and falling face-first into the frigid water.

He'd scrambled up the slope and sprinted across the highway. Only then had he seen the truck and heard the whining steel guitars coming from the open window. He dove away from the vehicle. His knees bounced once on the shoulder of the road and he rolled into the ditch, landing on his back, blinking into the winter-blue sky.

The music was still playing, painfully loud. Why doesn't someone turn that shit off? he felt like screaming.

Then there were footsteps coming down the slope and he hoisted himself into a sitting position. He blinked twice and looked at the woman who was now only a few feet from him.

She was a few years older than he, early thirties, maybe thirty-five. Short, careless haircut, androgynous clothing, feminine heart-shaped face with no makeup. Medium complexion, high color in her cheeks. And her eyes were enormous, the biggest eyes he'd ever seen. They filled her face, an intriguing blue-gray color. It was an oddly compelling face and it took Ryan a moment to figure out why—although the woman seemed calm and perfectly in control, she looked as if she'd spent her entire life walking on shards of broken glass. *Hurt.* She looked hurt, in a way Ryan couldn't imagine.

"You all right?" she said, and while the rural Oklahoma drawl was there, it was cultured at the same time, as if she knew how to lose the accent, but had decided to keep it anyway.

"I think so." He moved around gingerly, his foot throbbing. Now that he wasn't running, he began to realize how cold he was from tripping in the river. Water ran off his clothes, his hair, his beard.

"You could get yourself killed running out in front of traffic like that," the woman said mildly.

Ryan looked up at her. Those huge eyes, that wounded face, but still she was completely calm. It was unsettling. "Well, it's not exactly like rush hour out here." He tried to stand, took a step, winced. The pain in his foot made his eyes water.

"Leg?" the woman said.

"Foot. It's just sprained, I think. I actually hurt it a ways back." Watch what you say! he admonished himself.

The woman folded her arms. She didn't even seem to be cold. "So what are you doing, running around out here in the middle of nowhere?"

"Long story," Ryan said. "Sorry if I scared you."

"It'll take a lot more than that to scare me. You better let me take you to the hospital down at Elk City to have that foot checked out."

Ryan opened his mouth, then closed it. What did he do now? There was a dead man lying in the grass back there somewhere and a killer with a rifle.

Adam and Eve, Art Dorian had said with his dying breath. *Adam and Eve.*

At a hospital, they would want to know what had happened: "Mr. Elder, how did you happen to sprain your foot at the Battle of the Washita Historic Site? Didn't we have reports of gunshots out there?"

What if the woman wanted to call the sheriff or the Highway Patrol or whoever the hell had jurisdiction out here? Had Dorian's body been found? What about Ryan's car? So many questions. He could see himself sitting in a patrol car: "I was meeting this man, you see, and he was with the federal government. No, I don't know what department. We went for a walk and he was going to tell me something about my parents, who committed double suicide seven years ago. And look, I have this newspaper clipping here . . . my occupation? Well, I'm a radio journalist, but I was fired from my job. . . ." They'd lock him up so fast it would make his head spin. He'd had Dorian's blood on his hands, and even though it had washed off in the river, they could probably do DNA testing or something to prove it had been there. And, oh Jesus, he had Dorian's loaded gun in his pocket. He'd almost forgotten it in his mad flight across the plain.

"Hey," the woman said.

Another pickup truck zoomed past southbound, going at least seventy. He thought he saw the woman nod toward the driver, who continued on toward Cheyenne.

Target. Ryan was still a target out here.

"Shit," he whispered, then took a couple of halting steps up the embankment toward the woman. She reached out a hand to him, her right hand. The left never came out of her vest pocket.

Ryan stared at her hand. Smooth, with long fingers and very short, neatly clipped nails. No polish. His eyes flickered back up to her face and the decision was made.

He grasped her hand and she partially pulled him up the embankment toward the truck, then opened the passenger door for him. The radio was still blaring. The woman circled the truck and slid back into the driver's seat.

"You should probably be more careful about who you give rides to," Ryan said. "I could be a crazy man."

The woman's eyes widened, if that was possible, but not in fear. They locked onto Ryan and didn't waver for a full minute. Ryan had never seen a woman with such a stare.

Finally she turned from him, flicked off the radio, and put the truck in gear. "I've seen crazy, up close and personal," she said. "I don't know what you are, but that's not it."

For a fleeting moment Ryan wondered if he was the one who should be afraid. He shook it off, closing his hand around the butt of Dorian's pistol. "What's your name?"

"Cass. Cass Chambers."

"You live around here, Cass Chambers?"

"I do. Who are you?"

"Ryan. Just Ryan. That'll do for now." Both his foot and his head ached. He thought he could kill for a couple of Tylenol. "I don't want you to take me to the hospital."

"Oh?"

"Take me to your house and wrap this foot for me. It won't take long. Maybe you've got some aspirin or something."

She paused with her hand on the gearshift, looking over at him again. She said nothing, motionless.

Ryan blinked away the pain. He brought the gun out of his pocket and pointed it vaguely at her. For a moment he felt almost nauseated. He'd just pointed a loaded gun at another human being. "I can't go to a hospital. I need some time to sort some things out."

She kept looking at him. The gaze didn't flinch, the muscles of her face seeming almost frozen.

"Back up, get on the highway, and let's go," Ryan said. "Do you live alone? Don't try to tell me you're married to a big rancher who'll be waiting at the door with a shotgun."

"What if I am?"

"You're not wearing a ring."

"Lots of country women around here don't wear rings."

Ryan raised the pistol a couple of inches. "You're not married."

Her face was frozen again. Ryan felt like screaming.

"Drive," he finally said. The gun inched up farther and he leaned in toward her on the seat until he was no more than a foot away. "Do you still think I'm not crazy?"

"You're not going to shoot me," Cass said, a little too quickly.

"No?"

"No. That gun's an automatic and you haven't turned off the safety."

Ryan stared down at the weapon. He'd never held a gun before in his life. His parents hadn't allowed guns in the house and he'd never had an interest in them. He didn't even know what the safety looked like.

"Drive," Ryan said. "I just need a little time, then I'll leave you alone. Some time to get this foot wrapped and collect my thoughts." His eyes strayed out the window, back toward the river, toward Art Dorian lying out there, bleeding on the cold ground. *Adam and Eve.*

"What happened out there?" Cass said.

Ryan shook his head. The nose of the gun drooped a little. "I don't know," he said.

Cass kept her eyes on the pale ribbon of U.S. 283, stretching away to the north, into the wind. She knew he was still holding the gun on her and she also knew he didn't know how to use it. But it was just as clear that he wasn't stupid and he'd figure out the safety soon enough.

He could be a rapist. A serial killer. Anything.

She could stop the truck on a dime, reach over, and stomp on his injured foot before he could react, then push him out the passenger side door and drive to the sheriff's office in Cheyenne. It would be over before it began.

She eased off the accelerator just a fraction. He didn't seem to notice. It was as if he were looking through her, not at her.

What are you doing, Cassandra?

The last few years, nestled in her cocoon under the endless horizon of western Oklahoma, came back to her. The fingers of her left hand ached, or at least she imagined that they did.

She took a sidelong glance at Ryan. He frowned at her and motioned with the gun. She looked back to the road.

Chopin, Guillermo, her father . . . all the years had gathered into this tall, bearded young man who was holding a weapon he didn't know how to use and trying not to shiver.

She spotted the oil well on the Darnell property off to her right. One more mile to the turnoff. Only one other vehicle had passed them on the road. She checked the rearview mirror—the highway was empty. One more mile to make her choice.

The road rolled and the old Dodge truck took it smoothly. More than likely the man was right. He would take a little of her time and then be gone. He was no criminal, that was certain. But what was he, then?

Half a mile.

"How much farther?" Ryan said.

"Not far."

She spotted the turnoff. The gate was still open from this morning when she'd left to go to the school. That had been a long time ago, hadn't it?

She eased off the accelerator again. *Keep going*, she heard the voice again. *Drive on north, to Arnett, to the sheriff there. He'll never know.*

But whose voice *was* that?

Cass shook her head. She slowed and turned, leaving the blacktop for the gravel path to her house.

As the ranch style with the satellite dish beside it came into view, Cass thought she heard Chopin playing very softly.

8

THE WHISPERING MAN WAS WINDED. THOUGH HE'D never intended to catch Ryan Elder, it was important that the boy *believe* he wanted to catch him. Being careful to stay far enough back to avoid being seen, he'd kept up the chase for half a mile, until he heard Elder splashing into the waters of the Washita. That was when the Whispering Man had stopped and turned away.

He would find Ryan Elder again—he had no doubt of it. In fact, Elder might even find him first. He smiled a little at that. All the better, he thought. But first, he had other business.

The Whispering Man crept back to where he'd hidden on the ridge, retrieving the knapsack he'd secreted in some scrub. He broke down the rifle, stowed it carefully away, then walked back to where Art Dorian lay, staring lifelessly at the bright winter sky.

He had to hand it to Dorian. The government man had wanted seclusion and he'd achieved his goal. No one in their right mind, not the most die-hard tourist or history buff, would come out to this site in mid-January, with the day so cold and the wind so brutally relentless. It was a solitary place to begin with, but in January it seemed the loneliest place in America.

He poked around in the knapsack and came up with an old-fashioned Polaroid camera, the kind available at any discount store. Also in the bag, he brought out a box of rubber surgical gloves, removed a pair, and slipped them on. He took four pictures of Dorian, making sure the open chest cavity and all the blood could be seen clearly. He waited for the photos to develop, turning his head away from the wind, watching his breath in front of him. When he was satisfied with the pictures, he tucked them into the knapsack alongside the camera, the broken-down rifle, and the box of gloves. He walked up the road to his Escort, turned it around, and drove back toward Cheyenne.

Half an hour later he was back on Interstate 40, eastbound toward Elk City, the largest town in the region, when he pulled off at a desolate exit. Coming down the ramp, he noticed a widening of the shoulder where two large yellow trash barrels sat. He eased onto the shoulder next to the cans, put the car in park, and opened the glove compartment. He took out a cell phone and started to punch in the number for the Roger Mills County Sheriff's Department. But as his fingers hovered over the buttons, there was the vision again: the young boy gazing up at the man and saying, *Why, Daddy, why?*

The Whispering Man shook his head. The little boy and his larger-than-life father had nothing to do with the Revolution. Not anymore. If they'd helped to create the idea for the Revolution, so be it. But that was a long time ago, and they were both dead and gone now, weren't they?

For a moment the picture was so clear he almost felt he could reach out and touch the boy and the man. He wanted to put his hand on the boy's shoulder and tell him not to worry, that everything would be all right. He would take care of it. After the Revolution, things would be different. Everything would change, the land would be cleansed, and his father would listen. His father would not ignore his pleas anymore. *Just be patient, it's coming soon now. . . .*

The Whispering Man punched the buttons on the phone and the picture faded. When the phone was answered, he said in a thick Oklahoma drawl that was not native to him, "Yeah, I was just drivin' by the historic site out there, and I swear I heard some shots . . . that's right. Well, I know there's no huntin' allowed on the grounds, and I figured some kids might be out there shootin' beer cans. I hate to see the place get all littered up, you know? Anyway, just thought I'd call it in. Nope, gotta go. You just might want to send someone past there. Maybe it's nothin'." Before the dispatcher could say another word, he pressed the end button, then got out of the car and tossed the phone into the first trash can.

He slid back into the car and dug in the knapsack again. Three of the photos of Art Dorian went into a five-by-eight manila envelope, into which he'd already placed a single sheet of white paper with three lines of computer-printed text on it. Discount paper, printed from a cheap bubble jet printer, like millions of others in use all over the world. Untraceable.

He sealed the envelope with the paper and the photos, then eased the car back onto the highway. Ten miles east, he pulled off again and stripped his gloves into another trash can. He would put on a different pair of gloves before he made his delivery.

He figured distances in his head as he accelerated up the on-ramp. It was about 120 miles to Oklahoma City. He'd be there in less than two hours. Then the net would begin to tighten around young Ryan Elder.

Faith Kelly had drawn front desk duty, which was an utter abomination to any serious law enforcement professional. Even more so in the U.S. Marshals Service, where there was very little desk traffic of any kind. While others in her office were doing real work—two deputies had left on a prisoner escort that very morning, traveling to northern Minnesota to bring back a stockbroker wanted for forty-plus counts of securities fraud—she was stuck, staring through the bullet-proof glass.

In fact, in the ten months since she'd graduated from the academy and been assigned to Oklahoma City, she hadn't done much more than desk duty, community relations, and paperwork. She'd participated in one high-priority case, but that had turned out badly. The FBI had broken a case against a sitting U.S. congressman from Oklahoma, a case full of shady real-estate deals, extortion, and mail fraud. After the man was arrested at his office in the Rayburn Building in Washington, a team of deputy marshals was sent to pick him up and return him to Oklahoma for trial. Kelly was assigned as a junior member of the team.

She'd been disgusted by the congressman, who was known as a "family values" politician, but who began making overtly sexual remarks to her from the moment the team took him into custody. At the airport, with reporters shouting and jockeying for position, a photographer from the Associated Press had snapped a picture of the congressman staring openly at Kelly's chest. The photo had run in newspapers all over the country and Kelly was back to paperwork as soon as she arrived back in the office. As a prank, someone had blown up the photo and plastered it to her desk, with a comic strip balloon above the congressman's head and the words *You gotta have Faith!*

On today's front desk duty, Kelly had read a couple of

professional journals, fielded a few innocuous phone calls, read half of *U.S. News and World Report*, and made some notes for a TV reporter who was doing a series on women in law enforcement.

The phone rang. "Marshals Service, Kelly," she said into it, trying not to sound as bored as she was.

"Deputy Kelly, this is Clayton downstairs," said a gruff voice.

"Hi, Clayton. What's up?"

"There's a package here for your office. It's the strangest damn thing too."

Kelly's radar went up. The security forces at the courthouse entrance took everything seriously. "What do you mean?"

"Don't know where it came from. I mean, there's nothing wrong with it. We scanned it through already. Nothing in it but paper and what looks like photographs, so it's clean. But it was dropped in the revolving door. Judge Churchman and her big entourage had just come through, and a bunch of reporters covering the Nellis trial, and after everyone was gone, Deck turned around and saw this envelope in the revolving door."

"You checked with the judge and her group?"

"First thing. No one claimed it."

"How do you know it's for us?"

Clayton laughed softly. "No detective work on that one. It's got 'U.S. Marshals Service, Federal Courthouse, Oklahoma City' typed on the envelope."

Kelly sat back. "Send it up."

"It's on its way."

Five minutes later, she accepted the envelope from the messenger, pulling it through the opening in the bulletproof glass. She centered it in front of her on the desk, making observations as she'd been taught. There was nothing outstanding about it, a standard manila envelope with a tiny silver clasp to hold down the flap. There were no smudges or tears or perforations. It was crisp and seemed new.

Kelly undid the clasp, shook out the envelope's contents, and her lunch nearly came back up onto the desk in front of her.

There were three photos, at different angles, of a very dead Art Dorian. One clearly showed his face in a hard close-up, blood drying at the corners of his mouth. Another was a close shot of the chest area, all crimson against the snowy backdrop of Dorian's shirt. The third was from a few feet away, showing the entire body.

Control, Kelly thought. Don't lose your lunch. She'd never seen a dead body before, much less the body of a person she'd come to view as a mentor, friend, and surrogate father.

She clicked a nail against the desktop, the rhythm growing increasingly faster. Her mind churned. Her stomach rolled. What was the proper procedure? No one knew what to do regarding Dorian—he reported directly to Washington. Department Thirty was outside the normal hierarchy of the office.

"Hey, Faith, did you see the Svendsen file anywhere?" a voice said behind her.

Kelly jumped, banging her knees against the underside of the desk. She swept the photos into a pile under the envelope. "Don't sneak up on me like that," she said, turning around to face a tall, rangy, blond man.

Derek Mayfield was only two or three years older than Kelly, one of the more likable men in the office. He was easy-going if not the brightest deputy in the service and had won the agency firearms competition for three years running, ever since he'd come to Oklahoma City. "Sorry. You're jumpy. But then, desk duty can do that to you."

"Is the chief in?" Kelly said. The office was organized under the U.S. Marshal, who was a political appointee, and the Chief Deputy, who supervised the other deputies. Oklahoma City's chief deputy was a burly, no-nonsense man in his midfifties named Phillip Clarke.

"No, he had court, remember?" Mayfield said. "You okay, Faith? Any trouble up here?"

Kelly's heart pounded. What she said and did in the next few minutes could determine her future in the Marshals Service. She was the junior officer here. If she showed the photos to Mayfield, she'd be off the case before there even *was* a case. If Mayfield took the case to Chief Deputy Clarke, then Mayfield would get to work with the local authorities—and probably the FBI, since this involved the murder of a federal agent—in bringing the case in. She couldn't let that happen. Not for Art Dorian's sake and not for her own.

Kelly's grandfather had been a beat cop in Chicago for forty years. Her father was a captain of detectives in a Chicago suburb. Her older brother was a Customs agent, currently stationed in Arizona. Law enforcement was all she'd ever wanted, even more so after her father told her at age thirteen that a smart girl like her ought to be a schoolteacher. She'd been on full academic scholarship and at the top of her class, both undergraduate and master's level in criminal justice at Northwestern. Second in her class at the academy. *A schoolteacher!*

Chief Deputy Clarke would be back Monday morning. Kelly intended to be in his office at 8:00 A.M. She would use the weekend to prepare. For a moment she thought of Dorian smoothing his little mustache and she had to blink hard several times.

Don't cry, idiot, she thought. Don't blow it, not here in front of Mayfield.

"Faith?" Mayfield said.

"Sorry," Kelly said. She forced a smile. "I've worked up a pretty good headache. Desk duty does that to you."

Mayfield smiled back. "Tell me about it. You want some aspirin? I've got some in my desk."

"No, thanks. I think I'll take a break. I didn't take a lunch today, anyway. Cover me for fifteen minutes or so?"

"Sure, Faith. Glad to do it. Go get some fresh air."

"Thanks." Kelly shuffled the photos back into the envelope, slid it into her purse, and left the desk.

Two minutes later, she was in front of Dorian's door. *The mysterious portal to Department Thirty*, he sometimes jokingly called it. Quickly glancing to both sides of the hallway, Kelly let herself in with the key Dorian had given her three months ago. *Just in case*, he'd said then.

Kelly closed the door behind her and looked around the office. It was neat and unassuming as always, just like Dorian. Kelly went to the desk and shook the photos out of the envelope, then felt inside it. She inched the paper out. It had been folded over once and she carefully unfolded it.

In black twelve-point print was written: *Cheyenne, Oklahoma*. Then a double space and *Case # 73-00152*. Two more lines down, ominous in its presence in all caps, a name: *RYAN ELDER*.

Kelly felt her entire being tighten, like a fishing line whose bait was suddenly taken. Who had sent this? If it was indeed one of Dorian's cases, how did the sender know about it? Department Thirty's cases were kept so secret that not even the sister agencies knew anything about them. They knew Thirty existed, and that was all. Cases were never, ever discussed. Not even the case numbers were released. Kelly had tried to get Dorian to talk even in broad generalities about his work, but the little man never did.

Kelly's eyes roamed the desk. The computer looked like it was seldom used, a light film of dust coating the screen. The in-basket and out-basket were both empty. The telephone sat at a perfect forty-five-degree angle on the edge of the desk, and underneath. . . .

Kelly picked up the phone and slid the file folder from under it. She'd never seen even a hint of Dorian's work in this office. She knew he didn't like using the computer and she also knew the filing cabinet was always double-locked. She looked around—the blinds were open, looking down onto the Murrah Memorial. As always, tourists were milling about. All year round, all types of weather, there were people down there.

She reached up and closed the blinds, switching on the desk lamp as the room fell into shadow. She checked her watch: she'd been gone a little over five minutes. She had another ten before Mayfield might begin to wonder about her.

She looked at the file label. The number matched the one from the envelope. Beneath the number, in Dorian's fine, precise hand, was written: *Elder*.

Kelly opened the file.

Five minutes later, her mind burning with all the questions and an anger starting to form, she began to see possibilities. Ideas. Movements. The past and the present, fusing together.

She remembered the last time she'd seen Dorian in this office, a few days ago. He'd given her advice both about dealing with her father and her love life and managed to do it in such a way that it didn't even seem like advice. But he'd still been preoccupied. And there was something about a phone call. *From the past*, he'd said.

A phone call from the past.

She glanced at the file again, reading the case synopsis until she'd almost memorized it. Then she spied the photos out of the corner of her eye—Dorian's anguished face, his blood soaking the ground, a featureless ground of dry, brown grass.

But there were so many questions, not the least of which was: who had delivered this envelope? Where had they gotten the pictures? And how did they know the case number?

Ryan Elder. She wouldn't forget the name.

After a moment's hesitation, she reached for Dorian's phone, then stopped when she realized her hand was shaking. Without knowing it, she'd started to cry, silent tears that ran in straight lines down her face and dripped off her chin onto the desktop. She caught sight of the pictures again, reached out and pushed them off the edge of the desk.

Kelly made a fist and brought it to her mouth, pressing it several times against her lips. Her "cry reflex," she'd named it in college, when she'd been teaching herself how *not* to cry. In a moment the tears stopped, and in the cold-eyed aftermath, she reminded herself to stop in the ladies' room on the way back to the office. She'd have to repair her makeup. Mayfield couldn't see her this way.

She reached for the phone again and called information. When the operator asked what city she wanted, Kelly waited a fraction of a second.

"Cheyenne, Oklahoma," she said.

9

"PUT THE GUN AWAY," CASS CHAMBERS SAID AS THE
trail widened and ended at the house. "You won't need it."

Ryan jerked his attention back to her. He realized he'd
been holding the gun almost casually, with his mind miles
away. Art Dorian, Black Kettle, his mother's hands, the little
blue outfit with the car stitched on it, the pain in his foot. . . .

"You're not a criminal," Cass said, "so stop acting like
one." She coasted to a stop, put the truck in park, and turned
off the engine.

"You don't know that!" Ryan shouted, his voice bouncing
around the cab of the truck like a ball thrown by a toddler.
He raised the gun again.

Ryan's foot and head throbbed and now his hand—the
one holding the gun—was aching too. He blinked at Cass.
For a moment she was Art Dorian, chest blown open, bleeding onto the hard ground.

I'm trying to save your life, Ryan, Dorian had said as he
pushed him off the trail.

"Oh, Jesus," Ryan said, and the pistol slipped from his
fingers. He bowed his head and pressed his hands to his tem-
ples.

Cass breathed out slowly. "Come inside with me."

Ryan didn't raise his head. "What's happening? Someone
tell me what's happening—"

"You're not a killer. I know that. I don't know what kind
of trouble you're in, but—"

Ryan brought one of his hands down on the dashboard. It
sounded like a slap across the face. "I don't understand any
of this!"

Cass half turned in the seat. Glancing at the house, she

thought she saw movement behind the closed curtains that covered the kitchen window. "Any of what?"

Ryan acted as if he hadn't heard her. "Dorian knew things. The little jumper with the car on it. How could he have known about that? And the letter, the clipping, the phone number. *His* phone number. Department Thirty, and . . . what did he mean by 'Adam and Eve?' What the hell was that supposed to mean?" Both hands slammed the dash, twice, three times, four.

"Come on, let's go in the house. Let me get you something for the pain. You can get warm."

Ryan shook his head, then caught sight of the gun. It had lain untouched between them. He picked it up again. "Take it easy. Just get out."

"I've told you, put that away. You don't need it," Cass said.

"Just get out."

Cass took a deep breath. "I live with my father. He's not . . . well."

"What do you mean?"

"Please, for God's sake, you don't need the gun! If my father sees it, he might . . . I don't know. But I've said I'll help you. If you need to call someone, you can do it here."

The gun quivered. "I don't trust you."

Chopin had been niggling around the edges of Cass's mind, but it suddenly crashed to a halt as if someone had taken a hammer to the piano keys. "That's it! If this is how you are with someone who wants to help you, I'd hate to see you with an enemy, Mr. 'Just Ryan.' Look, my family has lived in this area for seventy years and I've lived in this house for . . . well, most of my life. People out here try to help each other. Even strangers. Even *strange* strangers. If you can't accept that, then I guess you'll have to shoot me in the back."

She reached across herself, opened the door, let herself out, and took a few steps toward the house. The movement flickered behind the curtains again.

Ryan froze, the gun drooping.

Cass took a few more steps.

"Wait," Ryan said softly, then raised his voice. "Wait a

minute!" He stuck the gun back in his coat pocket and got out of the truck, turning his head away from the wind. Cass was ten feet from him, almost to the edge of the simple rock garden in front of the house.

She stopped and turned halfway toward him. "Well?"

"You said your family has lived here for seventy years. You know Cheyenne, then. The people, the town."

Cass nodded. "Three generations of Cheyenne High School graduates. I was away for a few years, but I moved back after my father got sick."

Ryan's heart beat wildly against his ribs. The pain in his foot receded into some dark place. "Does the name Elder mean anything to you?"

She met his eyes. "No. Should it?"

Ryan came around the front of the truck. "No, I guess not. My father would have left here before you were born. What about your father? How old is he?"

"He's sixty-three. But he's . . ."

"My father would be sixty-two now. They probably grew up together. This is a small town, they'd have to know each other!" Ryan realized he was babbling. He took a few more steps. Ryan caught a little of Cass's scent—it wasn't perfumed, but simply *clean*. Too clean for a woman who spent her life battling the plains, he thought dimly. "Let me talk to him. Please, I need to ask him."

Cass's eyes settled on him again, those impossibly large round eyes with their blue-gray hue. For the first time since she'd been outside, she shivered. She finally nodded. "All right. But I need to tell you something. My father is . . . he has early-onset Alzheimer's. He was diagnosed about three years ago."

Ryan's face froze. "What?"

"His short-term memory is affected. Long-term isn't. He can't remember who I am sometimes, but he remembers fifty years ago like it was this morning."

Ryan shook his head. "I don't believe this." He raised his head and his voice to the sky. "Let me wake up back in Pensacola. At least there it was *warm!*"

"Come on," Cass said patiently. "Let me do the talking at first when we go inside."

The house was typical rural Oklahoma, blond brick and wood trim construction. Cass unlocked the front door, which opened into a hallway. Ryan smelled cigarette smoke and staleness, as if the windows were never opened. A watercolor of a mounted horse and rider commanded the left wall. On the right the hallway opened into a formal room. They moved quickly past it, but not before Ryan caught a glimpse of a piano.

"Is that a Steinway concert grand?" Ryan said. He must be hallucinating from the pain and insanity of it all, he thought. No one had Steinway concert grand pianos in their homes, certainly not in modest ranch styles ten miles outside Cheyenne, Oklahoma.

"Never mind," Cass said, and led him down two short steps into a den. A man's room, Ryan instantly thought. It was in a rustic motif, with an abundance of polished wood. It was filled with sturdy wooden furniture, a series of carved wooden flutes balanced on the curving stone mantel, framed photos of men, women, children, some studio poses, some candid outdoor shots. Ryan thought he saw one of a much younger Cass, with long hair, wearing a stunning emerald green formal dress and pearls.

In a wooden rocker covered with a handmade quilt in a Dutch doll pattern sat an old man. He was wearing blue jeans, cream-colored cowboy boots, and a thick flannel shirt. Bald on top, wisps of gray hair floated about his ears and down to his neck. He was very lean, the face more so than his body. His face looked as if it needed to have the slack taken out of it. The eyes were the same blue-gray as Cass's, although nowhere near as large. At the man's right hand was a small, round wooden table. On it sat a tiny lamp, a portable radio pumping out country music, a pack of cigarettes, lighter, and overflowing ashtray.

"Good, Cassandra, you're back," the man drawled. "Your mother's been hiding my cigarettes again."

"Daddy, where's Alice?" Cass said gently.

A woman came out of the kitchen, surprising Ryan. He closed his hand almost involuntarily over the automatic in his coat pocket. The woman was Native American, in her fifties, with coppery skin and ebony hair shot through with silver.

"Here, Cass," she said. Her voice was soft and cadenced. The two women exchanged looks, the older woman inclining her head slightly toward Ryan. Cass shook her head as if to say, Don't worry. Everything's fine. The Indian woman shrugged.

"Thanks for staying with him, Alice," Cass said.

"Always glad to do it," the other woman said, still looking at Ryan. She continued on toward the front of the house, taking a coat from a closet. A moment later Ryan heard the door open and close.

"Who's that?" Ryan whispered.

"A neighbor. She stays with him when I go to town."

"Cassandra!" the man barked. "My cigarettes! I don't know how many times I've told your mother. . . ."

"My mother's been dead nearly twenty years," Cass murmured, then stepped forward and knelt beside the man. She guided his hand to the pack of cigarettes. "Here, Daddy."

"Oh, good. I thought . . . never mind. Say, who's this?" His eyes fell on Ryan.

Cass stood up. "Daddy, this is Ryan. He's—"

The man stood and came toward Ryan with his hand outstretched. "Delmas Chambers. Nice to meet you. Say, I remember you. You took Cassandra to the senior dance."

Ryan looked at Cass, saw the pain on her face. "No, Daddy," she said. "Ryan's a new friend. He's . . ." She swallowed. "He's doing some research into his family background and some of his people are from around here." A sidelong glance at Ryan. "Isn't that right, Ryan?"

Ryan nodded and shook Chambers's hand. The grip was strong. Cass had said he was sixty-three, but he looked ten years older. "Yes, that's right."

"Ryan, you sit down. I'll get some things for you from the medicine cabinet."

Chambers's eyebrows went up.

"He had a little accident," Cass said.

"Got to be careful, boy," Chambers said, watching his daughter disappear into the hallway. "Fine girl. Have you heard her play?"

Play? Ryan thought, then remembered the Steinway. "No. No, I haven't."

"The best. Absolutely the best. Better than all those Russian piano players put together. She's got this thing about saving the world, though. I tell her not to worry about the world and worry about herself. Maybe she'll play when she comes back."

He motioned Ryan to a chair on the other side of the lamp table, then sat back down in the rocker and lit a cigarette. "Cassandra's mother, God bless her, keeps trying to get me to quit. But a man needs his vices. So you're from here?"

Ryan gripped the arm of the chair, trying to keep up with the man's jerky way of hopping from one subject to another without pause. "Well, actually, no. My father grew up here, but he left right after high school. His parents' house burned down, and he—"

"Just a minute," Chambers said, and turned up the volume on the little radio. "They're giving the news."

Ryan clenched his teeth. An ad for a furniture store ended and one for a car dealer came on. Cass returned with a bandage, Tylenol, and a glass of water. "Here," she said, and gave Ryan two capsules. He swallowed them and she pushed a small brown hassock under his injured foot. She looked questioningly up at him and he nodded. She proceeded to remove his shoe and sock, palpitating gently along the ridge of his foot.

The car ad ended on the radio and a droning newscaster came on. "A little breaking news now," the announcer said. "From Roger Mills County, there's been a report of a shooting at the Battle of the Washita National Historic Site just outside Cheyenne."

Ryan's heart skipped a beat, his entire body tensing. Cass felt it in his foot and stopped wrapping the bandage.

"Details are sketchy at this point, but one man is reported dead in the incident," the newscaster continued. "He has yet to be identified, but was said to be killed by a gunshot wound to the chest. Authorities from the Roger Mills County Sheriff's Department received an anonymous tip about gunshots in the area and arrived on the scene shortly after. A car with Ohio license plates was found in the parking lot of the historic site. At this time sheriff's officers aren't saying whether it's connected to the crime."

"What do you know about that?" Delmas Chambers said. "People gettin' shot, even around here. Time was, that sort of thing didn't happen. Used to be, you felt safe out here."

Thoughts tumbled through Ryan like water in a well: Anonymous tip . . . car with Ohio license plates. Who could have called the sheriff? There was no one there—he would have heard the sound of another car.

Like the blade of a dull knife, the realization sliced into him: the killer had called the sheriff.

Ryan's hand started to tremble and he had to grip the arm of the chair so hard his entire hand went white. Fear tramped up his spine on icy feet, settling at the base of his neck. Breath escaped him in a rush.

"Ryan?" Cass looked up at him.

Ryan folded both his hands together to keep them from shaking. "Go ahead." He nodded toward his foot. "Finish that up."

Cass slowly went back to wrapping his foot and Ryan held his breath against the pain, hoping the Tylenol would kick in soon. On the radio, the announcer was reading the weather.

Chambers took a drag on his cigarette and settled his gaze on Ryan. "Now, son, you wanted to ask me something."

"My father," Ryan whispered, then cleared his throat and said it again, louder. "He grew up here."

"How old is he?"

"He's . . . he would have been sixty-two this year. He died seven years ago."

"Sorry to hear that, son. Sixty-two, well I'm sure I knew

him. Cheyenne was a small school. Let's see, I graduated in 1958, so I guess he graduated in fifty-nine, right?"

Ryan nodded vigorously. "Yes, that's right. And that summer after he graduated was when the house burned down. My grandparents both died in the fire. My father had gone into Elk City with some friends and when he came back, the house was completely gone. He left town and joined the Marine Corps shortly after that."

Chambers stared at him, some of the slackness gone from his face. "What's your daddy's name?"

"Elder. Frank Elder. Francis Andrew Elder."

Cass slipped Ryan's sock back on his foot, over the bulky bandage. "Here," she said quietly, and put his shoe on. "You won't be able to lace up the shoe, but it shouldn't be too uncomfortable."

"Son, there must be some mistake," Chambers said.

Ryan unclenched his hands. Chambers ground out his cigarette and immediately lit another, exhaling smoke toward the lamp that sat between them.

"Maybe you've got your towns mixed up," he said.

"No." Ryan shook his head again. He remembered what Art Dorian said about how the Battle of the Washita Historic Site had always made an impression on Frank Elder. "My father . . . I know he played basketball in high school, and . . . and the historic site was a big deal to him."

Chambers stood up abruptly, knocking over the table. The lamp and the radio crashed to the floor. The ashtray upended, spilling its contents on the oval hooked rug under the chair. Chambers leveled a finger at Ryan. "You're trying to make a sick man look stupid. I may not know what I was doing an hour ago, but I remember high school just as clear as anything."

"But I don't—"

Chambers looked at his daughter. "Cassandra, take this young man back where you found him." He looked back to Ryan, eyes blazing. "Around here, we don't go into other people's homes and try to make fools of them. I don't know where you're from, but that's just not the way we do things." He looked around wildly. "Where are my cigarettes? Cassandra!"

"I don't understand," Ryan said.

"*I* played basketball," Chambers said. "I was on the team that won district in 1958. And there wasn't any fire in the summer of 1959. That would've been big news around here, two people dying in a house fire. And one more thing before you get out of my house: there wasn't a historic site then. Everyone knew where the battle was, all right, but there was nothing out there. It wasn't till the sixties that they put up any markers or anything."

Ryan felt as if he'd been punched in the stomach. Now the fear and the confusion were being stirred by something else, something he couldn't quite reach. Something dark. He stood up and Cass backed away from him. He took a few steps—his foot was still sore, but Cass had wrapped it well.

"Look," he said, "something's going on here, and I—"

"No!" Chambers shouted. "I don't know who you are or what you're up to, but let me tell you this, plain as day: I never knew any Elders. Not Frank or anyone else. Not in Cheyenne. Not ever."

10

RYAN CLOSED THE LAST BOOK AND LET IT DROP TO THE hardwood floor. The sound it made was hollow, like rain falling into a barrel, and Ryan thought he might as well have closed the book on everything he thought he knew about his father.

He looked up, saw Cass staring at him. They were in the front room of the house, cramped because of the piano. There was only space enough for two chairs and a tiny bookshelf. Cass was seated across from him, her back to the window. Behind her, the light slanted into shadows as the winter sun waned. They'd been looking through the books for over three hours.

"I know what you're thinking," Ryan said, "and I didn't kill that man."

"You don't know what I'm thinking and I know you didn't kill that man."

"Stop being so damn agreeable!"

"I'm not being agreeable. I'm being realistic." She leaned over and picked up the stack of Cheyenne High School year-books—"annuals," her father had called them—from the floor. She arranged them in order, 1955 through 1958, and placed them back on the shelf behind the piano bench.

Ryan put his head in his hands. It had taken time, but Cass had convinced her father to let Ryan stay at least for a while. "Nothing," Ryan said. "Not a damn thing. I looked at every page of every one of those books. Nothing with the basketball team, nothing in the class photo sections. He wasn't there." His face flushed a deep brick red. "Everything my father told me about his life was a lie. Why? Why would he do that? What possible reason—"

"Tell me what happened," Cass said. She waved a hand toward the window. "Out there."

Ryan shook his head. "You don't want to know."

"No, I don't, but if you tell me, maybe I can help."

"Why do you want to help me? You don't know me and I held a gun on you. That goes a little beyond the Good Samaritan bit."

"Maybe I like lost causes."

He pounded the chair. "Dammit, I need to think!"

Cass leaned back in the chair. "The news said there was a car with Ohio license plates, but earlier you said something about Pensacola. What's that about?"

Ryan stared at her.

Cass smiled. "It pays to listen closely. I've learned that les-son all over again with Daddy. There are always certain little signs that he's . . . well, drifting away from himself. But you have to pay attention."

Ryan shook his head. "I lived in Ohio until last summer. I've been in Pensacola since then, just hadn't bought new plates for the car."

"So it *is* your car."

"Oh, yes, it's my car." He sighed. "The dead man's name is Art Dorian . . . or at least that's what he told me his name was. He works . . . worked . . . for the government. He had asked me to meet him in Cheyenne. He said he had information about my parents. I know this doesn't make sense to you, but my parents committed suicide seven years ago."

Cass leaned forward, absorbing every word. "So you hadn't met this man before today?"

"Never. I didn't know he existed until a few days ago."

"You said he worked for the government. What part of the government?"

Ryan smiled emptily. "I don't know. He wouldn't tell me. But he *knew* things. I had to believe him. And then . . ." Ryan popped up from the chair, unable to be still any longer. He started to move back and forth between the piano and the door to the kitchen, his pace increasing as he related Dorian's murder.

Cass shifted again, her back almost touching the blinds covering the window. "If that's all there is, there's no reason you can't go to the sheriff and explain what happened."

"And how do I explain this loaded gun in my pocket?"

"Try explaining it to me."

Ryan stopped pacing. "It was his, all right? Dorian's. I grabbed it after he was dead. I thought I might need it!"

"If someone shot at you from the ridge, it would have to be a fairly long-range rifle. All you have is a pistol. They should be able to tell the kind of weapon from examining the man's wound. Plus there would be footprints on the ridge. All you'd have to do—"

"Don't you get it? That anonymous tip to the sheriff. That had to be the killer. Someone who knows about Dorian, knows about my parents . . . they didn't kill me out there, so they're trying to throw a net around me, to get the cops looking for me."

Cass leaned forward again. "Didn't you hear what I said? The evidence—"

"Not even as a suspect. They could arrest me as a material

witness. Look, I worked the law enforcement beat. But, dammit, I don't know what Dorian wanted to tell me. . . ."

Cass was quiet a moment. He sounded paranoid, one of those militia-type conspiracy theorists. But, she reminded herself, he didn't even know how to use a gun. He was flying totally blind, scared out of his wits. Sweat had popped out on his forehead and his lip was trembling.

"Tell me the rest," she said.

"What?"

"There's something else. What brought you here? How did this man Dorian get you from Pensacola to Cheyenne?"

Ryan thought of the newspaper clipping, the envelope arriving seven years late. "No. This is enough. I have to get out of here."

"I can't help you if you don't tell me."

Ryan's eyes burned into her. "Why do you always keep your left hand hidden?" he said abruptly.

Cass's fingers twitched in the pocket of her vest, but she said nothing.

"I notice things too," Ryan said. He sank heavily back into the chair by the piano. "I need to think. I need some answers." He patted his pockets, breathing out noisily. "I need a pen. Do you have a pen? I can't think without a pen."

"What does one have to do with the other?"

"Nothing. But I think better with a pen in my hand."

Cass reached up to the shelf behind the piano, pulled out a glass jar full of pens, and extended it to him. He took one between forefinger and middle finger and began tapping it up and down with his thumb.

Ryan thought about his father. His father's life, all lies. Up until seven years ago, his parents had been the bedrock of his life. He remembered his friend Jeff at the funeral, saying something in hushed tones to another friend: *They were always such a close family. I mean, he really got along with his parents. I don't know what this is going to do to him.*

Now, lies on top of the suicide. What else was a lie? Ryan's head throbbed, the pain in his foot muted for the time being. Then he thought of a name.

Ryan ran both hands through his beard. "I need to use your phone," he said to Cass.

Nearly a mile to the north of the Chambers house, Alice Nightwalker sipped her coffee and looked out the window, thinking about Cass and that young man. Ever since Cass had been a little girl, Nightwalker had worried about her. She was too trusting, too naive.

Nightwalker fancied herself a righter of wrongs and something was wrong at the Chambers house. She knew it from the moment she'd seen Cass drive up with that young man in tow. Something about him wasn't right.

Of course, she knew about the murder at the historical site. She'd heard it from a friend's daughter, who was a dispatcher at the sheriff's office. It had happened while Nightwalker was on her shift looking after Delmas Chambers, and then suddenly Cass had come home with a young stranger in her truck and they'd sat out in the driveway for a long time.

Nightwalker put down her cup of coffee and crossed the linoleum floor of her small but spotless kitchen. She didn't hesitate when she came to the wall phone. She called the number.

"Sheriff's Office," came the voice of her friend's daughter.

"Jeannie, it's Alice."

"Alice, it's crazy around here right now. Look, can you call back—"

"It's not a social call, Jeannie. Be quiet and listen to me. Get one of the boys to go out to Delmas Chambers's place. I think I know where you can find the owner of the car with the Ohio plates."

T. Jackson Coleridge, Attorney at Law, answered his phone on the first ring.

"Jack, it's Ryan."

"Ryan? Ryan, where in the world are you?"

"Jack, I can't talk long—"

"Ryan, are you in Cheyenne, by any chance?"

Ryan paused, listening to Coleridge's breath on the phone for a moment. "Yes," Ryan finally said.

"You left so quickly this morning and didn't tell me where you were going. When I got back to the office this afternoon, there were two federal agents waiting for me. They just left fifteen minutes ago. Ryan, a man was killed out there. The agents—"

"Who were they with? What agency?"

"Ryan, you're not—"

"The agency, Jack! What department were they with?"

"I don't see what difference—"

"Jack, for Christ's sake, I'm in trouble and I need your help! Who were they?"

Ryan heard papers shuffling. "One was with the FBI, a Special Agent Scott Hendler. The other was a woman with the U.S. Marshals Service, of all things. Her name was Kelly. Deputy U.S. Marshal Faith Kelly. They wanted to know if I knew where you were, if I'd talked to you."

"How did they even know we knew each other?" Ryan said. "Why would they come to you asking about me?"

Coleridge's voice turned hard. "Ryan, what happened? They mentioned this man named Dorian. Who is he?"

"I can't go into it, Jack. Things are happening and I don't know why. Tell me something. Did you find out anything about Dean Yorkton?"

"I hardly think—"

"Dammit, Jack!"

"Don't take that tone with me, young man. Now if you're in trouble, I understand, but you watch that mouth. You show me the respect I deserve."

Big breath into the phone. "I'm sorry. Jack, please."

More papers rustled down the phone line. "As a matter of fact, I was able to do some checking on Mr. Yorkton. You said he was a city employee, right?"

"That's right."

"Well, there's a computer database of employees of governmental entities nationwide. Tens of thousands, *hundreds* of thousands of names, from secretaries in city clerk's offices to the chief of staff for the president of the United States. I first found out about it when I was in the legislature. I went over to the university's library and accessed it."

"And?"

"I entered the municipal employees' database and put in Dean Yorkton's name. Nothing. I varied the spelling, used the broadest possible search, and still nothing. He wasn't carried on any records."

"But he died seven years ago. Would that—"

"Let me finish. These things carry deceased and retired employees. It was actually started by one of these government watchdog groups, to keep an eye on the kinds of benefits public sector employees received, and it just went from there. I thought maybe there was a data entry mistake, so I searched in county employees, then state employees. Still nothing. Then, just for the sake of thoroughness, I went into the federal section of the database."

"Oh my God," Ryan said after a moment.

"Yes, indeed. Yorkton was there." Ryan heard a tapping sound—Coleridge's pipe thumping against something, most likely the edge of his desk. "But here's what was strange. I've looked at a lot of these entries over the years, especially when I was in public service myself. There's a certain way they enter them, a certain formula, if you will. There's the name, the person's job title, the government entity and location which employs them, and below that, their salary and benefits. All public record. With Yorkton's, there was none of that."

"What do you mean?"

"I mean just what I said. Yorkton's name was there, but no job title or agency, not even a notation that the man was deceased. The only thing on the entire screen was the name and a number. The number thirty."

A slow and steady knocking came from the front door of the Chambers house. Ryan had just started to say something else to Coleridge—he wasn't sure what—when he spun toward the knocking sound, jerking the cord of the wall-mounted kitchen phone.

Cass muttered something Ryan couldn't hear and dashed back into the piano room, looking through a corner of the blinds. In the driveway sat a Roger Mills County Sheriff's Department cruiser. In front of the door was a slim young man in his late twenties, in black uniform pants and a pale blue shirt with a badge over the left breast. The holster on his hip was unbuttoned.

"Uh-oh," she said.

"What?" Ryan said, reeling in the phone cord.

"Ronnie Durland. He's a deputy sheriff."

"*Here?*"

"Looks that way."

"But how—"

"Alice," Cass said, shaking her head. "It has to be."

"I have to go," Ryan breathed into the phone. "I'll be in touch, Jack."

"Wait!" Coleridge said, but Ryan hung up the phone and disentangled himself from the long cord.

Cass listened to the knocking. Outside, a muffled drawl: "Cass? Mr. Chambers? Anybody home?" Cass looked through the blinds again. Ronnie Durland's hand was on the butt of his pistol. She turned back to Ryan. He looked stricken. Something in this man's world wasn't right, wasn't balanced. *My parents committed suicide seven years ago,* he'd said. She tried to imagine what it would have been like. She'd lost her mother to cancer when she was sixteen, but over the months Helen Chambers suffered, Cass and her two younger brothers had been able to prepare, and when the time came, the blow was softened. They'd already said their good-byes when the heart monitor in the Elk City hospital room went flat.

Cass looked at him again. Stricken, yes, but now there was something else. A resolve. He wanted to survive. She recognized the emotion—she'd felt it herself. The fingers of her left hand seemed to itch.

"I have to get out," Ryan said, his hand on the gun, barrel pointed downward. "Is there a back door?"

"Yes, but—"

"How about another truck? This is a farm, you've got to have another truck or two around, right?"

"No truck, but my dad's old car—"

"Does it run?"

"Yes."

"This way." He motioned her into the kitchen, away from the knocking. "Do you have any money in the house?"

Cass looked up at him. "Now you're robbing me?"

"No, I just want to stay alive long enough to figure all this out and I'm going to need money. A cookie jar? A rainy day fund?"

Cass's eyes widened.

"Go get it," Ryan said, gesturing with the gun. He peered through the kitchen door at Delmas Chambers, snoring in his chair, oblivious to the drama playing out around him.

Cass left the room and came back with a black nylon overnight bag. She held it out to him. "Look, why don't you take—"

Ryan's voice was rapid-fire, words almost tumbling over each other. "Hold on to it. Is there someone who can take care of your dad?"

"What do you mean?"

The knocking stopped, then resumed on the window, closer to where they stood.

Ryan jumped and lowered his voice. "Answer me!"

"Well, there's Alice."

"No good, not if she's the one who turned me in. Anyone else?"

"Well, a few times I've had someone from the home health agency down in Elk City come in and—"

"Okay, good. You're going to call them and tell them you have to go out of town suddenly and you need a nurse to stay with your father."

Cass took a step back. "What do you mean?"

Ryan raised the gun. "You said you wanted to help me. You're about to get your chance."

11

THEY MOVED SILENTLY THROUGH THE KITCHEN AND BACK down into the living room. "Wait a minute," Cass whispered. She went to her snoring father, knelt beside his chair, and said, "I have to go away, Daddy. I'll send someone over to help you." She kissed his cheek. He stirred but didn't wake. "I love you, Daddy."

Hoisting the overnight bag onto her shoulder, she led Ryan down a short, narrow hallway to a utility room and out onto a covered back porch. The yard consisted of a rusting barbecue grill and one small aluminum outbuilding. Ryan saw no fence, just more prairie stretching as far as the horizon. Fifty yards or so ahead and slightly to the left stood an oil well inside a wire enclosure. Its up-and-down pumping action and steady, rhythmic whirring sound reminded Ryan of the needle of a sewing machine.

"Come on," Cass said. "Ronnie's no genius, but he's not stupid either. In a little while he'll figure out something's not right and he'll call in for help."

They left the porch in as fast a trot as his foot would allow. The wind had died down and the air was left with a biting cold. Ryan didn't speak, straining to hear over the rhythm of the pumping oil well. No knocking, no pounding. Then, the slam of a car door.

"He's gone back to his car," he said.

"Uh-huh," Cass said. She reached the aluminum building, pulled out a ring of keys, and unlocked the large padlock. Throwing the door wide, she revealed a 1960s-vintage Ford Galaxie that had once been red, but was now surrendering to rust.

"Get in," she said. "It looks bad, but it runs."

"We can't get past him," Ryan said, sliding into the passenger seat. "He's still out front."

"We're not going that way."

"What?"

"Hold on." Cass tossed the bag onto the seat between them, and in one fluid motion, started the car while pulling the door closed. The large engine roared to life, even in the cold, and hummed smoothly. "Daddy comes out here and starts this car every single day. He hasn't driven it anywhere in at least a year, but it's in perfect working order. This car was his great joy when I was a girl."

She put the car in gear and pointed it across the grassland. Ryan braced both arms against the seat.

"Since you're the one doing the kidnapping," Cass said, "tell me where you want to go."

Ryan ignored the sarcasm, waving with the Sig Sauer. "Away from here. Get me to Oklahoma City." He stared through the windshield. "We have a problem, though."

"What's that?"

"There's no road."

Cass gave an exaggerated sigh. "You city boys. Of course there's a road."

Ryan squinted in the fading light. Two ruts, bisected by a straight line of brown grass, could barely be seen. "You call that a road?"

Cass didn't answer, steering the old Ford away from the setting sun. Ryan leaned back in the seat and closed his eyes. He began tapping Cass's pen with his thumb again. What did it all mean? Somewhere in his father's past, there was something he hadn't wanted Ryan to know, to the point where he'd fabricated a life in Cheyenne. But what about his mother? Had Anna known the truth, or had she been in the dark as well?

Ryan straightened slowly. What about her life? What about her past? Dorian had talked about both of them. And what of Dean Yorkton? How was he connected to Dorian and Department Thirty?

"Too many questions," he said, not realizing he'd spoken aloud.

"I'll say," Cass said, not taking her eyes off the ruts that were now curving slightly southward. "Fence coming up. I'll have to get out and unlatch the gate." She eased off the accelerator as the wood and barbed wire fence came into view. Beyond it was blacktop, the two-lane state highway. She braked, got out of the car, and unhooked a fencepost from a set of barbed wire loops. She pulled the makeshift gate aside, returned to the car, and drove through the opening, then closed the gate again and turned left—east—onto the highway.

"Where are we?" Ryan said.

"Highway Thirty-three, northeast of Cheyenne. Strong City's just a couple of miles away. Reach in my bag and hand me the phone, would you?"

Ryan unzipped the overnight bag. It contained a laptop computer, two cell phones, and two manila envelopes bulging with money.

"Good God," Ryan said.

"Sorry, I know you didn't expect that," Cass said. "The phone, please."

"Which one?"

"Either one will do."

"Who are you calling?"

"Just following your orders."

He handed her a phone and zipped up the bag, watching while she punched in numbers. After a moment she said into the phone, "Gayla, it's Cass Chambers from over at Cheyenne. I've had to go out of town suddenly and I need to set it up for someone to be with my dad while I'm gone. No, I'm not sure how long. That's right . . . Stephanie came last time and she was very good with Daddy. If she's available . . . okay, thanks. I'll check in when I can." She clicked the end button and placed the phone on the seat beside her.

"Who *are* you?" Ryan said.

"I'm someone who thought she might have to run someday. I guess I'm just running for a different reason."

"Why didn't you put up more of a fight with me? Why are

you so willing to just walk away from a sick father without resisting more?"

"You're a really lousy kidnapper, you know that? You're not supposed to care about the well-being of your victims and their family members. You need to reread that part of the kidnappers' manual."

"You didn't answer my question."

Cass cleared her throat. They were approaching the small town of Strong City, which was dominated by a huge, rusting water tower. "Like I said before, you're no criminal. I don't know what you are, but you're not a killer."

"Well, thank you for that insight. But your father's a sick man, and you just grabbed your little overnight bag full of money and ran off with a gun-toting stranger."

"Daddy will be fine until I get back."

"You're assuming you'll get back."

She glanced sharply at him. "Yes," she said. "I am."

Silence drew out, as long and straight as the country they were driving through.

"Well?" Ryan said.

"You're not going to let it go, are you?"

"No. The last person I trusted wound up with a hole in his chest."

Cass curled the fingers of her right hand tightly over the steering wheel. "A stranger helped me once."

Ryan waited. "That's it?"

"For now."

"That's all you have to say?"

"That's all I have to say."

They drove in silence for several miles, then Cass said, "We should be able to make the city by eight o'clock or so. Do you have a plan?"

"A plan?"

"To get yourself out of this mess, remember?"

"I remember." He sat back and closed his eyes again, his mind a momentary blank. After a moment an image appeared—Kirk Stillman, the corrupt contractor back in Pensacola who had gotten him fired on Tuesday, whose wife was the sister of the radio station's owner. Ryan would have nailed Stillman to the wall. He had him dead to rights. The paper trail led right to him.

He snapped his eyes back open. No one could exist in America today without leaving a paper trail. People's lives were held in files, in databases, in official forms and public records. People's lives . . . his parents' lives.

And Ryan knew where to start.

The Whispering Man was pleased. Deputy U.S. Marshal Faith Kelly had been a good choice to receive the package. He already had a file on her and by now he knew the two most important things about the young woman: she was ambitious and she'd looked on Art Dorian as a mentor, even as a father substitute. Daughter of a police captain, highly intelligent, driven, desperate to prove herself . . . she would do anything to bring in Dorian's murderer. She would be a valuable ally without even knowing it.

The Whispering Man's rental car was parked diagonally around the corner of Main and Broadway in downtown Edmond. The rush hour traffic was heavy with commuters returning from Oklahoma City, but he had an excellent vantage point. Kelly was sitting in her government-issue Ford, watching the door of T. Jackson Coleridge's law office. She was across Broadway and half a block south. She couldn't see the Whispering Man, but he saw her head of auburn hair quite clearly, and they could both watch Coleridge's door.

The FBI was already onto the Dorian case, but Kelly officially had no jurisdiction. She'd been able to tag along when the FBI visited the attorney, but after the FBI agent was gone, Kelly stayed. She was on her own—"off the clock," so to speak—and doing a minor surveillance of the Elder family attorney, one of Ryan Elder's only connections to Oklahoma. She wanted the case. The Whispering Man knew it by looking at her, sitting there in her car, waiting for Coleridge to return.

Many years ago, the Whispering Man had been known as one of the most dangerous men in America. No one knew who he really was, yet they had feared him. They feared the power he wielded. They feared the Revolution, the destruction of their carefully ordered society and its outmoded institutions, its way of compressing things into little ideological boxes. Radical left . . . extreme right . . . antigovernment crusaders . . . environmental activists. . . .

His breath quickened as he thought of what was to come. He would succeed where others failed. Finally, he would have his success and it would come because he didn't limit himself ideologically. Most revolutionaries were foolish, narrow ideologues with only their own agenda in mind. But the Whispering Man had discovered the truth that eluded them. He knew the *entire* system was corrupt and so the entire system would have to topple under the Revolution—a revolution for its own sake, beautiful and pure, not tainted by any political or ideological slant.

Just when he'd thought it would never happen, now it was within his grasp again. And it would be thanks to Ryan Elder, with a little help from Deputy United States Marshal Faith Kelly. The Whispering Man wondered if she would appreciate the irony of her helping to bring down the system she now served.

He settled in to continue watching the watcher and for a moment, like a breeze blowing through him, he thought he heard a voice, a tiny voice saying, *Why, Daddy, why?*

Soon, the Whispering Man thought. The Revolution will bring justice to you soon.

Ryan didn't even realize he'd dozed off until he felt the Galaxie's rhythm change, the engine slowing from its interstate pace. He opened his eyes, then blinked several times as Oklahoma City's downtown skyline came into focus.

"What time is it?" he said.

"A little after seven-thirty," Cass said. "Man, I have to say it again, you are one lousy kidnapper."

"What do you mean?"

"Going to sleep like that. I could have driven straight to the police while you were over there snoozing. I'm amazed you could sleep anyway. I go into overdrive and can't sleep during a crisis."

Ryan straightened in the seat, flexing his foot as he did. He grimaced—some of the soreness was coming back. "I guess it's a defense mechanism. I've always been able to sleep, even in high-stress times. I fall asleep quickly, and when I wake up, I'm totally awake. No gray areas."

"Good for you. You come up with a plan?"

Ryan thumped the pen, then walked it from one finger to another. "I don't know if it's a plan, but maybe it's the beginning of one." Ryan rubbed his face, scratching at his beard. "To get out of this, I need to know who killed Dorian and why."

"That makes sense."

"I think the 'why' will lead to the 'who,' not the other way around. And the 'why' has to do with my parents and me. If my father didn't really come from Cheyenne, I need to find out why he said he did. I need to find out what Dorian was going to tell me out there." He reached into his shirt pocket and unfolded the newspaper clipping. "And I need to find out what this means."

"What is it?"

"I'm not sure yet." He shifted on the seat. "Cass . . ." It was the first time he'd called her by name.

She glanced at him.

"This is where I need your help. I have an idea about what to do, but I need to disappear for a while to figure it out. I need you to . . . well, to sort of cover for me."

She said nothing.

"Please, Cass," he said, very quietly. "You're right, I'm no killer and you said yourself that I'm a lousy kidnapper. At this point I have no idea what's happening around me. But I need your help."

He told her what he had in mind. She shivered and nodded at the windshield. She thought she felt a warm prickling sensation in her left hand. Cass drove on toward the lights of the city.

12

"HOW DO YOU KNOW WE'LL BE ABLE TO FIND WHAT you're looking for here?" Cass said, driving south of downtown Oklahoma City on Shields Boulevard.

"I don't," Ryan said, peering out the window at convenience stores and run-down motels. "But I covered the police beat in Dayton for over two years and I found out that if you want do almost anything illegal, look for the part of town where the working girls are. For a price, you can find whatever you want." He nudged the black nylon overnight bag with his foot. "How much do you have in there and how did you come by it?"

Cass was silent.

"Look," Ryan said, "I'm not going to steal you blind. My parents left a sizable chunk of money in a trust. I haven't touched a nickel of it since they died. I'll pay you back every cent, with interest, when this is over."

Cass braked for a red light at Southeast Forty-forth Street. She looked at him. "I believe you."

"That's nice to know. How did you come by so much cash?"

"There's about twenty thousand dollars in there. As to where it came from, don't go there. It's none of your business."

"I guess it has to do with why you keep your other hand out of sight."

"I said, don't go there." The light changed and the old Ford moved ahead.

Ryan shrugged. "Oh, well. We should be able to find a way to get you some papers around here."

"Me? You're the one who's in trouble."

"Which is exactly why you're going to be getting the new

ID, so that I can be out of sight and you can conduct any official business."

"Look, I don't think—"

"Dammit, don't argue with me! I'm not going to hurt you, but you're going to help me."

Cass was quiet for a moment. "You have it all figured out, then."

"Actually, no. I'm making it up as I go. Flip a U up here, then come back and pull into this motel."

They tried two motels before pulling into The Oasis, whose *i* was missing from its sign. It was shaped like a rectangle with one open end facing the street. Toward the back of the parking lot were two miniskirted women on foot, one leaning against a door, one cruising the sidewalk.

Cass pulled the car next to them and rolled down the window. The cruiser sidled up next to them. Looking at her, Ryan didn't think there was any way this girl was over eighteen, in her tight black skirt and white faux-silk blouse, with stockings and black stiletto heels. But her long blonde hair was limp and stringy, her makeup a little off, her eyes dark slits. *What's your story?* Ryan wondered.

She leaned in the window. "I don't do threesomes," she said, looking down at Cass. Her accent wasn't Oklahoma, but upper midwestern. "You want to dump Ms. Short Hair and party with me, baby, we'll talk."

Ryan reached into the overnight bag and pulled out some cash. He peeled off a hundred-dollar bill and handed it to the girl. "No party, just information."

The girl stared at the bill as if it were foreign to her. "I don't do information. You want information, buy a newspaper, not a hooker."

"The newspaper doesn't have the information I need. I'd guess you're, what, about seventeen?"

She stiffened. "I'm nineteen and I can prove it. What are you, a cop, or some kind of soul-saving preacher or something?"

Cass thumped the steering wheel. Ryan leaned closer. "Neither one. I believe you can prove you're nineteen. You've got the ID and everything, don't you?"

"You got it, baby. Look, are we gonna fuck or talk?"

"Talk. I need some new ID and I need to know where to get it."

The other woman walked over to them. She was a black woman, a few years older, very tall, thin, wearing thigh-high boots, a suede miniskirt, and halter top. Ryan saw her shiver as she walked.

"Whatsa matter, Britt?" she said to the younger girl. "This one don't know what he wants? Take two, they're small, baby. Do Britt and me both, if you pay extra."

"I don't do threesomes, Monica," Britt said. "I told you that when I started."

"Come on," Ryan said. "The ID?"

"What do you need ID for?" Britt asked, still leaning in the window, letting the car's heater blow on her face. "You look respectable to me. Car ain't much, but you look like a real person."

A real person. If only you knew, Ryan thought. "I'm in some trouble."

Monica laughed. "He's in some trouble. Well, my, my, so is everyone else in the world. Come on, Britt." Another car had pulled into the lot and Monica swayed toward it.

Ryan pulled off another hundred. "Here, Britt. You need to go somewhere and get warm. And I need to know where to get some papers."

Britt pulled back and studied Ryan and Cass for a moment. "Monica's right, you know. We're all in trouble. One way or another, we're in trouble. The guy's on Northwest Twenty-third, around Robinson, over there close to the state capital. The place looks like it's all closed up, but it's got a red door."

"A red door."

"That's it. Don't say where you heard it."

"Thanks."

"Yeah, well." The girl pulled her limp hair back away from her face. "You decide you want to party, come back and I'll do you for no extra charge. You already gave me two hundred—wouldn't want to take advantage of you. Bad for business, you know."

• • •

An hour and a thousand dollars later, Cass had an Oklahoma driver's license, Social Security card, and birth certificate in the name of Alicia Rubinstein.

Ryan read the name off the driver's license. "Alicia Rubinstein. Where did you come up with that?"

Ryan couldn't see her face, but he thought he detected a hitch in her voice. "Two of the greatest pianists, Alicia Delarrocha and Artur Rubinstein. They inspired me. I know it sounds crazy."

"No, I understand."

"Do you?" Cass looked over at him, surprised.

"My mother was a musician. A violinist."

"Oh."

Within two hours, "Alicia Rubinstein" had purchased a fifteen-year-old black Jeep Cherokee with cash and Delmas Chambers's rusty old Galaxie was in the long-term parking area at Will Rogers World Airport. By midnight she'd rented a furnished apartment in a large complex not far from Oklahoma City University directly behind the monolith of Shepherd Mall.

Ryan was instantly struck by how much it resembled his own apartment back in Pensacola. Anonymous but contemporary furnishings, tasteful but sterile. Inside, he walked to the sliding glass door and did a quick glance over the parking lot. The Jeep was parked right next to the driveway that led back out to Thirtieth Street. "It'll do," he said finally, turning away from the door.

Cass, still standing, holding her bag, looked down at him. "You seem to know your way around the city pretty well. You're from here, then?"

Ryan nodded.

"So how'd you get from here to Ohio and Florida?"

"Jobs," he said curtly.

"You're not going to tell me, are you? After all this, you're not going to tell me."

Ryan shook his head. "No, I will tell you. I guess I owe you that much. But at some point you're going to tell me why you went with me so easily. I haven't held the gun on you for several hours and not once have you tried to run, or to attack me, or anything. If all kidnappings were this easy, everyone would do it." He watched her, thinking how out of place she looked with that short, simple haircut and wearing a sweatshirt and jeans.

Ryan sat down in the recliner, propping up his foot. "Seven years ago, I came home from college for Thanksgiving."

Cass turned slowly. She looked down at him in the subdued lamplight, then drew the curtains closed across the glass door. She sat down across from him and nodded at him to go on.

He spoke for nearly half an hour, telling her everything. When he was finished, Cass sat and looked at him in the quiet light of the apartment. It struck her that he was younger than she, but he seemed much older. There were lines etched around his mouth and a soft, strange pain in his eyes. Cass realized the look in his eyes reminded her of some of the kids she worked with on Fridays, especially the autistic ones like little Guillermo, who responded so well to Chopin. The look said, *Don't give up on me. There's more in here than you think. I can't communicate it to you right now, but it's here. Please keep trying and I'll break through the walls sometime.* An almost pleading look, she thought.

Ryan waited a moment and said, "My foot hurts like hell." He rubbed his beard. "I feel like I've just bathed in blood or something. Words are my business, but I've never put all that into words before."

It took Cass a few seconds to speak. "Someone once told me that most people in radio and television are actually introverted. Something about how you sit in a room with a microphone or a camera and talk to people you can't see."

"Maybe there's something to that." Ryan nodded. "Now you know as much about this mess as I do. I have an idea about what to do next, but I need a phone."

She unzipped the black bag and handed him one of the two cell phones. Ryan took a deep breath. "Here goes," he said, and punched in the number.

Four rings later, he heard Coleridge's voice, thick with sleep: "Jack Coleridge."

"Jack, it's Ryan."

"Ryan, where are you? What is going on? Don't you dare hang up on me again!"

"I won't, Jack. I need your help. Who was the woman with the Marshals Service who was asking you about me? Tell me her name again." He pictured Coleridge sitting up slowly in bed.

"Just a minute. I wrote it down. Good heavens, Ryan, why don't you call at a decent hour? Here it is, Deputy Marshal Faith Kelly. Why?"

Ryan scribbled the name on the back of Coleridge's business card. "I may need to contact her myself."

"Ryan . . . Ryan, listen to me. Were you involved in that man's murder?"

"I didn't kill him. I repeat, Jack, that I *did not kill that man.* I was there when he was killed, but I didn't do it and I don't know who did. But I'm going to find out and I need your help."

There was a hesitation on the line. "What do you need?" Coleridge finally asked.

Thank you, Ryan mouthed silently. "You still have power of attorney with Mom and Dad's estate, right?"

"Of course."

"All right, I need the papers from the safe-deposit box at First National in Edmond."

"Which papers?"

"All of them. Everything we put there. The birth certificates, the marriage licenses, insurance forms, Dad's military discharge, everything."

Ryan heard Coleridge tapping his pipe. "I presume you feel it would be dangerous for you to get these things yourself."

"That's right," Ryan said. "Whether it's the people who killed Dorian, or the FBI, or the Marshals Service, or whoever, I'm afraid to come up for air until I get this mess unraveled."

"Ryan, Ryan. My God, son, I just can't believe—"

Ryan cut him off. "Neither can I. Will you do this for me?"

"Of course I will. How do you want me to get the papers to you?"

"Let me think." Ryan closed his eyes, pacing the living room, walking in and out of the little sphere of light. He pulled Cass's pen from his pocket and began tapping it with his thumb. "What time does the bank open?"

"Tomorrow's Saturday, Ryan."

"Dammit! I can't wait until Monday."

"Just a minute. I happen to know the president of First National quite well. In fact, he contributed to my campaigns for the legislature. I know him well enough to call him at home. He'll do this for me."

Ryan breathed out. "All right, get the papers and take them to Reno and Indiana, west of downtown. Leave the envelope under the I-Forty overpass, up under one of the supports, on the . . . let's see, the east side of Indiana. Then get the hell out of there."

"Ryan, I want to see you."

Ryan shook his head vehemently. "No. Not yet. Jack, I've stepped into something very strange here, and until I know what it is, I want as few other people as possible dragged into it."

"Ryan, you're being foolish. As your attorney, I can—"

"Not yet. Bring me the papers tomorrow morning. I'll pick them up. If I find out anything, I'll let you know."

"Ryan—"

"Good-bye, Jack."

Ryan pressed end, then looked up at Cass again. "Tomorrow morning." She nodded. "Maybe tomorrow morning is when I get some answers."

"I hope they're the right ones," Cass said.

"You sleep in the bed, I'll take the sofa out here. But let me tell you one thing: if you try to go anywhere in the night, I'll hear you. I have my mother's sense of hearing, and if something so much as creaks, I'll be up."

Cass looked at him again. Pain and pleading, her fingers, her sick father, little dark-eyed Guillermo—they'd all gathered together right here, right now. "You don't have to start playing kidnapper again. I won't go anywhere."

Ryan didn't answer. He seemed far away until he spoke, seemingly without realizing it. "Adam and Eve," he said, almost in a whisper.

13

WHEN THE ALARM WENT OFF AT FIVE O'CLOCK SATUR-day morning, Faith Kelly was already awake. She'd been in and out of sleep for several hours and her thoughts focused on one thing in every waking moment: Coleridge had lied to her. Kelly knew he'd seen Ryan Elder, had talked to him, knew something about him. She'd seen it in the way Coleridge stared right through her.

The attorney was the key. He would lead her to Ryan Elder, and on Monday morning, Kelly would drop all of this into Chief Deputy Clarke's lap. Then she'd be assigned as the Marshals Service's official liaison to the investigation of Dorian's murder. Her friend Scott Hendler at the FBI was already on the case and already knew she wanted in.

Kelly put on a sweatsuit, pulled her hair back into a pony-tail, and walked into the dining room of her modest house in the Village neighborhood of northwest Oklahoma City. She made coffee and drank a cup, strong and black, standing at her kitchen counter.

Kelly stopped in front of the bookshelf and did a few stretching exercises. Her two passions were stored there: unsolved crimes and running. There were volumes of books on cases that were still technically open: Lizzie Borden, Sam Sheppard, the Cullen Davis case in Fort Worth, the Zodiac Killer, D. B. Cooper, even O. J. Simpson. Beside them stood one of her most prized possessions, a simple photograph of her crossing the finish line of her first Boston Marathon. Next to it, a photo from the New York Marathon last year.

She'd had to get a special leave from the academy to go.

She went for a half-hour run, then showered and dressed in black wool slacks, a simple cream-colored turtleneck, and low heels. On her way out the door, she nudged her foot against the plate she'd thrown at Mikael LeFlore. She'd cleaned up the omelet itself—at least that which hadn't stuck to Mikael's shirt—but left the plate where it had landed. Housekeeping held no allure for her and she only did the bare minimum. A tiny plaque in her dining room read DULL PEOPLE HAVE IMMACULATE HOUSES.

Strangely enough, she felt no sense of loss at the end of the relationship with Mikael, just relief. Oh, she'd miss the dinners and concerts and movies, and the occasional sex, but not the condescension.

It was still dark at 6:30 when she pulled out of her driveway in her gold Mazda Miata—no government-issue sedan on the weekends—and drove north on May Avenue toward Edmond.

She parked in front of a popular breakfast cafe in Edmond, where she could see Coleridge's office. At eight o'clock sharp, the attorney's steel-gray Cadillac pulled into the spot directly in front of the office. She kept up her surveillance on him through his quick business at First National Bank of Edmond, after which he emerged carrying a large manila envelope. She noted that the bank seemed to have opened specifically for him.

Twenty minutes later, she watched the Cadillac exit Interstate 40 at Reno Avenue in Oklahoma City. Reno marked the southern edge of the city's downtown and ran on a parallel east-west line to the highway. Kelly wasn't familiar with this area of town, though it was only a couple of miles from her office. It was primarily industrial sites and abandoned warehouses from the look of it, and she slowed as Coleridge did, five car lengths ahead.

When he turned north onto Indiana Avenue, back toward the interstate, Kelly kept going. If she stayed with him on a small, empty street like Indiana, he would spot her in a matter of seconds. Instead, she pulled into the first driveway along Reno. A high chain-link fence surrounded dozens of tractor-trailer rigs that looked as though they hadn't moved in years. She checked her sidearm. Even though she wasn't technically on duty, she was required to have her weapon with her at all times. Closing and locking the Miata's door very quietly, she inched her way back along the fence.

When she reached the corner, she found that one of the trailer rigs parked against the fence afforded good cover, but she could still crouch and see up the block. She was so close to the interstate she could hear the noise of the Saturday morning traffic, could smell the fumes of diesel trucks going by.

When she was in position, Kelly peered under the trailer. Coleridge's Cadillac was stopped in the middle of the north-bound lane of Indiana, underneath the interstate overpass. The lawyer left the driver's door open, took the envelope he'd picked up at the bank, and moved up onto the sidewalk. He looked in all directions—Kelly instinctively leaned back when he glanced her way, but there was no indication he'd seen her—then climbed the slope behind one of the columns that supported the overpass. She lost sight of him for a few seconds, and when he came back down the concrete slope, the envelope was gone.

Kelly sucked in her breath, heart pounding. *Maybe I should have called for backup after all,* she thought. *Be patient. Nothing's happening yet.* Dorian had often told her that patience would get her much further than action.

She ducked down again as Coleridge looked around, then got back in his car. She was prepared to run back to the Miata, but instead of turning around and coming back out to Reno, he drove north, up a slight hill. She watched him reach a stop sign, then turn right out of view.

She slowly made her way back to the Miata and slid inside to get warm. Even wearing a turtleneck, she felt the bite of the morning cold.

Sitting inside the car with the heater running, she doodled in her notebook, wondering about banks and lawyers, and what Coleridge knew about Ryan Elder.

She thought of Art Dorian, how she'd met him the second

week she was in Oklahoma City. She'd learned more about investigative procedure from Dorian than from six years of college and a year at the academy. After the embarrassment over the photo with the congressman, he'd spent an afternoon telling her about prisoner escort techniques, about always redirecting the prisoner's attention forward and down, and threatening to hang a coat or a blanket over the prisoner's head if they didn't cooperate. Kelly also thought Art had talked to Chief Deputy Clarke and she drew a couple of good assignments after that. She'd gotten to be out front on a property seizure that was a joint operation with Customs and she'd worked with Derek Mayfield on the investigation of a death threat against a federal judge.

Kelly's throat constricted as she thought of how Dorian had been everything her own father wasn't.

"Oh, Art," she said to herself.

Ryan couldn't be still. He scratched at his beard, dug at the cuticles of his thumbs, thumped Cass's pen. At 8:42 A.M., parked on Main half a block west of Indiana Avenue, he watched the gray Cadillac come to a stop, then turn east, away from the Jeep.

"That's him," Ryan said.

Cass, in the driver's seat, watched the Cadillac as it headed toward downtown Oklahoma City. "Do you think he got what you needed?"

Ryan put down the pen and picked at his cuticles some more. "I hope he got what I asked him for. Whether it's what I need or not. . . ." He shrugged into the car seat. The pain in his foot was quiet this morning. Cass had rewrapped it and he'd taken two Tylenol before leaving the apartment.

When he lost sight of the Cadillac, Ryan checked his watch. "Clock starts now," he said. They waited in silence while he counted off five minutes, then ten, then fifteen. Coleridge was long gone and only one other car had driven down Indiana, a decrepit pickup truck that drove all the way to Reno, then turned west.

After fifteen minutes, Ryan said, "Give it three more minutes." When his digital watch beeped at nine o'clock, he nodded to Cass and said, "Let's go."

She pulled the Jeep forward to the stop sign at Indiana, then turned right. They descended the short hill slowly. No other vehicles were in sight. To the right was a gray brick industrial building with concrete slabs extending toward the street. A weary real-estate sign was propped against it. Broken concrete littered the parking lot and tufts of brown grass jutted from the ground like prying fingers.

Past the gray building was a concrete lot filled with steel beams of various sizes, stacked in groups of five and ten, three rows deep. Forbidding NO TRESPASSING signs were planted at various intervals.

The Jeep crept farther down the hill and Cass eased it under the interstate. "Okay, let me out," Ryan said.

Cass spied a small street just the other side of the overpass, before Reno. A leaning sign identified it as California Avenue. "I'll pull in there."

The Jeep turned and she stopped just outside the shadow of the overpass. They both got out, listening to I-40 above. Ryan stared at Cass. "Stay here. I'll get it and be right back."

"I'm coming with you."

He shook his head. "Stay with the car. I want to get it and be gone as quickly as I can."

"But—"

"I'll be right back."

"You're trusting me not to run?"

Ryan waited a moment. "I guess I am."

Cass leaned back against the cold of the Jeep, hugging her vest around her as she watched him go. In a few seconds he was out of her sight.

"Be safe," she said quietly.

Kelly reached the corner, crouching behind the trailer at the fence. When she was in position, she took in the entire scene: the black Jeep parked on California, the short-haired woman standing beside it. And just entering the area of the sidewalk that ran under the overpass, a man.

She squinted in the hard morning sunlight. From here she couldn't make a real identification. He was tall, with a slim build, brown hair, bearded. Khaki pants, a dark green coat, running shoes of some sort. The only picture she'd seen of Ryan Elder was one taken at Frank and Anna Elder's funeral and given to Art to slip into the file. It had shown a serious, smooth-faced twenty-year-old, almost a carbon copy of his father.

Aside from the beard, maybe. . . .

Kelly shook her head. She couldn't call it. Not yet. She needed to get closer. But if she stepped out from behind the fence, she would be in open view of both the man and the woman.

She inched back a few steps from the corner and flattened herself against the fence, thinking.

A phone call from the past, Art Dorian had said. Art Dorian, dead in the middle of a field near Cheyenne, Oklahoma.

Kelly unsnapped her shoulder holster.

Ryan couldn't take two steps without crunching broken glass. The garbage littered the sidewalk, spilled over to the street and up the concrete slope that ran toward the highway. A lumpy pillow, sliced open with its ticking flowing out, sat squarely in the center of the sidewalk. Cardboard boxes, McDonald's sacks, a soggy, ripped *Penthouse* magazine, corn chips, and glass bottles: Budweiser, Coke, Snapple, Seagram's Extra Dry Gin.

Under the highway, Ryan listened to the rumble of the traffic above his head. Halfway across was an opening where a shaft of light poured down. His eyes followed it up to I-40.

He took two more steps, crossing behind one of the interstate supports. He began to climb the slope, the traffic thundering a few feet above his head. At the point where the support beam met the bottom of the highway was a little ridge, and above it, running the length of the overpass, a tiny opening, three or four inches wide.

He put his hand into the opening and began to work his

way down. He moved carefully, not wanting to cut himself on unseen glass shards. Halfway down, his fingers brushed paper. He pulled out the bulging manila envelope and turned it over and over. *Ryan* was written across the outside in a precise, masculine hand.

Ryan thought he heard his pulse roaring in his ears, intermingling with the traffic overhead.

He turned back toward the street below.

Cass didn't wear a watch, but Ryan couldn't have been gone much more than a minute, two at the most. She'd mentally been through at least three of the short Chopin waltzes, trying to hold Ryan and Chopin in her mind at the same time. The traffic sounds faded, the wind stilled, until there was only Chopin and Ryan Elder. Cass closed her eyes and leaned her head against the Jeep.

She didn't scream when the hand closed on her throat, and suddenly the music was loud and angry in her head before ending in the middle of a phrase. She expelled a rush of air, then she was spun around so that she was facing the Jeep, and the hand had been replaced by something sharp.

"One sound and I'll slit your throat," a man whispered.

Cass's eyes widened, her fingers tingled. She averted her eyes downward. The knife was long-bladed with a serrated edge. The hand holding it was encased in a black leather glove.

The serrated edge of the knife came closer, just under her chin. She felt it, cold, jagged, like the razor wire atop prison walls.

"Do you believe I'll kill you?" the man said, still whispering. "Just nod your head."

Cass nodded.

"Good," he whispered. The point of the blade danced ever so lightly across the surface of her throat. Cass tightened and sucked in breath.

"I don't know who you are," the man said, "but you need to give our mutual friend a message. Are you listening? Just nod."

Cass nodded again. Her hand was free, but the man was strong, muscular, and he had her pinned against the Jeep.

"He needs to work harder," came the whisper in her ear. "You see, his parents had something of mine, and they very rudely neglected to inform me where they left it before they lost their minds and killed themselves. With them gone, he's the only way I'm going to get it back. His parents left him a message. Somehow they told him and he's going to find my property. Whatever was in that letter will mean something to him. And that will lead me to my property. He may not like what he finds along the way, but if he doesn't . . . well, either the police will catch him, or I will. You're going to tell him that."

Cass nodded for a third time. She squirmed against the blade.

"No, no," the man whispered. Then in one motion the knife was gone and he shoved her in the small of her back.

Cass stumbled and went down into the gravel beside the Jeep. The man's foot—it felt like he was wearing heavy boots—went into her back, pinning her to the ground. As his foot came down, she let out a low groan. It was the first sound she'd made.

Patience only goes so far, Kelly thought, and made her decision. If she was wrong, she'd face Clarke and deal with it. If she was right. . . .

She ran for the Miata, grabbed her cell phone, and called the office. Derek Mayfield was on call this weekend and it took her less than a minute to explain. To his credit, he listened and didn't blurt out questions. He told her he'd alert Chief Clarke and call the FBI.

Kelly threw down the phone and ran back to the corner. She crouched down and felt as though an icy fist had grabbed her and squeezed.

She saw the man at the Jeep and watched as he knocked the woman down. She saw the sunlight glint off the blade in his hand. Now Kelly couldn't see the woman, but the man was reaching into the Jeep.

• • •

Back on the sidewalk, Ryan clutched the envelope and turned toward the south, crunching glass. He'd taken three steps when he heard the low sound, muffled, indistinct.

"Cass," he said.

With his foot still on Cass's back, the man leaned over her and whispered, "Remember what I said. Just so you don't forget. . . ." He took the knife and slit her vest down the back, from neck to waist, then did the same to her shirt. He tucked the tip of the knife under her bra strap and pressed just hard enough to draw blood. A bright red dot appeared and he slit the bra open.

Cass wriggled under him, clawing the gravel, her fingers tingling as if electrified. He was strong and she couldn't gain more than a few inches. Then the man was running, sprinting away toward Reno.

Cass rolled onto her back. "Ryan!" she screamed.

Kelly jerked as if she'd been prodded. The woman's scream rose above the traffic, and in less than a second, Kelly's nine-millimeter Glock was in her hands. She saw the man in the ski mask leap a low fence and not break stride, heading south toward Reno, and east, away from her.

She looked ahead. The young man—Ryan Elder, it had to be—came back around the edge of the overpass carrying the envelope. He started to run.

Where's that backup? Kelly wanted to scream.

She stepped out from the fence and began to run across Indiana. "Ryan Elder!" she shouted. "I'm a federal officer! Stop where you are!"

"Oh, shit," Ryan said.

He skidded to a stop at the edge of the overpass, taking in all he could see: Cass, picking herself off the ground; the woman with the gun who was shouting at him to stop, the man, growing smaller in the distance.

"Are you all right?" he shouted across to Cass.

"I think so!" Cass turned over her shoulder toward the woman with the gun.

Ryan pointed back to the Jeep, then up toward the interstate. He saw Cass hesitate half a second, then she was behind the wheel.

"Stop!" yelled the woman.

Clutching the manila envelope like a baby with a blanket, Ryan turned and started up the concrete slope. An eighteen-wheeler passed overhead.

Ryan was beyond conscious thought. Only instinct was keeping him alive now, he realized, and his instincts had a lousy track record to this point.

"Elder!" the woman shouted.

He didn't look at her. He didn't hear any others. A woman with a gun, identifying herself as a federal officer. The deputy marshal Coleridge had told him about. What was her name. . . .

He heard the sickening sound of the gunshot, and concrete flew all around him. He had one thought in his mind: Keep moving!

He reached the top, vaulted over the low retaining wall, and was almost run over by a motor home driving too close to the shoulder of I-40. The huge vehicle swerved back into its lane with a honk and a glare from the driver and Ryan began to run along the shoulder of the eastbound lane.

Kelly fired again, but put the Glock back in its holster after the second shot. She was too close to the highway and might hit civilians. She wondered how much grief Mayfield had to go through to get a team mobilized. It occurred to her for the first time that Clarke could have her badge for something like this.

"Dammit," she said, and jumped over the wall onto the highway.

Ryan hoped Cass had understood his message, that she knew what he wanted her to do. If not . . . well, he couldn't get very far and there was nowhere to hide on an interstate highway. Ahead, he saw the Oklahoma City skyline, the Colcord Building, the Renaissance Hotel. . . .

Green highway signs: WESTERN AVENUE, RENO AVENUE, EXIT ONLY. A diesel tank truck blasted close by him and he stumbled against the retaining wall. As his hands found the wall, he looked back. The woman was there, moving smoothly, gaining on him almost effortlessly. But at least she wasn't shooting, thank God.

His lungs aching from the cold, Ryan cut his eyes to the right. Coming up along the Western Reno on-ramp was the black Jeep. Cass had understood!

She was coming slowly, looking around for him. Their eyes locked and he made a merging motion with his right hand. She nodded and he took off in a full sprint. Cass twisted the Jeep sharply into the lane, cutting off a large van with the logo of a furniture store painted on the side.

There was traffic in the left lane and the furniture van went for the shoulder. Ryan heard the horn, heard someone screaming. Metal crunched concrete, and as the van bounced off the wall and back into traffic, Ryan angled himself between the van and the Jeep.

Ten more feet. The van was closing on the Jeep now, coming in behind it. Ryan looked back one more time—the woman with the gun was now standing on the shoulder a hundred feet back.

Five feet. The Jeep was almost stopped in the right lane of the interstate, barely creeping forward. Cass was looking back over her shoulder.

Ryan's hand closed on the door handle. The furniture van honked again. Ryan got the door open and threw himself headfirst into the Jeep. "Go!" he breathed.

Cass jammed the accelerator to the floor, the open door swinging in the wind. The Jeep shot across three lanes of traffic, Cass nudging it up to fifty, sixty, seventy miles an hour. Ryan got a hand around the door handle and pulled it closed, then slumped into the seat.

"Who—" he managed to say.

"I don't know," Cass said. Her back was sore, and with her

clothes sliced open she felt as if she'd been almost cut in two, but she didn't think she was injured. "How's your foot?"

"It hurts like hell. I hope she didn't get the license number."

"I don't think she got close enough. The man had a message for you."

"What?"

Ryan listened while she told him what the man with the knife had said.

"Son of a bitch," Ryan said when she was finished.

"My thoughts exactly," Cass said.

14

CHIEF DEPUTY PHILLIP CLARKE WAS A LARGE, POWER-fully built man in his fifties. Six-feet-four and 240 pounds, he was more fit than most of the younger men who worked under him. He wore his wheat-colored hair short and kept a bushy mustache, which was salted with gray. His voice was a gravelly bass rumble, his manner utterly no-nonsense. The first time Kelly had met him, she thought he fit every possible stereotypical image of a U.S. Marshal, from his appearance to his voice to his doubts about women in law enforcement.

Clarke parked his gray Ford and took his time getting out of the car. He was wearing a heavy flannel button-down shirt under a brown coat, faded jeans, and gray cowboy boots. His badge was clipped to his belt and his holster rode on the opposite hip.

He took in the scene: the FBI van with the Rapid Response Team had arrived just before him—a dozen agents in full riot gear. Two of his deputies, Mayfield and Stanton, were conferring with the leader of the FBI team. Two black-and-white Oklahoma City police cruisers blocked off the street. He spotted Kelly talking to one of the city cops, standing at the bottom of the slope which led up to Interstate 40.

Clarke walked with a deliberate stride toward her. Kelly caught sight of him and muttered, "Here we go."

Clarke nodded to the cop. "Morning, Sergeant. Could you excuse us for a minute, please?"

The cop moved away. "Chief, I—" Kelly said.

Clarke raised a hand. "Let's walk." He gestured northward, toward the overpass. They walked, crunching gravel and glass. Halfway under the overpass, Clarke raised his head but didn't break stride. "Deputy Kelly, would you mind telling me exactly what the fuck is going on?"

Kelly swallowed. "Chief, yesterday while you were out—"

Clarke nudged a piece of brown glass with the toe of his boot. "I know about Dorian. I know where and when and what."

Kelly cocked her head toward him as they emerged from under the highway.

"Did you think I wouldn't find out about what you were up to? Here you are, calling the sheriff out in Cheyenne, and your buddy Hendler at the Bureau, and you figure you'll do all this quietly and then present your big case to me. That pretty much cover it, Deputy?"

Dammit to hell and back, Kelly thought. "Yes," she said.

"Uh-huh." Clarke shook out a cigarette and ducked his head down with the ease of someone accustomed to lighting cigarettes in the wind. "Imagine what must've gone through my head at eight o'clock last night when Leo Dorsett over at FBI calls me at home and says, 'Phil, who the hell is Faith Kelly?' And I think, one of my young officers, one who's still in her probationary period, has lost her mind. She's inserted herself into a murder investigation where she doesn't have any jurisdiction."

"Chief, it's—"

"Close your mouth, Kelly. You could be gone right this minute, at my discretion. You're still on probation, so I don't even need to show cause. This kind of stunt has gotten smarter officers than you into more trouble than you can possibly imagine. You could very well be packing your bags to head back home to Grover's Corners or Walnut Grove or wherever the hell that suburb is that you came from. Maybe your old man could get you into a patrol car on the overnight shift."

Kelly clenched her teeth. Clarke stopped walking, exhaling smoke toward the sky.

"The only reason that's not happening," Clarke said, "is that I want to know what you've found. Tell me everything."

Kelly started with the mysterious phone call Dorian had received on Tuesday, the delivery of the photos, her reading of the case file, the surveillance of Coleridge. . . .

They kept walking the whole time, and before she realized it, they were at the corner of Main and Indiana. The rest of the officers were specks below them.

Clarke leaned against the stop sign at the corner. "I won't even start in on how many violations that is." He crushed the cigarette under his boot and nudged a stray piece of concrete. "Have you given this to the Bureau yet?"

"No, I—"

"Don't tell me you were waiting to see what I'd say. That would just be too much." He kicked the concrete piece into the street, then started back down the hill. "Shit, Kelly. You put me in an impossible position. But I'm not going to fire you. You knew Dorian better than anyone, not that anyone knew him very well."

Kelly held her breath.

"Understand one thing, Deputy. *I own you.* Is that clear?"

"Absolutely, Chief."

"Good. And do you know why I'm keeping you? Do you know why I'm going to assign you as a temporary investigative liaison to the Bureau? Answer that for me. And no patronizing bullshit."

"Politics. So that our office is there when this case is brought in and so the proper people know the role we played in it."

"To use your word, absolutely, Deputy. The marshal will be happy, the U.S. Attorney will be happy, and so on up the ladder."

They walked a few feet in silence. When they reached the overpass, Clarke took Kelly's sleeve and stopped her. "Be careful, Kelly. You know how Thirty is. Their cases are so secret that I don't even know how many are working in our jurisdiction. You know more than you're supposed to know, and Jesus help you, girl, if anyone in D.C. finds out you went into Dorian's office and got into a case file. Anything to do with Department Thirty is thin ice and you're liable to crash through and drown if you're not careful."

She nodded. "Thanks for the tip."

Clarke smiled. "That's not the best part."

"Oh?"

"D.C.'s sending someone. Another Department Thirty type. Someone who knew Dorian, apparently."

"When will he be here?"

"Beats the hell out of me. Thirty does things their own way."

Kelly shivered. "Then how do I find him?"

Clarke punted a beer bottle off the sidewalk and watched it shatter in the street. "I don't know much about Thirty's internal operations, but I do know this much. He'll find you, Kelly. Count on it."

15

THE MEMORY WAS AS HARD AND SHARP AS THE BROKEN glass along Indiana Avenue. The year Ryan was thirteen, or maybe it was fourteen. A year he'd played baseball in the summer, a thing ordinary suburban kids did. He and his parents had arrived at home after the game—his mother thought sports were a waste of time, but she attended all his games anyway—and there was Mr. Yorkton, sweating over his lawn mower. He'd waved them over.

Just want to talk to your mom and dad for a minute, Ryan, Yorkton had said. *Neighborhood association stuff.*

Ryan, would you go and water the roses, please? his mother had said. *Get the hose. We'll be along in a minute.*

The dutiful son, he'd gone and hooked up the hose, letting the water trickle onto his mother's prize red and yellow roses around the side of the house. Thinking about the ball game, about the ground ball he'd muffed at first base. Thinking about Allison McDermott's red hair and the way he'd sometimes catch himself staring at her during history class this past year. Thinking about how he'd decided he wanted to go into radio as a career. Jeff had laughed at him, Jeff who was going to be a surgeon.

Water dribbled into his shoe and he snapped himself back to reality. Then he straightened, playing the hose out over the flowers one last time, as he heard his mother's voice, the Czech accent biting down a bit, as it did when she was emotional: *Then when can we tell him?*

He turned his head toward the driveway. He heard his father making a shushing sound, then low murmurings, so low even he couldn't hear. They were whispering. He strained to hear, coming as close as he could to the corner of the house without being seen. But he heard no more.

He turned off the water and went in the house. The phone was ringing as he came into the kitchen. It was Jeff, who told him Allison McDermott had been at the game and was asking about him. His parents' whisperings with Mr. Yorkton in the driveway were promptly forgotten.

Then when can we tell him?

Ryan stepped away from the motel window. He sank into the overstuffed chair and propped his foot on the bed. Outside, traffic rumbled on Interstate 35. After hours of driving, zigzagging through streets and highways all across the metro area, they'd landed here, just outside the town of Guthrie, a few miles north of Edmond.

Cass came out of the bathroom. Ryan had gone into town and bought her new clothes from a discount store, replacing the ones that had been slit up the back. Her hair was wet, combed back after her shower. She looked so fresh, so natural. The girl next door.

"You look lost," Cass said.

Ryan looked up at her. "What did you say?"

She sat down on the opposite side of the bed. "I said, you look lost. Like you don't know where you are." She ran her right hand through her short hair, pulling it straight back. It looked darker wet.

"I don't. And I don't understand you either."

"Well, that's part of your problem. You shouldn't be trying to understand me."

"You could have left, or turned me in, a dozen different times today."

Cass looked at him pointedly. "Are you waiting for me to disagree with you?"

"No, I'm waiting to find out the real reason you're going along with me. Not some vague business about a stranger having helped you once."

"A stranger did help me once. That's a fact. There are a lot of reasons I'm here and I probably don't even know half of them."

"It's your father."

"What?" Cass stepped back from the abruptness of the words.

"Your father. You're young, you're talented and smart, and you've moved back to Cheyenne, Oklahoma, from wherever you'd gone, to take care of a sick man. You feel obligated to care for him because he's your father and he needs you, but you're stuck in that house, day after day, wondering why it has to be you. Does that cover it?"

"Keep your armchair psychology to yourself."

Ryan leaned forward. "That's it! You didn't resist, and you haven't run, because I've given you an out."

"Look, my brothers are both married with families of their own. They couldn't move in with him. The consensus in the family was that I should be there."

"Oh, the consensus. I see, the consensus. And I wonder if the *consensus* gave you any say in the matter. That's it, isn't it? It's hard dealing with a man who doesn't even know who you are half the time. And I bet the cigarettes drive you crazy too."

Ryan listened to her breathing, watching the enormous eyes. Dammit he thought. I pushed too hard, just like every other woman I've ever known in my life. Then he wondered why it mattered.

Cass finally pointed at the envelope on the bed between them. "Are you going to open that?"

Ryan didn't look at the envelope, keeping his eyes on her. "You know, if I were working on a story and I interviewed someone as vague as you are, I'd think they had something to hide. Other than your hand, I mean."

She blinked at him but didn't look away. "I don't have anything else to say about it."

Ryan finally shook his head and reached for the envelope, feeling an odd, unbidden sense of relief. "There's a Chinese proverb: 'May you live in interesting times.' It's a curse, not a blessing. I think I get it now."

He opened the manila envelope with his name printed in Coleridge's precise script. He shook out the papers and began to go through them one by one. Some of them were in their original envelopes from official entities, some were loose. There were many faded papers and some looked almost new.

With Cass's help, Ryan began to spread them out on the bed, arranging them in chronological order. When the envelope was empty, he sat back. There were less than twenty items.

"A family's lives, reduced to this," Ryan said. "A few papers on a cheap motel bed."

He leaned over the bed again and began shuffling through the papers. His father's birth certificate was the oldest document, and under "place of birth," there it was—Cheyenne, Oklahoma.

"You can't change people's memories," he said to himself.

Cass looked up from the papers. "What?"

Ryan shook his head, realizing he'd spoken aloud. "Documents like these can be falsified. People's memories can't."

Cass waited a moment. "Daddy."

Ryan nodded. "If for some reason my father had to create a different past for himself, he could find a way to make the paper trail. What he couldn't do was change other people's observations. A paper trail with no memory to back it up." He ran a hand over his face, subconsciously scratching at his beard. "Now I'm thinking like a reporter."

More paper shuffling: copies of Frank Elder's military records, transfers to various posts, his discharge papers, mortgage papers on the Edmond house. The first documents on Anna Malikova Elder were her formal request for political asylum in the United States, INS forms granting her resident alien status, and finally, her citizenship papers.

"It's all just like they told me it was," Ryan said. "All the dates, all the places . . . there's nothing wrong with it."

His voice began to rise gradually, like mercury in a thermometer. "It's all here. Every *t* crossed, every *i* dotted." Both hands slammed down on the bed. "It's like a two-way mirror."

"What do you mean?"

Ryan looked up and his gaze gripped hers. "You know those mirrors they use in police stations when interrogating someone? When I was in Dayton, the cops let me sit in a couple of times. You know, they put the suspect in a room, and to him the glass looks like a mirror, but on the other side it's a window. He can't see the people on the other side, but they can see him. And what's worse, the guy in the room *knows* he's being watched, but he can't see who's watching him."

Ryan flipped one hand across the bed. A few envelopes scattered. "Other people know about my life, my parents' lives. Dorian, this guy who attacked you, this deputy . . . Kelly. They're looking through the glass at me and I don't know anything about anything." He picked up an envelope from the far right side of the bed, the more recent documents. "My own birth certificate. What good is it?" He tossed it at Cass.

She picked it up, looked at the envelope, then started to put it down again.

Her hand stopped in midair, the blue-gray eyes growing wider.

"What?" Ryan said.

"You were born in California?"

Ryan nodded. "My father was stationed at Camp Pendleton. That was his last post before he left the corps. At least that's what—what are you staring at?"

Cass pulled the certificate itself out of the old white envelope, with the return address of the California Bureau of Vital Records. She unfolded the certificate, then handed it across the bed. "Is this your birthday? Is this correct?"

Ryan glanced at it. "Yes. I told you, all this stuff's in order. It was a bad idea. I don't—"

He looked across the bed. For the first time since he'd darted onto Highway 283 in front of her old Dodge truck yesterday, he thought she looked frightened. Even when recounting the way the man had held the knife against her flesh, she hadn't shown fear. Until now.

Cass held up the envelope.

"What?" Ryan said. "I don't understand."

She shook it at him. "If you were born on that date in California, why is the envelope that your birth certificate was mailed in postmarked nearly a year later in Washington, D.C.?"

Ryan's left eye twitched, then again, then he was utterly still. For once, he wasn't aware of every little background sound. There was no more interstate traffic outside, no people in the motel courtyard, no water dripping from the leaky faucet in the shower. It was as if he'd been sucked into a vacuum with no sound but his breathing and Cass's.

He extended a hand across the bed. Cass pressed the envelope into it, looking up at him.

There was the envelope: *California Bureau of Vital Records*, with a post office box in Sacramento. Then the fading red postmark—*Washington, D.C.*—and a date ten and a half months after his birth. Farther down the envelope was the address, as he'd seen it thousands of times—*Mr. & Mrs. Francis A. Elder*—their house number, their street, in Edmond, Oklahoma. The house in which he'd grown up.

For a moment Ryan's eyes seemed to go out of focus, the print on the envelope shifting from side to side. He squeezed his eyes closed—bright blackness, then a strange crimson. He opened his eyes again. He realized his teeth were clenched. His jaws ached.

Without a word, he dropped the envelope and the birth certificate back on the bed, then with both arms he raked across the bed and scattered them all onto the floor. He ripped up the cheap blue bedspread, grabbed the pillows, and threw them toward the bathroom door.

Cass ducked a flying pillow. "Ryan, don't." Her voice was calm, but straining. "Ryan, it's not—"

Ryan whirled around. His foot—not the injured one—made contact with the heating/air-conditioning unit just under the window. He kicked it again and again. Dents erupted on its surface.

"Ryan, stop it. *Stop it now!*"

He was sobbing, tears streaking into his beard, making the brown-gray hair glisten. He yanked the telephone from its little stand by the bed, knocking over the stand in the process. The cord ripped out of the back of the phone and Ryan cocked his arm.

"No," Cass said.

Then she was beside him and her arms were around his chest. He was nearly a foot taller and she had to reach upward from behind to get her arms all the way around him. She squeezed, her hands not quite meeting.

"Put it down," she whispered. "Put it down."

The telephone was behind his head, as if he were rearing back to throw out a runner at home plate. The receiver dangled on its cord, swinging free, bouncing crazily between the two of them.

"Put . . . it . . . down," Cass said again, squeezing his chest harder.

Ryan opened his hand and the phone fell onto the bed.

"But I—" he said, then he realized what Cass was doing. He grabbed her left wrist and spun away from her. He heard one sound, something from the back of her throat, as if she wanted to scream but couldn't.

Ryan pulled her left wrist up and said, "Oh, my God."

Cass's thumb and little finger looked like two peaks on

either side of a valley. Her second, third, and fourth fingers were gone, neat round stumps of scar tissue below the second knuckle.

Ryan dropped her hand as if it had burned him. He gazed down at her.

"Maybe you're right about my father, and maybe you and I are both using each other," she said as she folded her left hand back into a pocket. "And yes, my brothers decided before I even got there that I would be the one to take care of Daddy. And yes, I had money, time, and no other commitments. But do you want to know the real reason I haven't tried to get away from you?"

He nodded, a barely perceptible movement.

"After you ran out in front of me, when I got out of the truck and saw you in the ditch, I thought you were in pain."

Ryan's eyebrows arched.

"Not physical pain."

Ryan swallowed. He couldn't look away from her.

"I took one look at your face and I thought that you were so hurt that you probably didn't even know how hurt you were." She reached out tentatively with her right hand and touched his shoulder, then slid down to his hand. He folded his fingers over hers.

"It's funny," he finally said.

"What?"

"I thought the same sort of thing about you."

She slowly brought her left hand out of the pocket and covered his hand with it, so that it rested between both of hers. The touch felt strange, Ryan thought, with only two fingers. He made himself look at the stumps again. Neither of them moved for a long time.

16

FAITH KELLY STEPPED ONTO HER FRONT PORCH AT 5:30 Sunday morning, ready to start her run. She wore a heavy sweatshirt, leg warmers, and gloves. She'd pulled her hair back into its traditional ponytail and jammed a stocking cap on her head. The temperature had dropped overnight, and the thermometer just outside her front door read nineteen degrees.

She would go for her run, try to catch the early mass at St. Eugene's, and spend a few hours figuring out what came next. She went back in the house and put on a second heavy sweatshirt and another pair of leg warmers. She did her stretches, then started down the sidewalk.

She took her block at a moderate jog, then turned it into a lope as she rounded the curve, stretching out, letting everything fall away.

As she made the corner, she saw the truck sitting on the other side of the street, lights off. Although most people parked in driveways here, it wasn't that unusual to see a light pickup truck on the street. What was unusual was the lone man sitting in it, motionless in the dark at six o'clock on a winter Sunday morning.

Kelly quickened her pace, falling into her rhythm. There was no sidewalk on this stretch, so she hugged the edge of the yards she passed, pounding the concrete beside them. A quarter of a way up the block, the truck's lights sliced through the darkness.

Kelly made a sound under her breath, thinking of her Glock, securely tucked into its holster and sitting on her bedside table at home. She'd never taken her weapon out on her run and had always thought it foolish of other officers she knew who did.

"Damn," she muttered.

She crossed the next street and heard the truck's engine. Kelly made herself concentrate on her breathing. Steady, steady, she told herself. Just like the marathon, keep it steady, keep it controlled.

She glanced over her shoulder as the truck drew parallel to her. It slowed. She saw the window start to come down and the silhouette of a large man inside. She thought of the man yesterday at Reno and Indiana, the big man in the ski mask who'd attacked Ryan Elder's woman friend.

Then she had an image of Chief Deputy Clarke: *I own you.*

"Why, Deputy Kelly," the man in the truck said.

Shit! Kelly veered into a cul-de-sac that opened to her left. The truck turned sharply to follow, squealing tires. A light went on in one of the houses on the cul-de-sac.

Kelly tried to picture the neighborhood from an aerial view, the position of each house as it related to her own, and her position now. She was two and a half blocks from home.

The truck angled across the street toward her, coming slowly, deliberately. The high beams danced across her face. Kelly threw up her arms and spun away from the light.

Kelly sprinted up the driveway of the house whose light had come on, vaulting a low chain-link gate. In the dark backyard, she tripped on something, she couldn't tell what. Something with wheels. A child's wagon, a tricycle. It skittered away from her and crashed into the wooden deck.

An outside floodlight came on. Call 911, Kelly thought. Come on, be a good citizen and call the cops.

Footsteps along the driveway. The gate rattled. Then the footsteps retreated fast and the truck door slammed. A second later, the engine revved away down the cul-de-sac.

The back fence of the yard was made of wooden planks, about six feet high, as most were in this neighborhood. She climbed it, tangling her legs in a vine of some sort, then dropped to the ground on the other side. Behind her, she heard the screen door of the house opening, and a man's voice: "Hey!"

The yard she was in was similar to the other, except there was no deck. She found the gate, which wasn't locked, and opened it. Thank God she hadn't had to vault it too, she thought.

Her running shoes slapped concrete as she ran. In just under four and a half minutes, she dropped into her own backyard, which was bare except for the struggling peach tree she'd planted late last summer. Kelly bent over, hands on her thighs, and let her breathing slow down. After a few seconds, she jogged across her yard, under the covered patio, and fumbled the keys from the pocket of her sweatpants.

She unlocked the kitchen door and let herself in to a rush of warmth. She ripped the cap off her head and started toward her bedroom. She wouldn't screw up again. This time Chief Clarke wouldn't have cause to . . .

Kelly screamed.

The big man sitting at her dining room table said, "Why, Deputy Kelly, I can't believe you're so skittish."

Kelly didn't think. Pure instinct took over, making her feint left, then dodging to the right, toward the door that connected to the living room and hallway. She gained the hallway in five steps.

"It's not there," the man called, "so don't bother looking."

Kelly burst into her room, slamming the light switch upward. She launched herself at the bed, rolled once, and reached for the bedside table.

Her gun was gone.

In my house, he's in my house, she thought, the fear and panic breaking into a boil and turning to anger. She darted to the window and pulled aside the curtains. The truck was parked at the foot of her driveway, blocking the Miata.

"We're on the same side," said a voice from the doorway.

Kelly turned slowly, getting her first look at the man in the light. He was of indistinct middle age—fifties, she thought— and was overweight but not obese. He looked more like he'd just eaten a large meal and the paunch would recede after a few hours. He was bald on top, with brown-gray fringe around his ears, and brown horn-rimmed glasses magnifying large gray eyes. His clothes were brown pleated pants, navy blue shirt, large dark green overcoat. His speech was pinched, with the accent of the upper Midwest. Kelly recognized it from her years growing up in Chicago. She thought the only thing he lacked was a plastic pocket protector and several pens to make the picture complete.

"Your chief—Clarke, I believe is his name—told you I'd be getting in touch with you," the man said.

Kelly stood for a moment, breathing quietly through her mouth.

"I apologize for all the high drama," he said. "I have to be careful how I move around in this city. Let's talk."

Kelly didn't move.

The man sighed. "All right, maybe this will help. In Arthur Dorian's office, on the wall opposite the filing cabinet, there was a stuffed catfish, the only decoration of any kind in the office. It weighed over thirty pounds, and there was an engraving on the back of the piece of wood it was mounted on. 'Lake Texoma, July 4, 1981.' "

When Kelly had first met Dorian, she'd thought of how absurd the fish looked, mounted on Dorian's stark white walls, how out of character it was for him. It was only after he'd told her the story behind it that it made sense and that was her first exposure to his wry humor.

"Anyone could have been in the office and seen that hanging on the wall," she said. "That doesn't tell me anything."

The man's expression twitched slightly, then became non-committal. "Good for you, Deputy. That wouldn't have been enough for me either. The truth is, Arthur didn't catch that fish. He bought it from a taxidermist here in Oklahoma City. He used to say that his whole career was about making up fish stories, so he decided he needed a real fish in his office. Now, do I pass the test? Can we talk?"

Kelly snapped her head back to the big man, thinking of Dorian smoothing his little mustache on the day he'd told her the real origin of the fish. "You don't look like a field person," she said finally.

The man smiled. "Then that makes me the perfect field person, don't you think?" He gestured down the hallway.

They went back to the dining room, where Kelly made coffee. She took cups for both of them and they sat across from each other at the wooden oval table. The big man blew on his coffee, holding the mug with both hands. Kelly had already finished half her cup before he took a drink.

"Good coffee," the man said. He looked across at Kelly. "You read Arthur's file on this case?"

"Yes."

"And you think he took Ryan Elder to Cheyenne to tell him the truth, and when he did, Ryan killed him?"

"I'm not sure."

"Good for you, Deputy. You shouldn't be too sure. I'm not either, and may never be. But we do have a problem. Young Ryan is still out there and we need to bring him in."

The man began to drum his fingers in an odd pattern. He lay his hand flat on the tabletop, fingers splayed out, then tapped each finger twice before starting again. All the time, he was looking at Kelly.

"You'll be out front on this," he said, after he'd been through the rhythm four times. "I'm afraid I'm not able to be seen in Oklahoma City."

"Why?"

The man gave a thin smile, with some sadness to it. "There are reasons. Arthur was a friend for many years. Whatever happened in Cheyenne, I want to finish it. Whether Ryan Elder killed him or not, we'll only get Arthur's killer through him."

"Agreed. But—"

The man tapped again. "There are only two ways we're going to get to Ryan. You know one of them."

Kelly leaned back, finishing the last of her coffee. "The attorney. Coleridge."

The man nodded.

"And the second way? According to the file—"

Tapping, tapping, tapping. "No, no. Here's where we go past the file. I *know* Ryan Elder. We've even kept up with him the last seven years. I must say, it wasn't easy, the way he's been moving around." He stopped tapping, his eyes taking on a thoughtful cast. "His temperament has changed. Once, he was quiet, soft-spoken, inquisitive. A well-behaved, somewhat insightful boy. Gradually, over time, he's become . . . volatile. He responds angrily, then regrets it later. He goes through different phases. He tried various drugs for a while, but backed off when he realized he might lose control. He had a religious phase, fundamentalist Christianity. Decided Jesus didn't have what he needed either."

"Always looking for something," Kelly said.

"That's it. His parents' suicide left him without an anchor, with no center. No explanation, no understanding, so he's meandered from one thing to the next."

Kelly stood up and refilled their coffee mugs. "You said you knew him. You said there's another way besides Coleridge to get him in."

"There's one other person he trusts."

"The woman who's with him."

The man frowned. "No. I don't know what's going on there." The frown deepened, slashing lines across the thick forehead. "Strange. I don't quite understand . . ."

He tapped harder. Kelly reached across the table and brought her hand down on his, stopping the rhythm. "How do you know him? How do you know who he trusts? And you never told me your name, by the way."

"You're very ambitious." The man pulled his hand from under Kelly's, then reached under the table. When his hand reappeared, he slid Kelly's holstered Glock across the table to her. "Take it with you from now on, Deputy. You're working for me now, and you have to be very damned careful."

Kelly took the weapon, checked it over, then looked up again. "Who are you? I need to know what to call you, at least."

"What to call me. Well, that's good, you being concerned about such things. Try this. Maybe it'll help you get into Ryan's mind. Ryan used to call me 'Mr. Yorkton.' "

The man leaned back in his chair and tapped his fingers.

17

THE JEEP COASTED DOWN THE I-44 OFF-RAMP AT PENN
Avenue in Oklahoma City, and Cass turned south, gradually
making her way back toward "Alicia Rubinstein's" apartment.
"Still no company?" she said, as she had every five minutes
since they'd left the motel.

Ryan looked at both rear and side mirrors. "Not that I can
see." He looked back down at the legal pad in his lap while
she drove. He'd done what he always did when he was pursu-
ing a story—he made a list.

On one side of the page he'd written inconsistencies:
Dad/Cheyenne; my birth certificate. On the other side were
questions: *Who was Yorkton? How did govt. connect Jack C. to
me? What does Dept. 30 do? Man with knife? Newspaper article?*
Then, underlined three times: *Adam and Eve?*

At the bottom of the page, he'd written whom he thought
he could trust. The list, he reflected, was pitifully short. Jack
Coleridge's name was at the top.

He glanced at Cass, who was concentrating on the road
ahead, her forehead slightly furrowed, the fingers of her right
hand moving on the wheel every few seconds, as if in tune
with music that no one else could hear. He remembered how
her arms had felt wrapped around him, pulling him back
from the precipice of the hot black rage. For a split second,
before he'd thought to grab her left hand, he'd felt—safe.
He'd felt all right, and in that sliver of time, he'd thought for
a moment that he could just be plain old Ryan Elder, the
even-tempered, respectful kid from the suburbs.

What happened? he had finally asked, standing there in
the cheap motel with the official documentation of his family's life scattered all over the floor.

Cass had shaken her head, very slowly. *I can't. Not yet*, she'd said, and put her left hand back in her pocket.

He very carefully wrote *Cass* under Jack Coleridge's name.

Cass turned the Jeep onto Thirtieth Street. They were half a mile from the apartment complex. Ryan tapped his pen on the legal pad, then wrote *Jeff* under Cass's name. "Drive around a little bit more."

"Oh?"

"I want to make a call. If someone's trying to trace phone calls, they won't be able to pin down a cellular call while we're moving. They'll just get a general area of town."

"I hadn't thought of that."

"A cop in Dayton told me that. Cops absolutely hate cell phones."

Cass kept the car moving west. Ryan punched numbers on the phone.

"Memorial Community Hospital, how may I direct your call?"

Ryan closed his eyes and, for a moment, had a vision of himself and Jeff, at eleven, at sixteen, at eighteen, each being the brother neither of them had. "Is Dr. Jeff Majors in the hospital today?" Ryan knew there was a good chance Jeff was there. He was a second-year resident and most programs worked their residents a hundred hours a week.

"One moment, please."

A minute passed. Cass cruised onto I-44 again, glancing in the mirror and at Ryan alternately.

"Paging Dr. Majors now," the operator said in Ryan's ear.

What if they've gotten to Jeff too? Ryan thought wildly, listening to Muzak. Then: *No. That's too farfetched. I haven't seen Jeff in . . .*

"This is Dr. Majors," said a voice Ryan knew as well as his own.

He jumped in the seat. "Oh—"

"Hello?" Impatient now. "This is Dr. Majors."

Ryan watched green highway signs slide by. He took a breath. "Jeff, it's Ryan."

There was silence for a moment.

"Well, Ryan Grab-Ass Elder," Jeff Majors said.

Ryan closed his eyes and leaned his head against the cold window of the Jeep. Since the time they'd been preteens, the two of them had made up absurd, often vulgar, middle names for each other.

"Well, Jeffrey Hairy-Ass Majors," Ryan said. "I guess I should say *Doctor* Hairy-Ass."

Cass glanced at him. Ryan made a *be patient* gesture.

"Where the hell are you, Ryan? What's up?"

"Look, I'm in town, and I—"

"Here? In the city?"

"Yeah. Look, Jeff, I'm in some trouble and I need your help."

A few seconds passed. When Majors spoke again, his voice was lower, more serious. "What's going on?"

"Not on the phone. Do you remember my dad's lawyer, Jack Coleridge?"

"Remember him? Hell, *my* dad plays golf with him. He was our state representative for a long time. Of course I remember him."

Ryan nodded. Of course Jeff's father would know Coleridge. The senior Majors was a district court judge. "Can you get a message to him for me?"

"Message? Get a message to Jack Coleridge. Ryan, what's going on?"

"Trust me, Jeff. It's a mess and I don't understand all of it. Really, I don't understand *any* of it."

Majors's voice lowered further. "Why can't you talk to him yourself?"

"I just can't." Ryan felt his own voice rising. "Look, are you going to help me or not?"

"Jesus, Ryan. I only hear from you one time since—well, you know—and now you call me up out of the blue—"

"Jeff, please." Ryan hoped he didn't sound as desperate as he felt.

Majors breathed on the phone. "Okay, look. Let's get together. I'm on until eleven tonight, but I don't come back until noon tomorrow. Let's meet for breakfast. How's that sound?"

The Jeep turned back onto I-40. They were barely a mile from Indiana Avenue, where yesterday's blowup had occurred. "All right," Ryan finally said. "You remember where your dad took us for breakfast, the time we went to Career Day at his . . . his place of business?"

Majors was silent. Ryan imagined him thinking back, and at the same time wondering why Ryan was being so vague.

"Yeah, I remember. Ryan—"

"Don't say any more, Jeff. Seven A.M. tomorrow."

"And you'll tell me what this is all about?"

Ryan was suddenly very tired. "As much as I can."

"Okay, I'll see you then. Look, they're paging me. I'm working the ER and there's been a big accident—"

"Tomorrow."

"Okay, tomorrow."

Ryan pressed end, then looked at Cass. "I need to find out a few things."

Cass nodded toward the highway. "Where to?"

"Downtown. We've got work to do before tomorrow morning."

Dr. Jeff Majors hung up the phone and looked across the table in the on-call room at FBI Special Agent Scott Hendler and Deputy U.S. Marshal Faith Kelly.

"Ryan didn't kill anyone," Majors said quietly. "I've known him for—"

Kelly leaned forward. "But you haven't been around him much in the last few years, have you, Doctor?"

Majors shrugged. "He couldn't have killed anyone."

"We just want to talk to him," Hendler said. "Hopefully it'll clear everything up and we can be done with it."

"Then why do you want me to wear a hidden microphone?"

"It's more for your protection than anything," Kelly said.

Majors's eyes drifted down to Kelly's cleavage, then back up again. "Well, if you're just going to talk to him—"

"We just want to ask him some questions," Kelly said.

"Why don't I believe you?"

Hendler sniffed impatiently. Kelly leaned forward even farther and lay her hand over Majors's forearm. "He trusts you and you can trust me," she said. Her eyes burned into his. In Kelly's experience, most men were unprepared for a woman to meet their gaze strongly and directly. She couldn't force Majors to meet Elder wearing a wire tomorrow morning. He had to agree to it.

"As long as no one gets hurt," Majors said.

She had him! "Absolutely," Kelly said.

"And you'll let him call his lawyer?"

"Of course. That's his constitutional right."

Majors shook his head. "Ryan didn't have anything to do with killing anyone."

Kelly couldn't help noticing that Majors sounded less certain than he had a few minutes ago.

18

THE JEEP WOUND THROUGH THE MONDAY MORNING traffic, tightening like a belt through the construction zones approaching downtown Oklahoma City. Ryan slouched in the passenger seat, his brain fuzzy, nerves like old electrical wire. He'd lain awake on the sofa until well after 3 A.M., scribbling on his legal pad: questions, ideas, possible scenarios. Nothing made sense.

He glanced at Cass. He'd heard her turning restlessly in the apartment bedroom. Once, he'd even tiptoed down the hall and looked in on her. Asleep, but fitful. In the tiny shaft of light from the hallway, he'd seen both her hands on top of the covers. The right, with its long slender fingers and carefully trimmed nails; the left with its stumps, like clear-cut trees, never to return. And the face—younger, somehow, in sleep, not so much pain on the pale features, the huge eyes at rest.

He'd gone back down the hall, thinking of false identities

and the nylon bag full of money. Confusion. His entire life was confusion.

"Here," he said, and pointed.

They'd come to the corner of Robert S. Kerr and Robinson avenues, in the heart of the city's modest high-rise downtown. Cass pulled over, letting traffic wash past.

"You're sure—" she said.

Ryan held up a hand. "I need to go alone. Just follow the plan. If I'm not back by nine o'clock, gather up your things and disappear. Go back to your father, or start a new life as Alicia Rubinstein, whatever you want. But if you think you need to turn me in, at least wait a few hours. Please."

"I wouldn't do that, Ryan."

"Okay." He nodded, almost said something else, and realized he didn't know what he was going to say. He nodded again, and opened the passenger door into a rush of cold wind. He hugged his jacket tighter, got out, then stuck his head back in. "Nine o'clock. Don't wait around."

Cass nodded and blinked. "Nine o'clock."

Ryan closed the door and walked away, crossing the sidewalk and a brick courtyard before disappearing into the Bank of Oklahoma Tower's revolving door.

It was five minutes before seven o'clock.

Kelly thought Dr. Jeff Majors was considerably better looking in street clothes than in his hospital scrubs. Majors was short, but with a muscular build, and was wearing a navy blue turtleneck, black jeans, and brown leather boots. His hair was sand-colored, his eyes were a medium green-blue.

In the back of the white unmarked FBI van, Hendler finished running the wire from under the collar of the turtleneck down to Majors's belt. He clipped it under the sweater and said, "There, Doctor. You're ready."

"No, I'm not," Majors said, "but I'm wired, anyway."

"It'll be over before it starts," Kelly said. "As soon as he arrives, we'll come in. It won't be with guns blazing, Doctor. It'll be calm and efficient, and we'll hopefully be able to clear up some questions."

"Questions. Right." Majors stood up. "Let's get this over with."

There was a knock on the door of the van and Hendler opened it to let in the third member of their team. Nina Reeves was in her forties, a small woman with eyes the color of summer sky, contrasting sharply with her dark skin. She was wearing tan slacks and a green sweater under a heavy FBI jacket and was holding a steaming Styrofoam cup of coffee.

"Morning," Hendler said. "Faith, Doctor Majors, this is Nina Reeves, the Queen of Sound. She consults with our office on a lot of cases. Has all kinds of interesting degrees from places like MIT."

Reeves ignored Hendler and shook hands with Majors and Kelly. "Good morning. Faith, nice to meet you. I've heard so much about you already. Before you ask—and I know you're going to ask, because everyone does—the accent is Bermudan, spiced with ten years in Britain. And also before you ask, the blue eyes come from my grandfather, who was a Brit of European descent. That should about cover it."

Kelly smiled. "I guess it does."

Reeves sat down in front of the small console that hugged one wall of the van. The receiver that would capture the digital signal from Majors's transmitter was plugged into a portable Sony digital audio tape machine, only slightly larger than most personal portable stereos. The tape itself was smaller than a credit card, yet carried two hours of recording capability. Reeves slipped a pair of headphones over her head. Kelly, watching her, noticed that her straightened black hair held auburn highlights.

"Ready here," Reeves said. "Nice clear signal. Be sure to speak up, Doctor, but don't shout. You don't want to blow my ears off."

"I'll try to remember that."

Hendler held open the rear door and Majors climbed out. He started across Robert S. Kerr Avenue. A moment later he was inside the Oklahoma County Courthouse.

• • •

The bank itself wasn't yet open, only the outer building. Ryan nodded to a security guard, who nodded back and watched as Ryan walked the length of the wood-paneled lobby to a down stairway.

Holding the rail, Ryan started down. He turned a corner, descended another short flight of steps, and found himself in a subterranean foyer. To his left was a glassed-in room with a few tables and vending machines. Two women sat inside, smoking cigarettes, reading newspapers. Ryan guessed that in a few minutes they'd be upstairs, opening teller windows.

In front of him was a set of double glass doors, which led to the bank's underground parking garage. He could see, far across the garage, an identical set of doors. Ryan looked around, his heart thumping. He felt perspiration dotting his back. He unbuttoned his coat. The soreness in his foot was still there, humming like background music.

Ryan went through the first set of glass doors, assaulted again by the cold. He picked up his pace and instinctively felt inside his coat pocket for the letter he would ask Jeff to give to Jack Coleridge, the list of questions Ryan wanted Coleridge to ask, in official channels. Questions about Frank Elder's military record, Anna Malikova Elder's immigration, a fire in Cheyenne that never occurred, his own birth. Coleridge would be able to get answers that Ryan couldn't.

He crossed the garage, went through the second set of glass doors, and stepped onto the Metro Concourse. Built in the 1970s, the concourse was a series of interconnected tunnels that ran under most of downtown Oklahoma City.

The concourse walkway was carpeted in a tricolor weave: brown, beige, and a rusty orange. The walls were painted to match, but Ryan noticed a few water stains on the ceiling, with corresponding blotches on the carpet. He stopped to read a sign and get his bearings. Signs pointed south and east to Kerr-McGee, Sonic, Leadership Square. A westward-pointing sign said COUNTY COURTHOUSE. Ryan turned in that direction.

He passed a glassed-in Italian restaurant on the right and

memory flooded him. Judge Ray Majors, Jeff's father, had once said the place had the best food no one in town knew about. Ryan almost smiled. He and Jeff, inseparable as boys: swimming lessons; baseball; Jeff helping Ryan through science class while Ryan tutored him through social studies; Jeff making fun of Ryan's refusal to wear jeans, as early as the fifth grade; Ryan sneaking *habañero* hot sauce onto Jeff's scrambled eggs, Jeff who liked his food so bland it was almost without flavor. . . .

Then, in college, two kids from Oklahoma at universities on opposite coasts, they had talked on the phone at least once a week, covering the gamut: school, work, families, women, whether they'd return to Oklahoma after graduation. . . .

Ryan's eyes fogged. Christ Almighty, what had happened to his life?

He thought of the birth certificate, Cass in the motel room, staring at it. Return address, California. Postmark, Washington, D.C. *Confusion.*

Ryan flexed his hands, his breath coming rapidly. He felt for the letter in his pocket. He started to jog along the concourse.

Both Kelly and Nina Reeves sat under headphones in the van, listening to the sounds of Jeff Majors walking through the courthouse doors, turning a corner, descending steps. On the other side of the van, Hendler was reading the sports section of the *Daily Oklahoman.*

Reeves lay a dark hand over Kelly's forearm. "Lighten up, my friend. You're covered. Our man Sleepy Scott over there knows what he's doing and the other team is just around the block. First operation is always hardest."

"I know," Kelly said, "but this one—"

"Don't make it personal. Never let it be personal. It's a job. Do the job. Then forget the job and have a life."

Kelly was quiet. Easier said than done, she thought. For Art and for Mikael and for Captain Joe Kelly and for Chief Deputy Clarke, it's personal, all right.

Reeves adjusted the volume on the headphones. The DAT player slowly counted off seconds on the tape.

They listened to Majors's footsteps, now muffled on carpet, then they heard him mumble, "Okay, here we are."

"Ah," Reeves said, then was silent, listening.

The footsteps changed: a different kind of flooring. Then, a burst of music from a radio tuned to a classic rock station. Kelly recognized the song, CCR's "As Long As I Can See the Light."

"Will that—" she said.

"Oh no," Reeves said. "We'll still get this lovely signal. Wish they'd turn it down, though."

Kelly tapped her foot, thinking of Art Dorian, the mysterious package with the photos of his lifeless body. Then, Ryan Elder, running alongside Interstate 40. Chief Clarke: *I own you.* And the man called Yorkton. He'd given her a number where she could reach him in emergency. Otherwise, he said, he would be in touch with her.

In touch. Yeah, like breaking into my house, she thought.

And then her father, the captain of detectives. She remembered the conversation clearly: she was thirteen and had mustered every ounce of courage she had to tell her father she wanted to be a cop when she grew up. He'd gotten red in the face, as if he weren't sure whether to be angry or amused, and he settled on amused. *I don't think so, Faith Siobhan. You're a good girl and a smart girl and there are a lot of things you can do, but you don't want to be a cop. Maybe you could teach. You're smart enough to be a teacher. No, you can't be a cop, and you need to quit thinking about it.* His smug amusement had only strengthened her resolve.

Kelly shook her head, pulled her hair away from her face. Focus on right now—these things weren't good for her concentration. She winced as Jeff Majors cleared his throat in her ears. "Coffee, black," Majors was saying. "And a blueberry bagel."

A soft female voice, laden with Oklahoma drawl: "You got it. Best bagels in town, right here, you know?"

"I know," Majors said.

More music, a loud-mouthed announcer, listeners calling in to win tickets to something or other. An ad for a plumber.

Kelly gritted her teeth. The music faded a little. Majors was moving away from the counter.

Kelly grabbed the communications link, spoke into her own handheld radio. "Team Bravo, you there?"

Kelly didn't know any of the FBI agents in the other van, but Hendler had said they were all good. Dependable. "All quiet on the western front," said a scratchy male voice.

Kelly nodded. Hendler rattled his newspaper. Reeves closed her eyes, listening.

They listened to Majors, drinking coffee, chewing a bagel. Kelly had never been inside the Underworld Deli, but she felt as if she were there. The sound was so clear, so real.

A minute passed. Footsteps brushed past Majors. Kelly stiffened and thought, Here we go.

The footsteps stopped for a moment, then the drawl of the counter woman came through loud and clear: "Morning. What can I get you?"

Five seconds later, the radio volume increased to blast level. An old song by Kansas was playing: *Carry on, my wayward son . . .*

"Hey!" Reeves said, wincing at the volume. She reached for the controls.

They heard Majors scrabbling his chair back on a tile floor. *There'll be peace when you are done . . .*

A heavy, clunky sound, as if a box had been dropped on the floor, lost in the loud music. More chair scrabbling.

Lay your weary head to rest . . .

Footsteps. Staccato, rapid.

Majors: "You're not—"

"What?" Kelly said. "What did he say? I can barely hear over the damned music."

Reeves's hand froze on the control board. Hendler looked up, his attention riveted now.

A strange gurgling sound erupted into their ears. Then a crash against something heavy. A muted thump. Footsteps receding.

. . . *Don't you cry no more!* A scream of rock guitars.

Kelly sat paralyzed for a moment. Then she tore the head-phones off and screamed into her radio: "Something's going down! Move in!"

"Shit," Hendler said. In one movement he was on his feet, opening the rear door of the van and reaching for his gun.

Kelly followed, waiting for a break in the traffic. "Come on, come on," she murmured, waiting for the traffic light at the corner to change and the flow of cars to move a different direction.

The light changed. Kelly and Hendler ran.

Ryan turned at a sharp L junction of the concourse and heard the music instantly. Loud rock 'n' roll: guitars, bass, drums, strangely poetic vocals. He winced at the volume, then real-ized it could only be coming from one place. The Under-world was the last shop on the concourse before the court-house, the only thing open in this leg of the tunnel.

He moved faster, passing a sign advertising the Underworld: YOU'RE ONLY 16 STEPS FROM THE BEST BAGELS IN OKLAHOMA CITY!

Sixteen steps. The music was deafening. Who in their right mind would turn up the music that loud at this hour of the morning?

Ryan's heart quickened. Twelve steps, ten. The song by Kansas ended and "Slow Train Running" by the Doobie Brothers came on, so loud his ears were pounding in time with his heart.

Eight steps, six. He could see light spilling out from the door of the little deli where he and Jeff and Judge Majors had had breakfast on that long-ago morning, their junior year in high school. Ryan almost smiled. The judge was probably three floors above them, in the courthouse, right now.

Ryan turned into the doorway of the Underworld, the music hammering at him like a boxer repeatedly jabbing his opponent. The little deli was simple, with vinyl-covered tables and red vinyl chairs. Every available wall space was covered by posters. Posters for rodeos, operas, safe sex, anti-smoking, Oklahoma City's Festival of the Arts. There were even posters behind the counter. Ryan smelled strong coffee.

He was a third of the way into the place before he saw that a chair was turned over beside one of the tables. A large Styrofoam coffee cup was on its side, coffee dripping like dark rain off the edge of the table. A bagel with one bite out of it sat beside the cup on a white napkin.

Ryan stopped. He watched the coffee drip, wrinkling his brow. He raised his head, looking beyond the table.

Jeff Majors was sitting against the far wall, his knees drawn up, head bent forward. Ryan took a step. "Jeff," he said softly, unable to hear himself over the Doobie Brothers.

He stepped around the overturned chair and the puddle of coffee. "Jeff," he said, louder. "Jeff!"

Then he was at his friend's side, shaking his shoulder. Majors toppled away from him and Ryan saw the crimson smear on the wall where he'd been. Blood on the floor in front of him. Blood on either side of him. Why hadn't he seen it before?

"Oh God, Jeff—" He knelt down, flattening Majors onto his back, and he saw it: a slit like a cruel smile, all along the ridge of his throat.

Ryan screamed wordlessly and backed away, still in a crouch. He tried to straighten and fell over the upturned chair, banging his shoulder on the edge of the table.

Ryan finally gained his feet, pulling himself up on a wooden partition. He backed up, his eyes still on his best friend. He bumped into the counter, then whirled around. Behind the counter, more blood. A woman was lying face-down. All Ryan could tell was that she was blonde with dark roots. And that she wasn't moving.

His breathing started to come in rapid bursts, squeezing out of him as if someone were beating on his chest. They'd gotten to Jeff.

Memory: spring break their senior year in high school. It was the day Allison McDermott had dumped Ryan, saying that if he was really going to California to college, there was no way they could stay together. He felt as if he'd been turned inside out. His parents did what they could—*Hurt on your own terms*, his mother had said resolutely—but it was Jeff who sat up with him every night for a week, letting him cry his heart out, letting him curse Allison and then wonder what he could do to get her back, while still following his own dream.

Ryan wiped his hand across his mouth, then inched forward to where Jeff lay. The radio was maddening, Fleetwood Mac now, Stevie Nicks singing "Rhiannon." If Ryan screamed, no one could hear him over the damned radio anyway. He gingerly, almost tenderly, reached out a hand, and lay two fingers over Jeff's wrist. He already knew there was no life there, but he felt he owed Jeff this much.

He steadied himself with his other hand against Jeff's ribs, and he brushed something under the sweater. Ryan pulled up the sweater and saw the transmitter, with its wire snaking up his friend's back.

Ryan squeezed his eyes closed. His throat tightened. He took hold of the wire and pulled hard, disconnecting it from the little rectangular box.

"Oh, Jeff," he said. "I'm sorry. I'm—"

Ryan stood up and backed away. Fleetwood Mac finished on the radio, and there was a split second before the loud-mouthed announcer came on. In the flash of silence, Ryan heard sound, this time from outside the Underworld, on the concourse itself. Footsteps, coming fast.

Coming for him.

"I'm sorry," he said again, then backed out onto the concourse, turned, and ran.

19

HENDLER WAS THE FIRST ONE DOWN THE STEPS, RUNning at full tilt down the gentle incline onto the concourse. Kelly, three steps behind him, already had her Glock drawn. She was thinking: One block away from my own office. One block from the U.S. Courthouse, and we've blown it.

Hendler took a step into the Underworld and said, "Holy shit." Then, back over his shoulder: "Faith, he's—"

Still on the concourse, Kelly caught the movement out of the corner of her eye. Perhaps fifty yards down the tunnel was an L-turn, with a giant blue circle painted on the wall like a target. Just stepping around the circle was the tall, slender man in khaki pants, dark coat, and white running shoes.

"There he is!" Kelly yelled.

For a second, both of them froze in their positions. Kelly thought: We never believed he'd kill his own best friend. Then she remembered Yorkton: Never be sure of anything.

She raised the Glock and started toward the circle. "Don't move, Elder!" she shouted. "Federal officers!"

He jerked his head toward her.

She gripped the Glock in both hands, a good firing stance.

A man in a suit stepped around the corner in front of Elder, right into the line of fire.

"What's going on?" Kelly heard the man say. Then he turned, saw the gun, and yelled, "Hey!"

Kelly lowered her weapon. Elder was gone.

"Get a crime scene crew," she barked to Hendler, then realized he technically had seniority, not her.

Hendler didn't seem to notice. "Got it," he said, then he was talking into his radio. He called for backup, then alerted the other team that the suspect was moving toward them.

Kelly started down the concourse at a full run.

Ryan bounded off the blue circle on the wall, leaving the stranger staring dumbly at him. It occurred to him that he probably owed the man his life and certainly his freedom—at least for the moment.

He raced down the tunnel. The signs he'd read earlier were a blur. With every step the loud rock 'n' roll receded and all he could see was Jeff Majors, toppling sideways, leaving a trail of his blood on the wall of the Underworld.

His heart thundered wildly. His face twitched.

Whatever this was, it had swallowed up his parents seven years ago, and now it had left Jeff in a pool of his own blood. Dammit.

People passed him, on their way to work in banks or the courthouse or any of the other downtown office buildings connected to the Concourse. They stared at this strange young man, running for his life.

Somewhere, a scream.

Ryan's heart thudded, his eyes burned, his foot shrieked. Who are these people, with their ordinary lives? Then he thought that the people he passed were keeping him alive. Deputy Kelly and her troops wouldn't shoot, not down here, not with all these innocent bystanders around.

He pushed through the set of double glass doors without stopping or slowing. An elderly man on the far side said, "Slow down. Someone could get hurt."

Ryan swiveled his head to look at him. He was almost to the parking garage, almost free from the concourse. Far down the carpeted corridor, there were more running feet, this time from the other direction.

Voices: "Elder! Freeze!"

"What's the matter, son?" the old man was saying. He was stopped, one hand on the handle of the glass door, staring back at Ryan.

Ryan flapped a hand at him. Ahead on the left was the door to the parking garage. Down the tunnel, two men in suits, with guns.

Ryan angled across the tunnel and put a hand straight out in front of him, a halfback warding off tacklers. The long window of the Italian restaurant raced by. Then the garage, with its smells of exhaust and gasoline and, far above, the cold air of morning.

His outstretched hand slammed open the garage door and in two steps he was off the carpet, his shoes thudding on concrete.

Jeff, he thought. They killed Jeff, trying to get to me.

He turned the corner by the glassed-in smoking area and

ran into one of the women he'd seen there earlier. She tumbled to the floor, cigarette flying in Ryan's face, her purse spilling on the carpet.

"Hey, you!" she shouted. "Watch where you're going!"

"Sorry," Ryan mumbled, wiping ash from his face. I'm trying to stay alive, lady—give me a break, he thought.

Stairs ahead. Up. His foot started to scream. Then he was in the bank, a few more suits around. The suits stared, pointed. "Security!" one of them yelled.

Ryan loped across the bank lobby. He could see the outside world, Robinson Avenue, the bank courtyard, *escape.*

Kelly emerged into the courtyard, followed closely by the second FBI team. The cold, crisp air bruised her lungs and for a moment she stood completely still, scanning the street. Robinson Avenue was jammed with downtown office workers just arriving for the day's work. On an ordinary day, Kelly thought, she would be one of them.

Ryan Elder was nowhere to be seen.

Lost him, she thought. A block away from the office and we lost him.

One of the other FBI agents, a middle-aged black man named Merrill, stared up and down the street. "He can't just disappear like that."

"Obviously, he can," Kelly said.

"Come on, Kelly," Merrill said. "We'll get people onto all the transportation links out of the city—the airport, the train station. Kelly, are you with me?"

Kelly was staring south, at a tiny sign in front of Leadership Square, just across Robert S. Kerr Avenue on Robinson. A chill went through her.

"Kelly?" Merrill said.

"But what if he doesn't want to leave the city?"

"What?"

Kelly pointed at the sign.

Merrill squinted into the distance, then his face went slack. "Shit," he said softly.

The little rectangular sign, perched on top of a metal pole, was white with a logo of blue and green stripes and red lettering. The lettering read METRO TRANSIT.

The Oklahoma City Metro Transit bus transfer terminal isn't a terminal at all, but an open parking lot at Robert S. Kerr and Shartel avenues. Ryan took a moment to consider the location: the Oklahoma County jail was just west of the terminal, across Shartel. The Municipal Court building was just across the street to the south. The Oklahoma City Police Department main headquarters was a block away.

A few sagging wooden benches ringed the parking lot and a small temporary restroom stood at one end. Ryan had forgotten how wedded to their cars people were in Oklahoma. Public transportation was not a high-ticket item.

But this was the busiest time of day and buses were coming and going in and out of the lot. Most of the people waiting were minorities, black men in coveralls with their names across the breast, Hispanic women in hotel or fast-food uniforms. A few preppy-looking types, most of whom glanced nervously at the blue-collar workers. A few who looked homeless and hopeless. A man with a badly disfigured face sat alone on a bench, softly singing an old blues song.

And Ryan, pacing the line of benches, watching the line of buses and watching the eastern edge of the parking lot, waiting for people with guns to come racing across.

"They're always late," a man said near him. "Go to Atlanta if you want good transportation. They got these trains there—"

"No, Denver's better," said another man.

Ryan clenched his fist around the four quarters in his pocket, tuning out the debate. He tried to clear his mind. Survival was everything now.

He watched as the driver of his bus began to make her way back from the restroom. She was a tiny brunette with curly hair and a swinging step. She bounded across the parking lot and back to her bus. The display above the windshield read SHEPHERD MALL.

Ryan began to follow her, praying that she would leave

immediately. She settled into her seat and Ryan stepped onto the bus. The bus next to them pulled out and the driver waved. Ryan dropped four quarters into the slot, then slipped into the first row of seats.

He felt the bus drop into gear, then heard the driver say: "Wonder what that's all about?"

Ryan jerked his head up and looked out the window. Four buses away, Deputy Kelly and two men in dark suits were talking, making animated gestures to a Metro Transit supervisor.

The supervisor shrugged and pointed to the bus beside them. Kelly climbed onto the bus and the other two men fanned out to other buses.

Ryan's heart hammered. *Let's go!*

"I don't know what they're up to, but I got a schedule," the driver said, and pulled out of the lot.

Ryan sagged against the seat. *What's the secret?* he thought. *What's worth killing Jeff over, just because he was meeting me?* The man who attacked Cass had mentioned a message. Something about how his parents had sent him a message.

There wasn't a message. There was a phone number and an orchestra review cut out of a damned newspaper. What kind of message was that?

Ryan thought of Art Dorian, the way the little man had maneuvered him into the meeting in Cheyenne. A dramatic buildup, words about how important, how meaningful, the Battle of the Washita Historic Site had been to Frank Elder.

But he'd never heard that from his father. It took Art Dorian to tell him. Ryan realized he didn't know how his father had *felt* about most things.

Seven years ago, he'd stepped off the plane and had the startlingly clear thought: These are not my parents.

All he had were his own perceptions of who his parents were, not the reality. He remembered Professor Douglas, his communication theory teacher at UCLA, a good-natured, round-faced little man who'd devoted half a dozen lectures to the ongoing question of reality vs. perception of reality. Ryan could see him pacing up and down in front of the class:

In the broadcast media, does it matter who you really are, or only who your audience thinks you are? Then again, does your audience even care who you really are? They'll make you over in their own image anyway. . . .

Hell of an irony, he thought. He'd gone into a business in which he communicated to an audience, but for the first twenty years of his life, Ryan had himself been the audience—to a performance put on by his parents.

"Who were you?" he said aloud.

The bus driver glanced in the mirror at him. "What?" she said. "You talking to me?"

Ryan shook his head. "Nothing. Sorry."

She glared at him for a few seconds—oh great, another crazy man riding the bus—then turned west onto Sixth Street.

Lies, lies, and more lies. Ryan thought of a quote he'd read somewhere: There are lies, and then there are damned lies.

He could smell the bus fumes now, raw and pungent, as the driver put more distance between him and Kelly's people, taking him farther away from Jeff.

I'm sorry, Jeff, Ryan thought, and buried his head in his hands.

A few blocks north of downtown Oklahoma City, the Whispering Man pulled his car into the parking lot of a McDonald's at Twenty-third and Broadway. The knife, with traces of blood still clinging to it, sat on the passenger seat beside him. He was breathing fast, almost hyperventilating, both at what he'd done and at how close he'd come to meeting both Ryan Elder and the resourceful Deputy Faith Kelly.

He closed his eyes. He could see the face of the woman behind the counter, the classic "innocent bystander," her mouth twitching. And the face of Jeff Majors, the well-bred, well-scrubbed all-American face. The Whispering Man had watched his eyes, had seen the look change several times in the space of two or three seconds.

Now, perhaps young Ryan would understand just how serious the situation was. Instead of arranging class reunions, he would look in other directions, the directions that would lead him where the Whispering Man wanted—no, *needed*—him to go.

He began to think of the Revolution, but the faces of Jeff Majors and the woman melted into those of the little boy and the tall man.

The Whispering Man jerked, his knuckles rapping against the window of the car. Ever since he'd begun the plans for the Revolution so long ago, he'd had the visions and heard the voices of the boy and the man, but they'd come more frequently of late. They'd also become clearer, no longer just fuzzy images, but sharp, well defined, vivid.

The man was tall and broad-shouldered, with an ordinary, if somewhat blunt face. He always smelled of aftershave and tobacco and always wore white shirts with dark suits and slim dark ties. His eyes were also dark, and never still, always scanning the room as if expecting someone to jump out in front of him at any moment.

The boy was well built and would one day grow into a strong man, but for now he was small with a placid face, short dark hair, thin arms and legs. He was wearing short pants and a clean, pressed button-down shirt and his feet scuffed against the floor while the man paced up and down in front of him.

The boy and the man were in a small room with no windows and only the sparsest furnishings: a rough wooden table, two wooden chairs that seemed to have been scavenged from the dump, a threadbare rug on the dull hardwood floor. The room had a smell to it, damp, musty, *old*.

Why, Daddy, why? the boy always said. How many times had he heard those words? *Why do I always have to come way out here to see you?*

The man's voice was deep, gruff. *I've told you before. It's safer this way.*

Daddy, why do I have a different last name than you? All the other kids have the same name as their parents.

A touch of impatience: *Why do we have to go through this every time? You should be glad I see you at all. I have enemies, boy, many powerful enemies. If they knew I had a son, they'd use it against me.*

But Daddy—

Dammit, boy, I've told you to whisper! Even out here, there's no guarantee. The enemy is everywhere! Lower your voice, and whisper anything you have to say!

Please, Daddy, I don't want to go back to that school. I want to live with you.

Out of the question! Don't be foolish. I have work, important work, and I don't have time to deal with you. It's for the best. My God, if the enemy ever found out. . . .

The boy's eyes filled with tears.

Stop that, the man said, his voice soft but still commanding. He stood up and walked to the door. *Stop it, I said! I'll see you in six months.*

The boy launched himself at the man and wrapped his skinny arms around the man's legs. *Daddy!* he wailed. *Please—*

The man backhanded the boy across the face. The boy tumbled away, holding his cheek, where a welt was already rising. The tears oozed hard and hot down his face.

I told you to whisper, the man said, opening the door. *The driver will be here to get you in a few minutes, after I've left the area. Don't move until then.*

The door closed, and the boy was alone in the little room. *Why, Daddy, why?* he whispered.

The Whispering Man opened his eyes. *The Revolution.* The boy and the man. Justice for all. Soon, the system—the system the boy's father had spent his entire life serving and defending—would come crashing down, just as the man's hand had crashed down across the boy's face.

Oh yes, the Revolution will come.

The Whispering Man glanced again at the bloody knife, and it occurred to him that the Revolution was already beginning. In a few years, when the history books were rewritten, Jeff Majors and the woman behind the counter would be known as the first civilian casualties.

And how are *you* feeling right now, Ryan Elder? he wondered. Perhaps now you will begin to understand.

20

RYAN STEPPED OFF THE BUS RUNNING, IGNORING THE stares of the handful of other passengers. Shepherd Mall was a blur, the huge parking lot nearly empty before 8 A.M., like a great gray nest that all the birds had left. Running along Villa Avenue, he saw the apartment complex coming into view.

He crossed a grassy area at the corner of Thirtieth and Villa and came down into the apartment parking lot. He loped around the corner, saw the black Jeep Cherokee pointed toward the street. Inside the breezeway, he pounded on the door, and then he was staring into Cass's huge blue-gray eyes. She didn't speak.

Ryan veered away from her and collapsed onto the couch, his breathing as ragged as an old shirt. Then it all exploded: no longer running, he could see Jeff's blood on the wall, the little stream of coffee dripping off the table. He could feel the pursuers closing in on him at the concourse. He could feel his life receding, flowing away from him, a tide leaving the shore.

"What did you say?" Cass said.

Ryan looked up. He hadn't realized he'd spoken aloud. "I think I said, my life's not my own. I don't have an identity. I don't know anything."

Cass strode to the sofa and crouched beside him. "What happened?"

"Last Tuesday, I was going to go for a drive along the coast after work. I used to like to watch the boats on the bay."

"Tell me."

Ryan leaned back against the cushion, his eyes closed. "They killed Jeff. His blood was all over the wall."

"Oh God," Cass said, reaching out her good hand to cover his.

His eyes flew open at the touch and he jerked away. "Don't," he said roughly. "I can't—"

Cass pulled her hand back. Ryan began to feel numb. His face was cold. His hands were cold. His cheeks felt wind-burned.

He'd never considered a world that didn't have Jeff Majors in it. Even though they hadn't seen each other lately, he'd known that Jeff would always be there with a smart-ass remark, followed closely by a sympathetic ear. Doctor Jeff, the healer.

Ryan suddenly felt an overwhelming weariness, a fatigue that went beyond his bones, all the way to what was left of his core. He knew it was a function of grief. He'd read volumes about grief after his parents' suicide. Bitter irony: he might not be capable of grieving, but he knew all the stages, all the terms. He knew what he was *supposed* to do.

"What can I do?" Cass was saying in a soft voice.

Ryan had almost forgotten she was there, this enigmatic woman who had saved him twice, and about whom he knew next to nothing. "Leave me alone," he said.

She stared at him, her amazing eyes brimming with emotion.

"I can't think straight," he said. "I need some time. Please."

She nodded, turned, and walked down the hallway to the bedroom. Ryan heard the door close very quietly.

Ryan let his body sag against the sofa. He felt like throwing something, breaking something—his usual response—but he couldn't move. His mind, his body—they weren't cooperating. The overpowering fatigue was the only thing there.

I don't want this fight, he thought. Then he wondered: Maybe my parents didn't, either. Maybe they were just tired of fighting this battle, whatever it is.

Crazy. This is all crazy.

Ryan bit his lip, drawing blood. The coppery taste ran into his mouth.

He put his head down against the arm of the sofa. Ryan closed his eyes. He imagined himself running again.

• • •

Cass sat on the bed, staring at the blank white walls of the room. She had to know who Ryan was, *why* he was. She thought of her Friday class, of all those kids desperate to break out of whatever developmental shell they were trapped in. Little Guillermo, searching for Chopin in her boom box. Cass blinked. If not for the kids, if not for the class, she would never have left the house Friday morning and would never have run into Ryan Elder.

Cass reached for her cell phone and punched in the number of her father's house—*her* house. She spoke to Stephanie, the nurse from the home health agency, who said her father was doing well, had been "with himself" for most of the last twenty-four hours. The sheriff's officers had questioned him about a young man with a beard, though, and was she . . .

Cass hung up, guilt and relief fighting for control. Guilt that she'd left him, relief that she'd left him. Different sides of the same coin. Ryan had cut awfully close to the bone when he'd said she wanted to escape. He didn't know himself, but he'd figured her out pretty quickly.

While Ryan was gone, she had looked over his legal pad, with all its notes and questions and lists. The inconsistencies, the unanswered questions, they were all there in neat columns. But she came back again and again to one thing, the dying man's last words: *Adam and Eve.* That was the real enigma. It haunted her, a man who had been shot mortally invoking the name of the first man and woman.

Adam and Eve.

Cass took her laptop out of the black nylon overnight bag and powered it up. She logged on to the Internet, then sat motionless for a moment on the bed. She held up her disfigured left hand. She turned it around and around, palm in, palm out, palm in, palm out. For a moment she remembered the pain. For a moment she remembered her own blood, spurting as if it had been squeezed out of a tube.

"Stop it," she said aloud, in an even voice. She lowered her hand.

She tapped the keyboard of the laptop for a moment,

then went on. She pulled up a search engine and hesitated a moment. Then, using her right hand and deftly working the two remaining fingers of the left, she typed "Adam and Eve."

Cass sat back while the computer searched, then she almost smiled at the result: 10,963 websites containing the words.

She moved the cursor back to the search box, then asked it to search for pages containing "Adam and Eve" and "Department Thirty."

Zero.

Cass shrugged. She tried "Adam and Eve" and "U.S. Marshals Service."

Nothing.

She tried a dozen different combinations. A few of the expected biblical references popped up, as well as a smattering of pornographic sites.

She tapped her right thumb against the side of the keyboard, then without realizing it, tapped out the rhythm to the opening of Beethoven's "Pastoral" Sonata. She closed her eyes and the music took over, and she could feel the piano keys instead of the computer under her fingers. She'd played this piece in competition and she remembered seeing tears in the eyes of two of the judges when she finished. None of them spoke English, but she remembered the translation as they lifted the gold medal around her neck: *You speak the language of music like no other. You are one with the piano, you are one with the music.*

Cass snapped her eyes open. There was only the apartment, and the January chill outside, and a desperate man down the hall.

Ryan had shown her the newspaper clipping on Saturday night, the orchestra review his mother had sent to him a few days before the suicide, which took seven years to reach him.

The Beethoven faded. The apartment was silent as winter midnight.

Cass typed "Adam and Eve," then cross-referenced it with "music."

She swallowed. Her stumps itched. Her head tingled. She smoothed her short hair.

Six matches found.

She scrolled down the page. Five of the six websites were the text of songs that had references to Adam and Eve.

She squinted at the last one, then clicked on it. When the page settled onto the little screen, Cass frowned. It was some sort of an academic paper, written in the dry, slightly pompous style university graduate programs seemed to demand. The author was listed as C. J. Barrientos, M.A., assistant professor, Department of Political Science, State University of New York at Buffalo.

Cass read through the paper, looking for the reference she'd searched for. Finally, it came, some ten pages into her reading. It was a tiny reference, just one sentence in a long paragraph.

Cass sat back, feeling a sudden chill. "Oh, God, Ryan," she said. She thought she might have just glimpsed the first brick in the foundation of who Ryan Elder's parents really were.

21

CASS STARED AT THE COMPUTER SCREEN FOR A LONG time, willing herself to turn it off and forget what she'd seen. It would be easy. She'd take her overnight bag and just leave. Money wasn't a problem—she could exist as "Alicia Rubinstein" for a while until she figured out what to do.

Her stumps itched, and she absentmindedly scratched their tips with the fingers of her good hand. She looked back to the screen.

Adam and Eve.

She shook her head, thinking of the man down the hall. He'd lost his parents and never knew why. Then he'd found them again—or perhaps they had found him, she thought—

seven years later, and his world had spun crazily away from him.

And in the course of trying to chase down his life, he'd crossed her path.

Cass listened to her heartbeat, trying to summon Chopin, Beethoven, Mozart, Brahms. No music came. Just her heartbeat and Ryan Elder.

He needed her. Then a strange and unbidden feeling stole across her: And I need him, too.

What are you doing, Cassandra?

Her body tingled, a mixture of anticipation, fear, anger, confusion. All the same things *he* was feeling, she thought.

She found a pen and a notepad and wrote down the name of the paper's author, then she bookmarked the website in her computer, disconnected from the Internet, and turned off the machine. She snapped it closed and returned it to the overnight bag.

She quietly opened the bedroom door and started down the hall. Ryan was in the same position as when she'd left him, his eyes closed, head leaning back against the arm of the couch.

"Ryan," she said softly, and he opened his eyes wide, instantly alert.

"What?" He sat up. "What is it?"

Cass sat down next to him. "Tell me," she said. "Tell me about your parents."

He waited. "Why? What difference does it make?"

"I just want to know."

He looked at her, his brown eyes deepening, and for a moment she thought he was going to fly into another rage like he had in the motel, or worse, that he wasn't going to reply at all. Then, a tiny nod. "I guess . . . I'm not sure what to say. Since I don't know what's true and what's not anymore, I don't really know what to tell you."

"What they were like. Or at least what you thought they were like."

Ryan shrugged. "It's funny. When I was a kid, I thought we were a pretty ordinary family. Your ridiculously ordinary suburban, upper-middle-class family. My dad was quiet, soft-spoken. I never saw him lose his temper. He worked in insurance, starting out as an agent, then working up to corporate vice president just before . . . I know he liked the outdoors. We went camping, fishing. We used to vacation every summer up in the Ozarks. He'd say, 'This is my country. My country.' He was always there for me, supportive and all that, but feelings? Emotions? Forget it. He . . ." His voice trailed away.

Cass touched his leg. "What?"

Ryan waited a moment. He flexed both sets of fingers against his palms. "Don't have a pen. I can't think without a pen." He met her eyes. "Pretty silly, isn't it?" He smiled a little.

Cass held her breath—it was the first time she'd seen him smile. "Well, of course it's silly. But we all have things like that. My stumps itch or tingle when I'm nervous or excited."

"Yeah." Ryan leaned back, flexing his own fingers some more. "No, my dad . . . see, it's complicated. I don't quite know how to put it into words. I knew he cared, I knew he was doing the best he could for me, but he just couldn't ever say it. So I mean, he and I never had what you'd call heart-to-heart father-son talks. We talked about the weather and baseball and my friends, things like that. But at the same time, even as a little kid, I knew . . . I knew it was all he could do. And now . . . now I guess I understand a little bit more." He paused and scratched his nose. "No, I don't. I don't understand a damn thing. But I think part of the reason Frank Elder couldn't let me see more of who he was, is because Frank Elder didn't really exist."

Cass nodded. "Your mother?"

"My mom," he said, "was always more open, talked a lot more about a lot more things, but now that I think about it . . . even she never gave up very much. There were stories, always stories, but never how she related to the stories, how she felt at the moment. She *never* talked about Czechoslovakia. I tried to get her to tell me about it, but she always put me off. I figured she was still angry about how she had to leave. She was a great listener, though. Aggressive, occasionally overbearing, but still a good listener. I wonder if she was such a good listener to my problems because it kept her from having to face herself."

He stopped, leaning back, his hands still nervous. "Dammit," he said, then reached under the sofa and pulled out his notebook. He slid the pen from the ring binder and began walking it through his fingers. "But the music—when she picked up the violin, she was another person. It was like nothing I've ever heard. She would play folk tunes, a little jazz, and of course, the classical stuff. She taught at a couple of the local colleges for a while, but then gave private lessons at home. I used to go to the door of her music room when she was teaching and listen. I always wanted the kids she was teaching to shut up so I could hear her play."

"Did she teach you?"

"Never. Teaching a student who paid her money was one thing, but I think if she'd tried to teach me . . . it would have been giving up too much of herself. She would have been vulnerable to me. And she couldn't go that far. A minister once told me that you can't really have a relationship with anyone, whether it's God or someone else, until you're vulnerable, until you lay yourself open. My parents couldn't do that." He stopped, and the look that crossed his face reminded Cass of a lost motorist, staring at a road map. "As a kid, I thought they were just people. I never really thought any of this stuff until I went to college, and then—"

"You don't have to—"

Ryan shrugged into himself. "It was a tradition for Mom to make goulash on the day before Thanksgiving every year. That dish was about the only concession she made to being Czech. She'd make a huge pot of it. When I'd go back to UCLA, she'd send at least half a dozen little Tupperware containers of it back with me. My roommates brought back turkey, I brought back goulash. And then . . . then they were acting so strange that day."

Cass noticed he was flipping the pen faster and faster. A

deep ache began in her chest. She felt the unbelievable longing pour off him like melting ice.

He looked up at her. "They planned it," he said. "Whatever sent them over the edge, they waited and waited until I got home, then they sent me off to the store for that damned paprika. It's almost like they wanted to do it while I was nearby, but not right in front of me. One of the cops asked me where I was when it happened. 'In the spice aisle,' I told him. He looked at me like I'd lost my mind. Jeff was there, and Jack Coleridge, and they helped me get through it. Jeff took me home to his house and sat up with me all night. He was back in town for Thanksgiving too, and I remember his mother was already making dinner. She used to make this wonderful macaroni salad, you know, with cheese and pimientos and dill pickles and eggs and onions. The house smelled so good, and I just sat there at their kitchen table and Jeff held my hand. Isn't that a crazy thing? Two twenty-year-old guys, both straight as we can be, sitting there holding hands all night long."

"A good friend," Cass said, never taking her eyes from him.

Ryan nodded slowly. "Yeah. A damn good friend, when I needed one." His brown eyes shifted, boring into hers. "Sorry. You didn't want to hear all that. You ask me one question, and then I—"

She leaned in close to him. His body tensed, then froze. She covered his mouth with hers. Cass felt herself tremble, then felt his surprise, then something else. The longing again, the unrequited sadness.

She pulled back and looked at him. His eyes were wide and questioning.

"I don't—" he said.

"Hush. Yes, you do."

She kissed him again, longer, with a soft deftness. His lips were cool and firm. Cass shuddered. It had been so many years since she'd kissed a man, that she'd forgotten what it felt like. Forgot what it is to be a woman, she thought, and realized she'd even stopped thinking of herself in terms of being a woman.

She broke the kiss and leaned back. She pulled her sweatshirt over her head and tossed it onto the floor. She reached behind herself and unhooked her bra. She let herself feel amazed for a moment. She'd been hiding herself under bulky shirts and loose jeans for so long, she'd forgotten that she had a voluptuous figure. Her full breasts fell free.

Ryan's breathing quickened.

"Touch me," Cass said. "Please. I want to be close to you. I want to feel you."

"Oh God," Ryan whispered, his hands cupping her breasts. He began to rub in ever-tightening circles, taking her nipples between thumb and forefinger.

Cass moaned deep in the back of her throat. She closed her eyes and threw her head back, losing herself to his touch. She began to feel the heat spreading through her, as it radiated from Ryan as well.

She leaned forward and began unbuttoning his shirt, and he pulled his hands off her just long enough to throw it off. She worked her way down, undoing his pants. He kicked his shoes off. She pulled the pants down. She grasped him with her good hand, felt him swelling to the touch. Then she was standing, peeling off her own jeans, watching him watch her. Her nudity meant nothing by itself—she felt no embarrassment, no "shame." Ryan had already seen her left hand, so he'd seen her naked. The rest was just a matter of a few pieces of fabric.

"Oh God," Ryan said again, his eyes welded to her.

She slipped back to him, covered his entire body with hers on the sofa. Her mouth on his, his hands on her breasts, and in a few movements, he was inside her and they both cried out their surprise.

She'd been prepared for him to be a rough, even brutal lover. She'd steeled herself for it. He had so much anguish, so much rage, so much confusion in him. She'd been ready for it. But he was surprisingly gentle, almost tentative at first, then gaining confidence but never losing the fine touch. She began to ride him with intensity, with thoughts exploding in her head: I don't know this man. I don't know who he is, what he is. He may be dead tomorrow.

What are you doing, Cassandra?

Ever since she'd lost her fingers, lost her music, Cass had felt like she was in a state of suspended animation—waiting, then hiding, then dropped into the strange cocoon that was her father's life. His illness, her life, tangled together in a jumbled mess. Then Ryan Elder had run in front of her, in more ways than one.

She opened her eyes. Ryan was quickening under her. One of his hands snaked down, just above the spot where they were joined.

Sound and light crashed together in Cass's head. She was *feeling*. She was *living*. For a moment she could forget that this man didn't even know who he was. She could forget his pain, and her own, and there was only the incredible, almost spiritual feeling of oneness as they moved together, ever higher.

"Cass," Ryan whispered.

He raised his head and placed his mouth on her nipple, and then she was roaring toward the end. She screamed wordlessly, and a few seconds later she felt his body go rigid and electric, and then Ryan was screaming too.

Later, she lay on her back between his legs, her head resting on his chest. His hand traced lines across her bare shoulders.

"Who's F.C.?" Ryan asked.

"What?"

His fingers drew the letters on her shoulder. "F.C."

"Oh," Cass said. "That." She'd almost forgotten about the tiny tattoo, simple cursive letters in dark blue along her left shoulder blade.

"An old boyfriend, maybe?"

"You could say that. I had that done in New York, my first year at Juilliard. It created quite a stir. Concert pianists— especially female concert pianists—don't get tattoos. It's for Frederic Chopin."

"You're kidding. You had a composer's initials tattooed on your shoulder?"

Cass shrugged into his chest. "For a long time, he was the only lover I had. After I graduated from Juilliard, I lived with a conductor for a while. Six months or so. But conductors are control freaks and he wanted to control everything about me, from the music I played to the food I ate." She traced the fingers of her good hand along his leg. "What about you? A good-looking guy like you, off at UCLA. You must have had lots of college women."

Ryan shook his head. "Nothing very serious. For a long time I remembered my high school girlfriend, the one who broke up with me because I had the nerve to go to college out of state. I dated a couple of girls at UCLA, but nothing major. And then, for the last seven years, I was the guy in the apartment complex laundry room on Saturday nights, reading old magazines and watching the dryers go around. Little old ladies would come up to me—really, I'm not making this up—and say things like, 'What's a good-looking young fellow like you doing here all by yourself?' "

He sounded almost embarrassed, Cass thought, as the silence drew out. "But there was someone," she finally said.

Ryan looked at the ceiling. "Why couldn't I have kidnapped someone stupid, someone not quite so perceptive."

"That was probably in the section of the manual on choosing your victim."

"Guess I missed it. Her name was Melissa McNeill. I don't know what it is with me and women with 'Mc' in their name. I was working in Vermont, assigned to the state capital, and she was a media liaison to the speaker of the state House. I had a good capital source and I'd broken a story on how thirty or so legislators were going to stage a walk-out during open session. Literally, these guys were going to walk out of the assembly. They were protesting the governor's veto of an education bill. It had to do with funds for special education and they were furious with the governor. Well, I got this call from Melissa and she wants to know who my source is, and how could I broadcast such a thing. We went ahead and aired the story, and the legislators went ahead and walked out, and the governor screamed bloody murder.

A couple of weeks later, they very quietly got together and drafted a new bill and the governor signed it. So the special ed kids got their funding and I got my story. Best story I've ever done.

"Well, a few weeks later I got to thinking about this woman from the speaker's office. I decided I had nothing to lose, so I called up Melissa McNeill and asked her to lunch. We dated for a few months. I found out she was originally from Missouri. Here we were, two people from Middle America plopped down in New England. For a while I thought she might be . . . we might. . . ."

"What happened?" Cass said, when he didn't continue.

"Oh, you know. We went out to dinner at this seafood place near the capital, and she sat there with her shrimp salad and I had my grilled sea bass with extra-spicy cocktail sauce, and she looked at me over her salad and said, 'You are the coldest person I've ever known,' and got up and walked out. Two weeks later I was fired, and a month later I moved to Ohio."

Cass waited. "I'm sorry, Ryan."

"The truth is, I suspect she was right. I was on the verge of telling her about my parents, about explaining everything. I had hoped she would understand, at least a little. I've kept hoping for the last seven years that someone might understand, and that if they did, it might all start to make sense to me. I never got the chance."

Cass sat up, turning to face him. "I think we both needed to reconnect with life. I know I did." She touched his leg, his skin warm to the touch. "My God, Ryan. The things you've learned in the last two days, the things you've seen. . . ."

Ryan nodded. "I want to know you. All I know right now is that you're from Cheyenne and you've been taking care of your father and your family guilted you into doing it. You're a pianist, you went to Juilliard, you love Chopin. Your mother died when you were a teenager. You thought you might have to run away someday. The rest is speculation, that taking care of your dad is draining the life out of you, that you feel trapped, and that you feel guilty for feeling trapped because you think it's your duty to stay with him no matter what. How's that?"

A long moment passed. Cass felt her stumps tingling. "You do pay attention, don't you?"

"I do."

Ryan took her hand and touched the stumps, carefully running his own fingers over the round pads of scar tissue. He touched all three of them, then looked back up at her.

"I want to know you," he said again.

Cass didn't move, thinking about the knife, seeing the blood, seeing herself running, hearing herself screaming.

"God help me," she said.

Ryan kept looking at her, sitting naked before him. Naked now in more ways than one.

"I was stalked," Cass said, then lowered her head as the tears started.

22

KELLY SAT AT THE DESK IN ART DORIAN'S OFFICE. SHE closed her eyes and saw Dr. Jeff Majors's blood pooling beside his body. She saw the face she'd thought attractive painted a waxy gray. She thought of the Underworld woman, who'd been identified as forty-two-year-old Carolyn Wade, divorced mother of two teenage children. Dead, face-down in her own blood, two feet away from a basket of freshly baked cinnamon-raisin bagels.

She'd sent those people to their deaths: Jeff Majors, who thought he was helping to get his best friend out of a jam; and Carolyn Wade, who simply came to work and stepped into a nightmare.

And Ryan Elder, still one step ahead of her, had vanished into downtown Oklahoma City.

Kelly finished her incident report and took it to Chief Deputy Clarke's office. Thankfully, he wasn't there, in a meeting with the U.S. Marshal. When she returned to Dorian's office, the phone was ringing.

She remembered Dorian's protocol: *Never identify yourself on answering the phone.* "Yes?" she said as she picked it up.

"Faith, it's Nina Reeves. How are you holding up?"

Leave it to another woman to ask how she was, Kelly thought. "As well as can be expected, Nina. Thanks for asking."

"Nasty business this morning. Your first, I take it."

Kelly closed her eyes again. *So much blood.* "That's right."

"*Very* bad business. Say, I wonder if you could stop by this afternoon. I've been doing some tinkering with the tape and I thought you might like to take a listen."

"I guess so, but it seems pretty clear what happened."

"Does it?" Reeves said.

Kelly let the silence hang for a moment. "Okay, I'll bite. What is it?"

"You need to listen. I'm just a techie, you see, not an investigator."

Kelly caught the irony in her voice. "I'm properly rebuked. You're at the field office?"

"Oh my, no. I work at home."

"Really?"

"Really. You'll see when you get here." Reeves gave the address of a complex on Apartment Row in far northwest Oklahoma City. "Our man Sleepy Scott will be here too. Interagency cooperation and all that."

Kelly looked at her watch. "Give me half an hour."

She hung up and sat for a moment with her hand on the phone. She thought about what she'd read about Ryan Elder's parents. Everything depended on how much he knew. What had Dorian told him? She thought about Ryan Elder's unstable work history, his interpersonal relationships—or the lack thereof—these last seven years. Yorkton had filled in the holes in the file. Had Elder suspected Jeff Majors's betrayal? And in the end, wasn't that what it was all about? Betrayal, of one kind or another?

Kelly shook her head, cursing all the Elders. She wondered if Clarke was right, if she might not be better off in uniform, thumping teenagers for DUI in the suburbs. Or worse yet, perhaps her father had it right all those years ago. She could have been a teacher, after all.

Apartment Row consumed the entire mile along Northwest 122nd Street between Penn and May avenues. Built mainly during the oil boom days of the early eighties, the apartments were contemporary, stylish, mostly populated by young professionals as stepping-stones to homes in Edmond or the Village or Quail Creek.

Kelly drove the government Ford slowly west on 122nd, turned into the third driveway, and wound past four identical buildings. She was starting to search for the apartment number Reeves had given her when she saw Reeves waving from the bottom of a stone stairwell.

"Ah, Faith," Reeves said, after Kelly parked the car. "Glad you could make it. Have you had lunch?"

Kelly shook her head. "I'm not quite up for food yet."

"Come in," Reeves said. "I suspect you'll find this interesting."

They climbed the stairs to the apartment and Kelly instantly understood why the FBI granted Nina Reeves permission to work at home. The entire place was sound equipment and computers. Kelly counted at least ten sets of speakers and twice that many computer monitors. There were several boxes of digital audio tapes, diskettes, and compact discs. At least six DAT recorders were in plain view. There was even one ancient reel-to-reel tape recorder.

"I use the living room to work in because it's bigger," Reeves said. "The smaller of the two bedrooms is where I have a sort of living area, though I rarely use it."

"Did you buy all this yourself?" Kelly asked, scanning the room. Speakers even stood in front of the fireplace.

"Oh my, no." Reeves laughed lightly, a musical sound. "About half of it. The other half is strictly government issue. You'd be amazed at how much paperwork is involved in being able to actually use federal government equipment on private property. You want anything? Coffee, tea, soda?"

"Just some water, maybe."

Reeves returned with a cup of tea for herself and a bottle of Aquafina for Kelly. "Have some of this dreadful stuff. It's deadly, though. No fluoride, you know." She sat down across from Kelly. "I see you didn't take my advice."

"What do you mean?"

"This is all personal to you." She gestured with her teacup. "Your man Dorian, this Elder business, the whole affair."

"You didn't see those people's bodies this morning. That was my operation, Nina, and I blew it and those two people are dead. That woman behind the counter . . . we'd alerted her about what was happening and assured her nothing would happen. She had two kids, a boy and a girl. And Majors . . . God, how can it *not* be personal?"

"It seems to me you're learning the real world and your own vision of it doesn't always match up. That's the point where you start to question everything, including yourself."

"You're quite the observer of human nature, to be a techie." Kelly drank some water. "Nothing about this case follows the rules. Here I am, stumbling around in the dark, trying to figure out whether I should be a by-the-book Deputy United States Marshal and follow this policy and that procedure, or just say to hell with the book. I mean, I chucked the rules by following Coleridge on Saturday without talking to the chief first, and I lost Elder. Today, I planned the operation according to the manual, even brought in Bureau support . . . I lost Elder again, and those two people died. Somehow the academy forgot to cover all this Department Thirty gray-area stuff."

Reeves leaned forward and touched Kelly's arm. "Faith, my friend, that is the trick."

"What?"

"Knowing when to use the book and when not to. I'll tell you a secret. Most officers your age don't even realize they should be asking those kinds of questions." The apartment door opened and closed, letting in a blast of cold. "Ah, here's our man Scott."

Hendler came into the living room, holding a Burger

King bag and juggling a soft drink. "This better be good, Nina. Shit's falling out of the sky and landing all over me today."

"How colorful," Reeves said.

"Colorful, hell." Hendler found a canvas director's chair between two large speakers and sat down. He unwrapped a cheeseburger and took a large bite. He chewed quickly, like a man used to eating in a hurry. "The local cops were pissed about not being let in on the deal this morning. Dorsett and Clarke soothed them a little bit, gave them a story about how this was a possible interstate stolen-property ring we were infiltrating. That's the official line to the media too. That's been a fucking circus. Majors's dad is a judge. Did you know that, Faith? A judge, for Christ's sake."

"Have I ever let you down, Scott?" Reeves said.

Hendler shrugged. "Unless you can tell us where Ryan Elder is and produce a knife with his prints all over it, this is probably a waste of time. I don't imagine that's on your tape." He ate another third of the burger.

Reeves walked between them and sat at a horseshoe-shaped computer desk. Two computer monitors sat side by side, each flanked by a DAT recorder in a wooden rack.

Kelly pulled the director's chair close to Reeves. "I still don't see how we can get much from the tape. The music was so loud we couldn't hear a lot of detail."

"A common tactic," Reeves said, tapping one of the computer keyboards. "But we can work around that." She pointed at the DAT machine on the left, then pushed the play button.

Jeff Majors's muffled footsteps filled the speakers. Then his quiet voice: "Okay, here we are."

Kelly swallowed. It was the voice of a man who had less than five minutes to live. The music: Credence. Then Majors ordered his coffee. They heard him sit down.

Reeves pressed stop, then cue, and the tape raced forward. When she touched play again, the counter woman—Carolyn Wade, mother of two—said, "Morning. What can I get you?" Then the radio blasted out the song by Kansas.

Kelly winced.

Hendler balled up his burger wrapper and tossed it toward a wastebasket by the kitchen door. It bounced off the rim. "Nina, I don't—"

Reeves held up a hand. They listened to the chair moving, the sound of something heavy. Always the thundering music.

Majors's voice. What had he said? Kelly leaned forward, suddenly alert.

Screaming guitars. The strange gurgling: Majors's throat being cut.

Kelly made a fist, digging her nails into her palm.

Reeves pressed stop.

"So?" Hendler said. "What's the point?"

"This is where all of you bailed out, where the cavalry goes rushing to the Underworld. Being a simple techie, I don't do such things. I stayed with the van, as you know, and I listened. That is what *I* do. I listen."

"And?" Kelly said.

"Ah." Reeves steepled her fingers again, making a diamond shape. She looked at Kelly. "Tell me something, Faith. You're an observant officer. You caught sight of your man Elder before he gave you the slip, right?"

"Yes."

"Then answer me this. What kind of shoes was he wearing?"

Kelly stared at her.

"Come on, now. You chased him. Surely you—"

Kelly's heart started to pound. She saw Elder at the end of the concourse, standing in front of the blue targetlike circle, looking back at her. A second frozen in time. She'd mentally catalogued his khaki pants, the heavy coat. . . . "Sneakers. White ones. Running shoes."

"Ah." Reeves turned back to the console. "File that bit of data away. Now, what I've done is re-record this morning's tape onto the hard drive." She touched one of the computers. "Then, using this excellent all-American software, I've compressed some sounds, expanded others."

Now Hendler was paying attention. "You're not going to tell me you found a way to lower the volume of the music, are you?"

"Always charming, Scott. I won't tell you. You may listen for yourself." She moved the computer mouse, clicking it once. Black wavy lines filled the screen and sound flooded the speakers again.

The recording started at the point after Jeff Majors had sat down, when the other set of footsteps entered the Underworld. The steps were more pronounced, and the radio was a faint presence, far in the background.

Kelly leaned in even closer to the speakers. Alarm bells started to go off. Something wasn't right.

She heard Kansas on the radio, but it was muffled, as if a thick blanket had been wrapped around the radio. Majors scrabbled his chair on the tile. The heavy object dropped. Kelly realized it was Carolyn Wade falling behind the counter, dropping to the floor, stabbed through the heart.

The footsteps, quick.

Jeff Majors said: "You're not—"

They heard the knife tear into Majors's flesh, the ripping of skin and muscle and cartilage. Majors, gurgling, gasping for breath through a windpipe that no longer worked. A crash. The chair turning over. Majors hit the wall and slid down. A thump as his buttocks hit the floor. Footsteps, quiet, moving away quickly.

Reeves held up a hand again. "Listen," she said. "This is where you left the van."

Kelly put an ear as close to the speaker as she dared. There was only the music, background beat for a slaughter. Ten seconds, fifteen.

Thirty seconds.

Now the music was the Doobie Brothers. Kelly looked up at the black lines, rippling like summer corn in the wind across the computer screen.

Kelly heard something dripping—the coffee from Majors's cup. Then she sat upright.

A loud squeak sounded, very close to the microphone.

"Holy shit," Hendler said.

On the speakers, Ryan Elder said, "Jeff." Footsteps,

another squeak, then he said the name again, twice more, louder each time.

Then: "Oh God, Jeff."

Reeves pressed stop.

Kelly's stomach flip-flopped, and she was thankful she hadn't eaten. Everything they knew—everything they *thought* they knew—was wrong.

"Comments?" Reeves said quietly.

"Someone else was there before Elder," Kelly said.

"But why?" Hendler said, and took a swallow of his Coke. "I'll play devil's advocate here. What if Elder came back in after he did Majors and the woman? Maybe he came back to pick up the knife, or something else. There's no evidence of anyone else."

"Yes, there is," Kelly said, her mind straining.

Reeves and Hendler both looked at her, Reeves smiling faintly.

"The footsteps. Don't you get it, Scott? Nina, am I on the right track here?"

"You tell us," Reeves said.

Kelly nodded vigorously. "The shoes. Elder was wearing running shoes, with rubber soles. You know how shoes like that can squeak on certain floor surfaces. We *heard* it, right there!" She pointed to the speakers. "The other footsteps, the killer's steps, made hardly any sound at all. Leather. They'd have to be leather. Elder couldn't have done it."

"Come on," Hendler said. "You can't pin all this on the sound of a pair of shoes, for Christ's sake!"

"You have something better?" Kelly snapped, then backed down. Hendler was still the lead investigator on the case. "Look, Scott, it never made sense for Elder to kill Majors. I'm still not sure what happened to Art, but—"

"Why did he run? Why did Elder run from us? Why didn't he stop and say, 'I can explain'?"

"Wouldn't you run?" Reeves said. "He just found his best friend with his throat cut. He doesn't know what's happening around him, to him. It actually makes perfect sense for him to run." She leaned back and crossed her legs at the ankle. "But then again, I don't know about these things. I'm a techie. . . ."

"Not an investigator, I know, I know," Hendler said. "You keep reminding us all of that."

"He didn't do it," Kelly said, and she thought of a line her father used on her when she tried to slip things past him: *Who are you trying to convince, me or yourself?*

"Then we have a bigger problem," Hendler said. He looked at both of the women. "Who did?"

Kelly returned his look. She thought of the man in the ski mask, attacking Elder's woman friend at Reno and Indiana Saturday morning. "I think I have an idea," she said.

23

"I NEVER CRY," CASS SAID, USING A PAPER TOWEL FROM the kitchen to wipe the slickness from her cheeks. "Not anymore. I cried for years and then I just stopped. I can't tell you why or how, but it just seemed to turn off."

"Until now," Ryan said.

"Until now."

Ryan looked at her, her beautiful pale body in the lamplight, the tiny tattoo lying so incongruously on her shoulder blade, her strong legs and small feet. . . .

For a while he'd felt a sense of *oneness*. He wasn't sure he'd ever felt it before, and he certainly didn't know what it meant, but for a span of time that seemed frozen inside his chest he'd been a part of someone else. It was that simple, elation and terror slugging it out inside him. For a while, his parents' suicide hadn't been anywhere near him. The last seven years—confused, angry, bitter years—had sloughed off, fading away like an eroding shoreline.

Cass stood up and began to dress silently. Ryan found himself watching her left hand as she tugged on her jeans, the way her thumb and little finger hooked together, compensating for the other fingers. It seemed almost effortless.

He dressed himself, watching as Cass went into the kitchen. "You need anything?" she called.

"Given the situation, that's a loaded question," Ryan said.

"Anything from the kitchen, then."

"No."

She came back with a can of Diet Coke and sat beside him. "I'll tell you what I can," she said slowly.

"I understand."

A shadow crossed her face.

"My mother started me on the piano when I was four. She was a moderately talented pianist herself. She grew up in Tulsa and had studied quite a bit when she was a girl. Then she met my dad and they got married and he brought her back to Cheyenne, built her the house and everything. She was used to the city, to culture, and then all of a sudden she was living ten miles away from anything. So she had the piano brought in and away we went. When I was older she liked to say that she stood over me with a stick, threatening me to make me practice. Of course she never did that—she was a very gentle teacher, and after a while, the music was all I could think about anyway. She convinced me that we could change the world, really touch people, through music. I was the oldest and she barely paid attention to my brothers. I guess that's part of the reason they felt like it sort of evened the score for me to take care of Daddy when he got sick. Well, anyway, I practiced five hours a day, sometimes more. She took me to every master class within two hundred miles." Cass bowed her head. "Then she got sick when I was in high school."

"Look, I don't think—"

"No, listen. It's all part of this." She wiggled her stumps, making him wince. "On her deathbed, she made me promise not to give up the piano. Of course, by then I couldn't have if I wanted to. It was too deeply ingrained. Daddy had never cared much for that music—Johnny Cash is more his style. But he was always supportive, kept paying for my lessons, that sort of thing. I applied to the Juilliard School in New York, and it surprised all of us when I was accepted, on full scholarship. That's the only way he could have afforded it. I took two degrees in piano performance, and the year I finished my master's degree, my professor entered me in the Tchaikovsky Competition in Moscow. Do you know about that?"

"My mother told me that someone she had worked with was a finalist in it one year."

"Then you know how big a deal it is. And this was in the last years of the Soviet Union. Everything was changing all around. So I went to Moscow and I played, with no real thought that I could get past the first round. I was terrified. I hardly ate. But I kept playing well and I went to the finals."

"What did you play?"

Cass smiled a little. "Now I *know* you're the son of a musician. Thank you for asking. I played Beethoven, the 'Pastoral' Sonata. And I played it perfectly. I just felt surrounded by the music. It wasn't just my hands and the keys and the audience. It was *everywhere*. And when I finished, the audience just sat there for a few seconds. For a few seconds I thought I'd blown it, that my interpretation was way off. Then someone way in the back screamed something in Russian and the place just exploded. I looked at the judges and two of the men were crying."

Ryan watched her, imagining her hands on the keyboard.

"I'm not saying all this as self-promotion," Cass said. "It's who I am, at least who I was."

Ryan nodded.

"I won the gold medal," she said. "It was as if I'd climbed every mountain in the world in a single night. I called Daddy back home in Cheyenne and he cried on the phone. You have to understand, that's the only time in my life I heard him cry. He didn't even cry when my mother died. So I went back to New York and agents were calling and I signed with one and started touring. At first it was the solo recital circuit, then I started doing some orchestra performances. After about three years I finally got a contract to perform with the New York Philharmonic."

"Wow," Ryan said, watching her eyes.

"Wow, indeed. I played the Chopin first concerto, and it was amazing. I sat there, a few feet away from Kurt Masur, with one of the top orchestras in the world and played Chopin. What could be sweeter? For a girl from Cheyenne, Oklahoma, it was heaven. After the concert, I went out with a few friends, then I got back home to my apartment a little after one A.M. I had a little place in the Village, very chic, very bohemian. I could barely afford it, but I had a feeling that was about to change.

"As soon as I walked in the door, the phone was ringing. I answered it, and a man's voice said, 'I see you, Cassandra.'" Cass shuddered and wrapped her arms around herself.

Ryan leaned forward.

"I can do this," Cass said, hugging herself tighter. "He said, 'I see you, Cassandra. I heard you play tonight and now I see you.' Then he hung up. That's where it started. He would call at odd times over the next few months, sometimes twice a week, sometimes a month or more between calls. I called the police, I had my number changed. Nothing mattered. He always found me. He would always tell me how wonderful my playing was, and he'd talk about music, speculating about Brahms and Schumann. He sounded very well educated, very knowledgeable about music. And I was scared out of my wits. I was on the verge of having everything I'd worked for, and this lunatic was calling me and saying things like, 'One day we'll meet, Cassandra. And you will know.' Know what? I kept asking myself."

Cass unwrapped her arms and lay her hands flat on her pants legs. Ryan covered her right hand with his. "You don't have to—"

"Yes, I do," she said roughly. She stood up and paced the room a few times, then finally settled in the chair across from Ryan. Her eyes darted about the apartment, then she fixed them on Ryan again. "One night after a chamber music recital, I had come home. It wasn't too late, only around ten-thirty. I let myself in the apartment, and as I opened the door, I felt him push past me. I turned around and he slammed the door and locked it. Before I could scream, he said, 'Don't say a word, Cassandra. If you make a sound, I'll kill you. If you don't, I'll let you live.' I knew it was him. I recognized the voice."

Ryan gripped the arm of the couch. He could feel what was coming. He heard it in the way Cass spoke, faster, with lots of breaths.

"So I didn't say anything. He led me to the kitchen, made me sit at the table. That's when he took out the knife. It was the longest knife I'd ever seen, with a long black handle and this slightly curved blade."

Ryan thought of Saturday morning and the man who'd pressed a knife to her throat, who'd slit her clothes up the back. Anger began to simmer.

"He talked about music, the romantics versus the classicists. Haydn, Mozart, Beethoven, Schumann, Brahms, and of course, Chopin. Extremely well versed in music. He talked that way for half an hour, forty-five minutes . . . I don't know, I lost track of the time. All the time I was thinking, How do I get away from this nut? He was a big man, taller than you, and more muscular."

Cass rocked back and forth in the chair. "He talked and talked, on and on, then he just stopped in midsentence. He was saying something about Brahms and he just stopped and looked at me for a long time. I said, 'What is it?' I'll never forget what he said, as long as I live. He said, 'You are brilliant, Cassandra. You are feeling and emotion and mastery. *You are music.*' Then he grabbed my hand."

She held up her left hand, the thumb and little finger angled like the letter *y* in sign language. "He grabbed it and held my wrist. He was so strong, I thought he was going to break my wrist. And he didn't say anything else. The knife came down and I felt it slice through my index finger first. I actually felt my finger sever from my hand. And there was so much blood, it was everywhere, on the table, on the floor, on my blouse, on *him.* He brought it down again on my middle finger and then my ring finger. And he picked them up off the table and put them in his coat pocket. Just slipped them in his pocket like spare change! My head was spinning, I felt like I couldn't see, and my hand was just numb, like nothing was there."

Ryan shivered in the warm apartment. He couldn't stop looking at her, alternating his gaze between her eyes and the disfigured hand.

"He got up and walked to the door without looking back," Cass continued. "He got out into the hallway, and that's when I realized I was about to die. I was going to bleed to death right there in my apartment and the man who killed me was strolling away. I finally yelled as loud as I could and I stumbled out into the hall. I was yelling, screaming, out of my mind, and he was almost to the end of the hall, just walking casually along with my fingers in his pocket.

"The apartment door across the hall opened. This is New York City, remember, famous for indifference, that 'who cares' mentality. A young couple lived there. I knew they were about my age, but that's all. I'd never talked to them in all the time I'd lived there. The man came to the door, and he was wearing sweatpants and no shirt and he saw me and saw the blood. I looked up at him, and with the hand that was dripping blood everywhere, I pointed down the hall and said, 'Him!' That's all I could manage.

"He started down the hall and the man with the knife was just getting to the far end. He yelled, 'Angie!' and his wife came out. She was young and blond and had very long hair. The last thing I remember is thinking that I didn't want her to get my blood in her beautiful hair. I found out later that her husband chased the man with the knife for three blocks and tackled him and held him down until the police showed up. His wife, Angie, was a nursing student at Columbia, and had done her emergency room rotation at Bellevue the semester before. She stopped the bleeding and saved my life."

"The strangers who helped you," Ryan said, remembering what she'd said to him, back in Cheyenne.

Cass nodded. "The man who attacked me was named Steven Williams. Such a nice, common, all-American name. He'd been expelled from three different music schools for

threatening his female classmates. He'd wanted to be a conductor. The prosecutor later told me Williams was suspected of
murdering female musicians all over the country. A flutist in
Miami, a cellist in Chicago, a violinist in Denver. Here's the
irony of it—since I had the gall to survive, thanks to my neighbors, all they could charge him with was attempted murder.
They didn't have enough evidence to prosecute him for the
rest of them. He was convicted and sentenced to twenty years
to life. He's eligible for parole after eight years. As he was being
led out of the courtroom, he stopped at the prosecution table
and he said, 'We're not finished, Cassandra.'"

"And that's when you decided you might have to run
someday."

"I knew if and when he got out of prison, he'd come for
me. I saw it right there in the courtroom. He'd taken my
music from me and he was going to come back for the rest of
me. I filed a civil suit later against him and it turns out he
came from money. His family wanted the whole thing to just
go away and they paid out twenty million dollars cash."

Ryan's mouth dropped open.

Cass almost smiled. "My attorney had the jurors actually
crying, talking about my coming from this hardscrabble
town in Oklahoma. That's the word he used, *hardscrabble*.
Daddy hated that. The lawyer talked about how I'd worked
and worked and was one of the brightest up-and-coming
pianists, et cetera, et cetera. After that speech, Williams's family called and settled. I put the money away into trust funds
for my nieces and nephews and then I gave most of the rest
of it away. Musical scholarships, music programs for kids in
rural areas, public radio—you know, that sort of thing."

Her smile faded slowly. "After that I moved around a time
or two—Philadelphia, Atlanta. I managed a couple of music
stores, did a little teaching. But then . . ."

"Your father got sick."

She nodded. "Like I told you already, it was already
decided by the time I got to Oklahoma that I would be the
one to stay and take care of Daddy. My brothers figured I
had all this money and didn't really have to work, plus no

kids, and so on and so on. Plus, how could I not do it, 'after all he and Mama did for you'? So there it was, signed, sealed, delivered."

"And you started putting money aside."

"Money or no money, Philadelphia or Cheyenne, I couldn't forget what Williams said to me in the courtroom. I started putting aside hard cash, so I could disappear whenever I needed to and not have to worry about money. I'd arrange to have Daddy cared for and I could just go. I'm not giving Steven Williams the chance to finish the job."

Ryan shook his head. "Amazing."

Cass looked up at him. "If not for Angie and her husband, I would never have made it out of that hallway. I never really got the chance to thank them. While the trial was going on, I lived in a hotel room in midtown. I just couldn't go back to the apartment. After Williams was sentenced, I finally got up the nerve to go back. But they had moved."

Ryan was quiet a moment. "So you're thanking them now."

Cass shook her head. "There you go with the armchair psychology again. If that was all . . ." Her face changed, the eyes shifting. "Well, I would have bailed out a long time ago."

"Thank you," he finally said. "I understand why you didn't seem to be afraid of me, back when I pulled the gun on you, and why you were so sure I wasn't a psycho. You've already seen it and lived it."

Cass said nothing.

"I don't know what else to say to you."

"Nothing," Cass said. "Nothing at all. You're a better listener than I thought."

"My mother's influence, I suppose." Ryan suddenly had an image of Jeff Majors in the Underworld. "I'm not sure what to do now. Here we are, telling each other our life stories, and whoever is behind this—this guy who says my parents had his 'property'—is powerful enough to do damn near anything he wants."

"I found something," Cass said suddenly, her eyes lighting, remembering. "Come here."

They went to the bedroom and Cass brought up the laptop, logging onto the Internet.

"You're not going to tell me the answer is on-line," Ryan said, sitting beside her.

"No, but I want you to see this. I looked at your legal pad, at the notes you'd made, and just started fooling around, seeing what surfaced. I tried several combinations with 'Adam and Eve,' but nothing interesting came up until I cross-referenced it with music."

"Why music?"

"Your mother."

"I see. And?"

"This." The website she'd bookmarked came up, lines and lines of thick text, no graphics.

"What is it?"

"Read it."

Ryan took the computer from her, turning the screen around to face him. He put his hand on the touchpad and started to read.

24

THE ARTICLE FELL UNDER THE HEADING SECTION SIX AND was titled "An Overview of American Political Extremism—1960–1975."

"Political extremism?" Ryan muttered, thinking of Frank and Anna Elder. As far as he could remember, neither of them had ever talked politics.

He scrolled forward, reading the author's stiff introduction and remarks about the social conditions of the early 1960s, the impact of the assassination of President Kennedy, the Cuban Missile Crisis, and the deepening involvement in Vietnam.

"This reads like a dissertation or something," he said.

"That's what I thought too," Cass said beside him.

"Tell me again how you found this."

"I cross-referenced 'Adam and Eve' with 'music.' "

"I don't see anything about music."

Cass shifted beside him so she could see the screen. "Keep reading. It's about ten pages into it."

Political extremists? Ryan thought again. Were his parents the classic case of the student radicals who turned into calm, respectable suburbanites? *No.* That made no sense. There were thousands of such people all over America. And taking part in a few protests wouldn't lead to something so drastic as a completely fabricated past.

He read further. Three pages down, something caught his eye. The author listed the defining characteristics of extremists: 1.) They identify themselves in relation to who their enemies are; 2.) They use a double standard, wanting to be accepted without question, but refusing to do the same with others; and 3.) They emphasize emotional responses instead of reasoning and logic.

Ryan shook his head. Aside from his mother's music, Frank and Anna Elder were the least emotional, most reasonable, logical people he'd ever known. They'd had no prejudices that Ryan could tell, stressing to him the importance of respect and tolerance for all people and all points of view and to always get the facts before making a decision. Nothing in this treatise pointed to them.

He read a little further. The author went on at length about the "social ramifications" of such groups and the "tools" they used in spreading their message, whether from the far left or the far right. Another paragraph discussed the escalating violence among the extremist movements in the late 1960s.

Ryan looked up at Cass, ready to shut the computer off.

"There," Cass said.

Ryan looked at the screen again. He scanned halfway down it, suddenly feeling a chill.

When engaging in violent protest, many groups and those associated with them, either officially or unofficially, left behind "trade-

marks," in much the same way an artist signs
their work. Although their activities are outside the scope of this analysis, a good example
of this would be the notorious "Adam and Eve,"
who, in association with various groups over a
period of several years, would leave a copy of
a music score at the scene. Although this has
not been corroborated, contemporary sources reported the pages of music were usually compo-
sitions for the classical violin.

Ryan sat back. Everything went quiet.

He read the sentences again, then a third time.

He was aware of Cass beside him, heard her breathing.
Waiting.

"I don't—" he said, then he read the words again.

He thought: Dorian. Had Dorian meant Adam and Eve
actually were his parents, or that they had some connection
to Frank and Anna Elder? Or was this totally wrong? Maybe
it was a biblical reference, after all. . . .

"This isn't right," he said softly, almost in a whisper. He felt
Cass's hand in the small of his back, and for one instant that
passed like a sliver of dawn across a dark sky he thought it was
more intimate that the lovemaking they'd shared earlier. His
only thought: I'm losing my mind. I'm losing control.

Ryan abruptly put the laptop aside and slid off the bed. He
clenched and unclenched his fists. He went to the window,
pulled aside the thick beige curtains, and looked out into the
parking lot. The Jeep was directly in front of the window,
backed into a parking place. Otherwise, the lot was sparsely
populated. People with normal lives, he thought, were at
work at their normal jobs now. People who had families and
friends and knew with great certainty who they were.

Just past the apartment complex was a small park, with
two sets of swings, a pair of slides, an improvised baseball
diamond, two picnic tables. The kind of urban neighborhood park that was rarely used anymore.

Ryan let the curtains fall back into place. "This apartment

is suffocating me," he said without turning around. "You ever feel that way?"

Cass waited a moment before answering. "I guess that's part of being on the run."

"I guess so." He came back to the bed and sat beside her again, picking up the computer. He read the words again, for the fourth time.

He was ready to dismiss it all as speculative nonsense, except for three words: *the classical violin.*

Ryan began to dig at his thumb again.

"Stop that, you're making it bleed," Cass said.

Ryan looked at her, thinking of how her body had felt: warm, vibrant, *alive.* He stopped digging his thumb. "I've been doing that since I was a teenager. My mom used to make me tuck my thumb under the rest of my fingers and then close my fist over so people couldn't see how grotesque it looked when we went somewhere." He laughed softly, surprising himself, then sobered just as quickly.

"What?" Cass said.

"You know what scares me? I mean, what really scares the living shit out of me?"

Cass's eyebrows went up.

"Losing control. Not being able to be in charge of where I'm going, what I'm doing. That's why I keep losing good jobs. Someone else starts steering me somewhere I don't think I want to go and I blow up and tell them to shove it. I . . . I went through a time in Maryland, in the year after the suicide, when I was experimenting with drugs. Nothing really hard-core, pot, a few pills. Cocaine scared me, so I never tried it. But I quit doing the others because I realized they took the control away from me. Then, later on, I was in Wyoming, and a guy I worked with dragged me to one of those 'charismatic' evangelical churches. And I listened to this preacher, screaming and crying about the Holy Spirit, and I got down on my knees and cried too, right there in this tiny little church on the outskirts of Laramie. So for six months or so, every tenth word out of my mouth was *Jesus,* all the time. But finally, I realized that kind of religion was just another drug."

Cass put her hand on his back again. "That *is* scary. After your parents—"

"I had no control over them and then they were gone. Just like that! And it made me angry as hell at them. I mean, I was a grown man—sort of—when this happened. It's not like I was a kid. It shouldn't have that kind of a hold on me. But I just . . . I ran. I buried them, gave away all our things, put the house up for sale, got in the car, and drove away. I couldn't face the loss of control. That's why I didn't go back to college, why I never came back to Oklahoma."

He stopped and ran a hand across his face. Then he tapped the little computer screen. "Is this who my parents were? Violent political extremists of the hippie generation? Were they out of control themselves, back then? And if so, what changed them?"

"You?" Cass said softly.

Ryan snapped his head up. For a moment their eyes met. He shrugged. "And then what changed them again? What scared them so much that they got in the car and blew themselves up? I don't know, I've never known."

He got up and paced the room for a minute. "All right, none of this gets me any closer to knowing what's going on." He pointed at the computer. "This professor. Can we get in touch with him? Maybe he knows more than he put in the paper. Maybe there's some other reference to this Adam and Eve. Right now that's all there is. It may be nothing, but . . . I'll take anything right now."

"There's an address and phone number at the bottom of the page. I wrote it down."

"All right. All right." He stopped for a moment. Indecision crowded his face.

"What?"

"I have to get out of here. Let's go outside."

"Ryan, I don't know if that's—"

"Look, I've never done this before!" he shouted. "I don't know how long you're supposed to stay hidden and all that. I just want out of this apartment!"

Cass stared at him.

"Oh God, there I go again," he said, lowering his voice. "I'm sorry. I just want some air. Let's walk over to that little park next door. Bring the phone."

Cass hesitated, then picked up the phone and her notepad. They grabbed their coats and walked into the gray cold. Clouds had smothered the sun and the temperature was dropping. Ryan buttoned his coat to the collar.

They walked warily, watching the street and the apartment lot. There was no movement. No squealing tires, no fast-moving footsteps. By the time they crossed the baseball field of Swatek Park, Ryan was beginning to relax.

"They haven't found Alicia Rubinstein yet, I guess," he said.

The park ground was dry and hard in the freezing weather, but otherwise it was a pleasant place. There was none of the graffiti found in many urban parks and the play-ground equipment looked to be freshly painted: dark green for the slides, a bright orange for the frames of the swings, incongruous with the winter gray.

Ryan sat down in one of the swings and pushed himself back and forth a little. Cass sat beside him, quiet and still.

"Okay, here goes," he said. His cheeks were already stinging from the cold, but the sensation of real air, not the artificial heat of indoors, settled him. He swung a little more, listening to the rhythmic squeak of the chains above his head.

He took Cass's notepad and punched in the number for C. J. Barrientos, assistant professor of political science at the State University of New York at Buffalo.

After three rings, there was a click and the lead-in of a voice mail greeting. The voice was female, throaty, with a twinge of Spanish to the accent. "This is C. J. Barrientos in poli-sci. Leave a message, and if you sound interesting, I might call you back."

Ryan waited for the tone, then almost hung up. What was he doing?

He breathed into the phone. "Ah . . . Professor Barrientos, my name is Ryan Elder. I'm calling from Oklahoma. I read part of your paper about political extremism on your website and was calling for some information about the Adam and Eve you mention in section six. This is . . . ah, I'm doing some family research. Please, it's very important that I talk to you. Here's the number. . . ."

He pressed end. "Voice mail," he said. He pushed himself a little higher, then slowed down again, scuffing his shoes into the hard-packed earth. "I need to go back to the beginning."

"What do you mean?"

He stopped swinging altogether. "How did this all start? It started with the letter. The clipping and the Department Thirty phone number." He took the clipping out of his coat pocket and read through it again.

The reviewer was named Ron Rollins and the review of the Oklahoma City Philharmonic's performance was very positive.

Maestro Joel Levine and the Philharmonic were at the top of their form Saturday evening, proving once again that Oklahoma City possesses one of the finest orchestras in the nation for its market size. The lack of a guest soloist for the program meant it was an evening of large orchestral works. A full house in the beautifully renovated Civic Center Music Hall heard Beethoven's rousing "Fidelio Overture" to open the program.

Ryan read on, though he'd almost memorized the words by now. There were the usual phrases about "sensitivity" and "color" in the sound of the orchestra and a few side references to the good work of the new concertmistress. Ryan held tightly to the paper as a gust of wind threatened to blow it out of his hands.

The first half of the concert concluded with selections from Smetana's huge symphonic cycle, "Ma Vlast." These pictures of the Bohemian countryside were brought together in exquisite style. . . .

Ryan looked at Cass. She was sitting perfectly still in the swing, glancing down at the clipping as he read.

. . . .and after intermission, Tchaikovsky's last great masterpiece, the Sixth Symphony, the "Pathetique," was rendered in all its dark, tortured beauty.

"I still don't see anything," Ryan said. "I've been over this dozens, probably hundreds, of times and I don't see anything. None of these pieces mean anything to me." He turned to Cass. "This man who attacked you—he said that what was in this letter would lead me to his property, right?"

"That's right."

He folded the clipping and put it back into his pocket. "Maybe my mother just wanted me to think of her, to think of music. To, to . . . hell, I don't know." He moved the swing, listening to the squeaking chains.

"What about the phone number?" Cass said. "This Department Thirty."

Ryan looked at her for a long moment and he started to say something. Then he stopped, thinking of Art Dorian. It had really started with him, hadn't it? The meeting with him put everything in motion.

He squeezed his eyes closed for a moment, thinking of what Coleridge had said about the deputy marshal in his office. *Faith Kelly.*

He pulled another sliver of paper out of his pocket, smoothed it on his pants leg, and began to punch in the phone number.

"Back to the beginning," he said.

25

KELLY RETURNED TO THE OFFICE AT A LITTLE AFTER three o'clock, feeling the eyes on her back. At her desk, facing more paperwork, she spun the scenarios around in her head until she couldn't think straight.

"Faith?"

Kelly looked up. Deputy Derek Mayfield was sitting on the edge of her desk. All around the office, it seemed quiet, *too* quiet.

"How you doing, Faith?" Mayfield said.

Kelly managed what she thought was a passable smile.

"I'm okay. I'm guessing that everyone's either walking on eggshells because they feel like I'm about to fall apart, or they're pissed off because I screwed up the op and made the office look bad."

Mayfield shook his head. "No, it's not like that. You just haven't been here that long, and this was such a big deal, that . . ." He shrugged. "Plus, the chief was looking for you."

"I figured he would be. Is he in his office?"

"Nah. He's in a meeting with the Marshal again. I think the U.S. Attorney's in there too. He said he'd find you."

"Peachy." She thought: Shortest career in the history of the United States Marshals Service. That's one for the record books.

"Um, Faith?"

"What?"

"You okay? I mean, really okay?"

"I don't know. I just got back from going over some new evidence with Scott Hendler and Nina Reeves, and this may be an even bigger mess than it was before."

Mayfield picked up a paper clip from Kelly's desk and began unfolding it. Just as quickly, Kelly snatched it back from him and bent it back into shape. "Come on, I'm on the short end of the list for office supplies anyway," she said.

"Sorry," Mayfield said. "You really liked old Dorian, I guess."

Kelly nodded.

"I think I only talked to him a dozen times or so since I transferred in here and that's been nearly three years. Thirty's a little too far out in left field for me."

Kelly looked at him. "Maybe it is for me too and I just don't know it." She thought of Yorkton: *I have to be careful how I move around in this city.*

Mayfield got up from the desk. "Well, take it easy, Faith, okay? I know you and the Bureau are handling this case and we're not supposed to even ask about it, but if you need anything . . . well, my case load's light right now."

"Thanks, Derek. Thanks for the offer." Kelly closed her eyes for a moment. "I'm going down to Art's office for a while. I need to think." And I sure as hell can't do it here, with everyone staring at me, she thought.

Two minutes later, sitting at Dorian's desk, Kelly's eyes strayed to the absurd catfish mounted on the wall.

Fish stories, Art used to say. *My whole career is making up fish stories.*

A chill wormed its way down Kelly's spine. She looked back down at the desk, at the thick Elder file. Questions, questions, questions. For every answer, she had half a dozen questions. Who killed Majors? Did Elder really kill Dorian? Who sent her the pictures of Dorian and the Elder case information? The man in the ski mask Saturday morning? Her head began to throb.

Kelly took two Tylenol from her purse and swallowed them with a swig of bottled water, the same bottle Nina Reeves had given her. When the phone rang, it sent little jabs of sharp pain behind her eyes.

She picked up the phone, and as soon as the line was open, the microcassette machine in the desk drawer began to record. Yorkton had suggested it and Reeves had come over and installed it.

"Yes?" she said.

"Deputy Marshal Faith Kelly?"

"Yes. Who's this?"

"This is Ryan Elder."

Kelly sat up straight and suddenly the pain behind her eyes was gone. She opened the drawer and made sure the recorder was working.

"Don't try to trace the call. I'm on cellular, so all you'll get is a general location. I'll save you the trouble. My general location is northwest Oklahoma City. Listen to me, Deputy Kelly. I want to tell you something and I want to ask you something."

"I'm listening." Kelly's heart pounded. She caught sight of the fish again. *Dorian.*

"I did not kill Art Dorian and I did not kill Jeff this morning. Dorian was going to tell me something about my parents, and someone shot at us from the ridge. I know you set me up with Jeff and now he and that woman behind the counter are dead. They were dead when I walked into the place."

Kelly thought of the footsteps in the Underworld, of Jeff Majors saying, *"You're not—"* "I know," she said.

"Then why did you chase me?"

"Why did you run?"

There was a pause. Kelly heard noise on the phone line. She couldn't tell what kind. "If you were me, wouldn't you run?"

"Probably." Keep him talking! "If you'll come in, everything will be explained to you. We can straighten this out."

"I don't think so. The last time I agreed to meet with someone I talked to at this phone number, that person was shot and I was almost shot right along with him. Did you see the man on Saturday morning, the man who attacked the woman who's with me?"

"Yes, from a distance."

"He was a big man, strong, and never spoke above a whisper. He said my parents had some property that belonged to him and he wants it back. Do you know what that's all about?"

Kelly sat back, gripping the phone so hard her hand ached.

He never spoke above a whisper.

"Kelly? Are you still there?"

Kelly opened the Elder file and began turning pages quickly. She'd read something, a small reference, not part of the official reports but an addendum, a tiny piece of paper stapled to the back of something else. Written in Dorian's precise hand. . . .

"Who is he, Kelly? Who were my parents? Outside of the book of Genesis, does the term *Adam and Eve* mean anything to you?" There was another thundering pause on the line and Kelly heard the faint sound again.

Kelly turned more pages. There was something about a man who always whispered. . . .

"Who am I?" Ryan Elder said.

Kelly stared at the receiver. For a moment she thought it might slip from her hands.

"Who am I?"

It was almost as if Elder weren't there. Kelly kept going through the file. There was so much paper—medical reports, psychological evaluations, financial statements, annual updates prepared by Yorkton and signed by Dorian. Even Ryan Elder's school report cards.

"I see," Ryan Elder said. "Well, then."

"Wait," Kelly said.

The connection broke off.

Kelly held the receiver until it began beeping in her ear, then she hung it up slowly. The headache roared back, like a dragon that had been sleeping.

Toward the back of the file was the yellowed sheet of paper, stapled to the back of a copy of one of Dorian's reports to Washington. It looked like notes Dorian had made while talking on the phone.

Man who only whispers, poss. connection to "A & E?" Check this out!!

In typical Dorian fashion, the slip was dated: December 1975.

Kelly carefully pulled the handwritten note off the paper to which it was attached and slipped it in the pocket of her jacket. Then she popped the microcassette out of the recorder and it joined the paper. She scooped up the Elder file, crossed the office, and opened the door.

Chief Deputy Phillip Clarke was standing just outside, his face cloudy.

"Chief," Kelly said.

"My office, now," Clarke said, turned, and started down the hallway.

Clarke's moderate-size corner office was decorated in Western rustic, with a cherry wood desk, a wagon wheel commanding one wall, a rough-hewn shelf on the other holding several exquisite carvings Clarke had done himself: a rider astride a horse, a three-masted clipper ship, a young woman holding a child. In the handful of times she'd been in his office, Kelly had wondered at the paradox, how such an abrasive man could create such beautiful works of art from simple wood.

Clarke sat heavily at the desk. On the wall were photographs of him with the current and previous marshals, with the director of the Marshals Service, the U.S. Attorney General, and one of a much younger Clarke shaking hands with Vice President Nelson Rockefeller.

Clarke picked up a thin sheaf of papers from his blotter. Kelly saw it was her report on the incident at the Underworld.

"Deputy, I don't know how this could possibly have been fucked up any worse," Clarke said, his voice a truck in low gear. Kelly heard one of his bootheels thumping angrily on the floor under his desk.

Kelly sighed, but she didn't look away from him. "Yes, sir."

" 'Yes, sir,' " Clarke mimicked. "Two people dead, including one who had absolutely no connection to this case at all. And the other is a young doctor who happens to be the son of a district court judge." He abruptly leaned forward. "You play golf, Kelly?"

"Golf?" Kelly said, her stomach churning. "No."

"Personally, I think the only thing stupider than the game of golf is the obsession so many otherwise decent people have with it. Like the U.S. Attorney, for example. The man who ultimately has the jurisdiction over this office. But see, he uses golf as a way of getting together with like-minded people, forming these nice political friendships. And one of the people he plays with is Judge Ray Majors." Clarke threw the report across the desk and the papers scattered. "You come up with this stupid-ass idea all by yourself?"

"No, sir. Yorkton—"

"Oh, yes. Yorkton, your Department Thirty spook friend. I know all about him. But there's one problem. Since he doesn't exist, he can't very well take the heat for this, can he? No, that's where *you* come in."

"Sir, I—"

"Don't give me that 'sir' crap, Kelly. I'm tired of it. In two and a half days, you've managed to screw this thing up seven ways to Sunday. I thought you could handle being liaison to this investigation. I thought I could trust you to make it work for this office, to get the job done. And do you remember what I said to you out there on Saturday morning, after your little episode on the interstate? I said, 'I own you.' And I god-damned well meant it. Your master's-degreed, well-dressed little butt belongs to me. And thanks to your mindless, reckless behavior with Jeff Majors, you are off this case."

Kelly sat up straight. "Chief, you can't—"

Clarke held up a hand. "Save it. I don't care. Your stupidity got two people killed this morning, and you're no closer to being anywhere on the investigation into Dorian. Go back to community relations duty. You can't hurt anyone there."

Kelly winced, thinking of Carolyn Wade, the clerk at the Underworld. Thinking of Jeff Majors, how she'd so deftly convinced him he was doing the right thing. "Chief, I . . . look, I know I'll be thinking about those people this morning for a long time. I'm not ever going to forget Jeff Majors with his throat slit open. Never. But the case is—"

"The case is not yours. Surrender the case files."

Kelly reddened. "No, I—"

"No? *No?* You're not paying attention, Kelly."

"But Elder is—"

"I don't want to hear it. Give me the files. You're assigned to community relations."

She thought of Ryan Elder's voice on the phone: *"Who am I?"*

Who am I?

They stared at each other. Kelly thought of Art Dorian and Ryan Elder and everything she'd worked for, since the first time she'd ridden in her father's patrol car, twenty years ago. Her face felt hot and she suddenly had to get away from this office, from this man.

Kelly picked up the Elder file and tossed it onto Clarke's desk.

Clarke stood erect and folded his arms. "Take a couple of days to cool off, then I want you back on community relations. Go speak to Rotary Clubs and give tours to Boy Scouts and give interviews to aspiring writers. If I hear that you've met with Yorkton, you'll be gone faster than you can say 'bad career move.' "

Kelly turned around without a word. Outside Clarke's office, she avoided the eyes of the rest of the staff, even Mayfield. As she walked toward the door, her hand closed over the paper and the tape in her pocket.

Phillip Clarke watched Kelly go, then closed his office door. He shook a Marlboro out of the pack in his desk and lit it, inhaling deeply. To hell with the building's no-smoking policy.

He walked around the office, stopping at his shelf of wood carvings. He picked up the one of the horse and rider and ran a hand across the surface, feeling the tiny intricacies of the rider's face, the separate strands of the horse's tail. It had taken him nearly a year of nights and weekends to do this one. His boss, the political-appointee U.S. Marshal, fancied himself an art connoisseur and had told him such a piece would be worth several thousand dollars in a gallery.

Clarke closed his hand over the carving and carried it back to his desk. He centered it in front of him and stared at it from all angles while he smoked the cigarette down to the filter. He would spray some air freshener around later. The marshal was a fanatical antismoker. Goddamn politicians.

Goddamn that little Art Dorian. And goddamn Kelly. They shouldn't have let women into the Marshals Service in the first place, especially one like Kelly. Cop's kid, trying to prove a point. But he couldn't tell anyone that, not anymore. Not in this era of "sensitivity training."

When he picked up the carving again, Clarke noticed that his hand was trembling ever so slightly.

"Stop that shit," he said.

With his other hand, he picked up the phone and

punched in a local number. A moment later he said, "She's off the case. I don't think she'll do anything else. She's young and ambitious and doesn't want to screw up her whole career. Besides, she's scared of me."

"That's good," the Whispering Man said. "She was useful for a while, but after this morning, I believe things can move forward without her now."

"I got her to give me the files, just in case."

"There shouldn't be anything in the official reports."

"Can't be too careful. If you're going through with this, don't be careless."

"I'm not worried about that anymore," the Whispering Man said.

"Well, I sure as hell am. It's a little different for me than it is for you."

"So it is." There was a click and the line went dead.

Clarke put the phone down, leaned back in his chair, and ran his hands over the horse and rider again.

26

THE PHONE JARRED RYAN AWAKE AT A FEW MINUTES past seven on Tuesday morning. Cass found the cell phone, squinting at the caller ID readout.

"Barrientos," she said, and handed it to Ryan. "Here, I'll make some coffee."

Ryan sat up straight, fully awake, and spoke into the phone. "Hello?"

"Mr. Elder? C. J. Barrientos, calling from SUNY Buffalo."

"Yes. Thanks for calling back."

"Who are you with?" The woman's voice was more hard-edged than Ryan remembered from the voice mail greeting, the Spanish accent more pronounced.

"With?" Ryan said. "I'm not with anyone. I just had some questions."

"Are you with the government? If you are, I've already told you everything I know. It's a simple dissertation and I am an American citizen."

Ryan stared at the phone. From the kitchen, he caught the aroma of coffee. "I'm not with the government."

"Well. A reporter, then?"

Ryan had an image of himself, one week ago, throwing the WPSC tape recorder against the brick wall of the building. *One week ago.* "Not anymore. I called you for personal reasons."

"I listened to the message," Barrientos said. " 'Family research.' You'll have to come up with something better than that."

"Look, I stumbled onto your website and there was a reference to Adam and Eve in your paper on American political extremism. I just wanted to know more about it. Your reference was very brief."

"Do tell. The chair of my dissertation committee told me it wasn't pertinent to the body of the paper. I'd interviewed some Justice Department people in Washington, and then one of them seemed to think he'd said too much about a few things, so his supervisor came to see me here and wanted to know what I knew. I told him to ask his own employee. It's a classic case of the left hand and the right hand."

Ryan wanted to scream at the woman that he didn't care about her dissertation committee. "Look, what can you tell me about this Adam and Eve?"

Barrientos's voice lowered. "You still haven't told me why you're interested."

Ryan hesitated. "I think my parents may have had some connection with them."

"Do you, now?"

Ryan waited. Cass brought him black coffee in a Styrofoam cup. She raised her eyebrows at him as she handed it to him. He shrugged at her.

The silence drew out. "Can you help me or not?" Ryan finally said.

A rush of breath on the phone line. "You really don't know anything."

"No, I really don't," he said.

"Okay, look, I have a few minutes before class."

Ryan sipped coffee. "What are your sources? How did you get into all of this?"

"Second question first." Ryan heard Barrientos shuffling papers. "I was a teenager in Nicaragua in the eighties. Both sides were extreme. Sandinistas, contras, it didn't matter. Different ideology, same sorts of tactics. Keep in mind, the extremists were the government there. That's where I got interested in the subject. Now, jump ahead fifteen years. I'm teaching here and finishing up the doctorate at Cornell. So my dissertation's on fringe groups here in the States."

"All right," Ryan said. "Adam and Eve. You made this reference to music scores—"

"Interesting little trademark. But let's not get ahead of ourselves. Do you know *anything* about Adam and Eve?"

"Only what's in your paper."

Ryan thought he detected a note of satisfaction in Barrientos's voice. "I guess I know as much as anyone outside the government. But I warn you, it still isn't much. The first references to them start in 1969, but here I'm getting ahead of myself again. There were a lot of extremist groups operating in the States then, much more so than now. As for the overseas things, I know less about them."

Overseas? Ryan thought.

"There were groups on the left and the right, with varying degrees of destabilization as their goal. The Minutemen, the Liberty Lobby, the Christian Nationalist Crusade on the right. Students for a Democratic Society, the Revolutionary Communist Party, the Black Panthers on the left. Those are just some of the big names. There are three basic characteristics of all extremist groups, then and now—"

"I read that in your paper. Could you skip the lecture?"

There was a long silence and Ryan thought: Shit. I've blown it. She's going to hang up.

"You're a rude man," Barrientos finally said. "Why am I

spending time first thing in the morning talking long distance to such a rude man?"

"I'm sorry. I have a short temper to begin with and I'm dealing with what you might call a lot of stress right now."

Another long pause. "Where did you say you were from?"

"Oklahoma City." What does that matter?

"Hmm." Ryan pictured the woman nodding. "If you read the paper, you know that one of those defining characteristics is that the groups operate on emotion, not on logic or reason. And what's one of the hallmarks of groups of people who are centered around emotion? I'm crossing from poli-sci into sociology here."

Ryan thought for a moment, looking around the quiet, sterile apartment. Cass was across from him, sipping coffee, taking small bites of a cheese Danish she'd bought at a nearby grocery store yesterday morning. He watched a few crumbs fall into her lap, imagining a man chopping off her fingers and walking casually away with them in his pocket. His own fingers tingled at the thought.

"Well?" Barrientos prompted, bringing him back to the phone.

Ryan shook his head. "Disorganization," he said after a moment. "They're not very well organized."

He looked at Cass again and wished this phone call were over. He tried sorting out his feelings, as if he could toss them into different baskets within his mind. He and Cass had become lovers, of a sort. Or had they? Or were they just two desperate, shattered people grabbing onto whatever they could?

I don't know. I don't know anything, he thought.

"All right," C. J. Barrientos was saying, and she sounded vaguely irritated, as if Ryan had missed something. "So these groups aren't high on organization. But they have ideas, things they want to accomplish. Some of them are fed up with the whole idea of the political process and want to escalate into violence. But no one in the groups really knows what they're doing. Are you with me?"

Ryan began to think this call had been a mistake. Barrientos was a bored academic looking for a captive audience. "I'm with you."

"See, there's a whole underground network going on here. They're not sure how to get things done, but many of the groups on the left know each other. At least the leaders do. Same thing with the right. They have similar objectives, so they share ideas from time to time. They ask each other questions. They look for suggestions. 'None of my people can do this. Do you know someone who can?' 'Sure, here's a name.' And so on, through this little shadow world of extremist movements."

"Professor Barrientos, I—"

"Don't interrupt me again. I'm trying to give you some context. Without the context, you're like those people who insist that every word in the Bible is absolutely literal. And since I'm paying for this phone call and could hang up whenever I feel like it, it's a good idea for you to just listen."

Ryan accepted the rebuke. "I'm listening."

"So anyway, you have people associated with all these groups—a lot of very angry people—running around trying to figure out what to do. And let's say that through this little network, someone gives them a name or two. Someone who can help them. Someone who has experience in these sorts of things."

Ryan stiffened, his stomach starting a slow burn, the coffee pooling in it like hot oil. "Go on."

"I see I have your attention now. There it is. Adam and Eve enter the picture."

The picture was still cloudy, shrouded in the fog of Ryan's mind. For a moment he thought of Art Dorian's dying whisper, then the Battle of the Washita, Chief Black Kettle, and the Cheyennes. "So Adam and Eve went around and organized protests and activities for these fringe groups."

"No, no, no. See, you're not paying attention. I said, the groups sought out Adam and Eve when their focus turned violent."

Ryan stood up, clutching the phone, and paced across the room. "But I don't—"

"They weren't organizers, Mr. Elder."

"Then what—"

"They were assassins."

27

"ARE YOU THERE?" BARRIENTOS SAID.

Ryan slowly took the phone away from his ear and let his hand drop to his side. Like something from a cartoon, Barrientos's voice was still coming out of the earpiece.

"Ryan?" Cass said. "What? What did she say?"

The oil in his stomach bubbled. Suddenly he felt as though he'd been thrust into a blender, the power turned on just enough to shake him, not quite enough to rip him apart.

"Ryan?" Cass said again. Her hand was on him, somewhere on his body. His back? His forearm? He couldn't tell, he just knew she was touching him.

Barrientos's voice, tinny and ridiculous, burst out of the phone. Ryan knew his body wasn't shaking, but it felt like it was. A strange virtual reality—shaking inside his head. He lifted the phone very slowly.

". . . did you think I meant? Hello, hello!" Barrientos said.

"I'm here," Ryan said. His voice seemed to come from somewhere else.

"Did you understand what I said?"

"Assassins." Ryan saw Cass's eyes widen even more at the sound of the word.

"Yes." Barrientos sounded almost relieved. "Professional assassins. They were known to have been employed by—are you listening to me? Is there something I should know?"

"A mistake. It has to be a mistake. But tell me. How do you know all this? What makes you so sure?"

"I can be sure because of something most *norteamericanos*

don't appreciate—the Freedom of Information Act. If you're willing to fill out a lot of forms and then wait for several months, you can find out almost anything from the United States government. Adam and Eve are first mentioned in a State Department report from 1969. They're listed as possible suspects in the assassination of a Hungarian diplomat outside a nightclub in Budapest. The local police found a page from a music score pinned to the man's body. It was the first violin part to a string quartet by . . . I'm not sure how to pronounce this name. It's spelled D-V—"

"Dvorak." The blender kicked up to the next speed. Ryan's mother had loved Dvorak.

"That's it. A young man and woman were spotted near the scene of the assassination, but no one could remember much about them, and then they just vanished. Other reports started to come in every few months, from all over Europe. More assassinations: an Italian businessman, a member of the British Parliament, a labor organizer in Belgium. All different kinds of public figures, of all political stripes. The hits were all different too: point-blank shootings, sniper fire, explosives. And always a music score attached to the victim. Interpol code-named them Adam and Eve. The first man and woman to be a professional duo hit team."

Ryan was breathing hard. These were not his parents. Maybe his parents knew them somehow, but the people Barrientos was describing could not be Frank and Anna Elder. His gentle father, who refused to have a gun in the house. His mother, who was all grace and good humor.

Assassins.

Ryan tried to focus. He flashed on a picture of his father's car, crumpled against the side of the bulldozer, the flames enfolding his parents. The police and firefighters, chasing him down, tackling him. The two charred husks were removed from the car. Ryan remembered his mother's hand drooping from under the sheet as the gurney was pushed toward the waiting ambulance. The ruby ring that never left her finger was still on, and it dragged on the concrete. He remembered the scraping sound it made, dry and chalky.

Cass was watching him. Barrientos seemed to be waiting for him to say something.

The apartment suddenly seemed very small. He tugged open the sliding glass door and stepped onto the tiny covered porch. He could see the swingsets of Swatek Park. He gulped cold air and held the phone to his ear as if it were part of him.

"The States," he finally said. "How did they get here?"

"Good question. The State Department's official profile of Adam and Eve, pieced together from various 'sightings' and CIA stations in Europe, says the man, Adam, was most likely American, or possibly Canadian. The woman was eastern European. Hungarian, Polish, or Czech. They couldn't be more specific. These people were shadows, nothing more. Absolute professionals, accepting jobs for money. No ideology, no passion. There was even some speculation in the State Department that the KGB had used them on occasion. For that matter, one memo suggested a CIA liaison, but that went no further. The left hand and the right hand again. Anyway, early in 1973, two leaders of a radical left splinter group called October Force were blown up in their car in Providence, Rhode Island. A sheet of music was found taped to a nearby parking meter."

"But no one knows who they worked for," Ryan said.

Pause. "No. They'd by then built a reputation as two of the best killers for hire in the world. They wouldn't have come that far if anyone knew who paid them for their jobs." Barrientos cleared her throat. "It's worth noting that Adam and Eve never, ever had collateral damage in any of their jobs."

Ryan felt the wind on his face, drinking in the cold, trying to let it blow the fog away from his mind. "Collateral damage. You mean innocent bystanders."

"Exactly. They killed who they were hired to kill, and that's all. So they weren't terrorists. They were professionals. Now, remember that all of the United States was in upheaval then, in the early to midseventies. Vietnam, and then Watergate, had pulled this country apart, so there was lots of work for Adam and Eve. They hit the radical left and the radical right, industry,

labor, the government. Their highest-level hit was a deputy secretary of defense, shot in the head in broad daylight as he
unlocked the door of his townhouse in Georgetown. The
assassin was described as 'an attractive, slightly heavyset,
young dark-haired woman.' That was in the fall of 1975. In
fact, that was the last work attributed to Adam and Eve."

"What do you mean?"

"I mean they disappeared. No more music scores left anywhere. They just ceased to exist. The last official mention of
Adam and Eve in any of these records is late November
1975. A Justice Department snitch, who was planted in and
out of several radical groups, said he saw them, even talked
to them."

"What happened?"

"Nothing."

"Nothing? Just like that?"

"Just like that. The file was closed. And that, Mr. Elder, is
everything I know about Adam and Eve."

Ryan stood perfectly still for a moment, listening to his
heartbeat, watching the bare trees in Swatek Park bending to
the will of the wind.

Assassins . . .

Dvorak . . .

The woman was eastern European. . . .

Ryan swallowed. "Ah—"

"Go ahead," Barrientos said.

"This snitch. Is there anything more on him?"

"Ah, the last person to reportedly see Adam and Eve. He
was cut loose by the Justice Department shortly after that.
Evidently he had problems of his own. But there is a name. I
guess it wasn't kept a secret since they'd let him go."

"Tell me the name."

"Cyrus Graesner." Barrientos spelled it. "I tried to reach him
several times, but he wouldn't talk to me. I finally gave up."

"Where was he?"

Barrientos sounded surprised. "You don't know? No, of
course you don't. That's part of the reason I didn't hang up
on you."

"I don't understand."

"He's right there. Cyrus Graesner lived, and I guess still does live, in Oklahoma City. And one more thing that caught my attention. There was one interesting thing Graesner told his Justice Department contacts about Adam and Eve."

"What?"

"Remember how I told you about the deputy secretary of defense and how the witnesses called the woman 'attractive and heavyset'?"

Dates raced by in Ryan's mind. The fall of 1975.

The ground seemed to tilt up under him. He felt his stomach start to heave.

"Oh my God," he whispered.

"That's it," Barrientos said. "Graesner told them that Eve was pregnant."

28

FOR THE FIRST TIME IN AT LEAST A YEAR, FAITH KELLY slept past six o'clock and went for her run in full daylight. Her feet slapping the pavement of The Village, she heard Ryan Elder's voice on the telephone: *Who am I?* Interspersed with her dreams of the bloody scene in the Underworld, she heard those three words again and again.

Like a child's rhyme, it kept going through her head. *My parents were not who they seemed to be. They killed themselves seven years ago. I'm on the run for my life. Who am I?* A story, a riddle, a TV game show.

"I know who you are, Ryan Elder," Kelly said aloud.

She pushed herself harder through the end of the run, then circled back to the house. After showering and dressing, she swept up Art's memo and the microcassette recording of Elder's call and put on her coat.

Fifteen minutes later, she stood at the door to Nina

Reeves's apartment and said, "I'm sorry I didn't call first. I'm really not supposed to be here."

Reeves folded her arms, her face neutral. Her feet were bare on the carpet of the apartment and Kelly noticed a slim gold chain around one dark ankle.

"Please, Nina, let me in. We may have a break in this and I need your help."

Reeves stood aside and Kelly stepped into the warmth. Reeves closed the door behind them and faced Kelly in the foyer of the apartment. "There are so many things I like about not being tied to an office," she said. "One is that office politics rarely makes its way down to me." She turned back into the living room, leading Kelly into the amazing array of electronics. "However, it does happen on occasion. In my e-mail first thing this morning was a memo from our special agent in charge that you were no longer assigned as a liaison to the Bureau on the Dorian/Elder case, and that Bureau personnel were to have nothing to do with you."

Reeves sat down at the horseshoe-shaped table. "Now tell me, Faith, my friend . . . exactly whose balls did you step on over there?"

Kelly almost laughed. Hearing Reeves talk that way in her attractive, musical accent was a bit like bad wine coming from a beautiful bottle. "Clarke. But look, Nina, I don't blame him for pulling me from the case, not after yesterday morning."

Reeves arched her eyebrows.

"There's something else, though. He had me surrender Dorian's case files. The way the department is organized, he's not supposed to have the files. Department Thirty's completely self-contained."

Reeves leaned back, giving Kelly a long, shrewd look. "But you didn't give him everything."

Kelly smiled again. "You're very perceptive for someone who spends her life with electronics instead of people."

Reeves smiled back. "Indeed. You have something for me?"

"I don't want you to get in trouble, Nina."

"But you're still here."

"I have to know what's going on. Art used to tell me that gut feeling is better than all the hard evidence in the world. And my gut feeling says this is even more complicated than it seems. And trust me, it already seems pretty damned complicated."

"You never take my advice, my friend. It's always personal with you. Trust me, you will live a lot longer if your cases stay out of your personal life."

Kelly thought of Mikael LeFlore, standing in her dining room with eggs running down his shirt. "What personal life?"

Reeves shook her head. "My point exactly." She spread her arms out in an all-encompassing gesture. "Another fine thing about working here is that no one sees, no one hears, no one knows. As long as I produce results for whatever investigation I'm consulting on, no one cares what else I do." She extended a hand to Kelly. "Give it to me."

Kelly dug into her purse and passed over the microcassette.

"Ah," Reeves said. "So it was worth our while to put the recorder on your phone."

Kelly nodded. "It's him. Elder."

"How interesting." Reeves popped the tape into a small machine that seemed lost amidst all the other equipment on the horseshoe. Then she turned to one of the computers and manipulated the mouse until she'd accessed the recording program.

Reeves adjusted speaker volume, started the recording, and pressed play on the microcassette player. In a moment Kelly heard her own voice, answering the phone.

Reeves kept her eyes on the computer screen, watching the sound depicted in wavy black lines as it was transferred from the tape to the computer's hard drive.

At the point on the tape where Ryan Elder said, "Who am I?" Reeves glanced at Kelly and said, "Oh my."

When the tape finished, Kelly said, "That's it."

Reeves stopped the computer recording, then pulled the

cassette out of its machine and handed it back to Kelly. Reeves turned back to the computer, clicked several rectangular icons, assigned the recording a number and a name—Elder/Kelly, with the date—and clicked play. She turned up the speaker volume a little further and listened to the phone conversation again, then twice more.

Kelly shifted in her seat after the third time through, listening for the desperation in Elder's voice when he said, "Who am I?" She saw herself paging through the file, looking for the memo about the man who whispered.

"There's something here," Reeves said. "Underneath everything else, some kind of regular, rhythmic sound. A couple of them, as a matter of fact."

"I thought I heard something when I was on the phone with him, but I couldn't pick up what it was. It was too far in the background."

Reeves began tapping her keyboard. "Take off your coat, Faith. We're going to be here a while."

Just past three o'clock, Reeves drummed her fingers on the table and said, "There it is."

Kelly put aside the carton of Chinese take-out food and stood up, stretching the kinks out of her back. "How do you do it, Nina? You've barely moved for six hours."

"Hmm? Has it been that long?" Reeves glanced at the digital clock above her head. "So it has. Time has no meaning after a while."

Kelly shrugged and pulled her chair close to the horseshoe. She'd listened to bits and pieces of the two-minute phone call dozens of times. She'd heard her own voice and Ryan Elder's sped up, slowed down, run through filters that altered their character completely. She'd heard him say "Who am I?" at least fifty times.

Kelly shuddered. All her life she'd been able to identify herself in relation to the people and things around her. She was Sean Kelly's granddaughter. She was Joe and Maire Kelly's daughter. Her father's parents came from County Wicklow, Ireland, her mother's parents from County Donegal. She'd been there, had touched the grave markers of her great-grandparents. She had family stories, told again and again over time until they acquired the status of legend, of myth.

Ryan Elder had none of that.

Kelly shook her head. It had started as a simple investigation of the killing of a fellow officer, a man she respected. Now it was far, far beyond and out there somewhere was a man, only a couple of years older than she, who'd had everything he knew and understood pulled out from under him like a cloth from a table in a cheap magic act. First his parents' lives, in a spectacular ball of flames, then his parents' very identities, then his own.

Who am I?

"Hypnotic after a few times, isn't it?" Reeves said.

Kelly rubbed the back of her neck, pulling her hair back from her face. "It is that."

"Now you see how the time gets away." Reeves turned back toward the horseshoe. "I've reduced the foreground noise by about seventy-five percent. That's his voice and yours." She frowned, creasing her brow. "We'll lose a little bit of high and low frequency sound, but that can't be helped."

"How much?"

"Around three percent."

Kelly smiled. "I think we can live with that."

"I admit it. I am a slave to perfectionism. Anyway, I've broken down the sound into its various components and increased the background in proportion to the amount the foreground was decreased."

"So they're basically flip-flopped now."

"You could say that." Reeves smiled and clicked the start button.

The phone call filled the speakers, only this time Kelly could barely hear herself and Ryan Elder. She leaned forward, closing her eyes. She and Elder talked, again. He asked "Who am I?" again. The recording ended.

"Play it again," Kelly said without opening her eyes. She rolled her chair a few inches closer to the speakers.

This time, she forced the voices away, made herself abandon the natural human tendency to focus on human sounds.

Natural sound, a low rustle. She remembered yesterday had been blustery.

"The wind," she said, eyes still closed. "He's outside."

"Very good," Reeves said, and started the recording again.

They listened five more times and Kelly began to notice the strange rhythmic sound she thought she'd heard before.

"It sounds metallic." She sat up and rubbed her neck again. "Some kind of metal scraping. No, not a scrape. Almost a . . . what? Something like a squeak."

Reeves nodded. "I would go along with that. A squeak it is. Outdoors, some sort of metal squeaking. But there's one other thing here, almost on top of the metal sound."

"But I don't—"

"Put the metal out of your mind. You know what it is, so ignore it for the time being."

Kelly listened again. The metal sound, over and over, a rhythm as she and Elder talked. She could almost picture something moving . . . back and forth, back and forth. And there. . . .

"Outside," she muttered.

"Come on," Reeves prodded. "It's there. I know it is."

"Outside, moving. Back and forth. And, it's almost like he's . . ." She shook her head. "I can't get it. I can't quite reach it."

"He's not walking," Reeves said. "No one walks like that."

"No. It's almost like he's . . . scuffing his feet along on the ground. But that doesn't make any sense. . . ."

Reeves restarted the recording.

Kelly laid her head on the console, inches from one of the speakers.

Scuffing his feet along on the ground.

"But he would have to be sitting, somehow dangling his legs, to scuff the ground like that."

Reeves's eyes widened.

"And the metal," Kelly said. "That doesn't—"

"Moving back and forth," Reeves said. "There's a steady, constant pattern to it." She leaned toward Kelly. "He's outdoors. There's something with a steady rhythm, a back-and-forth motion, which causes him to scuff the ground."

Their eyes met. "Yes," Kelly said suddenly, adrenaline shooting through her like a laser.

"Yes. He's sitting in some kind of a swing."

Kelly stood up and began to pace a track around the equipment in the living room. "He's in the northwest part of the city. He said that much himself. How many swingsets are there? A thousand? Five thousand?"

"No, no. Think. He's on the run, Faith. You're in a strange place and you want to disappear. What kinds of places do you go?"

"Motels, rooming houses, even those no-questions-asked apartment complexes." Kelly stopped pacing. "Nina, that's it! We need a list of parks or playgrounds with swings located near motels or apartments in the northwest part of town. I need to use your phone."

"Very good," Reeves said. "But wait just one moment before you start making calls."

"What?"

"You, my friend, are off the case. You have no authority. As soon as you make a call and identify yourself as a deputy U.S. marshal, your man Clarke will know about it, and you'll be through."

Kelly let her arms drop to her sides. "I need that list. This could get me to Elder. It could lead me to Art's killer."

The two women looked at each other.

"Nina," Kelly said.

"No eyes, no ears," Reeves said. "It's a pleasure working at home. I can't promise much, being a simple technician and not a well-trained law enforcement officer, however." She paused, letting Kelly absorb the irony in her voice, then smiled. "Don't worry, I'll get you that list."

"Thank you, Nina."

Kelly started for the door. Keeping the tape had paid off, after all. She felt in her shoulder bag and closed her hand over the yellowed paper with Dorian's precise handwriting: *Man who only whispers.*

She had to get to the office, to the computer. She needed the Justice Department database. In a couple of hours the office would be nearly empty and Clarke would be gone.

Kelly could wait to go back to the office. She would have time to search the database while Nina Reeves found the other information she needed.

She sat in the Miata for a few minutes. Then she took out her cell phone and stared at it for a long time before punching in a number she'd committed to memory many years ago.

"Evanston Police," said a voice.

"Captain Kelly, please," she said.

Thirty seconds later, the booming voice she knew all too well said, "Joe Kelly."

She almost pressed end, then she quietly said, "It's me, Dad."

"Faith? Well, I'll . . . this is a surprise. Your mother didn't think you were calling until next week."

"Dad, I need your professional opinion."

Quiet rained down the line from Illinois.

Oh, God, she thought. This was a mistake. "Dad, I'm serious."

"Well," Joe Kelly said. "Well. I guess this is a first."

Here we go.

"I guess it is, Dad."

"You never wanted my professional opinion before. What's different all of a sudden?"

The old anger flared. "I never asked your opinion before because your opinion was that I ought to be teaching Shakespeare to high school kids and popping out babies every year."

"Man's entitled to his opinion about what his daughter ought to do with her life."

Faith doused her anger—there was no time for old battles. "I didn't call to argue about this."

"Why did you call? You've got your friend—your close *federal* friend down there—who gives you all kinds of professional insight. What's his name again?"

"His name *was* Art Dorian, and he was murdered last week."

Joe Kelly's tone bent like grass in high wind, and when he spoke again, it was more father and less cop. "Ah hell, honey. I'm sorry. I'm a grade-A jerk. What happened?"

She hesitated, wondering what she could say. "Dad, it's . . . it's complicated. He was working on a case and then I was pulled into it after he was shot."

"Any leads?"

"Oh, yeah. Lots of leads. But because of a bad judgment call I made, I've been pulled off the case now. I think it's political."

Her father sighed. "That's bad, but it's part of the deal. There's more politics than police work most days. What's your supervisor like?"

"He's . . . I don't know. He's done a couple of things that don't ring right." She thought of Clarke: *Surrender the case files.* "Things that don't add up. And Dad . . . part of this involves a man who wants some information. Information that I have. But he's in the middle of the case, and—"

"Is he a suspect?"

"Yes, but it's not that black and white. I could get in trouble if I pursue it."

Silence.

"Dad?"

A rush of breath on the phone. "What do you want me to tell you, Faith? I can't tell you what to do."

She thought about the two men, Phillip Clarke and Ryan Elder. One held her career in his hand, the ability to crush everything she'd worked so hard to achieve. The other could satisfy her need to know, could unlock what was happening around her. And she could finish the job for Dorian. The two men swirled around her like the dead leaves in the parking lot.

"I guess," she said, "I'm just not sure who to trust."

"Ah, by the saints, Faith Siobhan," Joe Kelly said, and Faith winced. He liked to affect Irish-isms, even though he was born and had lived his entire life in northern Illinois.

"Make up your own mind about the case and what to do. We've got all the manuals and the standard procedures and the proven techniques and all that crap, but at the end of the day there's only one thing. The best thing a good cop has going for him is instinct. That's all you can really trust."

Faith Kelly waited a moment. Something seemed to open, somewhere inside. "You know what, Dad? I think that may be the most useful thing you've ever said to me in my life. I wish you'd said it a few years ago."

"Yeah, well." Her father sounded vaguely embarrassed.

"I guess I need to go, Dad."

"All right. I'll tell your mom you called. Call her at home on schedule next week, you hear me?"

"I will." There was an awkward silence and for a split second she considered telling her father she loved him. But then the moment was gone. They'd never exchanged those words before, not once in her life. It felt almost hypocritical to say them now. "Well, thanks, Dad. 'Bye."

She pressed end, then opened her notebook, filled with scrawled notes about the case. Clarke may have confiscated the official case files, but he hadn't taken her notes. Not yet.

She flipped pages, then found what she wanted, not far from Jeff Majors's name where she'd first written it Sunday morning, with Yorkton at her dining room table. She conjured a mental picture of the handsome young doctor alongside the wall of the Underworld, with the coppery smell of blood hanging in the air like smoke after a fire.

Instinct. That's all you can really trust.

"Go on and do it," she said quietly.

Kelly double-checked the address, started the Miata, pulled out of the parking lot, and drove north.

29

THE SHADOWS WERE LENGTHENING, THE LIGHT ALMOST gone as Kelly rolled into Oak Tree, the last wooded subdivision before Edmond surrendered and suburbia became rural Oklahoma once more. It was the wealthiest part of a wealthy suburb, new money everywhere, ripening as if it were fruit.

The houses, Kelly thought, easily qualified as mansions, most of them built within the last twenty years. They had all the trimmings: curving driveways set behind huge, intricately landscaped lawns; cathedral-like entryways; pools; stables; guest houses. Kelly recognized it all. She'd grown up the middle-class daughter of a cop in a similar suburb.

She rounded a gentle curve, checked the address, and saw the house she was looking for. It was a Mediterranean-style mansion, set well back from the road and partially shielded by a grove of pecan trees. A line of cars—most new, all expensive—crowded the circular driveway and spilled into the street.

Kelly pulled off the street, cut the Miata's engine, and sat for a moment with her hands on the wheel, still warm from the drive.

Instinct.

"Get on with it," she said aloud, then stepped out into the cold, the light fading fast. Not quite 5:30 and almost totally dark. Kelly smoothed out her coat, picked up her notebook, and walked up the long driveway to the house.

The door was answered almost immediately and for a moment Kelly couldn't move. She stared into the face of a female version of Jeff Majors: the sandy hair, the blue-green eyes, the small, compact build. The woman looked out at her, tired, eyes puffy, numbingly weary. "Yes?" she said. "May I help you?"

Kelly was struck by the voice quality, the same tone as Jeff Majors. Behind the woman, people milled about, indistinct, talking in low tones. She smelled food, many different kinds of food.

I can't do this, she thought. Kelly remembered Majors, the way she'd put her hand on his arm Sunday in the hospital on-call room, convincing him he was doing the right thing.

"Are you a reporter?" the woman asked. "Because if you are, you can just leave right now."

"No." Kelly found her voice. "You must be Dr. Majors's sister."

"Jana Majors-Pearson. What do you want?" The woman's face softened, the defensiveness gone, wiped into grief.

Kelly showed her ID. "I'm sorry to disturb you now, but I was told I could find Jack Coleridge here."

The woman looked at Kelly's credentials, then at Kelly, then back to the little leather case again. Something indescribable crossed her face, then she said, "Wait here."

She disappeared into the house. Kelly stood dutifully on the porch in the cold, catching glimpses of crystal and cherry wood and a Renoir on the wall in the entryway. The buzz of conversation went on, soft and low, like ice cubes clinking together in a bowl.

In a moment, an angry visage came to her: Jack Coleridge in his black Brooks Brothers suit with the hazy chalk stripes, white shirt, yellow club tie. He was ramrod straight, striding forward.

"Why are you here?" Coleridge said. He came onto the porch and closed the door quietly behind him. "Don't you know what these people have been through?"

It occurred to Kelly: he doesn't know. He doesn't know that I was the one who set it up. The brass didn't tell them that part. She swallowed, tapped a nail against her leg.

"I need to talk to you and your housekeeper said you were here."

Coleridge's eyes stared right through her. "My housekeeper talks entirely too much. Can't it wait? Judge Majors and his family are close friends of mine."

Kelly took a breath. *Instinct.* "Mr. Coleridge, I know you can't tell me anything about Ryan Elder. I realize you're bound by attorney-client privilege and I won't try to compromise that. But I have to tell you, I believe *you* are in danger."

Coleridge stopped and took a step back. "What are you talking about?"

Kelly gestured toward the driveway and they began to walk. "Let me ask you something. You were very close to the Elders, is that right?"

"Why are you asking me this?"

"Were you?"

They walked a few steps farther along the drive. Coleridge stopped and leaned against a car, rubbing his gloved hands together. His breath fogged between them. He gave Kelly a look that was equal parts shrewd attorney and concerned friend. "What really happened to Jeff Majors?"

"He was meeting Ryan Elder," Kelly said.

Coleridge flinched as if warding off a blow. "You're not suggesting—"

"No," Kelly said quickly. "He didn't kill Dr. Majors. But that's why I'm here, Mr. Coleridge. Majors was killed because of his association with Elder. And you, sir, are the last connection between Ryan Elder and his parents. Maybe you know where he is, maybe you don't. But there is one thing I have to know. In all the years you were friends with the Elders, did they ever mention anything about a man who only spoke in a whisper?"

Kelly waited and watched, and she saw the flicker across Coleridge's face. It was nothing definite, a slight movement at the corner of his mouth, a subtleness of expression in the cloudy eyes. Then it was gone, like a wild animal running for cover.

"What kind of a question is that?" Coleridge said. "A man who only spoke in a whisper? Good Lord, Deputy, you're talking in riddles."

Instinct: he knows something. Her hunch—and Dorian's,

written on the yellowed paper in her pocket—was right. The connection was there, and at some point Ryan Elder's parents had spoken of it to Jack Coleridge.

But how much did he know? Could he know the Elders' true identities? Then, just as quickly: no, impossible. It would have been in the file, if Dorian had even the least suspicion.

Kelly's heart thumped, as if it were turning over. Suddenly she was no longer cold, feeling almost flushed.

"It's not a riddle," she said. "This is who's stalking Ryan Elder, and it's probably who killed Jeff Majors."

Coleridge's eyes shifted again.

"Mr. Coleridge," Kelly said, "this could help to save Ryan. You're the last—"

"When you first came to see me on Friday, you were treating him like a suspect. And today you want to save him? More riddles."

"A lot has happened since Friday. If you know anything about this man, I need to know it. I need to know who he is. It could explain the Elders' suicide. It could explain Art Dorian's murder."

Coleridge slowly shook his head. "I don't know what this is all about, and I can't help you."

Far up the driveway, the front door of the house opened and a man stepped out. Tall, silver hair, imposing, even without the robe: Judge Ray Majors. "Jack?" he called into the gathering dark.

"Be there in a minute, Ray," Coleridge said. He turned away from Kelly, back toward the house.

Kelly tugged at his sleeve. She lowered her voice. "Jeff Majors is dead because of this."

Coleridge half turned back toward her. He seemed to shiver. Something else passed across his face, that movement around his mouth again. But the eyes still stared right through Kelly.

"Frank said . . ." Coleridge bit back the words. His shoulders slumped forward ever so slightly.

Kelly held her breath.

Coleridge righted his posture. "Frank said something, a couple of days before . . . before he died."

"Yes?"

"I want you to understand something. This was not in the context of attorney and client. It was informal. We were at a recital of Anna's students, in Mitchell Hall at the university. Frank and I were sitting near the back, and he suddenly just leaned over to me, and out of the clear blue sky he said that there had been a brief time when he and Anna were involved in a few things they shouldn't have been. And there was this man he dealt with, a man he sometimes still dreamed about, and that he would not or could not speak above a whisper."

"That's all?"

Coleridge shrugged into himself. "He seemed to pull back then, like he'd said too much. It was so out of character for Frank. You have to understand, Frank was my closest friend for twenty years. But he rarely talked about feelings and he never talked about the past. That just wasn't him."

"Did he say anything else?"

"As I said, it was so terribly out of character for him, and it intrigued me, so I pushed him. He finally got agitated and practically ran out of the auditorium. I followed him into the lobby, tried to calm him down. But he was upset with himself, pacing up and down the lobby. I remember he kept slapping the back of his neck with his hand. I'd never seen him do that before. Finally I heard him say one more thing."

"What?"

"A name. He whispered it himself, and I barely heard it. Then he left the building, just walked out and left me. Didn't even take his coat. It was mid-November and the wind was up, but he didn't take his coat. That was the last time I saw him. But the strangest thing happened the next day. He called me at the office, made me swear not to tell anyone what he'd said, especially not Ryan. He said he'd been 'out of it,' but that now he was all right. That's what he said. 'Out of it.' He never talked like that."

Kelly's heart seemed to stop. Everything was still. "The name."

"Jack?" Judge Majors called again. Footsteps started down the driveway.

Coleridge leaned in close to Kelly, put his mouth next to her ear. She smelled his cologne and pipe tobacco, very faint, masculine and aristocratic. He lowered his voice and said two words, then backed away from her.

"I need to go," he said.

"You should have protection," Kelly said.

"The way Jeff Majors had protection?" Coleridge said, staring past her into the pecan trees.

Then Coleridge was hurrying away from her, putting his arm around Judge Majors's shoulders and guiding him back toward the huge house.

Kelly started down the driveway to the street, where she'd left the Miata. Halfway there, she broke into a run.

30

RYAN WAS SICK.

He'd retreated into silence, and Cass saw it and left him alone. Later she'd convinced him to eat and they ate in almost total silence, frozen pizza and Pepsi, college student food from yesterday's hasty shopping trip. Then he fell into sleep, his old defense mechanism. He lay contorted on the sofa while Cass went back down the hall to the bedroom.

Now, in the cold darkness of winter night, he hung over the toilet in the tiny bathroom, sending the pizza back. Cass stood in the doorway, almost translucent in a long white T-shirt and bare feet.

He kept retching after the food was all gone, dry heaving, like the hammer of a gun falling on an empty chamber.

He couldn't speak, finally pulling away from the toilet and leaning his head against the cool porcelain of the bath-tub. He rested his cheek there, was vaguely aware of movement: Cass. In a moment she was kneeling beside him, a cup of water in her hand.

He took the cup, drank the cold water. Neither of them spoke for a long time. She put a hand on his arm. With nothing more intimate than that, he felt connected to her, and was finally strong enough to sit up.

"I . . ." he said, and it was a rasp. He cleared his throat and for a moment his head spun like a ball in midair, and he thought he was going to be sick again. But he steadied himself, raised himself to the edge of the tub.

"Easy," Cass said.

He nodded uneasily, then brought her sharply into focus. A thought ran through his mind: I think I understand why my parents . . .

Ryan clenched a fist, tightened his jaw. "I . . ." He looked up at Cass. The huge blue-gray eyes were open wide, not even clouded by sleep. "I was . . . I was born the week before Christmas 1975."

Cass waited.

Ryan shook his head. "At least that's what I've always thought. If I . . . don't you see? Barrientos said that the deputy defense secretary was assassinated in October of seventy-five."

Cass expelled a little rush of breath and moved around, bare legs on the tile floor. "She would have been pregnant with you. But Ryan . . . you don't know that Adam and Eve were your parents. This is all—"

"No, I don't have proof. But there are too many coincidences. What else am I supposed to think?"

He squeezed his eyes closed, and behind the lids found a picture of his mother in her music room, absorbed in the violin, the music rolling over him like cool, fine water in summertime. Another picture formed: Anna Elder, young, heavily pregnant, with a gun to a man's head.

Ryan bowed his head and tapped his fingers against his forehead.

Had this been his parents' life? Political assassinations, extremist groups, murder for hire? Who were they? How did they get there? And from there, how did they become Frank and Anna Elder? Had they spent twenty years hiding from their past, and had the hiding caught up with them seven years ago, finally sending them over the edge?

"I don't know what to think," he said. His body physically ached, a hollow coldness that went all the way through him. "I don't know if I can . . ." He let the sentence die, leaning his head against the tub again.

"Come on," Cass said. She hooked an arm under one of his and helped him to his feet.

He staggered a little, then righted himself. "I'm okay," he said, but Cass didn't let go.

He made it to the bathroom door and felt a little better, moving slowly. A question formed in his mind. "Is there a phone book in this place?" he said.

"A phone book? I think I saw one in the drawer of the kitchen cabinet."

She got it for him as he came into the living room and turned on the floor lamp. He sat in the armchair, beside its ghostly ring of light.

"You don't really think he's still here, do you?" Cass said. "I mean, all these years—"

"It's worth looking." Ryan flipped to the G section of the White Pages, then turned pages slowly. He stopped near the bottom of a page. "Well, look at that."

"You're kidding."

"No. It's the only Graesner in the Oklahoma City phone book. Cyrus L. Graesner. The address is in the twenty-three hundred block of Northwest First." He looked up at Cass, silhouetted in the lamplight. "That's not far from here."

Ryan flung the phone book to the floor. "In the morning," he said, "we find him. I have to know. I have to finish this."

"In the morning," Cass said, nodding.

Ryan flicked off the lamp, and the apartment was dark but for the lights from the parking lot, filtering in under the curtains. He moved toward the sofa.

Cass reached for him, found a shoulder in the dark. He

felt her hand slide down and take his. Her good hand. She tugged slightly at him.

"No," he said. "I'm not—"

"Shhh." She pulled him a little farther, leading him through the hallway. "It's not a test. There are no right or wrong answers. Just lie down. Just rest with me. That's all."

Ryan opened his mouth to say something else, then realized he didn't really want to object after all. He wanted to be next to her, to just feel her beside him, to listen to her breathing and feel her warmth and be a human being again for a while.

In the bedroom, Cass threw back the covers and settled into the far side of the queen-size bed. Ryan stood for a moment in silence, then slowly climbed in beside her. They lay on their backs, and this time Ryan reached across and found her hand. She clasped it and he felt the stumps this time.

Cass squeezed his hand. Neither of them spoke. They lay with their hands clasped and both fell asleep that way.

31

KELLY SAT IN HER OFFICE, THE ONLY LIGHT COMING from the computer screen in front of her. She'd caught a break when she returned to the office after hours. The parking garage underneath the U.S. Courthouse was nearly empty. Using her key card, she rode the private elevator reserved for judges and law enforcement officers to the second floor. The Marshals Service office was quiet and dark.

Now, several hours later, she sat back and looked at the information she'd amassed from the Justice Department database.

When Jack Coleridge whispered the name to her, she'd recognized it instantly. Though not well known to the public, it was a famous name in federal law enforcement circles. Two of her books on long-term fugitives at home had chapters on him. At the Federal Law Enforcement Academy, less than a year ago, her instructor on fugitive apprehension procedures had spent three lectures on him.

The name was Terrence Ross.

Active in the domestic extremist community from 1971 through late 1975, he'd founded a shadowy organization called The New America (TNA). The group's specific ideological goals were never spelled out, but one thing was clear: The New America was dedicated to violent revolution. FBI reports put its membership at somewhere around three hundred in a dozen states, with Terrence Ross operating from somewhere near Washington.

TNA had claimed responsibility for bombings in and around Washington, for attacks on government offices, banks, corporations, and union halls across the country. A few low-level members were arrested and they all named Terrence Ross, but no one claimed to have ever seen him. He orchestrated all his maneuvers by phone or by reel-to-reel audio tapes sent to various lieutenants.

Kelly read the screen again. No one had ever seen Terrence Ross, but they agreed on one thing: he never spoke above a whisper on the phone or the tapes. In fact, several members of TNA referred to him as the Whispering Man.

Kelly paged down in the computer file, then read the account of one TNA meeting in Wisconsin, when Ross had allegedly been present, but insisted on making his speech from behind a screen. Kelly thought of the Wizard of Oz— *Pay no attention to that man behind the curtain. . . .*

The Justice Department knew nothing about Ross. He slipped away from them, leaving nothing except his whispers.

He was still out there.

Terrence Ross disappeared around Thanksgiving 1975 and TNA crumbled into dust, dissolving into a tiny blip, a footnote in history books about American extremist movements and a case study for students of law enforcement.

Thanksgiving 1975.

Kelly squinted at the screen, then rubbed her eyes,

fatigued from hours of staring at the glow. Her head throbbed from information overload.

Thanksgiving 1975.

Slowly she sat up straight. The timing. Ross had vanished at just about the same time as . . .

She shook the fog out of her head. Between Coleridge's statement that Frank Elder mentioned the name a few days before his suicide, and the dates . . . Kelly didn't believe in coincidence. Not anymore.

She leaned forward.

Ross was still out there. He'd never been found. Dorian had had a hunch that somehow "the Whispering Man" was connected to all this.

Kelly's head jerked. She held her breath. A door closed.

Someone was in the office.

Her body went rigid. She listened. Steps, heavy and hollow, muffled by the carpet.

She pulled a computer disk from the neat stack on the side of the desk and quietly inserted it into the disk drive. The click when it slid into place was as loud as a gunshot to Kelly.

She moved the mouse and began to download the DOJ file. Listening, listening. Her hand went to her Glock and undid the holster cover.

The footsteps came nearer, heavier, heading toward the main body of the office, the "bullpen" area.

Kelly crouched down in the opening under her desk, her hand never leaving the gun. A bead of sweat formed under her hairline and trickled down her nose.

The footsteps stopped. They turned, receding, stopping again. A rattling sound: keys.

Kelly's heart beat faster. A door opened. She peeked out from beneath the desk: the computer was still downloading. She remembered how Derek Mayfield had teased her about having the slowest computer in the office.

Bracing one hand against the edge of the desk, she swung her body part of the way around, where she could crane her neck and see into the bullpen area. A blade of light slivered out.

Clarke's office.

Kelly tucked herself back under the desk, heart thumping wildly. In a moment she caught a whiff of cigarette smoke from the direction of the light.

Clarke, here at midnight. Kelly's thoughts spun away from her, spiraling down like a staircase. If he caught her here, after he'd not only removed her from the case but placed her on leave. . . .

She twisted her neck around, looking up at the computer. The file was finished. She reached carefully up, removed the disk, and dropped it into the pocket of her blazer.

Now to get out of here.

The design of the bullpen area was in her favor. A row of large filing cabinets separated it from Clarke's office. If Kelly stayed in a crouch, there was no way Clarke could see her. She would have to open and close one interior door that led into the reception area, but then she was home free.

She'd been crouching for a long time and her knees were beginning to complain, but she stayed low and worked her way past the other desks in the office. Inching slowly, her mind flitted back to Terrence Ross, aka the Whispering Man.

Ross was still a fugitive. Frank and Anna Elder were dead and Ross was still out there, more than a quarter century after anyone had last heard of him. Had he surfaced to kill Dorian, and to stalk Ryan Elder? One step beyond that thought: What could he want from Elder?

She shook herself back to reality. There was only this deserted office, and Clarke—*I own you*, she remembered with a chill—in there smoking. She crept from behind the last desk. The wooden door was three feet away. She half hopped, half walked to it and reached up to enter her code on the key-pad lock. She turned back to look over the office one last time and her hand froze above the doorknob.

She could see the little shaft of light from Clarke's office, and another light, farther down, an eerie glow reflecting off the second-story window.

Her computer monitor. *Dammit.*

Kelly's breathing quickened. If Clarke walked out of his

office for any reason and came into the main body of the bullpen he would see it and know what she'd been doing.

Kelly paused with her hand on the door. Why not tell him? He's your boss, she thought, and by all accounts a good cop, even with all the "I own you" nonsense.

No.

She thought of Clarke demanding the case files. She remembered him kicking the empty bottle into Indiana Avenue Saturday morning, watching it shatter in the middle of the street. There was something in him that wasn't quite right. Something that didn't add up, not for a federal law enforcement officer.

She crouched low again and started back toward her desk. Sweating again now, like she did after a run. She felt it trickling down her back.

Kelly made it to her desk, reached around, and turned off the computer. The office plunged back into darkness.

She half turned, bracing her hand on the desk, when she heard Clarke's voice.

It was a low rumble, and from the distant quality, it sounded like he was still in the office. Kelly froze, straining to hear what he was saying, but it was too far away. She caught only a few words, then a long pause and more words, agitated.

The phone. He's talking on the phone, she thought.

She was perfectly still, breathing quietly through her mouth. Listening, she began to catch a few more words. She went rigid when she heard her own name murmured, followed a few seconds later, in a louder tone, by "fucking stupid bitch."

Kelly jerked involuntarily at the words, her head tilting toward the office door. Her hand, braced on the edge of her desk, slid forward toward her computer monitor and knocked over the stack of computer disks.

The sound was a whisper of hard plastic, but in the silent dark of the bullpen, it was an explosion. Kelly's hand went rigid, halfway off the desk.

Clarke's voice stopped in midphrase.

Several seconds of silence followed, then he said something that sounded like "later." Kelly heard the phone bouncing back into its cradle.

Kelly's head twitched again. She stood rooted to the spot in front of her desk, not breathing. A rivulet of sweat slid down her neck. She had a mad urge to reach out and slap it like a mosquito.

She heard a step. Clarke's boots, heavy even on carpet. Another step.

She moved. Long legs churning, she skittered across the bullpen area, setting her sights on the wooden door she'd been about to open two minutes ago.

Clarke's voice, still around the corner, but closer: "Hello?"

Kelly clamped a hand around the disk in her pocket. She had a clear shot to the door. No furniture in the way, she was moving silently. . . .

"Hello?" Much closer.

Kelly looked around wildly. A couple of steps and Clarke would be around the filing cabinets. She had three, maybe four steps to the door.

Clarke's heavy steps fell behind her, coming around the cabinets.

She blinked in the darkness. Her eyes, long since adjusted to the lack of light, fell on the reception desk, sitting parallel to the door. It was an L-shaped computer desk, with the leg of the L behind the all-too-familiar cubicle partition.

Two steps brought her into the reception area. She dropped down and squeezed herself under the L of the desk.

Clarke's boots thudded. Louder. He was in the bullpen.

Kelly squeezed her eyes closed. The steps halted abruptly. She imagined him at her desk, perhaps with his hand on the butt of his own gun.

Her knees, drawn up to her chin, began to cramp. Kelly bit her lip. Don't lose it now, she told herself.

Another explosionlike sound in the dark. The hard plastic sound of the computer disks. It sounded like he'd dropped one on the desk. Kelly tightened her hand around the disk in her pocket.

"All right, now," Clarke said in a low voice. "What's this?"

A long silence. He would be sizing up the office, wondering if he was hearing things or if there really was someone there.

Come on, Chief, you're hearing things, she thought. Go back to your phone and your cigarettes. Call me all the names you want, but go back in your office.

Then, like an electric shock, Clarke's voice again: "Kelly?"

Another whisper of plastic, then another, as if he were going through her disks.

A droplet of sweat ran into her eye, stinging with salt. She tugged at her lower lip with her teeth. The office was silent for a moment.

Kelly tried to think. What *should* Clarke have done in this situation? Call for backup, call building security downstairs. But he hadn't.

Her eye stinging, her lip hurting, Kelly's thoughts crystallized: You're dirty, Chief. You're in this up to your eyeballs. The reason for Clarke to be in the office at midnight became suddenly clear. Both the office itself and its phone lines were secure and he didn't want anyone to know what he was doing.

Fucking stupid bitch.

You're dirty, Chief.

Kelly ground her teeth.

A single step from Clarke. Kelly couldn't tell which direction it went. She shifted her position slightly, moving her weight around, trying to relieve the cramping in her legs.

A few more steps. They were closer, Clarke's heavy booted steps crossing the office.

For a wild moment Kelly considered drawing her weapon and confronting Clarke. *Never draw your weapon unless you intend to use it*, her firearms instructor at the academy had pounded into her. Would she do it? Could she shoot at Clarke? Kelly had never fired her weapon except on the gun range.

She shook her head, feeling her hair swish against the bottom of the desk.

Two more steps, three, four.

Kelly began to inch her hand out of her pocket.

A phone rang.

The steps came to an abrupt halt. Clarke made a grunting sound in his throat.

Kelly didn't move.

The rings were muffled, which meant they were probably coming from Clarke's office. An agonizing moment passed between the second and third rings, then the footsteps moved away quickly, bounding back around the filing cabinets.

Kelly didn't wait. She swung herself out of the small space, her knees snapping their anger. She heard Clarke grab the phone, heard his low voice. At the door, she punched in her code and twisted the knob carefully, silently. It opened and she stepped halfway through, then stopped, listening.

She caught a few words: ". . . thought I heard . . . get this over with . . . didn't think I could . . ."

Kelly pulled the door silently closed, then was out of the reception area in three steps and into the main hallway of the courthouse, her steps clicking like rain on an aluminum roof.

The Whispering Man sat in his car, parked along Harvey Avenue half a block from the courthouse, and watched Kelly as she drove out of the parking garage and turned north.

Persistent, he thought. An admirable quality. In another place and time, she might have done more important work for him. But then, he reminded himself, times had changed.

"You're under so much stress, Chief," he said into the phone. "Perhaps you're hearing things that aren't there."

"Don't get flip with me, goddamnit!" Clarke growled.

"I'm not being flip in the least. Don't worry about your Deputy Kelly anymore. Don't give her another thought."

"She can fuck up everything."

The Whispering Man spoke as if he were lecturing an inattentive child. "No, she can't. No matter what she finds out, no matter what she does, she can't possibly derail my plan. Even if she finds Ryan, which I seriously doubt, he'll play it out to the end. He has no choice. He's firmly in my grasp and he's going to stay that way until it's settled and I have my property."

"Yeah, but like I said before, I have a lot more to lose than you do. You know how it is with cops in prison."

The Whispering Man shook his head. For all his bravado, the man was pathetic. "That, my old friend, is your problem." He pressed end, tossed the phone onto the seat, and nudged his car out into the dark streets of downtown.

Half a block north, he passed the Oklahoma City National Memorial. Only now, in the middle of the night, did the tourists leave it alone. A section of the famous fence still stretched along Harvey, with its talismans: T-shirts, photos, crudely framed poetry, birthday cards to those killed in the bombing, and crosses—many, many crosses.

Timothy McVeigh was an idiot, the Whispering Man thought. A revolutionary, to be sure, but an idiot nonetheless. McVeigh had taken the simplistic approach that by striking at the government, he would somehow even the score for Waco and ignite a revolution at the same time. Foolish, short-sighted idiot. And then to drive up the road in a car with no license plate, carrying a loaded weapon, just waiting for an alert Oklahoma Highway Patrol trooper to pull him over. He'd wanted to be captured, of course, to be a martyr at the hands of the government he hated.

"You cannot watch the results of a revolution if you are dead," the Whispering Man said aloud in the car. He'd lectured his troops about that in the sixties and seventies, all the fiery young revolutionaries who were willing to die for the Cause. "Furthermore, you cannot emerge as a leader in the post-Revolution world if you are dead."

The Whispering Man smiled. Quoting himself was a bit silly, but they were words worth remembering.

The smile faded. The Whispering Man understood, where McVeigh and his ilk had not, that to bring about true revolution, you do not strike at one side or one institution. McVeigh was limited by narrow ideology: the government was too powerful, so the government must be attacked.

Not the government, the *system*. The government was only one part of the overall system that corrupted the society. To get to the government, go in a roundabout way. What does the government fear most? Not attacks on itself, but civil unrest, the people attacking *each other*.

Yes.

The Whispering Man had to pull to the side of the dark downtown street, as he considered the direction of the Revolution. He closed his eyes, thinking of what Ryan Elder must be doing now, but Elder was quickly replaced by the tall man and his son. Only now, the boy wasn't a boy, but a man himself, taller than his father and more solidly built. The young one had just graduated from college and there the two of them stood, in the windowless room, far out in the country.

You will join me, the father said. *I cannot publicly acknowledge you as my son, of course, but you will work with me. I think you're ready now.*

Work at what? the son said. *Jesus Christ, Dad, you don't really do anything. You sit around and formulate big plans and talk to people in Washington and—*

Watch your mouth! I've tried to impress upon you for your entire life how important I am, how critical my work is! There are elements of society that would destroy everything America stands for, and I must stand in their way. Have you seen what is going on in this country? Have you paid attention?

Destroy everything America stands for, the son thought. *Destroy everything you stand for is what you really mean, you stupid old fart. The rest of the country is as corrupt as you are. What we need is a New America, from the ground up, where people like you—you sorry sack of shit—don't have power over the rest of us.*

And the Revolution was born. In fact, it was perfect. The son couldn't have planned it better himself. His father—his father's ridiculous projects—provided him the perfect cover. He would plan it right under the old bastard's nose. In fact, the old man would think he was working for *him*, while all the time he was working to tear down everything he stood for.

The Whispering Man was born at that time, his persona as Terrence Ross. And what was so delicious about it was that his father actually encouraged him! The boy had finally come around and was working for him. Lovely, lovely irony.

Terrence Ross pulled back onto the street and he'd soon left downtown behind. He thought of Ryan Elder and he wondered what the boy's father would say now.

32

FINGERS OF HARD WINTER SUNLIGHT REACHED INTO THE apartment bedroom, slanting down through the blinds, when Ryan opened his eyes. Fully alert, he lay for a moment in the strange bed, blinking at the light.

He felt the coldness of the morning, but also the warmth of having another body next to him. He couldn't remember the last time he'd felt it. Yes, he could after all—he'd only slept with Melissa McNeill twice, but the second time he had awakened like this, deep in winter, a foot of new Vermont snow outside. Appropriate that it had been winter, he thought, remembering Melissa's last words: *You are the coldest person I've ever known.*

Ryan turned his head toward Cass and was surprised to see her eyes open and looking at him.

"Do you always do that?" she said, the sleep turning her voice craggy.

"Do what?"

"Just open your eyes and be instantly awake. No transition from being asleep to being awake."

"Always have. How long have you been awake?"

"A little while."

"Just lying there looking at me?"

"Just lying here looking at you."

They turned toward each other at the same moment and Ryan wrapped his long arms around her, pulling her close, her head against his chest. They stayed that way for a long time, and for a moment, Ryan thought Cass had fallen asleep again.

Then he felt her move her head slightly and he said, "What are we doing?"

Cass leaned away from him, propping herself on an elbow. "I'm not sure. But it's okay . . . I think."

He pulled her back to him, raked his fingers through her short, straight blond hair, pulling it gently away from her face. He ran his hand down the back of her neck, caressing its smoothness. His hand traveled down her back and he began to feel himself stirring. Evidently Cass felt it as well, for her good hand slipped between them.

"Tell me what you were really thinking about just now," she said.

Ryan smiled. "I was thinking about the last time I woke up in bed beside a woman."

"Were you, now?"

"I'm afraid so. What are you going to do about it?"

"You'll see."

"This is crazy, isn't it?" he whispered.

"Yes. But no more crazy than the rest of the last few days."

They came together slowly this time, gentle and quiet, wrapped in the quilt of early morning. The climax took a long time, and Cass bit the back of her hand to keep from crying out. Ryan buried his head in her shoulder.

When they were finished, they lay breathlessly together for a few minutes before Ryan said, "Let's just stay here and never leave."

Cass propped herself up again. "Yesterday you said this apartment was suffocating you and today you don't want to leave? Forgive me if I don't buy that."

"No, I didn't really mean that. If I don't finish this, it'll never leave me alone."

Cass's eyes widened.

"I know what you're thinking," Ryan said. "It may have gotten my parents, but it's not getting me."

Cass smiled slightly. "Do I detect a strengthened resolve?"

"I guess so."

Cass showered and dressed and had already made coffee when Ryan walked out of the shower with a towel around his waist. Without looking up, Cass said, "There are cups in the—"

She looked up at him and jumped, losing her grip on her

cup. It plopped onto the floor and coffee spilled on Cass's shoes. "What the—what did you do?"

"Thanks for buying the supplies yesterday," he said, and ran a hand across his newly smooth face.

Cass bent down and scooped the pieces of Styrofoam into the trash. Ryan came around the corner of the kitchen counter. "You look like you're about twelve years old," Cass said. "Even with the gray. Why did you do that?"

Ryan rubbed his face again, trying to get used to the way it felt. He'd started the beard a few months after his parents' suicide and had kept it continuously since. "Two reasons. Number one, our friend Deputy Kelly is looking for a guy with a beard. Number two . . . just a minute."

He vanished into the bedroom as Cass wiped up the coffee with a paper towel. When he returned he was holding his wallet. He opened it, pulled out a creased photograph, and handed it to Cass.

She stared at the two faces, Anna Elder's strong, dark Slavic features, and Frank Elder, the face wide but not fat, the pale eyes, squared shoulders. Behind them was the backdrop of a bookcase: a portrait shot. Frank Elder wore a serious expression and Anna had an easy, comfortable smile. Frank's hand was on Anna's shoulder.

Slowly Cass looked up from the photo at Ryan, then at the picture again, and she understood.

"It's uncanny," she said. "There's no doubt, is there?"

"None."

"You look exactly like him. The shape of your face, the cheekbones, the eyes, even the way you hold your bodies is the same."

"It got to be kind of a curse after a while. In high school I dreamed of growing a beard, just so I'd look different. Plus, no one I knew had one. Not too much facial hair in uptight, buttoned-down Edmond. As soon as I got to UCLA, I started one. When I came home for Thanksgiving that first year, I got off the plane and my dad said, 'Do you know how ridiculous you look?' On some level, I think he liked it that I looked so much like him."

Cass laughed. "Wish I'd known you then and got to see that first attempt."

"No, you don't."

"Did it come in gray?"

Ryan pointed at her. He'd forgotten what it was like to engage in simple, mindless banter with another human being. And he was glad he could talk this way with Cass. It made him feel nearly normal, whatever that was. "Don't push it, Madam Juilliard. I saw pictures of you on the mantel at your house, with long hair and wearing that green dress."

Cass made a face. "God, that was an awful thing. But I was on scholarship and didn't have money left over for wardrobe. I wore that for my senior recital. Some of the others in my class made cracks about it being made out of army surplus material."

"Was it?"

"Oh ho, very funny, Master Suburbanite. It was the best I had at the time." She handed the picture back and Ryan tucked it into his wallet.

Ryan turned serious again. "If and when we find this Graesner, we have to be able to convince him to talk."

"And if he sees you, clean shaven and the absolute image of your father—"

"It should tell us if Adam was my father. From there, I don't know."

Ten minutes later, dressed in his usual khakis and a dark blue button-down shirt, Ryan took a cup of coffee from her and leaned across the kitchen cabinet. "I really can't stand coffee. There's no more Pepsi?"

"Sorry. We drank it all last night with the pizza."

Ryan made a face and drank the hot liquid. "Sorry about your other cup. I really didn't mean to startle you."

"Yes, you did." Cass took a bite of her microwave waffle. "Or you would have told me before you did it."

Ryan waited a moment. "Maybe so." He smiled, then it faded quickly. "That address in the phone book for Cyrus Graesner? It's in the Flats."

Cass's eyebrows went up.

"You don't know about the Flats? When I was in high school, I had a civics teacher who was trying to talk to us about population flow, the flight to the suburbs, things like that. You know how when you drive around certain areas in the city that are considered 'bad' parts of town? A lot of times people will say things like, 'Too bad, it used to be a really nice area.' Well, the Flats was never a nice area. It's always been poor. I remember my teacher used to say that he knew the principal at the neighborhood school. Parents would go to her and say, 'Please help my child get out of the Flats.' That's where we're going."

"You think it's dangerous?"

"I'm not sure. It's been seven years since I lived here, remember? But as I recall, the Flats was never too violent, just depressing. But I don't know."

"I guess we'll find out," Cass said.

Ryan's face turned hard. "I guess we will."

Ryan drove the Jeep, moving slowly south on Villa Avenue. The change was gradual, from the middle-class urbanity of the neighborhood near the apartment complex, to the slightly bohemian district immediately south. Once they crossed Northwest Tenth, it changed rapidly. Ryan was reminded of the bridge at Reno and Indiana, a couple of miles east. Villa Avenue south of Tenth consisted of an industrial complex, an auto salvage yard, a couple of sagging churches, an open field of dead grass behind a high chain-link fence. Crossing the railroad tracks, he spotted the homes lying to the east of Villa decaying like rotting vegetables.

He turned on Northwest First, keeping a wary eye on the houses. Most were clapboard, many with peeling paint and sagging window coverings. Some windows were covered only with sheets of clear plastic. A few had tried to enliven the properties with flowerpots and attempts at landscaping, but in the January cold, even they looked weary. Broken toys sat in some of the small yards. Ryan couldn't help thinking of his own upbringing, clean and comfortable in the suburbs. The house he'd grown up in was only about fifteen miles from here, but it may as well have been fifteen thousand.

In the middle of the second block, like a mirage shimmering in the desert, was a small, neat house with a fresh coat of off-white paint and forest green trim, sitting behind a well-maintained chain-link fence. It seemed to Ryan as though an Oklahoma tornado had ripped the house from a working-class neighborhood somewhere else and deposited it in the midst of all this poverty.

He stopped the Jeep across the street from the pleasant little house and double-checked the address. "That's it, all right."

"Curiouser and curiouser," Cass said.

"You could say that." They looked at each other. "Well, let's do it."

Ryan hugged his coat around him and Cass put her left hand firmly in her pocket. Somewhere not far away, a dog barked once. Ryan thought he caught sight of a face in the window of the house next to Graesner's. Otherwise the street was still.

The gate was unlocked and they were on the small porch less than a minute after leaving the Jeep. There was no bell, but a brass knocker waited inside the storm door. Ryan lifted it and knocked three times.

There was sound from inside the house almost immediately. Footsteps, something heavy moving around, an interior door being slammed. In a moment the door opened and a young Hispanic woman said, "What do you want?"

Ryan looked at her. She was barely out of her teens, but her face seemed tired, careworn. The brown eyes were cold steel. She was wearing a green and white print dress with a small rip across the left sleeve. No makeup, no jewelry.

"We're looking for Cyrus Graesner," Ryan said. "Does he live here?"

The young woman's eyes opened wide, then narrowed, the skin around them crinkling. "Not here."

Ryan heard something else behind him, from the direction of the street. "Could you at least tell me if he lives here, or if there's another address—"

"Not here," she repeated, and slammed the door.

"Surly," Cass said, drawing out the word.

Ryan shrugged and lifted the knocker again. There was movement inside, but the door stayed closed. Ryan made a fist and pounded. Again, nothing.

"That would have been too easy, after all," he said, as they walked back to the Jeep.

As Ryan unlocked the driver's side door, he heard a step and turned. A very young black woman with blonde hair in cornrows stepped around the back of the Jeep.

"Well, look at this," she said.

Ryan looked at her. Like the young woman at the house, she was barely more than a girl, early twenties at the most. Unlike the other, she was attractive, with smooth skin, a classic figure, and dark eyes which seemed both shrewd and playful. She was wearing a heavy blue and green woven sweater, satin jogging shorts, and sneakers. Her right nostril was pierced with a tiny silver ring.

"May I help you?" Cass said, a couple of steps behind.

"And so polite," the girl said. "What you want Cyrus for?"

"You know him?" Ryan asked.

"I said, what you want him for?"

"I want to talk to him," Ryan said, looking up and down the empty street. He glanced back at the house and saw the curtains fall into place over the front window. "Who are you?"

"I'm T. That's all you need to know."

"T?"

"That's it. Wonder if Cyrus would want to talk to you or not."

"What are you to him?" Cass said.

The girl kept looking at Ryan, her eyes guarded. "Cyrus is my old man. We ain't married or nothing, but still. . . ." She shrugged.

"You live with him?"

"More or less. Hey, it's cold out here. How about we get in this nice little SUV you got here?"

"Are you going to tell me where to find him?"

T smiled, showing straight white teeth. "Maybe."

They got in the Jeep and Ryan started the engine, turning on the heater. "So tell me about Graesner."

"What's to tell? I take care of him. He keeps me away from my crackhead gangbanger brothers. So I stay with him. Got a decent place to live, even if it is the Flats. My brothers come 'round, he scares them off."

T twisted one of her cornrows and smiled. "Now you tell me something. What you want to talk to Cyrus about? I kinda screen people who want to see him."

"Do a lot of people want to see him?" Ryan said.

"Nah. But he gets crazy sometimes."

"Crazy how?"

"Crazy scared. Like he's afraid something he did is coming back to haunt him." T looked both of them up and down. "You two don't look old enough for that."

"So how does this work?" Cass said. "You give him a message and then he meets us?"

"Oh, kinda like that. Give me something to go on. I can't just say some tall, skinny white dude and his old lady want to talk. It won't happen."

"Tell him . . . tell him I want to talk about Adam and Eve."

"Adam and Eve. You don't need Cyrus for that, you need the Bible. I got two or three in the house if you want to borrow one."

Ryan resisted a strong urge to raise his voice. "Tell him the son of Adam and Eve wants to talk to him."

T stared over the seat at Ryan, her smooth features thoughtful. "You're serious."

"As serious as I can be."

"I get kinda protective of Cyrus. He takes good care of me. I might even love him. Don't tell him I said that part." She pulled at one of her cornrows again. "The son of Adam and Eve."

"He should understand what I mean."

"Cain or Abel?"

Ryan blinked at her.

"So?" T said. "You Cain or Abel?"

"I don't know yet."

The shrewd look from T again. "What I think is, you don't be careful, you might be Abel." She got out of the Jeep and shivered. "I'll talk to Cyrus. I were you, I wouldn't just sit there in your nice SUV on the street. Drive around a little. Come back in a half hour." She slammed the door and walked toward the neat little house.

Ryan and Cass watched her go. "You think she'll really get to Graesner?" Cass said.

"I don't know." Ryan dropped the car into gear. "But you heard the lady. Let's drive around a little."

Half an hour later, the Jeep eased down Northwest First through the Flats. Cass sipped scalding coffee, Ryan a Pepsi they'd bought from an angry-looking convenience store down the street.

"There she is," Cass said.

T was waiting on the house's porch. The jogging shorts were gone, replaced by pink sweatpants. A brown suede leather jacket covered the sweater.

"I believe she's dressed to go somewhere," Ryan said.

"Do tell."

T walked slowly, standing erect, across the street. She tapped on a back window of the Jeep and Ryan let her in. "Let's go for a ride," she said.

"He agreed to talk?" Cass said.

"Now, would I say 'let's go for a ride' if he didn't? He asked me a whole bunch of questions. How old you were, what you looked like, how you talked. That ain't like Cyrus, so you must know something about something."

"Where to?" Ryan said.

"Downtown. Go down to Reno, turn left."

"Where is he?"

"Leave it to me. Can I smoke?" She'd already lit a long, slim brown cigarette. "Cyrus won't let me smoke in the house. He don't really want me to smoke at all. Says I might get cancer."

"At least crack the window," Ryan said, the smoke burning

his eyes and irritating his nostrils. He caught a glimpse of T in the mirror. She held the cigarette close to her face, only inches from her lips. Ryan thought he detected a small smile on her face, an almost satisfied expression.

"You got it, Abel," she said.

Ryan drove south, then east on Reno, passing half a block from the bridge where he'd picked up the envelope from Coleridge on Saturday morning. *Saturday* . . . Jeff had still been alive and Ryan had still thought he knew who he was. It was a long time ago.

As they crossed Walker Avenue and came into the edge of downtown, T pointed and Ryan swung the Jeep into a parking lot that adjoined the Myriad Gardens.

An anchor of the southern end of downtown Oklahoma City, the gardens were a sculpted, landscaped plot that sported an idyllic, well-stocked pond. A round concrete stage floated in the center of the pond, connected to the rest of the park by a slender walkway. Commanding the scene was the Crystal Bridge, a three-story tubular structure filled with tropical flowers and plants.

Ryan looked up at the tube as they walked up the slope into the park. He caught a glimpse of a memory, coming here with his father as a preteen, neither of them speaking, looking at all the exotic plants. He'd never wanted to leave. Talking was unnecessary—just being beside his father was enough.

"Where?" Ryan said.

"Down by the water stage," T said.

They passed through a breezeway by the tube and down a set of concrete steps. Ten steps down, the walls formed a windbreak and it felt warmer. Ryan spotted a lone figure sitting on the steps of the amphitheater that surrounded the floating stage.

T brushed past them and led them around the back of the amphitheater. The man was facing away from them and he hadn't moved. Ryan saw a gray ponytail, tucked into the back of a heavy black coat. A bright multicolored scarf circled the man's neck.

"His hearing's not too good," T said quietly. She raised her voice: "Hey, Cyrus."

The man slowly stood and turned toward them. At first his expression was neutral and he was still far enough away that Ryan couldn't read his eyes. Then, he caught sight of Ryan.

The man's face went slack and the color drained from it. His hands froze in front of him, held waist-high.

"Cyrus?" T said. "Cyrus, you okay?"

Graesner let his hands fall to his sides and he muttered a word, so softly even Ryan could scarcely hear.

"Adam," he said.

33

RYAN STARED.

Cyrus Graesner's age was impossible to tell. His face was sallow and wrinkled, his skin papery. His gray hair was sprinkled with a few fading grains of brown, the hair combed straight back to meet the ponytail. The face was commanded by a nose that looked as if it had been broken multiple times, with burst blood vessels spreading like a spider's web on one side. He wore silver oval glasses, which appeared too big for his face. He was gaunt, and even standing still looked awkward, as if he were about to fall over.

"Adam," he said again, louder, and his voice was a resonant baritone, betraying his appearance.

In three steps, T was at his side, holding his arm. "Cyrus? You okay? You want me to take them out of here?"

Graesner seemed to come to himself, color edging back onto his face. He shook his head, pulling the ponytail a little ways out of his coat collar. "No, Tanis. I'd better talk to them." His eyes stayed on Ryan.

The girl lowered her voice. "Don't call me that in front of people."

"It's your name, honey. It's nothing to be ashamed of." Still looking at Ryan.

"Well, I still don't want you to call me that in front of people."

"Go on home, Tan . . . T. I may be a while."

T put on a pout. "I rode with them."

Graesner pulled keys from his pocket. "My car's in the lot on the east side of the tube." He finally dragged his eyes from Ryan and looked at T. "Go on. I'll be home later. You and Linda take care of each other." He kissed her lightly on the lips and made a shooing motion with both hands. She took the keys, climbed the steps past Ryan and Cass, and disappeared into the breezeway.

Graesner's gaze was riveted to Ryan again. "Sorry for staring," he finally said. "It's just that you look so much like him. You have a little more gray in your hair, but other than that. . . ." He shook his head, seemingly amazed.

"Then you are the Cyrus Graesner who worked undercover for the Justice Department?"

Graesner threw back his head and laughed, the sound coming from deep in his chest, booming out over the pond.

"Was that funny?" Ryan said. His own heart was starting to hurl itself against his rib cage. He was the son of Adam and Eve, professional assassins. He'd known it, as soon as he saw Cyrus Graesner's face go slack. Any doubt he'd had was gone. He looked down on the little man by the pond. He seemed to be laughing from a great distance.

Graesner slapped his legs as the laughter subsided. Then he wiped the back of his hand across his nose. "I'm sorry. What I did was sleep with women, do lots of good drugs, play with guns, and listen to a bunch of crazy SOBs plot the overthrow of the U.S. government. I wouldn't quite call that working." He waved a hand. "Come on down."

Ryan and Cass came down the stairs and sat on the cold concrete, a few feet from Graesner. "Don't mind Tanis. She's a good girl. I got her away from a bad home situation and now she's overprotective of me." He rubbed his nose again.

"Another cold. It's one cold after another, all winter long. I'm paying now for everything I did to my body back then. So tell me, what name did they give you?"

"Ryan Elder. Who's 'they'?"

"You know."

Ryan leaned forward. "No, I don't know."

Graesner narrowed his gaze. "How much have your folks told you?"

"Nothing." Ryan took a breath. "They're dead. They committed suicide seven years ago. Drove their car into a bunch of construction equipment. There was an explosion."

Graesner watched Ryan closely, as if gauging whether he was telling the truth. Then he dropped his eyes and looked off toward the pond. He looked away for a long time, and when Graesner turned back to Ryan, he had the look of a man faced with an unpleasant chore. "Adam and Eve committed suicide." He shook his head slowly. "How much *do* you know, son?"

"Very little. They sent me this." He pulled the clipping out of his pocket and handed it to Graesner. "Evidently I was supposed to receive it right after they killed themselves, but because I . . . I sort of moved around quite a bit, it only caught up with me last week."

Graesner examined the paper, reading over the tops of his glasses. He handed it back to Ryan. "Doesn't mean squat to me. I knew Eve was into music, but hey, I was listening to Dylan in those days. Tell me, what do you do in real life?"

"I'm a journalist."

A tight smile from Graesner. "Of course you are. Newspaper or TV?"

"Neither. I'm in radio. At least I was."

"Radio. Well, that's refreshing. How'd you get my name?"

"There's a professor—"

"Oh, you mean the Nicaraguan woman in Buffalo? 'I'm a child of the Contras' and all that? She's a stubborn one. I hung up on her at least five times. I should send Tanis around to talk to her."

"Look, I just want to know a few simple things. Like my

parents' real names, *my* real name, how they became what they were—"

"Just a minute . . . is it Ryan? That's the name you grew up with? What did they call your parents?"

"Frank and Anna."

"And the last name?"

"Elder."

"Elder, right. Well, you want to know more than just a few things, and not one of them is simple, Ryan Elder." Graesner looked at Cass, who had sat silent the entire time. "Who's this?"

"A friend. She's saved my life a couple of times in the last few days. Talk to me. I have to know."

Graesner's nose was running and he wiped it this time with his coat sleeve. "Wish I weren't sick all winter long." He looked up at Ryan again. "No, you really don't *have* to know, son."

"Don't call me son. Your meeting in the fall of 1975 is the last trace of Adam and Eve. I want to know what happened, before and after."

Graesner sighed, and it seemed to come from deep within his scrawny body. "They're dead. Let them rest." He stood up abruptly and started to walk away, toward the steps on the far side of the little amphitheater.

"Graesner!" Ryan shouted.

"Leave it alone. Go on with your life. Go home." Graesner sniffled again.

For a few seconds Ryan stood immobile, then suddenly, like a storm from a clear sky, the old Ryan was back, the angry young man who threw things and got in people's faces and told them what he thought, consequences be damned. With clear-eyed rage, he bounded off the steps and grabbed Graesner's coat.

"Hey!" Graesner shrieked.

Ryan took double handfuls of the older man's coat and whirled him around, slamming his back into the concrete wall at the base of the steps. "Talk to me." His voice was low, dangerous. "You know what they were. You knew what they did, and somehow, you know why they changed. My whole life has been a lie, Graesner. One big, carefully plotted lie. You are going to talk to me."

Graesner's eyes were wary but showed no fear. "What do you want out of it? You think you'll get some kind of revelation, some huge insight into yourself? Well, you're wrong. You'll only have more questions, and some of them don't even have answers, much less answers I can give you."

Ryan tightened his grip. "No, you're the one who's wrong. This isn't just some screwed-up kid who's just found out these terrible things about his parents. Someone else is moving around in all this, a man who always talks in a whisper. He's after me, and he wants me to find something for him. He killed Dorian, he killed my best friend." Ryan swallowed hard, and then the rage was draining away, like fluid from an abscess. "I think somehow he pushed my parents over the edge. I think he's the reason they killed themselves."

Ryan let go of Graesner's coat and backed away a few steps. He made his eyes focus and realized that Graesner's face had changed. Now the man looked scared.

"What?" Ryan said.

"A man who talks in a whisper." Graesner coughed violently, hacking out a wad of yellow phlegm onto the ground. He smeared it around the sidewalk with his shoe. "Is that what you said? Oh, sweet Jesus, boy, you have stepped in it."

"You know him?"

"I knew him back then. As much as anyone could."

Ryan held his breath. "Who is he? What does he want?"

"The name I knew him by was Terrence Ross. As to what he wants . . . oh, hell. You better tell me what's happened." Moving stiffly, he sat back down. "I thought all this was behind me. I've got my little house, my garden, I live with two young girls who are crazy about me, and I'm totally clean." Graesner crossed his legs. "I'm getting goddamn arthritis too, I think. I guess we all pay for our sins in different ways. Me, my body's giving out, piece by piece, and now here you are, dredging up Terrence Ross and Adam and Eve."

Ryan told him what had happened over the past week,

then said, "Tell me. How did you meet them? How did you meet this Ross?" Ryan sat down beside Graesner.

Graesner shook his head and looked around the water stage. They were alone. The park was quiet. Only faint sounds of traffic from Reno on the south and Sheridan on the north came to them. "I did two years in Army Intelligence. I was in Berlin from sixty-eight to seventy-one. I didn't do very much, mainly listened to officers brag about the size of their balls and what they'd done with German women. But they sent me on a few runs into the DDR, you know, the old East Germany. At twenty-one, I looked sixteen. Also, my dad was German, so I spoke the language like a native. They liked that."

Graesner coughed and wiped his nose. "When I got out of my hitch, I didn't know what to do. I figured I'd come back home to Oklahoma and see what shook out. But Uncle Sam answered that little dilemma for me. The Justice Department was forming a special task force right about then. The government's big on task forces, you know. They'd seen a lot of growth in fringe groups and with the little discussion going on in southeast Asia, they figured it was going to get worse. They wanted to infiltrate. Now, keep in mind that this wasn't J. Edgar and the FBI. This group reported directly to the Attorney General. There was a controller, a guy not much older than I was, and then the A.G. Nice, streamlined power structure, none of the usual bureaucracy. I didn't care about politics one way or the other, and they liked that too, because they said I wouldn't sympathize with one group over another."

"So you went undercover."

"Oh, yeah. I was all over: Berkeley, Madison, New Haven, New York, Mississippi. I hung with the Weathermen and with DePugh and the Minutemen. Now that's about as far apart as you can get. I fed little bits of data back to Washington, and for the most part, the government could stay one step ahead of these groups. What was so funny was that they didn't really need me in there. They were paying me all this money and I was getting dope and booze and women, and it wasn't even necessary."

"Why not?" Cass said.

Graesner looked at her. "I'd feel a lot more comfortable if you'd take your hand out of your pocket."

"I don't have a weapon. If I did, I might have used it on our whispering friend."

Graesner cocked his head, as if listening for a far-off sound. "You've seen him? I mean, seen him up close?"

"You could say that," Cass said.

"What did he look like?"

"He was wearing a mask. But he was muscular, strong. Not really big, but very strong."

"Interesting. Because no one ever saw Ross. Never, in all the years I was working."

"You said it wasn't necessary for you to be there," Ryan said, and he began digging at his thumbs. "Why was that?"

"Yep, you're a journalist, all right," Graesner said. "Direct the conversation the way you want it to go." He shrugged, his shoulders small inside the huge black coat. "The groups were always bickering amongst themselves. Their petty little internal squabbles did most of them in. Just like the Soviet Union, for God's sake. Self-destruction from within. But I spent a few years drifting around and feeding things to D.C."

"What about Adam and Eve?"

"What about them? They changed everything. When you put professionals into the middle of a bunch of amateurs, the world starts to spin in a different direction. The first hit of theirs that I knew of was paid for by the Revolutionary Communist Party. They wanted to show how capitalism was destroying the world, so of course they had a businessman killed. The president of one of the big retail chains. He was shot sniper-style at a football game at Ohio State University in Columbus. A page of music was stuffed in the pocket of his coat. No one could figure out how he was shot from far off, but someone was close enough to put sheet music in his pocket." Graesner looked at Ryan squarely. "You sure you want to hear this?"

Ryan nodded, fighting nausea.

"All right, then." Graesner shifted on the concrete step.

"Eve was always said to be the better one with guns. And since people didn't expect a woman to be skilled with a gun, she could get into a lot of places. Adam was the explosives expert. Car bombs, pipe bombs, little tiny firecracker bombs. He was also supposed to be better at tracking, at setting up the targets. I don't like telling you this. I want you to know that. I don't get off on this kind of thing."

"I know," Ryan said. "Go on."

"It went on for a couple-three years. I met them once. It was in L.A., somewhere down around Newport Beach. This would've been in about seventy-four, I think in the spring. Or maybe it was fall. Sorry, the memory's not what it should be. Too many good drugs back then. I was in one of the weird little offshoots of SDS at the time. This was a tiny little group, but one of the honchos was a kid who came from money. His dad was a big Hollywood producer. His idea was to start assassinating members of Congress. He wanted to go down a list of every state's congressmen, pick out one who had been a supporter of the war in Vietnam, and just blow them away, one by one. In all the years I was underground, that was the single stupidest thing I ever heard. The logistics of it. . . ."

Graesner's tone had turned matter-of-fact, as if he were discussing an expansion of the family business instead of mass assassinations. "But he'd managed to make contact with Adam and Eve, and they came to this big beach house we had there. It belonged to the guy's father. After he outlined the plan, I remember this—Adam and Eve looked at each other like they'd just wasted a lot of time. Your mother very politely declined the contract, and they got up and walked out."

"Did you meet them? Did you talk to them?"

"There wasn't time." Graesner sneezed and wiped his arm on his sleeve again. "Goddamnit, I hate being sick. No, I didn't talk to them. But I remember thinking how gorgeous Eve was. Those blue eyes, and the accent when she talked. And she seemed so cultured . . . sophisticated, I guess. Adam was another story. He was quiet and sat very still. I've never seen anyone who could be as still as he was that night at the beach."

Ryan thought of his father's long silences and of the way he could be so still it seemed as if he'd stopped breathing.

"I didn't see them again until . . . well, you know, I suppose. Thanksgiving of seventy-five."

Ryan leaned in. He caught Graesner's scent, stale and sickly.

"But then, I'm getting ahead of my story. This is where Terrence Ross, also known as the Whispering Man, comes in. I'd been hearing Ross's name for a while. He was the head of a group called The New America, and he set about slowly building a small group of people committed to violent revolution. But like I told you, no one ever saw him. He worked by phone, or he'd make tape recordings to send to his people in the field. I was ordered to stay away from TNA. Very explicit instructions from the task force controller: Do not try to infiltrate The New America. Do not associate with Terrence Ross. Do not pass go. It was very clear."

"Why?" Ryan's mind raced ahead. "It seems this is just the kind of group they would want you to infiltrate. Violent revolution, you said."

Graesner nodded. "That's what I said. But under no circumstances was I to touch them."

"Why?" Ryan said again.

"I found out in the spring of seventy-five, but not from my controller. I was in a motel in Jacksonville, Florida. I'd been under with a group protesting at the naval training ground there. The phone rang, and here was this whisper. 'I know you,' he says. Ross had already gotten this 'Whispering Man' identity, so I knew who it was. He told me he knew what I was and who I was working for and then he told me something else." Graesner gazed off into the distance. "Dammit, I haven't thought of this stuff in so long. He told me I was lucky, and that he was going to tell me all about something big, something *huge*, that was going to happen within the next few months, something that would reshape American society."

Ryan straightened slowly. "Reshape society."

"That's what the man said, or whispered. Then he sort of laughed and said that he and I were like brothers, that I was sort of like his protector."

"What?"

Graesner sneezed and pulled his coat around him. "I think it's getting colder. Damn, I hate winter."

"But what—"

"Like brothers, he said. And then I understood what he meant. Terrence Ross, the Whispering Man, was also under the protection of the U.S. Department of Justice."

34

TERRENCE ROSS.

The Whispering Man.

The U.S. Department of Justice.

Ryan felt light-headed. It was conspiracy theory stuff, the kind of story for people who were obsessed with Waco and Ruby Ridge and the Murrah Building bombing. But then again—

Think like a reporter, dammit. You haven't forgotten how, he said to himself.

The notorious Adam and Eve were professional assassins, who had by then been operating in the U.S. for over two years. Wouldn't the government do everything in their power to stop them?

Ryan squeezed his eyes closed, reminding himself that his parents were the ones who were the criminals. But his mind flitted back to Cheyenne, to Art Dorian. Is this what the little man had meant to tell him?

Rifle shots, on the ridge. Dorian, running along the path: *"I'm trying to save your life!"*

"It's not what you think," Graesner said, as if reading Ryan's mind. He stood up. "It's almost noon. Let's get something to eat. I may be sick, but I still need to eat."

Ryan didn't move.

"You opened this can of worms," Graesner said, standing up. "If I have to show you what's inside it, I at least want a lunch out of the deal."

Ryan nodded, too numb to speak. He and Cass stood and followed Graesner up the steps. Outside the amphitheater, the wind blew steadily. "Let's go across Sheridan to the Lunch Box. I don't guess you've been there."

"Yes, I have," Ryan said.

Graesner looked over his shoulder at him.

"My father worked downtown and I remember him taking me there a few times."

"You lived here? In Oklahoma City?"

"I grew up in Edmond. My dad worked in insurance."

"Well, I'll be damned. Guess you've got me to thank for that. I never would've thought—"

"What do you mean?" They were approaching the corner of Sheridan and Hudson Avenue, at the edge of the Myriad Gardens.

"That part comes later," Graesner said, and pushed the button for the light on the corner.

They crossed Sheridan going north, skirting the Stage Center Theater, with its circular structures and multicolored walkways connecting the buildings, and its strange assortment of aerial tubes. Ryan had always thought it looked more like a power plant than a theater.

Graesner then turned back to the east, passing the Union bus station and stopping before a small glass-fronted restaurant. The Lunch Box looked as if it belonged on the courthouse square of a small town instead of the heart of the inner city. It was a cafeteria-style restaurant, with hot food under glass to the right just inside the door, a row of booths on the left.

Ryan stepped in behind Graesner, and he realized he was still holding Cass's hand, and had been ever since the Myriad Gardens. He blinked at the restaurant. It was just past eleven o'clock and the lunch rush was still a few minutes from beginning. A few men over sixty sat at a center table, coffee cups in front of them. Ryan remembered his father had said it was a popular spot for discussing local politics. His father, the political assassin.

He squeezed Cass's hand. Ahead of them, Graesner was saying something about meat loaf. The young woman behind the steaming trays of food was looking at him expectantly. He glanced down: creamy mashed potatoes, assorted vegetables, meat loaf, fried chicken, salads, pie, cake. His stomach turned.

"Just something to drink," he finally said. "A Pepsi."

Cass took a green salad, paid for the meals, and they crossed to the rear of the room. Cass picked at her salad and Ryan simply watched as Graesner off-loaded meat loaf with potatoes and brown gravy, green beans, fried okra, peach pie.

"Good stuff," Graesner said, and cut into the meat loaf.

Ryan slammed his glass of Pepsi onto the table, spilling cola and ice cubes. One cube streaked across the table and dropped in Graesner's lap.

"Hey!" Graesner said, then lowered his voice. "Boy, you're not very good at this game, are you?"

"This is no goddamned game. Do I have to sit here and watch you stuff your face before you explain all of this to me?"

Graesner stopped with another forkful of meat, dripping gravy, halfway to his mouth. He met Ryan's eyes, and Ryan saw Graesner's face had turned hard. He thought for the first time that there was more to Graesner than a simple snitch. The man had swung from aloofness to fear to matter-of-fact storytelling, now to something darker.

Graesner lowered the fork and set it silently on the plate. "You want to start being careful, now." Ryan thought his Oklahoma drawl had thickened.

The two men glared at each other until Cass leaned in and quietly said, "This isn't a school playground and this is no time for playing king of the hill, you two. Ryan's right—this is no game. You said Ross worked for the Justice Department. Was he part of some elaborate sting to catch Adam and Eve, or what?"

Graesner swung his gaze to Cass. "Sting, huh? Honey, no one talks that way. You've read too many spy novels." He looked at Ryan again. "There's something you have to know about the underground. It wasn't like life here in the real world. No one was who you thought they were and *everyone* had an ulterior motive. There were layers and layers and layers of this stuff."

Graesner sniffled and moved some green beans around on his plate. Then, in a sudden jerky movement, he dropped his fork squarely in the center of his plate, sending a distinct, resonant sound through the restaurant. Several of the men at the next table looked over.

Graesner leaned across the table, his face inches from Ryan's. "Look, boy, let's just end this little dance right now. I can pick up the phone, and with one call, have the FBI and federal marshals and a few other agencies all over you. I have a hunch they're anxious to meet you."

Ryan stabbed his finger into the Formica tabletop. "That's bullshit, Graesner. The government cut you loose. You weren't even important enough to them to conceal your name. I doubt the Justice Department today even knows who you are."

Graesner's face reddened. "Is that what you think?"

Ryan spoke slowly, deliberately. "Yeah. It is." He glanced at Cass. "Let me have the phone." She handed it to him and he placed it on the table between himself and Graesner. "Here. Make the call."

Graesner didn't move.

"Go ahead. I won't stop you. Call them."

Graesner stared at the phone, then at Ryan, and finally his face softened again. He picked up his fork, stabbed a piece of fried okra, and pointed it at Ryan. "When I was working underground, the groups on the left wouldn't play poker if you played for money. Money was irrelevant and personal gain was poisoning our society, all that shit. The rightists, of course, said 'deal' and you took your chances. Of course, if you won, you took the risk that someone would shoot you in the name of America. I was a lousy player." He ate the okra, chewing slowly. "Called my bluff, didn't you?"

Ryan took the phone and gave it back to Cass. More people were trickling into the Lunch Box, men and women in power suits, laborers in jeans and down vests. The noise level rose.

Graesner ate another piece of meat loaf. "Ross didn't exactly work for the Justice Department. At least not the way you're thinking. Not the way I worked for them. He just used it as a cover."

Ryan waited.

"What's that supposed to mean?" Cass said.

Graesner ate more meat loaf. Some brown gravy dribbled down his chin and he wiped it with his sleeve. He took a sip of water. "First things first. Ross didn't want to arrest Adam and Eve. He wanted to hire them."

"Hire them?" Ryan leaned in again. "For what?"

"Well, what the hell do you think? They were assassins, so obviously he wanted them to do a job."

"But if he was—"

"You don't pay attention very well, boy. I don't know what kind of reporter you were, but you sure don't pay attention. I told you before that everyone, and I mean *everyone*, had an ulterior motive. Nothing was what you thought it was. Ross would call me at odd times over the next few months, after that first time in Florida. I never knew how he got my location. I guess he got it from my controller, but he always found me. He told me this story over that spring and summer." Graesner belched softly, then ate more okra.

"And?" Ryan said.

"And Ross was part of what he called a 'foundation.' I always got a kick out of that, he made it sound like some kind of a charitable group, like the United Way or some such. This foundation had been set up a few years earlier by Ross's father."

Ryan felt his blood begin to hum in his ears. "His father?"

"Ross's father had evidently been in the OSS in World War Two. You know what that is?"

"The forerunner of the CIA."

"Good, so you know at least a little bit of history. Around 1960, the old man started to get pissed off at the way the country was going and he suddenly quit the government. Just took early retirement and moved out to Richmond, Virginia. Set up this foundation there. Ross told me about it: it was called ACE."

"ACE?"

"Americans Combating Extremism. You see, as we got into the sixties and the world started going crazy on all sides, the old man convinced himself that extremists were ruining the country. Didn't matter whether they were on the left or the right, he wanted everything back to the middle-of-the-road Eisenhower politics of the fifties, when things just sort of sailed along. That's a load of shit, of course, but it's what the old man believed."

"What did this ACE do?" Cass said, leaning over her salad.

"Well, the way Ross told this story to me, the old man still had a lot of friends in the government. Very powerful friends, if you know what I mean. Particularly in the Justice Department. About the same time the task force was created that gave me a job, Ross's old man came to an 'arrangement' with the department. ACE would do everything in its power to stop extremist organizations. Where normal channels failed, ACE could step in and do anything. *Anything.* Get my drift?"

"I think I do," Ryan said. "If your information couldn't stop a group from doing something, ACE could step in and do things that you, as a government employee, couldn't do. And the Justice Department would have perfect deniability, since ACE wasn't part of the government."

"You understand. Now, the government never gave ACE a dime. It was an informal arrangement, you see. Just the thanks of a grateful nation. They ran around and set fire to a few meeting halls of some of the groups, plopped bullets into a few heads—"

"I'm sorry," Cass said. "I can't buy this. I don't believe the government was involved in something like that. It doesn't make sense."

Graesner tapped his fork against the table. "Does anyone

here listen to anything I say? Write this down, girl: *the government wasn't involved.* Say someone high up in the government had a meeting with Ross's father, a respected former public servant, and this person chanced to say, 'I sure wish such-and-such extremist group would stop making so much noise.' And Ross's father says, 'So do I.' And then they talk about sports or the stock market or who's screwing who in Washington or who knows what. No one in the government told ACE to do anything, they didn't give ACE any money, ACE didn't report to them. You see? Informal."

Ryan sat back, trying to digest everything this strange man was saying. His mind raced, shifting into reporter mode. "So The New America was Ross's cover for ACE. He built up an extremist movement of his own to give him credibility in the underground network, to make a name for himself, so he could . . . do what? Destroy the groups? Obviously, that didn't happen."

"Ah, you see, this is where it gets complicated."

"It's not already complicated?" Cass said.

Graesner smiled. "Honey, until you've been under with some of these people and heard some of the plots they hatched, you don't know what complicated is." He looked back to Ryan. "You're not quite right, but you're on the right track. He said he wanted to hire Adam and Eve to do one big job, something huge. But first let me give you a little background. These people, Ross and his old man, were strange birds. The old man was so paranoid, so sure his enemies would do anything to get him, that he gave his only son a different name from his and sent him off to boarding school. A different last name. Can you believe that? Just so no one would know he was his son. Then he would meet the kid way out in a broken-down cabin out in the woods about twice a year. The kid had to be blindfolded before he could see his own father! The old man was screwed in the head, if you ask me. Then, a few years later, the old man sent the kid away to college, and after all that, he finally brought him into ACE. So the kid cooked up that name, Terrence Ross, and got into the underground."

"The big job," Ryan said. "That has to be it. That's what he's after now. Something to do with the big job."

"But the big job didn't happen," Graesner said, and cut off another slice of meat loaf.

"And now, after all these years, he wants to make it happen." Ryan felt flushed. He'd never been this close to knowing what was happening to him. "What was the job?"

Graesner slowly shook his head, chewing. "Can't help you there. But there's one last twist—as far as the old man was concerned, The New America was this great cover for the work his son was actually doing, wiping out extremists and all that crap. But Ross told me, and here's the kicker, that he was serious about it. He really *did* want a violent revolution and the old man's contacts in the government were giving him the perfect cover. They thought The New America was a scam, but in fact it was the other way around. Ross wanted to screw his old man, tear down everything the old SOB had worked for. This is when Ross got really weird, talking his grand revolution that would strike at every part of the system and bring the whole country crashing down." Graesner pushed himself back from the table. "At the time, I thought Ross was like me, that he'd taken way too much dope and was out of his head. But he wasn't. Man, he was as straight and serious as could be. I was relieved when he dropped out of sight. I never talked to him again after September of that year, and as far as I know, he just faded away. My controller wouldn't talk about it, and after that I ran into a few problems, so they cut me loose."

"What kind of problems?"

Graesner sniffled and put down his fork. He unbuttoned the cuffs of his loose-fitting shirt and rolled up his sleeves.

Ryan stared at the needle marks, which ran like a connect-the-dots puzzle up and down both arms.

Cass sucked in her breath. "Oh—"

"Don't say anything," Graesner said, and rolled down his sleeves. "I've been clean for nearly twenty years now, and I don't blame Justice for letting me go. I started missing assignments because I was too strung out to do anything." He shrugged. "Past history, just like all this stuff."

Ryan shook his head. "Your controller. You've mentioned him several times. Why wouldn't he talk about Ross? Who was he?"

"The controller? Big guy named Clarke, Phillip Clarke. He was some kind of a whiz kid, destined for greatness. After all the shit with ACE and Ross and Adam and Eve, he was transferred out somewhere, to some other agency. I never heard from him again."

"Thanksgiving 1975," Ryan said. "You said you met my parents."

Graesner sighed and wiped his nose. "I was back home then, right here in good old Oklahoma. I was between assignments, just hanging out in my little house, mostly stoned. It was Thanksgiving Day and I was about to go to my mom's place. She and my baby sister thought I had this great job selling typewriters for IBM, traveling all over the country selling typewriters to small companies. Typewriters!" Graesner snorted out a laugh, which devolved into a fit of coughing.

"I walked out onto the porch of my little house and there was Eve, with this big goddamned automatic pistol in my face. 'Let's go back inside,' she says in that beautiful accent. We go in and Adam's already there. Somehow he'd gotten in my house and I thought I was dead. My cover was blown and someone had paid them to kill me, simple as that. Then Adam says, 'We know what you are.' I *knew* I was dead. But Eve puts the gun down, sits at my kitchen table, and I just then noticed."

"Noticed what?" Ryan said.

Graesner smiled crookedly. "That she was pregnant. *Very* pregnant, like she was about ready to pop. I knew they'd done that Pentagon guy a month or so before, and I remembered how the witnesses said the woman who shot him was pregnant. Amazing. Hell of a woman. And she looks at me and says, 'We're quitting.' Just like that."

Blood roared in Ryan's ears, drowning out the restaurant noise. "Quitting?"

"That's what I said. They said they'd had enough, that they were going to retire and Adam and Eve would just fade into the sunset. Adam said they'd agreed to do this one last huge job for Terrence Ross and The New America, but it was too far out and they weren't going to fulfill the contract." Graesner leaned forward, his murky eyes suddenly alight. "Get this, boy. They weren't just going to retire, but they were going to the government. They wanted to make a deal."

Ryan gripped the edge of the table. The restaurant seemed to spin. "Department Thirty," he finally managed to say.

"And so it goes." Graesner wiped his mouth and tossed his napkin onto his plate. "I thought they were crazy. The government wouldn't deal with the two most notorious assassins in the world. No way in hell. But Eve—your mom—explained it to me. They knew more about the world than any government agency. They had names, they had dates, they had places, they had account numbers. They had *dirt*. Serious dirt, folks. They were going to turn it all over to the U.S. government in exchange for new lives. They figured, would the government want a couple of hired hands, or would they want to know who hired them?"

"But . . ." Ryan was struggling, the thoughts only half-formed. "They were professionals. They'd been living underground for years. They didn't need the government to give them new lives. They could have just disappeared. Why did they—"

"Guilt," Cass said.

Both men's heads turned.

"The lady wins the prize," Graesner said. "That was one part of it. Guilt, and—"

"Me," Ryan said.

"Yes, sir. Here's our grand prize winner. I never knew why they got into the killing game, but I know why they got out. They'd had enough of the blood, and the baby was due any time, and this was their . . . what's the word? *Atonement*, is what my good Jewish friends would call it. Their penance." He sat back in his seat and folded his hands over his stomach. "You've heard of WITSEC, right?"

"What?" Ryan said.

"Witness Security. Sometimes you hear it called the Witness Protection Program, but that's not the real name. It started in 1970, you know, to protect people who saw things, who knew things. It was designed to help in prosecuting the Mafia, mainly. Ah, but they put together Department Thirty at the same time, specifically for people like Adam and Eve. I bet Congress never dreamed they'd be holding hands with the world's best assassins, but there it is. Thirty was supposed to create new identities for criminals, while the regular WITSEC program was strictly for witnesses. Adam and Eve went into Department Thirty protection and right there is why your name is what it is. Some clever public servant in Department Thirty probably named you."

Dorian, Ryan thought. "You said earlier that you were the reason they were in Oklahoma. What's that all about?"

Graesner snorted. "Adam told me that day in my kitchen that I was to spread the word that Adam and Eve were gone. Just gone, not available for any more work. Adam and Eve weren't going to exist anymore. I was to tell the underground, through my contacts on both sides. Then I asked them if they knew where they were going to settle. They didn't. I was being a smart-ass and said they ought to come right here to Oklahoma. Clean air, nice people, low cost of living, and no one would look for them here. I remember Adam said that he'd thought of that as they were driving across the country to get to me. Something he'd read had really gotten to him, about one of the big Indian battles out west. 'We just might,' he said. I never knew that really happened until you showed up. Be damned if strange things don't happen all the time."

"So," Ryan said, "Department Thirty created Frank and Anna Elder, my dad's background in Cheyenne, the story about my mother in Prague, the whole thing. In exchange for information."

"I don't know, but that's the deal they wanted to make. I'd say they probably made it. You know, as I think of it, there were an awful lot of arrests made in the six months after that."

"The big job," Ryan said, feeling flushed again. He ran a hand over his face, momentarily puzzled by the lack of a beard. My father, he remembered. I look like my father. His stomach lurched again. "What was the big job?"

"I already told you, I don't know that. But I do know this, boy. If it made Adam and Eve decide then was the time to retire and give it up to the government, then it must have been one hell of a job. As for Ross, who knows? He disappeared too. He probably went back to his real identity, whatever it was—"

"So Terrence Ross wasn't his real name?" Cass said.

"Oh, hell no. He told me that the first time I talked to him. Like I said, layers and layers."

"Did you ever get his father's name?" Ryan said. "In all those phone calls, did he ever mention any names?"

"Of course not. He gave me just enough to want more, then he'd pull in. Arrogant son of a bitch." Graesner looked at Ryan, clear-eyed. "Boy, I'm sorry for what's happened to you, and I don't know what to say about your folks' suicide, but you were born into a weird world."

Ryan felt Cass's hand on his arm. He glanced at her, felt his eyes burning. Suddenly the restaurant seemed very warm. He swallowed. "Now I know why the government's so anxious to bring me in."

Graesner nodded. "I don't reckon they'd want it to be public record that they made a deal with people like your folks. They may have gotten some good convictions out of it, but the public has a habit of not going along with things like that. Congressional hearings, indictments, careers ruined . . . and then there's you, Ryan."

Ryan looked up. It was the first time Graesner had called him by his name.

"And you'd be the star of the show. So, yeah, I guess that along with your troubles from Ross, if that's really him jerking your chain, old Department Thirty probably wants to visit with you." Graesner picked up his fork. "I don't know another goddamned thing. But I do know this pie's getting cold." He began to eat again.

• • •

When Ryan and Cass had gone, Graesner finished his pie and drank two cups of coffee before putting on his coat and heading back into the cold. He found a pay phone at the bus station and pulled his crinkled leather wallet—same one he'd had for thirty years—out of his pocket.

He searched through the pockets until he found a business card with one edge torn away and a brown stain across the bottom. The name and the phone number were clear, though. He called the number.

When he heard the voice on the other end, Graesner said, "This is Cyrus. Remember me?" He waited, then said, "Just like old times, huh? Looks like you may have a problem."

35

THE WHISPERING MAN, AKA TERRENCE ROSS, WAS DRIVing across Hudson Avenue on Sheridan when he saw Ryan Elder and the woman come out of the Lunch Box deep in conversation, Ryan making insistent hand gestures.

Ross U-turned in the middle of Sheridan and pulled in at a parking meter. He was breathing hard, his heart racing, and he knew why.

The boy had shaved his beard. Ryan looked just like Adam-Frank. It was his father all over again!

Ross gripped the steering wheel. He hadn't seen the boy since Cheyenne, but he'd followed the investigation through Clarke and the ever-resourceful Deputy Kelly. What was he doing? He watched Ryan and the woman as they crossed the street by the bus station, Ryan still talking, shaking his head occasionally.

Ross was about to pull the car back into traffic and follow at a reasonable distance when he saw another figure come out of the Lunch Box. Yes. Ryan Elder had found Cyrus Graesner.

Ross was almost shaking with anticipation. It was coming together. The boy was gathering information. By now, after talking to Graesner, he would have Terrence Ross's name. He would know what his parents had been, some of what they had done. He would be aware of the unfinished business.

Even better, Ryan Elder showed no signs of falling apart the way his parents had seven years ago. Ross remembered when he had finally called Adam and Eve—Frank and Anna Elder. He'd known their identities for years, thanks to one tiny mistake by Art Dorian. But the timing hadn't been right until seven years ago. Ross had waited patiently until everything was right, biding his time, waiting, year after year. Then he simply picked up the phone and called the home number of Frank and Anna Elder.

I know who you are, he'd whispered when Anna came on the line. *I've always known. And now it's time to finish what we started.*

There had been a pause, and he heard Eve—*Anna*—breathing on the line before she hung up. Three days later the Elders' car crashed at the construction site. Three days later his plans literally went up in smoke. Until. . . .

Ross watched as Ryan Elder vanished into the Myriad Gardens. The boy would be angry now, confused, and he would want to confront Terrence Ross, the Whispering Man.

"Good," he said aloud, in a clear voice. "Very good, Ryan." No whispering needed now.

Ross watched Cyrus Graesner go into the bus station, saw him on the phone, watched him come out again, wiping his nose. The old fool looked pathetic, with his long gray ponytail and his ill-fitting clothes.

Graesner, my old confidante. No doubt he sang to Ryan like a soprano at the Met. Graesner, who had thought of himself as a great weapon in the battle against extremism. But he'd surrendered to the needle and the lure of unbridled sex.

Ross's head began to throb, as it did more and more often of late. There were moments—snippets of time which flashed by like bullets—when he wasn't sure who he was supposed to be. Before Adam and Eve's betrayal, he'd submerged himself into Terrence Ross, the Whispering Man. Even though he'd been living under his own name for years now, he still caught glimpses of Ross, more so lately, since he'd caught up to Ryan Elder in Pensacola.

He remembered when he'd told his father that The New America was blown, that he'd have to find another project. He'd stood there with his head down, hands folded in front of him, just like he'd done as a child when the old man insisted that he always whisper.

Veins had popped on the old man's neck, his eyes bulged. *We've invested nearly two years in this project, in infiltrating these low-life subversive groups, and all you can say is "There's been a setback"? That's not good enough!* he'd screamed.

Still he'd stared at the floor. *I'm sorry, Dad,* he'd said. But he was thinking: You sorry son of a bitch, if only you knew that The New America was real all the time, that your friends at the Justice Department gave me cover. If only you knew how close I came to starting the Revolution. If only Adam and Eve hadn't gotten scared, the Revolution would be in progress now, and you and your whole precious fucking system would be as dead as the Roman Empire, as dead as Hitler and Stalin and Kennedy, as dead as all those thousands of soldiers in Vietnam.

Sorry? Sorry! The old man had begun to splutter. *It was a mistake to think I could trust you, boy! You have no idea how important this is, how important I am! You will have nothing more to do with ACE. Nothing, do you hear me?*

But Dad, I can—

No, you can't, idiot! I'll continue my work here without you! Get away from me, get away from ACE. He'd lowered his voice and stabbed his finger into the teak surface of his immense desk. *So help me God, as long as I live, you will have nothing more to do with me, with my work.* Then, as if he were stabbing the words with a knife: *You . . . are . . . a . . . disgrace!*

He'd left the office with his head down, and outside, he'd begun to smile. The old man, who saw conspiracies and enemies everywhere, hadn't seen what was right in front of his face. All the better—Ross would have time to get the information he needed to set the Revolution back on the right track. He was patient.

Watching Cyrus Graesner, Ross shook himself out of the past and felt the stirring of pain behind his eyes again. He rubbed his hands together. Ryan Elder and the woman were gone. He leaned back against the fine leather of his car seat and watched Graesner standing by the door to the bus station, wiping his nose.

Ten minutes passed before a battered, ancient pea-green Chevy Monte Carlo pulled up. A very young black woman with blonde hair was driving. Graesner leaned down, said a few words to her, and got in the car. He kissed the woman, then the car headed north on Walker.

Ross followed carefully, watching as the Monte Carlo wound into the Flats. He stopped at the end of the block and noted which house Graesner and the black woman entered.

He picked up his cell phone. A moment after punching in the number, he said aloud, "Let's go visit an old friend."

Ross was sitting in his car in the parking lot of a pizza place at Tenth and Villa when Phillip Clarke pulled in. Clarke wasn't driving his usual government-issue sedan, but a new white Dodge pickup truck.

Ross chuckled as Clarke slid in next to him, ducking his head down so he wouldn't scrape the roof. "No company car today?" Ross said.

"This is all a big game to you," Clarke rumbled, "but it's goddamn serious to me. I want it done. I want it over and I *don't* want to hear from you anymore."

"Oh, you'll hear from me, even after it's over, my good old friend. We're like an old married couple, you and I. They may bicker and scream and throw things at one another, but they can't ever get a divorce."

Clarke's mouth twitched under his bushy mustache. "You're a goddamn riot, you know that? What do you want?"

Ross sighed. "Ryan has been talking to Cyrus Graesner."

To Ross's surprise, Clarke nodded. "I know. Graesner called me."

"You knew he was here? Why, of course you did. They probably sent you out here to keep an eye on him, didn't they?"

Clarke shrugged.

"How clever," Ross said. "Rather fortuitous, I'd say. So nice for us to all be 'together' again, in Oklahoma City, of all places."

"Fortuitous, my ass. They transferred me into the Marshals Service and Graesner was blown out of the task force and they plunked us down in one city, so each of us would be a reminder to the other. That's what the Attorney General told me, right to my face. But it's not like I've been *hanging out* with Cyrus. And I sure as hell didn't know what Adam and Eve's names were, or where they were living. I gave you what you wanted back then and I wanted out. Hell, I want out of this now. For you it's a damned crusade."

Ross's anger flared. "If you and your kind hadn't already failed, there wouldn't be any need for me to do anything. But you have, and so I will."

"Save the speeches. I don't care anymore. What do we do about Cyrus?"

"I think we should visit him," Ross said slowly. "Three old friends, veterans of some of the same battles. We should find out what he told the son of Adam and Eve. We should find out what names he mentioned."

A shadow crossed Clarke's face. "If he told them that I was in charge of the task force, that could get back to my office. No one here knows I was hooked up with it. Hell, the Bureau's still investigating Dorian's murder. They could—"

Ross looked with satisfaction at the anger crossing Clarke's big face. "Let's go, then."

Cyrus Graesner lay back on his bed and propped himself against three pillows. He looked at the two young women—Tanis with her striking skin contrasting with the bleached cornrows, wearing a white silk sheath and nothing else; and

Linda, in a black lace bra and panties. She was a little more slender than Graesner liked, but Tanis had brought her home six months ago with no explanation other than, "She's going to stay here for a while."

Graesner watched them standing in the doorway caressing each other, but for a moment he was distracted, thinking of that kid, Adam and Eve's son.

The son of Adam and Eve. He remembered Eve pointing that big automatic at him so long ago, just a few feet away from where he was right this minute. Adam and Eve had killed themselves and now Terrence Ross himself was chasing the kid, trying to finish the last big job. But why now?

And hadn't Clarke sounded scared shitless when Graesner called him from the bus station? A blast right out of the past. He'd had no reason to call Clarke in all these years, but now, he couldn't resist. The whole program—ACE and the task force and all that—was a fucking house of cards, and it had been from the word go. Ross and all his well-bred talk about reshaping society, about starting a revolution against a system that was corrupt. Graesner had just gone along because it was a job and it beat the hell out of selling typewriters.

And now the house of cards was about to tumble down on their heads, all because of that tall, skinny kid that looked just like Adam.

I love it, Graesner thought, and sighed with satisfaction as he turned his attention back to the girls. Tanis was taking the lead, as she always did, kissing Linda deeply, one of her hands squeezing the Latina's buttocks and the other teasing her nipples. Graesner reached under the sheet and found that he was already hard. He began to stroke himself, his eyes locked onto the two young women.

Tanis turned slightly toward him, guiding Linda, and Graesner had the full view of both of their young bodies. Even ten feet away, he thought he could feel the heat coming off them. Linda murmured some sex talk to Tanis—they knew he liked that—and Tanis applied both hands to the other girl's breasts.

Tanis's back was to the doorway now and she began kissing her way down from Linda's mouth, to her throat, sinking lower and lower. . . .

Graesner caught a tiny movement behind the girls and stopped touching himself. "What—" he said.

The two large figures appeared in the doorway and Tanis half turned from Linda, just in time to see the gun butt come crashing down on her head.

Linda screamed something in Spanish and the gun came down on her. The two women fell in opposite directions and blood began to pool on the hardwood floor.

Graesner rolled over, scrambling toward the bedside table. His .38 was in the drawer, if he could just—

"Don't do that, Cyrus," said the first man.

Graesner jerked as if he were a horse being reined. He knew that voice.

Then Clarke stepped fully into the room.

"Guess it's old home week," Graesner said, then sneezed.

"For Christ's sake, Cyrus, at least pull your pants up," Clarke said.

"You didn't have to hit my girls. You want me, you take me, but you leave my girls alone."

"How noble," the other man said, and looked at Graesner. "You know who I am?"

Graesner's heart roared in his ears and then he had it. Who else could it be? "So you finally decided to show me your face, Ross. Well, better late than never."

"Timing is everything, isn't it?" Ross said. "Pleasant little house you have here, Cyrus. I can't say much for the rest of the neighborhood, but you have a nice little corner of the world."

"Not much, but it's mine. News travels fast. Not like the old days."

Ross smiled. "You had a nice chat with Ryan Elder, I take it?"

Graesner wiped his nose and swung his legs off the bed. "You boys are just shitting your pants over that, huh? Wouldn't it be terrible if John Q. Public found out that the United States government gave new identities and jobs and a home and everything to the two most notorious hired killers in the world? I love a good scandal. Maybe I'll make the talk show circuit. Can't you see me talking to Oprah? I love Oprah."

"You always were a smart-ass, Cyrus," Clarke said, red-faced. "You're in no position to say anything. We're running the show here and you're just a stupid old fool who spends his time jacking off while young girls play with each other."

"Oh, that's good, Philly. Does anyone still call you Philly?" Ross had been standing silently by and Graesner noticed a small smile on the man's face. "And you, Ross, or whatever your real name is. You set all this up, chasing around after Adam and Eve's kid? You ought to know by now you're never going to get that wonderful society you always wanted to make. It's a fairy tale."

Graesner moved a few more inches toward the table.

"It's no fairy tale, Cyrus," Ross said, and his voice had dropped to a whisper.

"Oh, so now you're The Whispering Man again." Keep them talking! "What have you done all these years? Still pissed off at your old daddy? Aren't you a little old for all that now?"

Ross's mouth twitched.

"All right," Clarke said. "What did you tell Elder?"

"Yeah, I knew we'd come back to that," Graesner said. He gained a few more inches in the direction of the table. "Well, I told him everything I could think of. The task force, Adam and Eve, The New America, ACE, even you, Philly."

Clarke came another step closer, stepping around Tanis's legs on the floor. "You gave him my name?"

"Of course I did. No reason not to. I figure the kid deserves to know everything."

Clarke's voice rumbled like distant thunder. "Goddamn you, Cyrus. You're still bound by security clearances. Don't you know that? You signed an oath—"

"Oh, fuck that oath, Philly. You come in here to my house, knock my girls around, and you talk to me about security clearances and oaths? You're a real piece of work."

"Shut up, Cyrus. You're about to—"

Tanis moaned and moved slightly on the floor, one of her legs brushing against Clarke's foot.

Graesner blinked, thinking first of Tanis—he would make this up to her. As Clarke looked down at her, Graesner saw the opening he needed. He rolled off the bed and clawed open the drawer of the bedside table.

"Cyrus—" one of them said. Graesner couldn't tell if it was Clarke or Ross.

He wrapped his hands around the butt of the old S&W .38 and swung it around to Clarke. For a second, his gaze strayed to the floor again. Tanis's eyes were still closed. Well, thank God for that. He didn't want her to see. . . .

His hand shook the butt of the gun and he had to steady it with the other one. Goddamn heroin, he thought. All those years he'd abused himself and now he couldn't keep his hands from shaking. He lifted his eyes, and the gun, and saw Clarke holding a big automatic, probably a nine-millimeter. Oh, shit.

Graesner squeezed off one shot, but his hands were shaking too badly and it went wild over Clarke's head, splintering the wood of the doorway. Then he saw Clarke's weapon come up, rock-steady. He didn't hear the sound, but he felt an enormous pressure in his chest, as if someone had dropped an anvil on him. Then his shirt was all wet, and Graesner didn't care anymore. He barely felt the second shot. As his eyes closed, he thought, I'm sorry, Tanis. I'll make it up to you.

Tanis Harper lay on her side, and through the drumbeat of pain in her head, she knew.

Pistol-whipped. She'd been hit with a gun butt once before, when she was fifteen and her gangbanger brothers beat her bloody and then let some of their friends take turns with her. Gang-banged by gangbangers, she'd thought at the time.

She opened her eyes slowly. At first she couldn't see anything but a gray blob, and she knew better than to move.

Play dead. That was the way to survive. She knew it too well.

Her eyes finally focused and that seemed to make the pain increase. She bit her lip to keep from letting out another involuntary moan. Her cheek was resting against the cold hardwood floor, a few feet from the bed, and the first thing she saw was a boot, then another. Gray shit-kicker cowboy boots, and a couple of legs in gray pants.

Then the boots moved a couple of steps away and she had a clear view of the bedside table.

Cyrus. Cyrus! No! screamed inside her head.

He was all crumpled up and blood was everywhere. It was on the shirt he was wearing, the one she'd bought him for Christmas. It was on the bed, the bed she shared with him. All over the floor, the table, even the lamp.

Tanis felt an overpowering emptiness, as if a part of her had been ripped out. He was just a skinny old white man, but he'd given her a real home with a little fence and a vegetable garden, and he'd bought her nice clothes, and he didn't get mad when she told him what she thought about things.

And he was stone cold dead.

The emptiness began to give way to something else and she blinked against pain and rage. The two men in the room were talking. Arguing, it sounded like. The voice closest to her—the voice that belonged to the shit-kicker boots, she thought—was a real rumbly, low voice, like the man had been gargling gravel. The other man was just an average white man's voice, kind of quiet. Tanis couldn't tell what they were saying, but Boots sounded strained and Quiet Man was in charge.

The boots stepped over her, seemed to hesitate for a few seconds, then moved on. The other man followed, a lighter step—not as big. In a minute, she heard the front door slam. Outside, a car started and drove away.

Tanis waited a few more minutes before she opened her eyes again. She moved her head around a little bit. Linda was beside her, still out cold, but she saw her chest moving. Tanis tried to crawl, but the pain was too intense.

Cyrus. Shot dead. Why?

She remembered that skinny guy from this morning and his girlfriend with her short hair. This wasn't him—his voice didn't sound like the two who'd just been here. But what was it he said? Hard to think. . . .

Just the past meeting the present, Cyrus had said when she picked him up at the bus station downtown. *Don't worry about it, T. Let's go home.*

The son of Adam and Eve.

The pain was too great, and Tanis finally gave in to it and closed her eyes.

36

TERRENCE ROSS . . . THE NEW AMERICA . . . THE JUStice Department . . . one last big job. . . .

Ryan's mind couldn't stop working. At the apartment, he wrote pages of notes from what Cyrus Graesner had told him. He wrote until his hand ached from gripping the pen. He wrote until his eyes throbbed with the strain. He filled pages of his notebook and it felt more real once he had written it down.

He was oblivious to Cass moving about the apartment in a nervous flutter. He didn't hear her using the cell phone to call her father's nurse, didn't hear her say, "I don't know how much longer I'll be away." Just like being on a big news story, his entire being was focused on what was before him.

But at the end of this story, when he'd gathered all the data and put it all together, there would be no quiet, solitary editing booth where he created a narrative with sound. This story was his life, and his life was the story. He'd be damn lucky to be alive at the end of it.

Some clever public servant named you, Graesner had said.

Art Dorian. This was what Dorian had wanted to tell him in Cheyenne. He wanted to tell Ryan who he really was.

Maybe he would explain what that last big job was, the thing that finally drove the infamous Adam and Eve to retire.

Ryan turned it over and over in his mind, facts sifting through like flour. He tried to think in terms of Adam and Eve's world. The challenge was divorcing Adam and Eve from his parents, thinking in terms of shadowy underground movements, money changing hands, and sudden, horrible violence. . . .

"I don't think so," he suddenly said aloud.

"What?" Cass said from the kitchen.

Ryan looked up and felt bathed in shame. For a moment he'd forgotten her, this woman who'd done so much for him, who'd saved his life in more ways than one. "I'm just going over what Graesner said. The key to what Ross wants from me has to be the last job, the job Adam and Eve backed out on. At first I thought that Dorian was probably going to tell me about it, but the more I think about it, that doesn't make sense."

Cass came into the room. "In what way?"

Ryan tapped his pen on the notebook. "When I showed Dorian the newspaper clipping my mother sent me, he seemed honestly puzzled by it. Didn't have a clue as to what it might mean. I think my parents didn't tell the government about the last job. I think that whatever it was, whatever this 'property' is that Ross keeps talking about, never came out."

Unable to sit still any longer, Ryan shot out of the chair and began to pace the room, rapidly flipping the pen between his fingers. "What was it Barrientos said about the government? She said something about the left hand and right hand not knowing what each other were doing. So my parents went to this brand new Department Thirty to purge their souls and give out information in return for new lives, but they didn't give up that last bit. It was too big."

Cass was nodding. "So Ross, and maybe this controller at the Justice Department, knew what it was about—"

"But Dorian and Yorkton and whoever else was in Department Thirty, which is also part of the Justice Department, didn't know." He spread his hands apart. "The left hand and the right hand. So Dorian didn't know that part. I don't think he knew what the 'property' was, or is. He just knew who Frank and Anna Elder had been. That's all he could have told me." Ryan stopped at the sliding glass door and rapped his knuckles against it. "Dammit! I need to think. . . ."

He sank back into the chair again, paging through the notes, the pen dancing against his palm. Cass watched him silently. "What did he say?" he muttered, turning pages. "What was it . . . Ross's father . . . this ACE that was behind Ross, it was something like a foundation. I wonder if the foundation would still exist." He looked up sharply. "Barrientos. Her research is on extremist political movements." He flipped back to the beginning of the notebook, where Barrientos's phone number was scribbled on a margin.

"Ryan—" Cass said.

He was reaching for the phone. "Just a minute." He punched in numbers, not noticing the troubled look on her face.

"C. J. Barrientos," said the voice a moment later.

"Professor Barrientos, it's Ryan Elder. We spoke yesterday."

"I remember. How's your . . . research?" The last word was drawn out and heavily accented.

Ryan cleared his throat. "The information you gave me was very helpful. I found out several things this morning. But I do have one follow-up question."

"Go ahead." Barrientos sounded guarded, wary.

"Have you ever heard of an organization called Americans Combating Extremism, or ACE? I think they're headquartered in—"

"Richmond, Virginia. Yes, I'm familiar with them."

"So it still exists."

"So far as I know. I tell you, though, that's an odd group. I came across them about a year ago. They're supposed to be a research foundation, with an archive of primary source material, and most places like that are very open to visiting scholars. ACE wouldn't give me the time of day. No one ever returned my phone calls or e-mails, and I finally gave up. I think it started out as some big shot's personal project and evolved from there."

Ross's father, the OSS agent, Ryan thought. "Do you have any contact information for them?"

"You won't get anywhere with them."

"I have to try."

"You're not a scholar, Mr. Elder. Why would they talk to you if they wouldn't talk to me?"

"Please, Professor. If I get anything—anything at all— from them, I'll pass it on to you."

There was a long pause. "You're an interesting man. I wonder if sometime I'll find out what it is you're *really* after."

"Maybe sooner than you think."

"Maybe so. Hold on." He glanced at Cass and shrugged. She was looking at him strangely, as if she wanted to say something. He held up a finger as Barrientos came back on the line. "All right, here's a phone number and a website." She read off the details and Ryan repeated them back to her, then thanked her and hung up.

"Okay," Ryan said, tapping the notebook against his leg. "I'm going to call this ACE—"

"Ryan," Cass said.

"And she said they have a website too. Every scrap of information helps, even if it doesn't seem important at the time. So I'll—"

"Ryan!" Cass screamed at him.

Ryan jerked, dropping his notebook and the phone. "Jesus! What? What is it?"

For a moment Cass seemed inarticulate, unable to find words. "All this," she finally said. "I need to know—what happens when it's over?"

Ryan stared back at her. "What kind of a question is that? I want my life back. I want to find out what the last big job was that my parents were going to do with Ross. I want to find out what his damned 'property' is, and—"

Cass leaned forward. "And then what?"

Silence filled the three feet between them. Ryan stood up, dug at his thumb, walked around the room, sat down again.

He made his voice tight. "Then I'll turn it all over to the cops. I'll give it to Kelly. I'll find Ross. I'll watch them arrest him. I'll find out my real name. Then I'll walk away, get another job, and try to have a life."

"That's what I'm asking. This life you're going to have— am I in it?"

Ryan took a step back as if she'd struck him.

"What I mean is, after Ross is gone and you have whatever you're looking for, then what?" She was almost pleading, as if searching for words that were hiding from her. "Look, my situation with my father may be difficult, but you could come back with me. You could help me. It would be easier with two of us and you could learn how to be connected to a family again. I could bring you to the school where I work with the special ed class. You could get to know my brothers and their kids—"

"Are you out of your mind? Good God, Cass, listen to what you're saying! I'm the only son of the two best assassins in the world and you're talking about creating some kind of Little House on the Prairie scenario."

"You are not your parents. Who they were or weren't, what they did . . . that doesn't define who you are." Her eyes bore into him. "Unless you let it."

Ryan stared for a moment, then looked away. "Look, I'm sorry I dragged you down. The kidnapping's over. Go on back to Cheyenne if you need to, but I have to end this."

Cass came out of her chair. "I know you have to end it. I never said you didn't. I—"

Ryan seemed not to have heard her. He pulled his hands back through his hair. "I thought you understood this. I thought you were the only other person who did. I guess you can't, but that's not your fault. All your life you've at least known who you were."

Cass thrust her left hand and its ruined fingers at his face. "This is who I was," she said. "The music is who I was, and now I don't have it! So I haven't known who I was for five years now, since Steven Williams sliced off the part of me that mattered. Don't you get it? I understand everything! And yes, I've used you just as much as you've used me, getting away from an intolerable situation with my father. There, I said it! But God help both of us, I've come to care about you and I'm afraid you're going to get killed, and I don't want to lose that too."

She backed away from him and Ryan saw for the first time the tears streaming down her beautiful, wounded face. "I don't—"

Cass continued backing away, sank into the couch, and held her head in her hands.

Ryan stood uncertainly in the center of the room, like a tree in a desert, suddenly feeling lost. "Cass, I—"

He went tentatively to the sofa. He sat beside her, not touching her. "I don't . . ." He cleared his throat—it was suddenly full of gravel. "Maybe we can have a future . . . after. But I don't know who or what I'll be when this is finished." She looked up at him. "Look, if you want to go back to Cheyenne and get *your* life back, I'll understand. I'll—"

She reached out and put her good hand over his mouth. "My God, but you are a stubborn and extremely frustrating man."

He pulled her hand down and enclosed it in his. "Yes."

"I'll bet those qualities made you a very good reporter."

"I think I was. And who knows? Maybe I will be again."

Approaching five o'clock, the shadows lengthening, Cass went into the bedroom to take a nap and Ryan called the number Barrientos had given him for Americans Combating Extremism.

A pleasant female voice said, "Thank you for calling Americans Combating Extremism. We're not able to take your call . . ."

Ryan disconnected the call, then went to get Cass's laptop. He logged on to the Internet and typed in the web address Barrientos had given him. A flashy red, white, and blue logo announced AMERICANS COMBATING EXTREMISM, "dedicated to mainstream American values for forty years."

Ryan read several pages, which talked about archives, visiting professors—why hadn't they talked to Barrientos?—and their close relationship with Congress and various Cabinet-level departments.

Impatiently, Ryan spotted an icon labeled HISTORY and clicked it. Again, it was very sparse.

```
Decorated military veteran and public ser-
vant Ross Mobley began ACE in 1960. A true
American visionary, Mr. Mobley anticipated the
turmoil of the decade and sensed a need for a
private organization to help maintain balance
in society. ACE has been involved in hundreds
of projects over the years, including lecture
series, university seminars, corporate work-
shops, and public-private partnerships with
the U.S. government, to stop the spread of
extremism through our nation. Mr. Mobley per-
sonally headed ACE until his death in October
1995, at the age of eighty-nine.
```

Ross Mobley. Terrence Ross's father. At least now Ryan knew where he'd picked up part of the pseudonym.

He read the passage again: . . . *public-private partnerships with the U.S. government.*

Ryan shook his head, then his eyes focused on the last line. October, 1995. Just over seven years ago.

"What the hell . . ."

The father of Terrence Ross, the Whispering Man, had died one month before Frank and Anna Elder—Adam and Eve.

With trembling hands, Ryan clicked on a box that read, FOR A PHOTO OF OUR FOUNDER, CLICK HERE.

The picture that materialized was of an older man with thin gray hair and horn-rimmed glasses, wearing a suit that seemed slightly too large. He was seated at a desk, on which sat an old-fashioned rotary telephone and nothing else. Behind him, spreading across the entire length of the photo, was a huge American flag.

Ryan stared at the picture, tilting the screen to get the best light.

Confusion, his old friend, came running back to him.
Ross Mobley . . . Terrence Ross.

"Oh God," Ryan said.

I've seen this face before.

37

"CASSANDRA CHAMBERS AND ALICIA RUBINSTEIN,"
Nina Reeves said as Kelly walked into her apartment at eight
o'clock Thursday morning.

"What?" Kelly's mind was racing in dozens of directions,
still thinking about Clarke in the office two nights ago. And
Jeff Majors still haunted her. I didn't kill Jeff Majors, she had
to remind herself. And neither did Ryan Elder. Terrence Ross
did.

"The woman who's with our man Elder," Reeves said.
"Her name, depending on whom you ask, is Cassandra
Chambers or Alicia Rubinstein."

Kelly sat down at the horseshoe and took out her notes. "I
don't understand."

Reeves, wearing a soft blue denim dress, was, as usual,
barefoot. She leaned forward and tapped Kelly's knee. "Faith,
my dear, where are you this morning?" she said with her
musical accent.

Kelly shook her head. "Too many things running through
my head, Nina. I'm sorry, what do you have?"

Reeves's slim dark brows knitted. "Two separate reports. A
woman named Cassandra Chambers, thirty-four, of Cheyenne,
left her home rather abruptly on Friday. She lives with and
cares for her father, who has Alzheimer's. A neighbor who
sometimes stays with the father called the Roger Mills County
Sheriff's Department and informed them Ms. Chambers had
brought home a strange man around one o'clock Friday afternoon. Not long after that, the same Ms. Chambers phoned a
home health agency and said she had to leave town suddenly

and needed someone to stay with her father. The description of the 'strange young man' matches your man Elder. Ms. Chambers's father's car was found last night at Will Rogers World Airport."

Kelly remembered Saturday morning, the woman beside the Jeep. "She's not under coercion. Just during the few minutes I saw her, she could have gotten in her car, driven off, and left Elder. So he somehow convinced her to go with him of her free will."

"Perhaps."

"And the second report?"

Reeves pulled a piece of paper from the stack beside a computer printer. "Yesterday afternoon, a man named Cyrus Leonard Graesner, fifty-six, was found shot to death in his house on Northwest First. His common-law wife, Tanis LaNita Harper, twenty-two, was knocked unconscious and Graesner was shot twice in the chest. The officers canvassing the area were told by two different neighbors, both elderly Mexican ladies, that a black Jeep was seen on the street and parked in front of Graesner's house, earlier in the day."

Kelly made some notes. "Go on."

"One of these public-spirited ladies wrote down the license number of the Jeep. She told the uniformed officers at the scene that she'd been afraid the Jeep belonged to drug dealers, since it was 'too nice' to belong in the neighborhood. The other woman gave a rough description of the two people in the Jeep to the officers. One, a woman in her thirties, short ash blonde hair. Two, a man, a few years younger, tall, slim, brown hair with quite a bit of gray for such a young person. The officer said the lady spoke very bad English but was quite observant."

"A beard?" Kelly said. "Did the man have a beard?"

"Clean shaven, according to this." Reeves rattled the paper. "One of the local officers realized something was going on here and remembered a bulletin about our case. Through channels, the Oklahoma City PD called our mutual colleague Sleepy Scott, and this has been circulated."

"He could have shaved. Makes sense." Kelly looked

intently at Reeves. "They traced the Jeep's registration, then?"

"Indeed they did. It was in the name of a southside used car dealer. The Jeep was purchased with cash on Friday night by one Alicia Rubinstein. Ah, but the address this Rubinstein gave was fabricated, a fictional Oklahoma City address."

Names, Kelly thought. Names rolled through her like parts on an assembly line. Cyrus Graesner. She knew the name instantly from the case file, the last person to see Adam and Eve before they went to Department Thirty.

And why had Cyrus Graesner been murdered? According to the file, he'd just been a low-level informant. But he'd known Adam and Eve, had talked to them just before they became Frank and Anna Elder. And Ryan Elder had sought him out, no doubt pumped him for every bit of information he could. Hours later, he was dead.

Circles inside of circles. A maze with no exit.

Kelly sat back. She needed Elder.

"This means things are tightening up," she said, "and it means I need to get to Elder before the Bureau or the local cops do."

"Faith, Scott knows that Elder didn't kill those people in the Underworld. He sat right there and listened to the tape the same time you did."

Kelly shook her head. "Doesn't matter. Elder's still considered the prime suspect in Art's murder."

"I might also remind you that you have no authority to do anything at all. You're on leave and off the case."

Kelly took a breath. "Nina, there's more to it than that."

Reeves raised her eyebrows again.

"It's Clarke. I think he's connected to it." She told Reeves what had happened in the office two nights ago.

Reeves listened, laying a forefinger across her lips. "Faith, I—"

"Don't tell me I'm losing my mind. There was no legitimate reason for him to be there at midnight except to be in a totally secure environment."

"Ah, but there was no legitimate reason for you to be there either."

The two women stared at each other. "What am I supposed to do?" Kelly finally said. "What am I supposed to think? He may be a sexist and a jerk, but this goes beyond even that. Did you get the information on the playgrounds?"

"Faith, I—"

"I have to find Elder. Right now. I have to get to him before Clarke does. I have to find out what he knows, what Graesner told him, how far this thing goes. If Graesner knew Terrence Ross. . . ." She trailed off again, thinking of the computer disk with the data on Ross. She'd been in such a rush to finish downloading it, she hadn't been able to read the complete file.

Her mind raced. She pulled the disk from her purse and waved it at Reeves. "Do you have a computer where I can view a file?"

Reeves gave a wry smile and swept a hand around all the equipment. "Do I have a computer?"

Kelly put the disk into a drive and accessed the file she'd downloaded from the Justice Department database. She scrolled through the material she'd already read about Terrence Ross and The New America, then came to the end, the part about Ross's disappearance in the fall of 1975.

While Reeves sat to the side, Kelly read the report about how The New America was unlikely to present much further threat to people or property, as Ross was the driving force behind it, and all indications were that he was gone forever. How could they be sure? Kelly wondered, thinking the report was a little too pat, a little too sure of itself.

She read further, then stopped cold on the last entry.

It is recommended that the task force cease operations with regard to Terrence Ross and The New America, and that the task force itself be dissolved, folding operations into other areas of DOJ.

Kelly read it again. Why would they fold up the task force just because one terrorist suddenly disappeared? Others had done the same thing, and the groups went on. What was so special about Terrence Ross and The New America?

The last line of text on the screen was: Prepared and

submitted by P. Clarke, Case Officer C-7, DOJ Domestic Extremism Task Force, November 30, 1975.

"Oh, shit," Kelly whispered.

Reeves made a *tsk-tsk* sound. "It can't be that bad, Faith."

Kelly pointed to the screen, to the last line, then explained the task force, the Whispering Man, Terrence Ross, and The New America.

Reeves's face grew animated. "I remember, on the tape when Elder called you. He said something about a man who whispered. This is him?"

"This is him. He disappeared right about the same time Adam and Eve went into Department Thirty, and Clarke was part of the task force investigating him."

Reeves sat back and folded her arms. "All right, I would say that's a few too many coincidences."

"I can't believe this. Clarke, tied up with the Whispering Man. This is even messier than I thought."

"Why don't you just ask Clarke about it?"

"You didn't hear him the other night, Nina. He's . . . somehow he's mixed up with Ross again, in the here and now, and they're after Ryan Elder." She looked up. "The list of playgrounds. I have to get him. Now. Today."

Reeves plucked a printout from the horseshoe desk. "I came up with thirteen locations in the northwest part of the city, parks or playgrounds located within two blocks of apartment complexes, motels, or rooming houses."

"I have to get onto them. I'll start canvassing—"

"Faith," Reeves said.

"What?"

"Perhaps you should share this with the Bureau. Scott Hendler's your friend, isn't he? He'll—"

"No, not yet. I need more evidence. If I go after Clarke without having enough information, the old boys will close ranks and I'll be lucky to get a job as a mall security guard somewhere. After I have Elder and find out what he knows, then I'll go to Scott. I need to get going."

"Wait a minute," Reeves said, and left the room. When

she came back, she was wearing shoes and holding her coat.

"What are you doing?"

"We can cover the ground more quickly if there are two of us. I'm going with you."

They split up the list of thirteen locations, Kelly taking seven, Reeves six. In the apartment parking lot, Reeves said, "Ah, Faith, there's a man sitting in your car."

Kelly snapped her head around, then relaxed. "Yorkton. He's Department Thirty. He has an odd way of coming and going. You take your car, I'll take mine, and we'll keep in cell phone contact."

"You're the investigator," Reeves said wryly, took her list, and got into her car, a blue Honda.

Kelly went to the Miata and slid in.

"Not much room in this car," Yorkton said mildly.

"Did you get my message?" Kelly said.

"Oh, yes. Had a little scare with your chief deputy, did you?"

"It's more than that." She explained Clarke's connection to Terrence Ross.

The big man grew quiet, then said, "Well, I'll be damned."

"There's more." Kelly pulled out of the parking lot and turned south. She told Yorkton about Cassandra Chambers/Alicia Rubinstein.

A troubled look crossed Yorkton's face. "So that's it," he finally said. "She managed somehow to get new identification and that's why no one's been able to track her. Very clever of Ryan." He leaned back against the seat, drumming his fingers against his leg. "I don't think you'll see me again until this is over. You're making the case on your own quite well."

"Wait a minute now—"

"Give yourself some credit. You may have a future in Department Thirty after all this is over."

Kelly waited, hands clamped to the wheel. "I'm not sure I'm interested in that."

"Guilt feelings. Well, that's normal. We'll see, after this is finished."

Kelly wanted to throw something at the man. "If you're gone, who do I report to?"

"Yourself. When it's done and Elder is in, write your report and I'll file it. For now, I'll be leaving town. Since I lived in Oklahoma City as Dean Yorkton for twenty years and people here still know me, it's not good for me to stay too long. I'm supposed to be dead, remember?"

"But what—"

Yorkton held up a hand. "That's enough. You're in an interesting position, Deputy. Not only do you have to deal with Ryan Elder, but you're going to find a way to bring down your own boss."

Kelly gripped the wheel, the Miata moving south on May Avenue toward The Village. "I know," she said.

Nina Reeves took the six locations that were closer to downtown, inner-city areas, while Kelly decided to work The Village, Quail Creek, and other outlying neighborhoods.

The first one on Reeves's list was the kind of hotel that had once been called a "fleabag," located just west of downtown. She drove slowly past the playground, with its sagging chain-link fence, ruptured garbage bags, broken bottles, and run-down swings and slides.

She was in and out of the hotel in five minutes after she determined that the desk clerk, a teenage boy who wore an earring shaped like a penis, hadn't seen Alicia Rubinstein.

She moved down her list, driving from one place to the next, rooming houses populated by old men in undershirts, crumbling apartments inhabited by single mothers with too many children, near-empty motels with wary-eyed clerks. The life of a street investigator. For a moment Reeves wished she were back in her warm apartment with her computers and her sound equipment.

It was nearly noon when she drove up Northwest Thirtieth, passing Swatek Park, thankful that the neighborhoods had finally improved. The woman at the desk in the apartment leasing office was in her late forties, with advancing wrinkles she had desperately tried to hide under makeup.

Her hair was light brown, with a few stray grays. She was stylishly dressed in a navy blue suit and jacket with a cream-colored silk blouse, but her pale blue eyes were terminally weary. Soft country music played from a radio on the desk.

Listening to songs of lost love all day long would make anyone weary, Reeves thought, then smiled at the woman.

"Can I help you?" she drawled, attempting a smile of her own.

Reeves read the nameplate on the desk: SHARON FLYNN, LEASING AGENT. "Oh, I hope so. Are you Ms. Flynn?"

"You don't have to call me *mizz*, honey. I'm just Sharon." She rolled her chair a few feet back from the desk. "Single woman? Say, we're running a special on one-bedrooms this month. There's no deposit."

"Oh, no, I'm not here to rent an apartment. You see, I'm looking for a friend of mine."

"Does she live here?"

"Well, you know, I'm not quite sure."

Flynn pursed her overly red lips. "Don't know how I can help you, then."

"I suppose I should explain. She was living with this horrible man. Just horrible. He would go out and drink five nights a week, then come back and beat her for no reason at all." Reeves watched the woman's eyes. She had her full attention now. "Once he even broke her collarbone. She's a smart woman, but she just wouldn't leave him. She stayed with him for two years. Horrible man. But then, about a week ago, she calls me and says she can't stand it anymore, that he's gone over the edge and she has to leave."

"Good for her."

"Yes, of course. That's what I told her. Of course I offered to let her stay with me, but she said she had an apartment in the northwest part of town, that she'd rented a while back but never used. She said it was near a park, but she didn't want to tell me any more than that. I've been so worried about her and I've been searching apartment complexes all over this part of the city."

Reeves felt Flynn's eyes on hers and knew she was thinking, Black woman, blue eyes, funny accent. But she was also struggling, thinking of a battered woman escaping an abusive relationship, and standing before her now was a concerned friend.

Flynn chewed a nail, which like her lips was far too red. She exhaled a weary breath. "You'd think the cops could do more about these jerks."

"Oh, the police weren't very helpful at all. They said if Alicia didn't want to press charges, they couldn't pursue it."

"Tell me your friend's name. This is a big complex, but I could look her up on the computer."

"Oh, would you? Her name is Alicia Rubinstein."

Flynn applied her nails to the computer keyboard. "Well, look at that. I guess you've found your friend."

Reeves's heart skipped a beat, thinking of Kelly, of everything at risk here. In a careful tone, she said, "Thank heaven. What's her apartment number? I want to make sure she's all right."

"Number one-thirty-two. That's around the corner here to the right. It faces the park."

Reeves clutched a hand to her breast. "Thank you so much. I hope she's all right. I can't believe I've finally found her."

"Glad I could help. You see her, you tell her not to ever go back to that scumbag. My daughter lived with one just like that. I had to drive all the way to Dallas to get her once, 'cause he'd beat her black and blue. But you know what? She wouldn't dump him. Now she says he's changed and he's wonderful and she wants to marry him." The weary look was back. "You tell your friend what I said."

"I will," Reeves said.

Half an hour later, Kelly and Reeves had made two circuits of the parking lot, with no sign of the black Jeep Cherokee.

"Where are they?" Kelly said, slapping the steering wheel.

Sitting in the Miata beside her, Reeves laughed lightly. "A couple of years as a freelance investigator in New York taught me two things, Faith. The first was that most of what you do is waiting. Waiting for something to happen, waiting for someone else to do something or say something. Terminal waiting."

Kelly pulled her hair back and began twisting strands of it around her fingers. "And the second thing?"

"Ah." Reeves took a small black leather bag out of her coat. "The second thing was how to get past almost any locked door."

Kelly considered for a moment. Breaking and entering. Just a few days ago, she would have never considered such a thing. But then again, in the world of Department Thirty, proper procedures and warrants seemed to mean very little.

She flashed on an image of Clarke in the darkened office, saying her name. She remembered the photos of Art Dorian's body. Clarke and Ross and whomever else had twisted the system around until it was almost unrecognizable.

She remembered her father's intense anger a few years ago when he'd broken up a ring of corrupt cops on his own force. And that had been a relatively small protection racket. Kelly felt her own anger rising. Now I understand you better, Dad, she thought.

Kelly looked at Reeves and said, "Let's do it."

38

THE TEMPERATURE WAS DROPPING AND THE SKY DARK-ening, as if a gray sheet were being gradually pulled across it, when the black Jeep crossed Tenth Street and entered the Flats.

The picture of Ross Mobley from the ACE website never left Ryan. He knew he'd seen the man—but *where?* It was buried somewhere deep in memory and he couldn't get to it. There were so many other things in his mind that there was simply no room. Ryan thought of a computer: eventually you put so much data into it that it ran out of memory and just couldn't take anymore.

Then there was Cass. She was quieter, strange. An uneasy

resignation settled over her. Ryan listened as she called her father, watched the pain on her face. He offered again to go it alone, to let her go back to Cheyenne, but she silenced him again with a look.

"Don't you think Graesner would have told us yesterday?" she said as they drove south on Villa.

"He knows," Ryan said forcefully, then softened his tone. "It doesn't make sense that Ross would confide in him, give him all this information, then cut him off cold. They were both hooked up with the Justice Department and Graesner even said Ross made that comment about them being like brothers. No, I think Ross wanted someone to know what he was up to, what the last big job was, and Graesner's the logical choice."

"There's nothing logical about any of these people."

"No, but I think Graesner knows."

"Then why didn't he say it yesterday when he was telling everything else?"

Ryan shrugged. "I don't know. Maybe he got cold feet at the last minute. Did you notice how abrupt he was at the very end? It felt incomplete."

Cass shook her head. "Reporter's instinct?"

"Maybe, maybe not. But I think he knows."

But where have I seen Ross Mobley's face before? Ryan thought.

Cass driving, they turned onto First Street and Ryan said, "Look."

Yellow crime-scene tape covered the gate to Graesner's house.

"I have a bad feeling about this," Cass said, slowing the Jeep.

Ryan's thoughts tumbled and churned. Art Dorian, Jeff Majors . . . now Graesner too? He began to clench and unclench his fists. "Drive around the block. I need to think." The pen began tapping between his fingers, a hard staccato pattern.

Cass circled the block, driving slowly past Mark Twain Elementary School and turning back onto Villa.

"I need to find out what happened," Ryan said. "But you're right, this doesn't feel good."

Cass parked in front of the house and they pushed aside the yellow tape. At the door, Ryan raised the brass knocker and rapped three times, just as he'd done yesterday.

When the door opened and Tanis appeared, Ryan started to say something, then he took in the girl's puffy eyes and the large bandage on her head. He saw the eyes go from emptiness to rage.

Ryan said, "I don't know if you—"

Tanis balled up both fists and slammed them into his chest.

He was nearly a foot taller than she, but he stumbled backward, more in surprise than pain. She took a step forward, hit him again, and began pounding his chest with a steady rhythm.

"Bastard," Tanis whispered. "Bastard, chickenshit, son of a *bitch!*" As she cursed, she kept pounding.

"Hey, wait," Ryan said, putting out his hands.

She knocked his hands away and kept pummeling his chest.

"That's enough! Come on, that's enough!"

He grabbed her wrists and she squealed. Cass rushed forward and pulled her away from Ryan, toward the door.

"Look," Ryan said, "I don't know what you think—"

"Ryan," Cass said, very quietly. "Look at her."

The bandage, the eyes, and tears streaming down her cheeks. The fight had left Tanis, and she was standing with her hands at her sides, letting Cass hold her.

"Come on," Cass said to her. "Let's go in."

"What happened?" Ryan said. "T, what happened?"

They stepped through the door and into the house. Ryan looked around. The furniture was cheap, discount-store vintage, but it was all clean. Hardwood floors were covered by a brightly colored rug, frayed at the edges, but again, spotless. No dust was visible anywhere in the room. Over the mantel of the fake fireplace was a portrait: Graesner and Tanis, the two of them a study in contrasts: age, race, personality.

The only disarray in all the order was in front of the small wine-colored sofa. On the floor was an upended silver strongbox, with a semicircle of envelopes and papers, and one videotape case, fanning out around it. Beside the box was a white ceramic bowl with at least a dozen slim brown cigarette butts in it.

"What happened?" Ryan said again.

Tanis backed away from them, toward the sofa. Hands shaking, she took a pack of cigarettes from the wooden stand beside it, shook one out, and lit it. "Cyrus wouldn't let me smoke in the house, so we never had no ashtrays." She nodded toward the bowl.

She sounds almost apologetic, Ryan thought.

"He left me the house," Tanis said. "I never owned nothing in my life and he left me this whole house."

"Look," Ryan said. "Tell us what—"

"Stop asking me what happened!" Tanis screamed, kicking out from the sofa and knocking over the bowl with the cigarette butts in it. "Oh shit, now look what happened." Crying again, she slid down and began to pick up the butts from the rug, dropping them back into the bowl.

Ryan sidled down next to her and helped her clean up the mess.

"Ash all over the rug," Tanis said, still crying. "I always tried to keep this place clean. And now look, ash all over the rug. Oh Jesus, Oh God." Through the tears, she looked up at Ryan. "You, Abel. You done this. Cyrus—"

Graesner dead. Ryan squeezed his eyes closed. Graesner dead, and his parents dead, and Art Dorian and Jeff Majors and that woman in the Underworld. . . .

"Where's your friend?" Cass said gently. "Linda, is that her name? Is she all right?"

Tanis shrugged, dragged on her cigarette, wiped her cheeks. "They knocked me and Linda in the head. When I woke up, Cyrus was shot dead and Linda was gone. She probably got scared they'd find out she didn't have papers."

Ryan looked at the bandage on her head. "Did you see a doctor about your head? It looks—"

"Cops wanted me to go to the hospital. I told them I

couldn't go to no hospital. Ambulance guys gave me some heavy-duty Tylenol and cleaned it up. Cops was here till midnight, then they finally, how did they call it, 'released' the house. Ain't that a kick? Released the house."

"Who did this? Did you see them?"

"I saw nothing but feet. Two big white dudes, older. One with business shoes, black with little tassels. Normal white dude voice. One had gray shit-kicker boots, talked like he'd been suckin' gravel." She raised her head. Her eyes were clear. "You come along, Abel, and a few hours later someone comes in and knocks me in the head and shoots Cyrus. He never done nothing. He liked to talk, that's all. He used to talk big, but he never done nothing."

"Listen, Tanis—"

"Don't call me that! Only Cyrus could call me that! He was the only one that ever gave a rat's ass about me. Nobody else ever treated me good and now he's shot dead, Abel. You hear that? *Shot dead after you came here.* I ought to told the cops about you, but I never did. Cops don't know shit about shit. They won't never find who did Cyrus." She leaned forward, putting her hands on her knees. "Damn, my head hurts. Little dizzy sometimes. No, the cops won't find out 'cause the cops don't care. Just another shoot-up in the Flats. Kept asking me a bunch of questions about dope. I ever see cocaine in the house? I ever do cocaine? What about meth? Cyrus dealin' meth out of here? They don't give a shit. But you do, Abel. *Don't you?*"

Ryan's head ached, almost as if he could feel the pain in Tanis's head. "T, my oldest friend was killed last week. By these same people, I think. My parents killed themselves seven years ago, because of this . . . this whatever it is. Cyrus gave me some information yesterday, information I need to track down who's behind all this. But I don't think he told me everything. That's why we came back. I didn't know—"

Tanis ground out her cigarette, only half-smoked, in the white bowl. "What you want from me? I don't know nothing about what Cyrus did a hundred years ago. We been together 'bout two years, that's it. He used to talk a lot, but mostly about how much dope he did back then and how many hippie women he had. Trash talk, just bullshit."

Ryan's eyes fell on the strongbox and the papers.

Tanis followed his look. "Shit," she said. "I'm just going through some stuff. That's what you're supposed to do, right? I found out he left me the house. There's a will in there, got signed by a notary and everything, and he left me the house. I never owned nothing. Most of it's weird shit, insurance and bank statements and shit like that."

"Can we at least look?" Ryan said, thinking of the papers Jack Coleridge had gotten from the safe-deposit box. His birth certificate, all those falsified official documents. . . .

Tanis sat back. "You think something here helps you find out who did Cyrus?"

"I don't know, T. Maybe."

"Maybe. You know what, Abel? I believe you. I believe you're desperate enough to do just about anything."

"What's this?" Cass said, going through a pile of papers and laying a hand on the videotape box.

Tanis, sitting cross-legged next to her, shook her head, wincing against a wave of pain. "Don't know. I hadn't got that far yet. It was in the little box with everything else. Cyrus told me this was where all the important stuff was."

"Let's find out," Ryan said.

Tanis shrugged. "Probably a porno movie. Cyrus liked the ones where a whole bunch of girls get it on together with no men."

Cass shook the tape out of the box. Affixed to one end of the tape was a white label with TRANSFERRED TO VIDEO—JULY 1995 written on it in a precise hand. She tapped it. "Look at this."

"Transferred to video?" Ryan said. "So maybe it was originally on another format?"

"What's all that about?" Tanis said.

"Let's see," Cass said, taking the tape to the small television and VCR, which sat on a cheap rolling stand across the room.

After a few seconds of blue screen, the picture appeared. It was grainy, the colors tinted a little strangely, but it was this room, the living room of Graesner's house. Much of the furniture was the same, though on the screen it looked almost new.

"Hey," Tanis said. "That's—"

"Yes," Ryan said.

Then a shadow moved and Cyrus Graesner stepped into the frame and settled onto the same wine-colored sofa. Tanis put her hand over her mouth and stifled a sob. Cass put her arm around the girl's shoulders.

The on-screen Graesner was much younger, the gray ponytail then somewhere between blond and brown. He wore the same style of round glasses and they still slipped down his face. There were fewer burst blood vessels in the nose, and the man sported several days' growth of beard. He was wearing a red-and-black flannel shirt, blue jeans, and sandals. Around his neck dangled a set of military dogtags.

Graesner reached up and ran the back of his hand across his face, almost the exact gesture he'd used in wiping his nose yesterday. For a ludicrous moment Ryan thought of the man suffering from the same cold for nearly thirty years.

"Okay," Graesner said on the screen, "I guess it's running. Well . . ." He rubbed his hands together. "Well, here goes." Graesner shifted on the sofa, crossing his legs at the ankle, then putting an ankle on a knee, then placing both feet flat on the floor.

Graesner coughed, the sound slightly distorted. "Okay, okay, this is it. Ah, my name is Cyrus Leonard Graesner. It's . . . ah . . . what the hell day is it? Okay, it's the second day of December 1975, and I'm making this film at my house in Oklahoma City, Oklahoma."

A week after he saw Adam and Eve, Ryan thought.

"Okay," Graesner continued. "There's some heavy shit about to come down and I guess I might be the only one that knows all the sides of it. Maybe not, but I've found out some strange stuff in the last few months and I think I better make a record of it in case anything happens to me."

Tanis sobbed again and Ryan thought: Something happened, all right, Cyrus. It took a long time to happen, but happen it did.

"I've been working underground for the U.S. Department of Justice . . ."

Graesner went on to tell essentially the same story he'd told Ryan yesterday. The man on the screen stood up from time to time, wandered out of the frame, then back, talking all the while.

Ryan sat up straight when Graesner said, fifteen minutes into the tape, "I don't think Ross was going to tell me all the details about this last big job he was cooking up, but I finally got it out of him." He rubbed his hands on blue-jeaned legs as if trying to generate warmth. "Jesus, this is heavy shit. I'm telling you, I don't really know what to think about all of it. Ross is . . ." Head shake, as if confused. "I hope none of this comes back to haunt me, man. I just don't know what to think."

"Come on, Cyrus," Ryan whispered. "Tell me, tell me."

"A few weeks ago, around the first week of November," Graesner said, wiping his nose, "Ross called me. I was still under with the Revolutionary Workers Party and we were in Detroit. I was in this rooming house and it was three o'clock in the morning and the phone rings and it's Ross. He was all wired, like he was on speed. He said it was in the works and it was about to go down. And I said, 'Ross, you stupid shit, I was asleep. Either tell me what this is really all about or let me go back to sleep.' And he did."

Ryan held his breath. On the screen, Graesner coughed again, then looked straight at the camera. "Terrence Ross wants to start a war."

39

RYAN STARED AT THE VIDEO SCREEN, AS IF HE COULD absorb Cyrus Graesner's essence through it. He was barely aware of Cass and Tanis, less than five feet away from him. He tuned out the sleet that was beginning to pelt the roof of the house.

A war.

On the screen, Graesner stood up, made a circuit around the sofa, and sat down again. The man laughed in his throat. "Wish I was stoned right now," he said, "but I promised myself I'd be straight when I did this." He sniffled and coughed into his hand. "Hell, I can't believe I said it out loud. Well, okay, I thought Ross was crazy. I mean, Saigon fell and Nixon fell and it seems to me like everything's falling apart on its own. But no, Ross says to hear him out, that he's got the perfect plan."

Graesner stood up again, paced a little more, and finally sat down on the arm of the sofa, at the far right side of the screen. "He tells me about his old man, the former OSS agent, and how he's started this ACE group, right? And ACE is giving him this perfect cover for what he's really going to do. He keeps talking about 'rivers of blood' and 'America's Second Revolution.' He wants to topple the whole country, the 'system,' he calls it. What he really wants to do is get back at his old man for being such a jerk when Ross was a kid. So here's his revolution, and the way he's going to start it . . . he wants to start this war between the extreme left and the extreme right. Get it? To get all the far-left groups and all the far-right groups fighting with each other. And not just bull-shit fighting. Real, serious violence with lots of people getting killed and buildings getting blown up all over the country. Right there's the beauty of it—Ross is really into irony, always quoting Shakespeare and people like that. The New America was created as a cover, but in the end, the result would be exactly what their so-called agenda was—violent revolution, with the left and the right destroying each other piece by piece in this war. Then the government gets involved and you've got your 'rivers of blood' and the whole thing just collapses."

Ryan thought of the picture of Ross Mobley, the huge American flag draped behind him. *Where have I seen that face?*

"I told Ross he was full of shit and that it wouldn't ever work, that every country has extreme groups and it's been that way forever. Hey, after all, what about Jesus? He was a real radical in his time, right? That's why they killed him." Graesner rubbed his hands on his legs again. "Anyway, Ross wants to start this war in a big way, and this is where I got scared. He said he's hired Adam and Eve—you know, the big-time professional killers—to do this."

Ryan's breathing quickened.

"Ross contacted Adam and Eve and told them he wanted them to make a bomb. Adam's supposed to be good with explosives, so I hear. But not just some little pipe bomb." Graesner shook his head and slid back onto the sofa. "He wanted them to make a nuclear bomb. There, there it is, out in the open."

"Ryan?" Cass said, and her voice was far away.

He heard Tanis say something as well, but it was lost. Outside of controlled tests, nuclear weapons had never been detonated inside the United States. And Terrence Ross had wanted Adam—soon to be Frank Elder—to be the first to do it. To start his war, his revolution. *The Second American Revolution.*

"Okay, okay," Graesner said on the screen, his head bobbing up and down. "Ross has these contacts all over the world, plus he's got money, and those two things mean he can do damn near anything he wants. He's hooked up with this Russian dissident group and he offers them a couple hundred thousand American dollars to smuggle some weapons-grade uranium out of the country. One of these guys is actually a nuclear scientist who's fed up with the Soviet system. He can arrange it so that a little bit of uranium at a time is smuggled across the border into Poland. Once they had enough, the stuff's put on a boat and brought over here. The boat docks somewhere up in New England— Maine, I think—and Adam and Eve meet the boat. The crew doesn't know what they're carrying. Hey, they're smugglers, it's a no-questions-asked kind of operation, right? The uranium is all packed in lead cases, with something like forty or fifty pounds of lead to a half-pound of uranium, 'cause the shit's dangerous, you know? But if it's inside the cases, you can handle it and transport it without it doing anything to you. They're going to take these cases and put them on a truck and take them somewhere so Adam can make a bomb, and then it's going to be set off at one of the leftist camps somewhere in Texas, and one of the rightist groups gets the blame, and they set off more and more and more of these things and this war, this goddamned war between left and right, is going all over the place. Then the government will send troops in to put down the violence, and then other groups will fight back against the government, and . . . and Ross sits back and watches his revolution."

On the little screen, Graesner leaned forward. Ryan heard his voice break. "Look, a lot of people would get hurt—hell, a lot of people would *die*—in a deal like this. Ross is a crazy bastard, and he's got it in his head that only he can fix America, and he's gonna do it by tearing it down. I'm nothing but a snitch, a nobody, but this . . ." He flapped a hand. "This is some heavy shit and I can't let it go by. Someone's got to know."

Graesner wiped his nose again and sat back. "Ross said part of it had already gone down, that Adam and Eve already had the uranium and it was on its way to wherever they were making the bomb."

Ross's "property," Ryan thought, his heart thudding wildly. My parents took the uranium and hid it, then didn't follow through with the rest of the job.

"But hey, it gets even better—" Graesner said on the screen.

Ryan leaned forward again, then swiveled his head as a knock, sharp and metallic, sounded from the front door.

A muffled voice: "Ms. Harper? It's the police, Ms. Harper. Are you in there?"

"Shit, the cops," Tanis whispered.

"The tape," Ryan said. "We need the tape." He looked around wildly. He met Cass's eyes and he knew she was thinking the same thing: the Jeep was parked on the street in front of the house and the police stood between them and it.

"A way out," Cass said. She placed a hand on Tanis's shoulder.

Tanis looked at both of them, settling her gaze on Ryan.

"Ms. Harper?" Louder knocks. "Are you all right?"

"We're not done, Abel," Tanis said. "We got work to do." She pointed. "Back door, through the kitchen. Your nice little SUV is history. Bet one of those busybody old Mexican ladies across the street spotted it and called the cops. Get to the parking lot at AMC. You know where that is?"

Ryan thought for a second. "The big flea market, Tenth and Penn."

"That's it. Get behind the building, Tenth Street side. I'll get you. I can't keep them from chasing you, but I can give you a head start. Now go on." She slapped Ryan's buttocks. "Remember, we ain't done, Abel."

"I remember," Ryan said. Cass had stuffed the videotape in her purse and he took her good hand as they ran for the back door.

The next three hours were a blur of cold and ice, pellets of sleet stinging them like little bullets. Block by block, the police had cordoned off the Flats, until Ryan and Cass had to scale a fence and drop into the back of a massive auto salvage yard. There they stayed, huddled freezing in the back of a burned-out Aerostar minivan, while the manhunt went on around them.

When a wrecker truck rumbled into their section of the junkyard, Ryan uncoiled his legs—they were so cold they were cramping—and took Cass's hand without speaking, inclining his head toward the truck. With the videotape tucked securely into her purse, they crouched and climbed onto the passenger side of the wrecker while the driver talked on the radio to his dispatcher. It was one of the new style of tow trucks with a flat bed that could be lowered and angled to pull up a disabled vehicle. The two of them hid under a tarp that was stowed just behind the cab, right beside the controls for lowering the truck's bed. Ryan breathed out a deep, frosty breath and squeezed Cass's hand as the truck began to move again.

Ryan occasionally poked his head out one corner of the

tarp, taking care to stay low, away from the driver's line of sight in the rearview mirror. When the wrecker driver turned east on Tenth, Ryan closed his eyes and silently mouthed, "Thank you." He and Cass held tightly to each other. At one point, Cass's foot slipped and dragged the street for a few seconds before she could right herself. Ryan winced at the sound, thankful that the driver had his windows up, the heater on high and the radio blaring loud country music.

The driver was careful and began slowing well before the intersection at Penn. The AMC building, a huge white brick conglomeration with red and blue trim, loomed on the right, their side of the truck. The parking lot was empty, as the huge flea market only operated on weekends.

Ryan watched as they pulled parallel to the lot, and he caught sight of an old green Monte Carlo wandering aimlessly through it. Tanis's blond cornrows against her dark skin were unmistakable behind the wheel.

Ryan breathed out, for what seemed like the first time in hours. The truck was coming to a stop, coasting, the driver giving himself plenty of space with the icy streets.

"Now," he whispered, and Cass unfolded her legs, jogging alongside the truck, then jumping onto the curb.

Ryan rolled himself down to where Cass had been, then swung himself out behind her.

"Hey!" someone yelled from a passing car.

They darted up the embankment and into the AMC parking lot. The Monte Carlo made another aimless turn, then headed in their direction. It went into a skid on the ice and narrowly missed them. Tanis threw open the passenger door.

"Nice to see you," she said. "I nearly got tired of waiting. But then I thought: old Abel, he'll find a way, and Quiet Girlfriend, she'll make sure he gets here. I got nowhere else to go, anyway."

Ryan climbed into the backseat, felt the warmth of the old car's heater and a blast of loud hip-hop from the radio. He leaned his head back and closed his eyes.

"Where to, kids?" Tanis said over the music.

Cass gave her the address of the apartment complex.

"Here we go," Tanis said, and slid out of the parking lot.

• • •

Fifteen minutes later, Cass put her key in the lock of apartment 132 and swung open the door. "Finally," she said. "I can't wait to—"

Ryan was two steps behind her, Tanis another couple of steps behind him. "What?" he said.

Ryan stepped into the doorway and stopped cold at the sight of the tall woman with the red hair and the well-tailored suit.

"Welcome home, Ryan," Faith Kelly said.

40

RYAN STOOD STOCK-STILL, AND FOR A MOMENT HE thought, It's over.

He and Kelly met each other's eyes for a long time, then he heard Tanis coming up behind him.

"The fuck's going on?" Tanis said, then she stepped into the apartment. "Oh—"

Kelly broke eye contact first and glanced toward Cass. "You must be Ms. Chambers. Or I guess I should say Ms. Rubinstein."

"How did you get in here?" Cass demanded. "What do you want?"

Kelly reached into her pocket and flipped open her identification. "Deputy U.S. Marshal Faith Kelly." She indicated the slender, urbane-looking black woman in the chair behind her. "This is Nina Reeves. She's a consultant to the case."

"Shit," Tanis said. "From one set of cops to another."

"And you are . . . ?" Kelly said.

"T," Tanis said. "That's all you need to know. You know who did Cyrus?"

"Ah, you're Cyrus Graesner's . . . companion," Kelly said, then she looked back to Ryan. "I guess I could say something like 'we meet at last,' but that doesn't ring quite right, does it?"

"Am I under arrest?" Ryan asked, his throat raw.

"It's not quite that cut and dried anymore," Kelly said. "Come in and close the door."

No one moved.

"I know you didn't kill Jeff Majors or Art Dorian or Cyrus Graesner," Kelly said. "I understand that now. I know who your whispering man is. His name is—"

"Terrence Ross," Ryan finished. "I found out who he is and what he wants. Since no one in your Department Thirty could or would tell me, I had to find out myself. And Graesner's dead because of it."

"I know. Ross—"

Ryan closed the door and turned back around to face Kelly, his eyes blazing. It wasn't over after all, not by a long shot. Not after all he'd seen on Graesner's video. As Tanis had said, we're not done yet.

"No, not Ross," he said, and took a step, watching Kelly's body go tense. "Go ahead, pull your gun on me. I'm not armed. None of us are. But first you're going to listen to me, Deputy Kelly of the U.S. Marshals Service or Department Thirty, or whoever you really work for. And you're going to watch a little home movie."

"But Ross—" Kelly said.

"Just watch," Ryan said as Cass put the videotape in the combination TV/VCR, rewound it, then pressed play.

They watched silent and motionless as Cyrus Graesner told the story again, then Ryan leaned in close as Graesner said, "But hey, it gets even better," the point when the police had come to the door.

Graesner said, "Last week, out of the blue, Adam and Eve showed up on my doorstep, right here. Hell, I don't know them, barely met them once. And they tell me they're quitting the game, getting out of the business. Eve's big as a house—pregnant, I mean—and they say they had one more job to do, but it's too much and they can't do it. So they're giving up and going to the government, cutting a deal to get new identities.

"But you know what? They didn't say anything about this

war of Ross's, or any of it. Just that it was a really big job and they weren't going to go through with it. I don't think they were going to tell the feds about it. I think they were going to give them all kinds of names and stuff to cut a deal, but not this. They wanted to just bury it, make it go away. Maybe it was some kind of leverage, maybe they had guilty consciences, maybe they were thinking about their kid, who knows?"

Cass and Kelly both looked at Ryan. His hands were clasped together so tightly that his knuckles were the color of paste.

"And it's funny," Graesner said. "After all this happened, now I can't get hold of my controller, Phillip Clarke. Something's happening and I think maybe he's about to cut me loose. Adam and Eve have gone under, and now Ross has gone under, and outside the three of them, I think I might be the only one who knows all this. Maybe Clarke does too. Hell, I don't know. I know Ross knows him. Once I mentioned Clarke's name to Ross and Ross laughed and said something like, 'Don't worry about Philly.'"

A strange look crossed Tanis's face. She touched the bandage on the back of her head as if it were alive.

"So I don't know," Graesner said. "It's all mixed up and I'm afraid somebody's going to come in here and shoot me. Every day, I think Ross or Adam and Eve or Clarke or someone I've snitched on, they're just going to blow me away. I guess that, whoever's watching this, if you're seeing it, that means I'm gone, one way or another. I hope I die in my bed at age ninety-seven, with lots of young girls hanging off me, but . . ." He gave a crooked, hopeless smile. "I'm not betting on it."

Graesner stood up and walked toward the camera, then out of view. A moment later the tape ended, replaced by a blue video screen.

No one spoke for a moment, then Cass pressed the stop button on the VCR and pulled out the tape.

"Philly," Tanis said.

They all looked at her.

"I was on the floor after they'd knocked me in the head, and I think I sort of came to a couple of times, like when I saw the shit-kicker boots. But I remember. . . ." Tears welled, but she blinked them back fiercely, wrapping her arms around herself and rocking back and forth. "It was before the gunshots and Cyrus said something about Philly. I remember I heard it, and I thought, That's a stupid thing to say, Cyrus. Then the other voice, the shit-kicker with the gravel mouth, he was saying something else, and he was pissed off, and I think I kind of faded out again."

"Philly," Ryan said. "Phillip Clarke, Graesner's controller in the Justice Department."

"And the other man," Cass said. "The one with the tasseled shoes. Isn't that what you said, T? And that he had a softer voice."

"Yeah," Tanis said, still hugging herself and rocking.

"Terrence Ross, in person," Cass said, shaking her head.

Ryan looked at Kelly. "Do you know this Phillip Clarke?"

Kelly's face flushed. Ryan couldn't tell if it was from anger or embarrassment.

"I see that you do," Ryan said. "Who is he? I mean, now, today. In 1975 he was Graesner's controller and he knew Terrence Ross. He had to have known what Ross was doing. But he's here, in Oklahoma City, and he's hooked up with Ross again. And he killed Cyrus Graesner yesterday, just because Graesner talked to me."

"Damn," Kelly said softly.

Ryan sat back and thought of his father making a nuclear bomb. Uranium. Lead cases. Ross's "property."

That was what Terrence Ross wanted with him. He wanted the uranium back. Twenty-seven years later, he wanted to find the uranium and start his war, his revolution, all over again. And he wanted Ryan to find it for him.

He remembered something else Graesner had said yesterday, that Adam and Eve never killed innocent bystanders in any of their assassinations. Assassins, not terrorists. And there was the answer: that was why they didn't follow through on the last job. A nuclear blast would injure and kill innocent people.

Morality from assassins? Ryan thought bitterly, then shook it away. He couldn't afford to be bitter, couldn't think about it. It led down a road he wasn't sure he could navigate. His parents, the people who didn't talk about feelings. Maybe it was because they didn't *have* feelings. Maybe something in them had been hollowed out, leading them to take other people's lives and view it as a business. Maybe now the same hollowness lived in him. He glanced at Cass, caught her looking at him.

He tapped the arm of the sofa with the pen. But what had happened seven years ago? Ross Mobley, founder of Americans Combating Extremism and father of Terrence Ross, had died. A few weeks later, Ryan's parents committed suicide. Something was still missing. His parents hadn't been Adam and Eve for twenty years at that point and nothing was heard of Terrence Ross again. What did the death of Ross's father have to do with Frank and Anna Elder going over the edge? He looked across the room at Faith Kelly and saw that confusion had slashed furrows into her forehead.

"Who is Clarke, Kelly?" Ryan finally said. "Tell me who he is."

"Damn," Kelly said again. "I knew he was somehow involved in all this, but I didn't think—"

"Who *is* he?" Ryan said again.

Kelly sighed. "He's my boss. He's the chief deputy marshal for the Oklahoma City office of the U.S. Marshals Service." She backed into a chair.

Ryan stepped forward. "Are you arresting me, or are you here to kill me, or what?"

Kelly looked up at him. At first he thought she looked defeated, resigned, then angry. He knew the look well—he'd seen it in his own mirror quite a bit of late.

"I'm not here to kill you, for God's sake," she said. "I'm a federal law enforcement officer and I take my responsibilities seriously."

Tanis snorted, and Ryan said, "Forgive me if I don't buy that sanctimonious bullshit."

"Look, I don't speak for Clarke. I speak only for myself.

You want to know something? I'm technically off this case. Clarke pulled me off it because of what happened down on the concourse. I'm not supposed to be here. Clarke called me, and I quote, a 'fucking stupid bitch.' Clarke thinks I'm a nuisance and maybe now I understand why."

"Then why *are* you here?" Cass said.

Kelly looked at her. "I could ask you that, Ms. Chambers."

Cass looked uncomfortable. "Look, I—"

Kelly held up a hand. "Never mind. I'm here because Art Dorian was my friend. He was my mentor, my teacher, and I owe it to him to find out what happened. Under the law, I need to find out what happened. It's my job."

"Huh-uh," Tanis said, and they all looked at her. "It ain't your job no more, Ms. Deputy. It's what you want. Like what I want is to bring down whoever did Cyrus. You want whoever did your friend-mentor-teacher guy. Abel here wants to find out who he really is, and talk to this Ross about his mama and daddy, so he don't have to look over his shoulder his whole life. Way I see it, we need to cut through all the shit flying around in here and figure out what we're gonna *do*."

Reeves stood up and spoke for the first time. "I wouldn't have put it that way, but I believe the young lady is right. None of us are really here officially." A glance at Kelly. "Faith, I think we're going to have to be creative, operate outside protocol. That little discussion we had about breaking rules? This is where it's led us. And you have a decision to make."

Kelly crossed to the counter that separated the living room from the kitchen. She leaned on it as if she were very tired, tapping her nails, looking at Ryan.

Cass came up behind Ryan, her hand in the small of his back. Ryan realized he ached all over and the pain in his foot was merciless, as if angry at having been denied for the last few days. "I need to sit down," he finally said, and hobbled to the sofa.

"Are you hurt?" Reeves asked.

"Oh, just a little." Ryan managed a crooked smile.

"I'll rewrap it for you," Cass said, and went into the bathroom to get the supplies.

Kelly watched the entire operation, took in the body language between Ryan and Cass. Finally she shook her head—Ryan couldn't tell if it was frustration or disgust or what—and walked to the chair beside him while Cass was working on his foot.

"Two things have to happen," Kelly said.

"What about the rules, Deputy Kelly?" Ryan said.

Kelly waited a long moment before speaking. "No rules." She ran her hands through her long red hair, pulling it straight back. "Not anymore."

"I'm listening."

"Clarke will have to be brought down. I can't believe I'm saying this, but we have to have solid evidence to bring him down. I think . . ." She tapped her fingers on the lamp table. "I think he hides behind the fact that he's a big man with a big voice, but he gets rattled easily."

Ryan looked into her green eyes. "Then let's rattle him."

"I'll have to convince. . . ." Kelly's voice trailed off. "Never mind. Leave that to me. He has to fall, and fall convincingly. Then, the second thing."

"Ross. He wants me to find the uranium for him. And I'm going to do it, because the only way I'm going to find out what made my parents lose control the way they did . . ." He lowered his voice. ". . . is to ask him. And the only way I'll be able to look him in the face is to take him where he wants to go."

An idea opened in the back of Ryan's mind. Ross Mobley. ACE. Terrence Ross—the boy whose father gave him a surname different than his own. Ross's disappearance, at the same time as Adam and Eve's.

Disgrace . . .

humiliation . . .

the war that didn't start . . .

the father. The son.

Ross Mobley's picture, imprinted on his mind like words stamped into metal.

Folded into Ryan's shirt pocket, as it had been since the day he received it, was the newspaper clipping. He took it out and opened it, read it again.

"It's here," he said, shaking the little rectangle of paper. "The uranium's right here. My mother sent this to me the day before she and Dad killed themselves. It's right here. Ross knows about it, but he doesn't know what's in it. It's something only I would know. Something . . . something from the past. It's right here, something from my life growing up. Right in front of my face, and I still can't see it." He looked from the paper back to Kelly. "By the way, Deputy, who is Dean Yorkton?"

Kelly twitched, her knuckles rapping the lamp table. "You tell me."

"Clever. See what he knows before you admit to anything. Okay, I'll play. He's Department Thirty, like Dorian. Dorian was the controller, the paper czar, and Yorkton was some kind of a field person. Since my parents were such high-profile and dangerous people, they assigned someone to them permanently, made him the next-door neighbor. So for twenty years there he was, mowing his lawn and talking about the neighborhood association and local politics and sports. He even came to some of my baseball games. No kids of his own, you see. The good neighbor. How am I doing?"

Kelly smiled thinly. "Pretty well. He was in town for a few days, helping me with the investigation. I just saw him a few hours ago." The smile faltered. "It was his idea to use Jeff Majors to get to you."

Ryan's face darkened. "Son of a bitch. So he is still alive. I thought that story about being shot in front of the Lincoln Memorial was a little too cute to be real."

"Ryan," Kelly said, "I'm sorry. If that sounds trite, then so be it. But I'm sorry for what's happened to you." Kelly looked around the room and settled her gaze on Cass. "If Nina and I put together who Alicia Rubinstein was, Clarke won't be far behind. We need to get you to a safe house. I don't think you're safe here anymore, any of you."

Ryan nodded. He'd been in the warmth of the apartment for a while now, but he still felt cold and cramped from the hours spent huddled in the salvage yard. It was a chill that he thought might never go away. Florida, he thought. Sunny and warm in Pensacola. The city that had been his home most recently, not that he ever really had a home. Just like the people who lived under the bridge.

He'd left Pensacola a week ago Tuesday. The day he was fired. The day he received his mother's letter, seven years late.

Thoughts of Pensacola, of WPSC, of his buffoonish boss Earl Penders and the corrupt contractor Kirk Stillman, began to intermingle with Ross Mobley and Terrence Ross and his parents, burning to death in their car.

The idea began to bloom a little further. Ryan thought he caught some of its scent.

Connections, he thought. Who was Terrence Ross, really? Who were any of them?

Connections.

"I want two things," he said to Kelly.

"Go ahead."

"I want to know my real name, if I have one, the name my parents gave me. I want to know who I was before they went to your friend Dorian." He thought of Dorian, at the Cheyenne battlefield, talking about being there with his parents, and he, Ryan, as a baby in his mother's arms. "And I know you must have some kind of a debriefing report from when my parents went into Department Thirty's protection. Somewhere, I'll bet someone—maybe even Dorian—asked them why they started killing. I want a copy of that report."

Kelly blinked at him. "All that may still be classified."

"I don't care if it's classified or not. My whole life is classified, isn't it? I'm not really supposed to exist, am I?"

"I don't know if I have the authority to get it for you."

"Then find someone who does."

Kelly nodded. "For what it's worth, I think it's a reasonable request, given what's happened. I'll ask Yorkton."

"When you talk to him, tell him . . ." Ryan stopped, and he thought of a summer, a long time ago. "Ask him if he remembers the summer he went on vacation to California. At least that's where he told us he went. He was gone for two weeks. I volunteered to mow his lawn for him. He had some strange-looking plants in his backyard and I mowed them down. I thought they were weeds. Later my dad saw what I'd done and nearly had a heart attack. Turns out they were some kind of rare, exotic flower just a few days short of blooming. I felt so bad I wrote Mr. Yorkton a note, apologizing and offering to buy him some new flowers out of my own money. I taped the note to his door. When he got back, he told me not to worry about the flowers, but he told me how responsible and mature I was for leaving him a note like that." Ryan bowed his head. "Ask him if he remembers that, will you?"

"I will," Kelly said.

Ryan nodded, barely listening as Kelly began telling him about moving to the safe house.

Memory.

Ross Mobley. Terrence Ross. Fathers and sons.

Connections.

And Ryan began to understand.

41

THEY TOOK TWO CARS, KELLY'S MIATA AND REEVES'S Honda, driving slowly on the slick streets. Kelly rode alone in her two-seater and the others rode with Reeves. No one spoke except Tanis, who sat beside Reeves and peppered her with questions.

Ryan watched the dark, icy streets of the city slide by without really seeing, aware of almost nothing external but Cass's head against his shoulder, her arm linked through his.

Ross Mobley.

Terrence Ross.

Father and son. What would it have been like to have a father like Ross Mobley? A "hero," a man so paranoid about his enemies that he gave his only son a different surname and sent him away for most of his life. What kind of expectations would a father like that have for his son, as an adult?

He'd pressured his son into joining him in his master creation, ACE, but then the son decided to turn the tables on the father. Instead of The New America being just a cover for anti-extremist infiltration, it had truly been about the violent overthrow of American society.

It was like looking through a new, clean pane of glass, so clear it seemed as if it wasn't there. Adam and Eve had taken the uranium, hidden it somewhere, and gone into Department Thirty protection. After Ross's failure to start the war, the great conflict that would see the extreme left and the extreme right destroy each other and create a second American Revolution, he disappeared. Of course, he went back to his real identity, leaving Terrence Ross and his whispers behind for many years.

Then the old man had died.

Seven years ago, at the end of October.

Terrence Ross, now growing old himself, would have finally been free from his father's obsessions and tyranny. In his own twisted worldview, he was free to try to find Adam and Eve, who had betrayed him so long ago. Free to go back and finish the job he'd started twenty years earlier, no longer in need of his father or ACE or the Justice Department to provide cover. He would have spent all the intervening time building a cover of his own.

Ryan closed his eyes. There were still holes to fill in, so many holes. But he thought he understood Terrence Ross a little better.

Now, where had he seen Ross Mobley's picture?

He couldn't reach it, as it danced carefully away from him, a demented ballerina on the stage of his memory.

The car was slowing and Ryan was vaguely aware of Tanis talking to Reeves in the front seat. He opened his eyes and turned his head. Kelly's little Miata was just ahead of them and they were turning into a driveway on a quiet suburban street, the kind where "soccer moms" and their families lived. The house was simple, brick, with an attached garage. A real-estate sign stood by the curb.

Ryan's heart almost stopped.

He disengaged himself from Cass and scrambled out of the backseat almost before Reeves had stopped the car.

Ahead of them, Kelly was just getting out of her car. "Art told me about this house," she said. "Both WITSEC and Department Thirty have used it for—Ryan? What's the matter?"

Ryan walked into the middle of the front yard. Next door, a minivan sat in the driveway. He remembered the Hispanic woman with the three boys.

It's a nice neighborhood, she'd said.

He turned on Kelly. His voice was low. "Is this some kind of a sick joke? What the hell are you trying to do?"

Kelly's eyes widened. "What do you mean?"

Ryan swept his hands around in an all-encompassing gesture. Cass was just getting out of the Honda. "This! For Christ's sake, why did you bring me here?"

"I don't understand."

Ryan took a few steps toward her, watching her body go tense again, just as it had back in the apartment. "This is my house."

"What?"

"The house I grew up in! You brought me to my own house. I can't believe—" He broke off, staring at her face. "You didn't know. My God. You people . . . Barrientos was right. The left hand and the right hand."

Kelly was stricken. "No, I . . . I never had your address. I just . . . all I knew was that this was a department safe house. Art didn't—"

"If we're supposed to be out of sight, we ain't doing a very good job of it," Tanis said, getting out of the Honda.

"Nina," Kelly said, her voice still unsteady. "The back door."

Reeves jogged around to the back of the house.

Ryan stared up at the house, ordinary, unremarkable, ridiculously suburban. *His* house. The house where he'd lived his lie of a life for eighteen years.

A safe house.

"Ryan," Kelly said, and she was closer to him. "You have to believe me. I didn't know. It's just—"

Ryan held up a hand.

His house.

His life.

"Come on," he said. "Let's go in."

Nothing remained that he remembered. It was a shell, an empty hulk with nothing in it but memory.

Ryan walked from room to room, opening closet doors and cabinets, touching the walls.

His life.

Empty.

Appropriate, he thought.

In his bedroom, he stood in the center and looked at the emptiness. His bed had been here, his dresser there, his tiny desk by the window. His collection of baseball caps had hung on wooden hooks his father made, all around the room. The CD collection, the UCLA pennant, his autographed photo of Bob Edwards. . . .

He'd lain on the bed, right about here, and practiced reading fictional newscasts in his best radio voice, from the time he was ten years old. His mother had bought him a tape recorder with a microphone when he was eleven and he'd worn it out within two years, interviewing himself, interviewing Jeff—Jeff had thought he'd lost his mind. There was no money in radio, after all.

Here was the spot where his mother had sat on the edge of the bed and said, *Hurt on your own terms.*

"Ryan, are you all right?" Cass said gently, from the bedroom doorway.

He nodded. "Let's sleep in here," he said.

Half an hour later, Reeves returned with a trunkload of sleeping bags and blankets.

"The best we can do," Kelly said. "Since this is outside official channels. . . ." She shrugged. "Nina's agreed to stay with you."

"You think we'll try to run?" Ryan said. "You don't trust us. Well, that's all right, because I don't know if I trust you either. Nothing personal, you understand."

"I understand."

"But I'm not running anywhere, not until I figure out where that uranium is."

Kelly nodded. "Can you come in the living room for a minute, please? I'd like to talk to you alone."

Ryan stared at her for a moment, then looked at Cass. "Hang on, I'll be right back."

In the empty living room, Ryan leaned against the wall and studied the tall, well-dressed woman.

"I've risked everything on this," she said, "to find you, to put all these pieces together. Last Friday I was sitting there on desk duty when this envelope was dropped in my lap. Since then, nothing has made sense to me. Not even the things I've said and done myself have made sense to me."

"Well, then." Ryan smiled, surprising himself. "Welcome to the club, Deputy."

Kelly stood there stiffly, hands at her sides. Finally she shook herself, brushed her hair back with both hands. She handed Ryan a card. "Here are my home and cell phone numbers. Call me when you have some answers."

"Where are you going?"

Kelly's face was grim. "Everything we've seen says my boss murdered Cyrus Graesner. He has to answer for that."

"What are you going to do?"

"Leave that to me. I'll need Miss T to make a statement." She started toward the hallway. "I'll be back here by ten o'clock tomorrow morning. Call me if you think of anything."

"You already said that," Ryan said.

"Ryan." She hesitated a moment. "I just want to make this right. To just get things back to . . ." She groped for the words.

"Don't," Ryan said. "There's nothing to say."

"Maybe that's best," Kelly said, called to Tanis, and left the house.

42

KELLY DROVE THE MIATA SOUTH ON MAY AVENUE, LEAVing Edmond behind and coming back into Oklahoma City proper.

"Tell me," Tanis said. "What's the deal?"

Kelly braked for a light, pumping the pedal lightly on the ice. Ahead of her, a sand truck rolled slowly through the intersection. Child's play compared to Chicago, she thought.

"The deal," she said, "is that you're going to help me get to Clarke. You remember I said I thought he could get rattled easily?" Tanis nodded. "Well, we're going to rattle him. I'm going to need you to talk to someone."

"He's the one did Cyrus, I'll talk to the devil himself."

"I think if he's confronted with your statement, the day after he assaulted you and killed Cyrus, and then he sees Cyrus's videotape, we'll have him. First, though, we have to do the official things."

She turned west, then back to the north onto a quiet Quail Creek street. She'd memorized the address the first and only time she'd been here, a little over a month ago. She stopped in front of the house. Red, green, and white Christmas lights still adorned the well-trimmed hedges and the edge of the house.

"What's this about?" Tanis said, hugging her coat around her as they stepped out of the Miata.

"You'll see."

Kelly rang the bell, checking her watch. A little after eight o'clock. Not too late. Come on, open the door, she thought.

The man who came to the door was in his early forties, with razor-sharp blue eyes and movie star looks. He was wearing a white dress shirt with a loosened red tie below it, and tailored gray suit pants.

"Mr. Springs," Kelly said.

"Yes?" the man said neutrally.

"You may not remember me. We met at your Christmas party." She flipped open her ID case. "Deputy U.S. Marshal Faith Kelly."

A shadow crossed the man's face. "Kelly. The Majors incident."

"Yes, sir, that was my case."

"Why are you here, Deputy?"

"I'm sorry to bother you at home, sir, on a night like this, but some evidence has come to light and I want to bring it directly to your attention."

The man's eyes cut to Tanis.

"Oh, let me introduce you," Kelly said. She hoped her voice sounded smoother than she felt. "Tanis Harper, meet Mr. Owen Springs, the U.S. Attorney for the western district of Oklahoma. Sir, may we come in? I need a few minutes of your time."

"No, you may not. Go through channels, Deputy."

"Mr. Springs, this is very sensitive."

"I don't care. This is very improper, and you have no business being here." Springs began to close the door.

Kelly took a breath. "Do you think your friend Judge Majors would like to know who really murdered his son?"

Kelly watched the man. His jaw worked, and Kelly knew she had his attention. Springs hadn't given up his political ambitions. He'd narrowly lost a U.S. Senate bid just last year, but the governor's seat would be coming open in the next election cycle. Springs liked the image of the crusading prosecutor and Judge Ray Majors was a powerful friend to have.

"I'm listening," Springs said.

Kelly reached into the pocket of her coat and held up the videotape. "I assume you have a VCR, sir. I'd like to show you a home movie and then I'd like Ms. Harper to tell you a story."

An hour later, Kelly and Tanis emerged from the house

into a night that had grown colder. Kelly thought of the strange series of looks that had passed over the face of Owen Springs.

"I do all right?" Tanis said.

"You did great. I don't think he likes the term *shit-kicker*, but you know what? I don't care."

They both laughed. "Now what?" Tanis asked.

"I have some calls to make."

They climbed into the Miata and Kelly drove back to the brightness of May Avenue. She parked in the lot of an all-night donut shop and pulled out her cell phone. The first call went to Reeves's own cellular, back at the safe house.

"Our friends doing all right?" Kelly asked.

"Nine o'clock and they're sleeping like the proverbial babies," Reeves said.

"Good. I guess we're on for tomorrow morning. Between T's statement to the U.S. Attorney, and the videotape, Clarke won't know what hit him."

"Good luck, my friend."

"I'll need more than luck. I should be back there by ten in the morning."

The second call was to Scott Hendler at home. The FBI agent picked up on the first ring.

"Scott," Kelly said, "it's Faith."

"Well, Faith Kelly. How's community relations duty?"

"Always charming, Scott. Does everyone know about that?"

"Pretty much. What's up? You finally decide you want to go out with me? No conflict of interest, since you're off investigative duty."

"Scott, you are full of shit."

Hendler laughed. "Yes, I am. Nice of you to say so, and so good to know you can curse with the big boys. What's up?"

"Where are you on the case?"

Hendler's voice turned wary. "Look, since you're off this thing, I'm not really supposed to talk to you about it."

"Fine, Scott. Don't talk to me about it. I'll talk to you about it. You want to break it wide open?"

The line was silent.

"Come on, Scott. I don't have all night."

Hendler sighed. "You haven't been doing something you shouldn't, have you?"

"No, I'm not the one who's been doing things they shouldn't." Kelly's voice started to rise. "Do you want to know what I have or don't you?"

"I was just sitting here watching the basketball game and Oklahoma State's up by six points on Kansas, there's only five minutes to go—"

"If you'll agree to meet me at the courthouse tomorrow morning, you can go right back to it."

Another sigh. "I suppose. What time?"

"Seven-thirty. In the basement, by our elevator. One question, Scott. Any leads on where Ryan Elder might be?"

"Oh, hell, Faith. Not a one, and I've had trouble getting through to your boss over there."

Kelly smiled. "You can talk to him tomorrow."

Kelly pressed end, then looked at Tanis. "One more call."

"Okay. Can I go in and get some coffee?"

"Go ahead."

Kelly watched her go in the little shop, then called the last number.

"Hi, Mom," she said a moment later.

"There you are," Maire Kelly said. "You're late."

"Sorry, Mom. It's been kind of hectic."

"Oh, I guess. Your dad told me you called him."

"Is he around?"

"Oh no, cop talk. Sure, honey, he's right here."

"Faith?" Joe Kelly's voice said a moment later. "Is everything all right? Are you okay?"

"I think so, Dad." Kelly closed her eyes. "Actually, I have no idea."

"What about your case?"

"It's bigger and crazier than I thought." There was a long silence, the same kind of silence that had lingered between them for most of her life.

"Well?" Joe Kelly finally said, just as he had always done.

"I just . . . I just wanted to hear your voice. Tomorrow's going to be strange, and I . . . I don't know." She waited again. "Oh, by the way, Dad. . . ."

"Yeah?"

"I just wanted you to know that I paid attention to you the other day."

"Oh?"

Kelly squeezed the phone. "I followed my instinct."

The net was closing . . .

The Whispering Man sat in his car, not fifty yards away from Kelly's Miata, and watched the young woman's head of red hair bob up and down as she talked on her phone.

The oh-so-resourceful and clever young Deputy Kelly had proven her worth once again. He'd followed her to the apartment complex, watched as she emerged with Ryan Elder and the woman, followed her to the "safe house" in Edmond—what a deft touch, that being the Elders' old house!—then to Owen Springs's home, and now here.

He knew what she was doing, of course. The visit to the U.S. Attorney cemented it. She wanted to bring Clarke down through the right legal channels and she was planning to do just that. The Whispering Man knew Owen Springs well, and he could just imagine the man considering what his own political fortunes would be from breaking open such a case. Yes, he would have fallen for whatever plan she brought him.

And most important of all, Kelly had Ryan Elder. She would be gaining his trust by now. He would begin to believe they were on the same side. He would tell her things. Whatever Ryan knew, *she* would know.

The Whispering Man smiled into the dashboard lights, then glanced back toward the donut shop. The black girl with the blond cornrows, Graesner's sexy little friend, was sliding back in next to Kelly, holding a steaming cup of coffee.

You're brilliant, Deputy. You've done just what I needed you to do.

The Whispering Man picked up his own phone and punched in a number. When he heard Clarke's drawling voice, he said, "Phil, my old friend. I believe there's one last thing you need to do."

43

AT 3:00 A.M., RYAN HAD BEEN UP FOR AN HOUR, SITTING in what was once his dining room, Cass's laptop in front of him.

He'd passed by the master bedroom—his parents' room—and glimpsed the sleeping form of Nina Reeves, wrapped in a brown sleeping bag. Now, with the glow from the computer the only light in the house, he sat digging at his cuticles and knowing that something was wrong.

Frank and Anna Elder. Adam and Eve. Professional killers.

He'd been betrayed twice, he thought. First by his parents' lives, then by their death.

Ross Mobley. Terrence Ross. The Whispering Man's nuclear war.

Uranium in lead cases.

Lies inside of lies.

His good, decent upstanding parents. The insurance executive and the music teacher. A modest home in the suburbs, an only son, money in the bank. Then what? A phone call, a knock on the door seven years ago? The past insinuating itself into the present. Panic. Fear. The house of cards crashing down. A cryptic letter to Ryan, away at college, waiting for Thanksgiving, waiting for him. A fiery, bizarre, spectacular death.

Ryan thought of the life he might have had, if only he hadn't allowed that one fiery moment to define the man he had become. He might have been a network radio anchor by now. He might have married Melissa McNeill or come back to Oklahoma and tracked down Allison McDermott. He might even have children of his own. He might not have spent the years sitting alone eating spicy food or in apartment laundromats by himself.

Ryan put his head in his hands and began to weep.

Cass found him there, asleep, at a few minutes after four. His chin was on his chest, his back against the dining room wall, the computer still on. She gently took it off his lap, glancing at the screen, at the ACE website he'd been viewing.

As soon as she moved the computer, he was awake. "What is it?" he said.

"Nothing. You fell asleep out here. I was just moving the computer."

Ryan lifted his head, wiped his face, felt the tear streaks.

"Are you okay?" Cass said, then added, "Is that a stupid question, or what?"

Ryan looked at her, seeing just a silhouette of her face in the light from the computer screen. A beautiful, compassionate, wounded, yet incredibly strong woman. And if not for all this, he would never have met her. What a strange thought to have. "I think this is going to be over soon. I have some ideas about what happened in 1975, and about seven years ago. It's like I've got the pieces of the puzzle that go around the edges and now I need to fill in the middle."

He heard a sound, then lowered his voice. "I think our gatekeeper is stirring. Let's go out into the garage."

They walked through the kitchen, Ryan instinctively feeling his way along. How many times had he come in too late as an adolescent, fumbling in here through the dark, only to find one or both of his parents asleep on the sofa with a lamp on? It was the kind of thing normal parents did, worrying about their teenage children. It made him stop for a moment, with his hand on the door that led from the kitchen to the garage.

"What?" Cass whispered.

Ryan shook his head. "Nothing."

They passed into the garage and he closed the door quietly behind them. It was utterly dark and Ryan felt along the wall until he found the light switch. He flipped it and the garage was bathed in buttery light.

"Kelly said not to use the lights inside, so the neighbors don't get curious, but you can't see this light from outside," Ryan said. He walked around, inhaling the musty smell. "I wonder who the family was who were here after us. More people with new identities, I guess. Coleridge said they 'outgrew' the house. I wonder what that really means. I guess the money I thought came from the sale of the house really came from the government. What a mess."

He scuffed his foot around an old oil stain. "Right here," he said.

"Right here what?" Cass was next to him, crossing her arms over her chest against the cold.

"Here in the garage, this is the last place I saw my parents alive. They'd been acting so strange, ever since they picked me up at the airport. My mother never came to airports. She hated them. And then that damned paprika for the goulash. And my mother . . ."

He froze, a flash of memory hurtling toward him, then brushing by like a passing train. The garage. His mother. But what did it have to do with any of this?

He sat down on the cold concrete, Cass beside him. "This is insane," he said. "Why are you still here?"

She smiled. "Good question. Maybe I just want to see what happens."

He nodded silently, trying to retrieve the memory, the little sliver of something he'd seen a moment ago.

He pulled the newspaper clipping out of his pocket. "It's here. Whatever they wanted me to know is right here, but I can't see it. I don't know why they sent it to me, but it's here."

They read the words again. "All those pieces of music," Cass said. "Beethoven, the Coriolan Overture, Smetana from 'My Country,' the Tchaikovsky 'Pathetique.' It was Tchaikovsky's last piece. I wonder if that has something to do with it." She crossed her legs in front of her. "Smetana was Czech. But . . ."

Ryan turned to look at her, at the amazing eyes. "But what?"

"Nothing. It doesn't make any sense."

"Neither does anything else. Tell me."

"It was a stupid random thought. I was thinking, your mother was Czech. But there's no possible way they could have shipped the uranium there, to Czechoslovakia—I guess it's the Czech Republic now. If what Graesner said was true, it just came from eastern Europe. They wouldn't have turned around and sent it right back."

"You're right, it . . ." Ryan looked at the page again, the words he'd stored in his memory a week and a half ago. "Wait a minute. What did you just say?"

"Which part?"

"The music. The piece. The one by Smetana."

" 'Ma Vlast.' It's a series of tone poems for orchestra, based on the—"

"No, no. That's not what you said."

"Oh, the translation of 'Ma Vlast' is 'My Country,' or sometimes, 'My Fatherland.' That's why I thought . . . Ryan?"

"My country," Ryan whispered.

Memory: ancient, rounded mountains, trees with branches spread heavenward as if begging, twisting roads of two-lane blacktop, blue waters, roadside stands selling tourist trash. His father behind the wheel: *This is my country, Ryan. My country.*

He felt a sudden stillness, and Ryan knew.

"That's it," he said, so softly Cass had to lean forward to hear him. "My father always said it was his country." He looked at her. "The Ozarks. The Ozark Mountains, Missouri, Arkansas. Remember I told you we went there every summer? Dad loved the hills and he always said it just that way: This is my country."

Cass sat back. "My God. And you think they put the uranium somewhere there?"

"It has to be. There's no other . . . but where? It's a big area. We used to range all over the place. There are so many little valleys and back-country places, it could be anywhere." The stillness gone, he began to feel the adrenaline shooting through him. "A map. Don't you have a map in your bag?"

"A road atlas, yes. I thought I might—" She was up in a moment, vanishing into the house. Then she was back, cat-like, silent. They opened the atlas to the page for Missouri.

Ryan ran his finger to the bottom of the page, the far southern end of the state, where it met Arkansas. He caught names that had been a part of his childhood: Table Rock Lake, Mark Twain National Forest, wavy blue against splotches of green. In red lettering were the tourist attractions: Talking Rocks, Silver Dollar City, Shepherd of the Hills Farm. And so many roads, twisting like serpents across the page.

He and Cass leaned close to the map, their faces inches apart, Ryan looking for anything. Looking for connections. Dammit, where are you? We're so close!

"This is impossible," Cass said. "There are a million tiny little towns on here. Look at some of these names: Walnut Shade, Rocky Comfort, Blue Eye, Clever, Viola. . . ."

Ryan went rigid. "Let me see that."

He took the map, bowing his head as if praying to it. He traced his finger to a spot on the Missouri–Arkansas state line, then dropped the map and backed into the center of the garage.

"Right here," he said.

Cass looked up, puzzled.

"I was sitting in my mother's car, getting ready to pull out of the garage to get the paprika. My dad had given me a twenty-dollar bill, and I was in the car, and the garage door was up. I'd started the engine when she came over and tapped on the glass. I rolled down the window and she leaned down. I remember smelling her perfume, White Shoulders, the kind she'd worn ever since I was a little kid. And she leaned over and whispered in my ear. The last words my mother ever said to me."

Cass waited, watching him.

" 'Remember these eyes' is what she said, and she pulled back and I looked at her, and that was it. 'Remember these eyes.' "

Cass shook her head. "I don't—"

"My mother had blue eyes."

Ryan picked up the map again and traced his finger down the page. South from Springfield, south from Branson, then a twisting jog west and south again, all the way to the Arkansas line. A tiny black dot along State Highway 13, sitting exactly on the border.

The town of Blue Eye.

Ryan began pacing the garage. "I remember now. It was away from all the tourist hype, far enough from Branson to the north and Eureka Springs to the south to be just a tiny little Ozark town. Half of it's in Missouri, the other half in Arkansas. The state line is a road that cuts through the middle of the town. I remember we stopped at a little store. It was sort of a cross between a 7-Eleven and an old country general store. There was a big purple awning out front and it sat on the state line. The road that splits the town extends right across the highway from the store. Every time we went through there, up until I was a teenager, I used to go and stand at the state line marker and have Dad take my picture. That was just amazing to me, to have one foot in one state and the other foot in another state."

"Any landmarks?" Cass said. "Anything your parents paid special attention to when you were there?"

"There wasn't much to it, really. A little white post office on the Missouri side. That store, a little park with a pavilion right across the highway, on the Arkansas side. And we would always drive out along that road. It was a kick to think we were actually driving on the state line." Ryan paced, thumping his forehead with his fingertips. "A cemetery. There was a cemetery on the Missouri side, and when I was older I remember thinking that it was really well kept, with more flowers on the graves than anyplace I'd ever seen. I guess the town took care of its dead."

Oblivious to the cold, Ryan felt flushed. He glanced at Cass, and was surprised to see that she looked like he felt. Memories crowded him, elbowing for space like children at a candy counter. "That road went for a ways, a mile, maybe two miles before it dead-ended, and there was a huge old elm tree just at the point where the road stopped. Biggest tree I've ever seen, looked like it could stop a tank. A little gravel road led off from it to the south. We would drive all the way to the end and Dad would say, 'End of the line, troops!' and we'd turn around and drive back to town. I thought it was so . . . so hokey, so corny. So unlike my father. But. . . ."

The sentence died, and Ryan had a clear vision of his father slowing the car and pulling to the side of the narrow road as they were driving back toward Blue Eye.

What do you think? he'd say. *Is that our new house? You ready to move in? Come on, Anna. Ryan, how about you?*

Dad, you're weird.

I agree with Ryan. You're weird, Frank. Laughter from all three of them.

He saw it clearly: a dilapidated, long-abandoned house, a small white frame structure with a roof of green shingles, the sagging porch supported by green-painted posts. The windows were gone, there was a huge gash in the roof, and whatever paint was left was peeling in long strips.

It sat behind a barbed wire fence with NO TRESPASSING signs bolted to it. A trail—just two ruts broken by a line of grass—led past the shack, winding up to a barn, barely visible from the road. From what Ryan could see, the barn seemed to be in better repair than the house. Other than squirrels and birds, there was no sign of life around the place.

Come on, I want to take a picture.

Frank, it says "no trespassing."

Dad, it's just a run-down old shack.

It'll make a great picture. I'll be right back.

His father, climbing a tree that stood just outside the fence, then dropping to the ground on the other side.

We ought to take a picture of him climbing the tree, Ryan had told his mother, and they laughed again.

Frank Elder had disappeared from view and came jogging back down the path ten minutes later.

He'd done it every year they went to the Ozarks, insisting it was a forgotten corner of America, and the pictures were snapshots of a disappearing life.

Looks like everything's already disappeared from this place, Dad.

Yeah, well, you'll appreciate it someday.

It had all been for his benefit, Ryan thought. The jokes about "our new house," the charade of taking pictures, blathering about Americana.

Frank Elder had been going up to that barn to check on what was inside it.

Dozens of lead cases.

"I know where I have to go," Ryan said to Cass.

Cass came to him and put her arms around him. He let himself be held for a long moment.

"Blue Eye. I . . . we . . . have to go to Blue Eye."

"Yes." Still holding him.

"But before we go, I have a few more things I need to do."

She looked up at him. His body had gone rigid again, tense as telephone wires in high wind. They went back into the house and retrieved Cass's phone from the sleeping bag. Ryan pulled the card out of his pocket and called the home number Kelly had given him. While he was punching in the number, Nina Reeves appeared, fully dressed, in the doorway.

When Kelly's voice came on the line, remarkably free from sleep for 4:30 in the morning, he said, "Did you do what you needed to do?"

"I don't know if it's what I needed to do," Kelly said. "But it makes the best use of the evidence we have. We'll see what happens in the morning."

"You sound pretty awake for an ungodly hour like this."

Kelly breathed into the phone. "After I dropped T off at her house, I came home to pack up a few things, thought I'd try to rest before everything hits the fan."

"But you can't sleep."

"What's sleep?"

Ryan nodded. "Point taken. I know where the uranium is. It's in an old barn about a mile west of the town of Blue Eye, in the Ozarks on the Missouri–Arkansas state line."

"How do you know?"

"I'll explain later. But that's where it is, Kelly. I know it. That's where Ross wants me to take him."

Kelly cleared her throat. "Okay, stay put. After we deal with Clarke, we'll get a haz-mat team and Special Operations Group people moving there."

"Haz-mat?"

"Hazardous materials. I'd say we need them, don't you?"

Ryan thought of Ross's nuclear war, his second American Revolution. "I would say so, yes."

"Thanks for calling me, Ryan. Thanks for trusting me."

"When you get Ross, I want a few minutes with him."

"Ryan—"

Ryan's voice rose. "This is no ordinary investigation and you know it. You can get me a few minutes with him."

"Look, I'm guessing that by that point, I may not be able to do anything. The investigation may belong to the Bureau by then."

"That's a cop-out."

"Pun intended?"

"Dammit, Kelly, this isn't funny—"

"Okay, I'm sorry. I'm tired. Look, Ryan, the truth is, they're not going to want you anywhere near that uranium. As soon as the whole Clarke issue is settled, we'll deploy SOG—that's Special Operations Group. That's an elite Marshals Service unit headquartered in Louisiana. Scott Hendler will bring in Hostage Rescue from Quantico, and the Bureau's haz-mat teams. I have it all planned out. Between the videotape and Tanis's statement, we have enough evidence to arrest Clarke, for conspiracy if nothing else. After he's in custody, the U.S. Attorney will drop all outstanding warrants against you. But even though you're free, you're still a material witness in this whole business, and I can guarantee you there's no way they'll let you anywhere near Blue Eye or Terrence Ross."

"But—"

"You'll get your day, but it won't be tomorrow. For God's sake, just rest. After everything that's happened, I'd think you'd welcome the chance."

Ryan began to feel the anger, like shards of glass pricking his skin. "You can't deny me this. Everything I've ever known was a lie, and Ross is the only living connection that might be able to tell me some truth."

"Just stay there. I told you, I'll be back to the house by ten o'clock. We'll talk more then."

"I don't believe you."

"Fine, don't believe me then. I still have a job to do. For what it's worth, yes, I believe you should have the opportunity to look Ross in the eye. Common decency says that's the fair thing to do. But the cop in me says it's not going to happen." She cleared her throat, and for the first time Ryan thought her voice sounded tired. "Look, I'll see what I can do. I can't make any guarantees. But I give you my word I'll talk to the U.S. Attorney."

Ryan started to argue, then realized he wasn't likely to get a better deal than that. "All right, I'll buy it. At least for now. Good luck with Clarke."

"See you at ten."

Ryan hung up, looking into Cass's huge eyes, catching a glimpse of Reeves hovering a few feet away. Like an unexpected knock at the door, he felt another tiny blip of memory: the far past and the recent past melting into one another.

"Come on," he said to Cass.

"Where?"

"I need your computer again. I think I just figured out where I've seen Ross Mobley before." He took her by her good hand and led her back through the house.

44

AT 7:15 FRIDAY MORNING, PHILLIP CLARKE SAT PARKED in his new white Dodge Dakota on a quiet street, smoking one cigarette after another, right down to the filter. He'd been sitting here since midnight, watching the one lamp that was on in a corner of the house. He watched the car in the driveway, imagining what the layout of the house would be like inside. Once, at around 4:30, he'd seen a light go on in the front room and saw a shadow crossing back and forth.

Talking on the phone, he thought. Just like at the office, she paces when she talks on the damn phone. Damn her, a cop's kid trying to prove a point. And Graesner. And Ross. Damn all of them to hell for dragging me down.

After ten minutes, the front light had gone off again.

"Don't tell me you think you're going to sleep," Clarke said aloud to the interior of his truck.

There had been no movement since, and now, with the jagged edges of winter sunrise just showing behind him, Clarke ran his hands over the smooth wood finish of the clipper ship he'd carved nearly twenty years ago. He felt the three masts, the boat's prow, the detail he'd put into the cabin, right down to the portholes. A beautiful piece of work. He'd brought it from the office, a tiny connection to reality in the midst of all this muck.

After a few minutes he closed his fist around it, then tossed it onto the floorboard.

Clarke splayed his hands out on the steering wheel, trying to keep them from shaking as he thought about how he'd killed Cyrus Graesner.

He could have justified it as self-defense. Graesner, the stupid old fart, had gone for his gun first, had even fired first. But then Clarke would have had to explain why he was in Graesner's house in the first place and why he'd clubbed two nearly naked, unarmed girls over the head.

Well, see, he would say, it all started a long time ago. I was a young hotshot working on this special task force. Things were rolling along, we were getting good information from Graesner and our other snitches in the field, when I got a visit from this very strange guy. He told me his real name and who his father was, but then said he was going to adopt the name of Terrence Ross, and he was going to build a great cover, and then he was going to make sure the fringe groups in America destroyed each other. And he had a lot of money, and his father was a legend, and some of his ideas weren't bad. . . .

Clarke cracked his knuckles. Ideas, hell. He was fooling himself. It was the money. He may have been a young Justice Department hotshot, but even young Justice Department hotshots didn't get paid very well. Coming as he had from hardscrabble west Texas, son of a part-time carpenter and full-time drunk, Clarke took the money and ran.

And, all things considered, he hadn't had to do very much for Ross. A few snippets of information here and there and that was it. The biggest was at the very beginning, when Adam and Eve double-crossed him and decided to go under with the newly created Department Thirty. Ross called him one day, mumbling about his so-called revolution, and then he whispered, "I need Adam and Eve's case officer. Just the name. I'll take care of the rest."

What harm could the name do? he'd thought at the time. No one else knew about Ross's little war, and Clarke thought all his talk about "a second American Revolution" was so much bullshit, more of the same nutty stuff that everyone was spouting in those days. So it couldn't really hurt anything for Ross to know who was handling Adam and Eve. The task force was being shut down anyway and Clarke was quietly transferred into the Marshals Service.

Clarke closed his eyes, thinking of everything that had happened because he gave Art Dorian's name to Ross so long ago: Adam and Eve's suicide, then Dorian's murder, the fiasco in the Underworld, and now Graesner. Graesner had given Clarke's name to Adam and Eve's kid. And he, Phillip Everett "Philly" Clarke, son of the town drunk from Spearman, Texas, had blown two holes in Graesner's chest.

Ross had manipulated him, had been manipulating him for nearly thirty years. Clarke slammed his fist down on the wheel, then again, and again.

And now, Kelly.

Clarke flexed his hands against the wheel, then watched as the light came on at the front of the house. He checked his watch, then scanned the sky, watching the ragged light steal over the city.

"You're not taking me down, girl," Clarke said, then looked around. He'd only begun talking to himself lately. Had to watch that.

To hell with it, he thought. He got out of the truck, closed the door very quietly, and began to cross the street.

Kelly contemplated making coffee, then decided she was already too jittery and didn't need any more caffeine. She'd finally dozed for an hour or so after talking to Ryan, after jotting down directions to the location he'd given her for the cases of uranium. But it was a restless sleep, and she finally woke up bathed in sweat.

She showered and dressed quickly, keeping one eye on the clock. She was due to meet Hendler and U.S. Attorney Springs at the courthouse at 7:30. Clarke was always in his office early—she knew he'd be there.

Clarke was about to fall, but Kelly couldn't get excited about it. She felt none of the big-case exhilaration, but a profound weight, a deep sadness. This would smear the name of the Marshals Service, the oldest federal law enforcement agency in the country, and one she'd fought inordinately hard to get into. She pictured headlines: "Federal Lawman Indicted for Murder in Death of Ex-Informant. Federal Marshal said to Be Involved in Terrorist Conspiracy."

Kelly shook her head. These days, *terrorist* was the worst thing one could be called. She didn't know why Clarke had veered off the path and she decided it didn't really matter anymore.

She put Graesner's videotape into her coat pocket, put on her coat and scarf, and as she always did just before she left the house, made sure the Glock was fully loaded.

She fished her keys out of her purse, wondering if she'd have to scrape frost off the Miata's windshield. Have to actually park it in the garage someday, Kelly thought as she opened her front door.

Kelly screamed.

Clarke reached out with both of his massive hands, grabbed double handfuls of Kelly's coat, and shoved her backward into the house. She tumbled to the side, gashing her hip against the oak end table by the door.

Clarke slammed the door so hard that it bounced back open a few inches. Oblivious, he bent over Kelly and snarled, "Going somewhere, Kelly, you little bitch?"

Kelly rolled onto her back and aimed a kick at his groin, but her aim was off and she barely clipped his shin.

Then Clarke was on her, his thick legs straddling her chest, pinning her arms to her sides. "First things first, now," he said, and his hand brushed her right breast as he reached inside her coat. When he found the shoulder holster, he snapped it open and had the Glock out in one smooth motion. He held it over his head and threw it overhanded across the room. It bounced once and landed in the doorway between the dining room and kitchen.

"You went to the U.S. Attorney," he said, bending his head down. She could smell his breath. "Stupid, girl. That was really stupid."

Kelly's mind bounced like a crazy ball in a child's game: How did he find out? Then: What does it matter?

"Chief—" she said, and her voice died in her throat.

"Listen, Kelly. You listen to me. You've got Elder. I know you've got him. Now tell me where that fucking uranium is."

It was hard to breathe with the 240-pound Clarke sitting on her chest.

"Don't know," she mumbled. "He didn't tell me."

"Don't fucking lie to me!" His right hand formed into a fist and crashed into her cheek. "Where is that uranium? I saw you in here at four-thirty fucking A.M., pacing back and forth on the phone. Who else would call you at four-thirty in the morning? Tell me, Kelly! I'll kill you. I swear to God, I will kill you!"

Kelly's vision was blurred. Talking was useless. There was no reason in Phillip Clarke anymore. Whatever humanity had been there before was long gone. His big face was twisted into something out of a horror movie, his nostrils flared like a wild animal's, his eyes beyond comprehension.

Clarke's fist came down again, and at the last moment it

opened and he slapped her across the bruise he'd just given her. "Talk to me, Kelly. You tell me where that uranium is and we can end this."

Kelly shook her head through the pain, but she realized that when he'd hit her, he'd put so much of his body into the blow that his right leg had loosened its grip on her left arm.

Clarke leaned back again, bellowing without words, and as he did, Kelly's left hand snaked out behind her. Her fingers raked the carpet. Clarke's hand flew downward, this time angling for the other side of her face.

Her hand closed on cold hardness. She got two fingers around the outer rim of the ceramic plate she'd once thrown at Mikael's chest, and she pulled it to her.

She solidified her grip, turned her head slightly, and flipped the plate at Clarke's head.

He roared in rage and staggered to the side.

Kelly was off the floor in a second, stumbling toward the hallway. She was almost home free when she felt his hand on her ankle. She didn't even think—she'd trained for this at the academy. Before his hand closed, she jerked her foot backward, extending her leg as far as it would go and grinding her heel into Clarke's face.

He howled and clutched his nose. "Dead!" he shouted. "You're dead, you bitch!" He staggered against her bookcase.

She surveyed her options—Clarke was between her and the kitchen, so she couldn't get to the Glock. She dashed down the hall to her bedroom and slammed the door, but it popped back open as if on springs. Clarke, blood streaming from his nose, filled the entire doorway.

"Just tell me," he breathed. "Tell me where that damned uranium is and we'll be done with it."

Kelly backed up and found her voice. "I can't believe you'd be a party to this, Chief. If Ross does what he's planning to do—"

"I don't care!" Clarke screamed. "I just want it over, and when I'm finished with you, it's *over!*"

Kelly backed against her night table, feeling around for

something—*anything!*—she could use as a weapon. On an ordinary night, she would have had a glass of water on the table, but this had been no ordinary night. Nothing there—a few cosmetics, the new lipstick she'd bought at Foley's but hadn't tried yet, a month-old copy of *U.S. News and World Report* which she hadn't gotten around to reading, a couple of pairs of earrings, a small cube of notepaper. . . .

The directions Ryan Elder had given her, the directions to the uranium.

She snatched the top sheet off the cube and jammed it in the pocket of her slacks.

Clarke was closing in on her. "What's that, Kelly?" His voice was even more gravelly than usual. "Something for me?"

She feinted to the right, then moved left, toward the bed. But Clarke, even injured, moved fast for such a big man. One arm caught her across the ribs and flung her onto the bed as if she were a rag doll.

He hit her hard across the face again, and she could feel one of her eyes beginning to swell. The room started to tilt at an odd angle, then all she could see was Clarke on top of her again. He slapped at her breasts.

"Like that?" he snarled. "Too bad we don't have more time. But business is business. Now where's that paper?"

Her hands were free this time and she dug a nail into his wrist, but it didn't seem to faze him. He backhanded her and her ears rang from the blow. One of his huge hands went into her slacks pocket, fingers out and searching.

No! Kelly screamed inwardly. She ran through the directions in her head. She had a terrible memory for directions—that's why she'd written them down. Had Ryan said the barn was a mile east or a mile west of the town? And was it one mile or two miles?

"Here we go," Clarke said in an almost singsong voice. "The Ozarks. Well, how absolutely fucking quaint that is. It's good to keep written records, Kelly. You always were efficient at that sort of thing."

He tightened his legs' grip on her body and pulled a cell

phone from his coat pocket. He punched in the number and a moment later said, "This is it. I've got it. This is it and I don't ever want to hear from you again." He read the directions into the phone. "Do you have that? Good. Now leave me the fuck alone! It's over!"

He put the phone back in his coat and turned back to Kelly as one of her hands came up against him. He slapped it away, the way he might have slapped at a mosquito. "You stupid little bitch," Clarke hissed. "You might have had a career and done something your daddy the detective would be proud of. But you screwed it up, girl. Talking to the U.S. Attorney. That's bad, that's outside channels. That's not playing by the rules."

She raised her head, he slammed it down on the bed, and his hands went around her throat.

Kelly gagged. My God, he's trying to strangle me!

"Should have just stayed quiet and done what I told you to do," Clarke said, and his voice had grown softer.

The pressure around her neck intensified and Kelly began to feel dizzy. She squirmed, but movements were getting more and more difficult as her oxygen supply dwindled.

"You and that Dorian," Clarke said, almost whispering now.

Kelly jerked at the mention of Art's name and she summoned a burst of strength, flailing her arms at Clarke's chest. Clarke seemed not to notice.

She tried to make a fist to hit him with more force, but her movements were slow, drugged, as if she were encased in cement. Her vision was ragged, the room blurring before her eyes. All she could see now was Clarke.

I'm going to die, and all of this will have been for nothing, she thought.

She squeezed her eyes closed, so she wouldn't have to look at her murderer. She thought of the uranium and Terrence Ross and the people who would die—who had already died—because of his twisted view of the world. She saw poor Ryan Elder's sad face and brown eyes. He'd never even known who he was. . . .

She thought of her mother and her father and her brother. They would ship her body back to Evanston, and she'd be buried in the cemetery by the church where she'd grown up. . . .

Hail Mary, full of grace, the Lord is with thee . . .

Kelly snapped her eyes open. The pressure around her neck seemed to have lessened a fraction, and Clarke seemed to be breathing harder.

The thought dripped into her mind. Clarke was nearly sixty years old. Strong, yes. In good shape, yes. But nearly sixty, and he probably hadn't exerted himself this much in years.

One hand left her neck altogether. Kelly looked into his eyes and she saw the change. His face softened, his mustache drooped, and he began to look almost human again.

Kelly couldn't speak, floating in a cool blue mist, but somehow she registered that sweat had popped out on Clarke's forehead. His face was red, veins bulging in his neck.

She felt Clarke's legs loosen their death grip on her ribs.

Kelly sucked in a breath. The room began to spin a bit more slowly. The blue mist started to break up.

Oxygen flowed back into Kelly's brain and her thoughts cleared. Tried to kill me, she thought, and a moment of wild, thoroughly unprofessional rage burst out of her.

"Bastard," she whispered through her damaged windpipe.

Her eyes focused between his legs. He'd stopped squeezing, his legs were holding her loosely, his breath ragged. Kelly concentrated every ounce of strength into her arms and hands, visualizing them as indestructible, as weapons of mass destruction. She reared them back until they were even with her head, then swung forward and slammed them with all her force into Clarke's crotch.

He sucked air—just like I was doing a few seconds ago, she thought—and toppled off her, crashing into the night table, sending the lamp reeling to the floor.

She rolled off the other side of the bed, landing on all fours, then shakily stood up. Her legs weren't working properly and the room had started its crazy careening again. She stumbled, went down again, and half walked, half crawled past the bedroom door into the hallway.

Behind her, Clarke grunted.

Halfway to the dining room.

"Dead," she heard Clarke say. "You are fucking dead, Kelly."

But his voice was a rasp, a low, gravelly whisper.

Kelly staggered into the dining room, kicking the plate out of her way. She finally collapsed against the table. She crawled toward the kitchen door.

Footsteps sounded from the hallway. Clarke just wouldn't stay down.

Kelly rolled onto her side, her ribs aching. No longer able to even crawl, she scooted along the carpet. When her hand touched the linoleum of the kitchen floor, she almost fainted.

Clarke rounded the corner.

The blood was drying on his face from where she'd kicked him and he seemed hunched over. But he's standing and I'm not, she thought.

"I'm going to kill you, Kelly," he rasped. "I may be getting old, but you think a little kick in the balls is going to stop me? You are dead, girl. I think I may even call your daddy the detective and tell him you died in the line of duty. What do you think about that?"

He began to close the distance between them. Kelly scooted, one arm out in front of her. She turned her head slightly—pain shot through her neck—and spotted the Glock.

Clarke was coming, slowly, deliberately.

"Nowhere to fucking go," he growled, his voice stronger this time.

She pulled the gun to her, and before she even had a firm grip, had flicked off the safety with her thumb.

"Stop," she said, except her voice wouldn't work, and it came out as nothing more than a rush of bruised breath.

She rolled onto her back, bringing the Glock down into a two-handed firing grip. A bad stance, with the glass-topped dining room table above her. But she couldn't move anymore.

"You going to shoot me, Kelly?" Clarke said. "I don't

think so, Miss Pretty Girl. You don't have it in you." He reached the far edge of the table.

Kelly squeezed the trigger. The gun bucked only slightly—the Glock was a smooth-firing weapon. Glass shattered. She felt shards pricking her face. Clarke howled. Kelly closed her eyes and heard something heavy falling.

Another set of footsteps sounded.

"Faith?"

Kelly tried to open her eyes. Bits of glass from the shattered tabletop were embedded in her eyebrows, her cheeks, even her *nose*, for God's sake.

She tried to raise her head and saw a man in a dark suit bending over Clarke.

"Holy shit," the man said, and Kelly almost smiled as Scott Hendler turned toward her. "Faith, what happened? You didn't show at the courthouse and I got worried."

"Dead?" Kelly rasped.

Hendler shook his head. "No. He's hit in the shoulder. Shattered his collarbone, I think."

Then Hendler was kneeling beside Kelly. How did he get from there to here so fast? she wondered as her mind drifted again. "I called nine-one-one and for backup," Hendler said. "Just take it easy, Faith. What happened? Can you talk?"

Kelly tried to speak, but couldn't anymore. When she heard the sirens, she passed out.

45

TEN A.M. CAME AND WENT.

Ryan paced the empty living room like a caged predator. "I don't like this," he said.

"Patience," Reeves said.

"Patience, hell. She's not back, there's no answer at either home or cell numbers. She told me she'd talk to the U.S. Attorney. Dammit, she gave me her word!"

"Ryan," Reeves said, "if Faith Kelly gave you her word, you can bet she meant it. I don't know what's going on, but you need to wait."

Cass came out of the bathroom. "What about those other calls you wanted to make?"

Ryan shrugged, digging at his thumb. "I give her another half hour. If she's not here by then . . ." He met Cass's eyes, wondering if she could tell what he was thinking: *Then I go myself, Kelly or no Kelly.*

"What calls?" Reeves asked.

"A couple of things that have been bothering me since a week ago Tuesday, the day this all started for me. The day I lost my job. The day I got my mother's letter."

"The same day?"

"The same day."

"I should mention," Reeves said, "that I no longer believe in coincidence."

"Wise woman." Ryan took Cass's phone and called WPSC in Pensacola. In less than a minute, he was talking to Earl Penders, the station manager who'd fired him.

"Earl, it's Ryan Elder. Earl, did someone set me up? Maybe they gave you money to get rid of me? That whole story, with Kirk Stillman and the highway project. It was all phony, wasn't it? A complete setup."

Penders cleared his throat. "Oh, Ryan, come on now. You were a good reporter, you just didn't—"

"Don't, Earl. I don't have time for that. Since I left there last Tuesday, my best friend was murdered, had his throat cut just because he was meeting me. At the very least, you're looking at some kind of labor law violations. At the worst, you could be an accessory to murder and conspiracy. So save the bullshit and answer my question. Was there a setup?"

"I don't know anything about a murder, Ryan. Let's not get carried away here. I'm just a businessman."

"How much, Earl? How much did he offer you to set me up?"

Deep sigh. "Reckon I should talk to my lawyer."

"No, I *reckon* you should talk to me, and right now. I can

place one phone call to the U.S. Marshals, they could place a call to Florida and have some agents at your door in fifteen minutes." He shrugged at Cass and Reeves. Reeves smiled— *nice bluff.* "They could shut down the radio station, Earl, off the air just like that, your FCC license pulled until the investigation was complete. Now you talk to me!"

"Oh, hell, Ryan. Don't try to bluff a poker player. I do feel bad about the way all this happened, but you have to understand—"

"How much, Earl?"

Penders's tone remained even. "See, that temper of yours is what made it easier for me to fire you. It was three hundred thousand, Ryan. The guy called me about a month ago, offered me that much if I'd find a legitimate way to get rid of you. I thought he was full of it and told him so. I stand by my employees, all that bit. He talked a while, and I started thinking that young reporters are a dime a dozen. This is a small market, Ryan, and I've never seen three hundred thousand dollars in my life. Just fooling around with this guy, I told him that if he was serious, to set up an account and direct deposit a down payment of ten thousand into a bank on Grand Cayman. I hung up and laughed at him. Wonder who Ryan pissed off now, is what I thought."

"But he was serious."

"Yep. The money was there the very next day. He called me back and said the rest would be on its way. One condition: the firing had to be done on a certain date. Last Tuesday."

"So you fed me those rigged numbers about Stillman and let me pursue him into holding that not-so-impromptu press conference downtown, and presto! A reason to let me go."

"Yeah, I guess that's it." Penders coughed into the phone. "Look, Ryan, it's not like you won't get another job. In this business, someone with a little talent can always get a job. And with you, you've got no ties anywhere. I mean, you're mobile, you can—"

"Did you get your money, Earl?" Ryan's eyes were burning. No ties anywhere. "Did you get it?"

"Well, now I—"

Ryan jabbed at the end button, then looked up. Cass and Reeves were staring at him. "Ross wanted me to have all ties severed. No job, no home, so I could just pull up stakes and come do his bidding. The only thing I don't understand is why it took him seven years after my parents' suicide."

"Ryan—" Cass said.

"One more call."

"Who this time?"

"The post office."

"Excuse me?"

Fifteen minutes later, Ryan pushed the end button again and sat back, his heart thumping.

There was no truth. Everywhere he turned, more lies and betrayals.

He knew exactly where he had seen the face of Ross Mobley and it chilled him to the bone. So clever, so painstakingly, brilliantly executed. Terrence Ross had made it his life's mission, and would fulfill it no matter what he had to do, and no matter how long it took.

And in the end, Frank and Anna Elder, Adam and Eve, were betrayed as well.

"It's nearly eleven o'clock," Ryan said. "I don't know what's happened to Kelly, but I'm not sitting around here with all my old ghosts. I'm going to Blue Eye."

"I don't think so," Reeves said softly.

"And are you planning to stop me?"

Reeves shook her head. "No, I won't try to stop you. But you're not thinking clearly. There's a good reason why Faith hasn't come back. And if you'll just—"

"No, sorry, I won't just. Ross has had my whole life in his hand for a long, long time and I'm about to get it back."

"You're making a mistake. If you go, you'll be alone."

Ryan looked at Cass, asking a silent question.

"Oh, God help us," she said. "I'll go where you go."

Reeves sighed. "I mean, you won't have official protection."

"I'll—we'll—take our chances."

Reeves stepped forward, and it took Ryan a few seconds to realize that she'd extended her hand to him. He clasped it gently.

"I don't know if I'll be seeing you again," Reeves said. "Since you're serious about this, you should know that Faith did manage to get your Jeep released from the local police impound yard. It's in the driveway."

Ryan nodded. "Thank her for me when you see her."

"Take care."

Ryan nodded again. He and Cass gathered up their few belongings, Cass clutching her black overnight bag. Ryan checked to make sure Art Dorian's gun was loaded, and they left Reeves in the house.

They climbed into the Jeep. "Just a second before we go," Cass said. "I want to call and check on Daddy."

She punched in the number, and Ryan watched her sit up straight, the color draining from her face. She muttered a few indistinct, urgent syllables.

She pressed *end* and looked at Ryan. "He's had an accident," she said.

46

KELLY WOKE UP IN THE HOSPITAL. ONE SIDE OF HER face felt strange, as if she were a doll that hadn't been stuffed properly. One eye remained blurry, and when she breathed, she felt an ache in her ribs.

She blinked and the room focused.

Two shadows took shape around the bed. What an odd duo, Kelly thought vaguely: a gorgeous blue-eyed black woman; and a thin, young, yet slightly balding man in a dark suit.

Nina Reeves and Scott Hendler.

I don't understand, Kelly thought dully, then began to remember.

She tried to say something, but her vocal cords wouldn't cooperate. Reeves put a hand on her wrist. "The doctor said you shouldn't try to talk."

Kelly mimicked writing. Hendler took a pen and a pad of paper embossed with the FBI logo out of his suit pocket.

"How you doing, Faith?" Hendler said, putting on a nervous smile.

She shrugged and accepted the pen and paper. *Clarke?* she scribbled.

"He's a few doors away, right on this very floor," Hendler said, then grinned. "We were all waiting for you at the courthouse, even Owen Springs. At this point I don't know that the chief will ever get out of jail."

Kelly looked grim. She tapped the pen hard against the paper and wrote, *Ryan???!!!*

Reeves sat beside the bed. "He's gone, Faith."

Kelly's eyebrows went up instinctively, and then she realized it hurt when she did that.

"When you didn't show up at ten o'clock, he decided to go to this place Blue Eye. He took the Jeep. Ms. Chambers's father had some sort of accident, and she left for Cheyenne. I drove her to the airport, where she'd left her own car."

Kelly sat up, pains stabbing her from all directions. She shook her head and scribbled furiously. *He can't go up there alone!!!*

Reeves shrugged. "How could I stop him?"

Kelly blinked against pain and confusion. She looked at Hendler.

Hendler held up his hands. "Springs said that, if you're fit, you're to coordinate the rest of the investigation."

Kelly waited a moment, then wrote, *SOG. Hostage Rescue— Quantico? Will Bureau help?*

Hendler took the pad. "Wouldn't miss it for the world."

Kelly took the pad back, started to write the directions Ryan had given her. East or west? One mile or two? Was it a barn, or a house he'd said? Her head began to throb again. Kelly put down the pen.

Hendler scooted around the edge of the bed and looked

at what little she'd written. He smiled again and very gently touched her shoulder. She looked up at him.

Hendler pulled a plastic baggie out of his pocket. In it was a badly crumpled piece of notepaper. "In Clarke's pocket," he said.

Kelly sagged back against the bed. *Get moving,* she wrote. *Ryan's up there by himself.*

"Got it," Hendler said, and ran out of the room.

It was nearly two o'clock when Ryan crossed from Oklahoma into Missouri on Interstate 44. The turnpike driving had been mindless, sightless, and as he kept the old Jeep pointed relentlessly northeast, images danced before his eyes in a ghostly minuet: his father along the country road, the camera around his neck, dashing up the trail to the abandoned barn; Yorkton talking to his parents in the front yard while he watered the roses, his mother whispering, ". . . tell him?"; his mother leaning toward him in the garage, a cloud of White Shoulders trailing her, saying, *Remember these eyes;* the explosion of his father's car and his own screams; last Tuesday, opening the letter, looking at his mother's scrawled handwriting. The images came faster: Jeff with his throat cut, coffee dripping off the table in the Underworld; the chase through the concourse; Cyrus Graesner; Cass.

He wanted her here with him. He wanted her hand on his arm, or in the small of his back, pressing with the lightest touch. He wanted her father not to have been injured. But she'd had to go. He knew she had to go to Cheyenne. He knew he would have done the same thing—if he'd had a father.

He'd seen the conflict raging behind those huge blue-gray eyes, and he'd told her, *Go. I understand.*

He looked back through the windshield as an eighteen-wheeler blew past him and his thoughts turned to the man he would no doubt see shortly at the old barn near Blue Eye.

The Whispering Man.

Terrence Ross.

The master manipulator.

Soon, Ryan thought. Pretty soon, one way or another, it'll be over.

An hour later, he left the interstate and drove straight south on U.S. 65 from Springfield, keeping the Jeep just over the speed limit. The mountains surrounded him, ancient rounded hills covered in trees that were January bare. They were still amazing, Ryan thought. Like many others raised in flatlands, his fascination with mountains was eternal. *Just like my father before me.*

He passed tiny towns, billboards advertising country music shows and Ozark arts and crafts. Tourists were the main art and craft of these hills now. Then he skirted Branson, an odd combination of Nashville and Las Vegas, many of the showplaces and theaters closed for the winter.

South, approaching Arkansas. Beyond Branson, he left the highway, remembering the route his father had taken, the little two-lane state road. It ran west, crossing an arm of Table Rock Lake, then bent sharply south again.

He passed a few mobile homes, set back from the road in stands of trees, silver mailboxes atop wooden posts standing guard by the driveways. Occasionally he saw a truck tire tossed to the side of the road. A beer can here, a liquor bottle there. His mother had often complained about people who lived in such a beautiful place, yet couldn't pick up their trash.

The sign read: BLUE EYE, POP. 129.

Ryan shook his head. There had been five times that many in his high school graduating class alone.

He slowed the Jeep, passing a liquor store, then the little white frame post office. Ahead on the left was the store he remembered. The bright purple awning was still there, and looked practically new. Across the road, he saw the large rectangular sign welcoming travelers to ARKANSAS, THE NATURAL STATE.

Another sign pointed west, announcing that the Mount Olivet Free Will Baptist Church was one block away; and just below, WELCOME—ANNUAL BLUE EYE REUNION HELD HERE.

It was all the same as when he'd been a boy, as if the surrounding hills had shut out change from this place. He could see the appeal to his parents, people whose lives had been fashioned out of turbulence, blood, violence.

Almost trembling, he stopped at the store, still on the Missouri side of the line, and went in. Dusty shelves stretched away, filled with canned goods, diapers, headache medicines, candy, chips. One change from his childhood: a lunch counter and grill to the right. He reached into the old-fashioned cooler and pulled out a twenty-ounce bottle of Pepsi.

An elderly man in a plaid flannel shirt took his money. "Nice day," he said, the accent a little softer, a little more rounded than that of Oklahoma. "Least we got some sun."

"Yes," Ryan said, looking around the store. He pictured himself, seven years old, pulling on his father's sleeve, begging for a package of Genuine Ozark Spicy Peanuts from the snack aisle. "You still sell the spicy peanuts?"

"Spicy peanuts," the old man said. "I don't think so, and we've had the store for nine years now. My wife and I moved down from Kansas City to retire." He looked over his round glasses at Ryan. "You been here before?"

"When I was a kid. We used to—" He shook his head. "It was a long time ago."

The man looked Ryan up and down. "Couldn't be that long ago. You're not that old."

Ryan took his change and went back to the Jeep but didn't get in. He swigged the cola, then walked across the empty state highway to the Arkansas sign. He planted one foot on either side of it, remembering.

Take my picture, Dad.

Inside the store with the purple awning, the old man watched Ryan go across the highway, watched him stand at the sign, like he'd seen many others do, although most of the ones who did it were kids. Then he watched him get back in the Jeep and turn west, driving along the state line.

The old man picked up the phone.

• • •

There were two churches, a dormitorylike stone building with a historical marker in front of it, a few frame houses, and that was all there was to Blue Eye. Ryan pointed the car to the west, Arkansas on his left, Missouri on his right.

I'm coming, he thought.

He almost missed the house two minutes later, and pulled the Jeep off the narrow blacktop a hundred feet or so beyond it, on the opposite side of the road.

This is it. This is what it has all been about.

He got out of the car and pulled his coat around him. The temperature was around thirty, but the day was cloudless under bright, bracing cold sunlight. Cold as January, bright as July.

Ryan stopped when he'd crossed the road. There was the tree Frank Elder had climbed, its thick branches leaning out across the fence.

The gate was wide open.

It looked as though it had been rammed with a car, more likely a truck. It was bowed in the center and one of the posts that had held it to the fence was ripped out of the ground, trailing barbed wire.

Ryan's heart beat faster. He could see the house, a little older, a little shabbier than in his memory, another section of the green-shingled roof collapsed.

Is that our new house? You ready to move in?

You're weird, Dad.

Ryan walked through the gate.

In her hospital room, Kelly stared up at Hendler, who looked grim. Kelly tapped the paper and wrote, her letters looping furiously: *What does that mean? An hour delay????*

"First it was authorization problems," Hendler said. "They didn't want to talk to me, since I'm not Marshals Service. Then they said they'd only take authorization from the chief deputy. I told them that would be sort of a problem. I tracked the U.S. Attorney down and he called their director and they finally got that worked out. But then their chopper was in for maintenance today. It'll be an hour before they can get it out."

Quantico? Kelly wrote.

"Working on it. My SAC put in the request. But remember, they're a lot farther away. Even if they deploy right away, it'll take a while for them to get into the area."

Kelly threw down the notepad. "Dammit," she rasped.

The door to the house was off its hinges and lying on the concrete porch. Ryan looked inside. Only one interior wall was standing. Garbage filled the place: chairs with the upholstery ripped out, old lumber, twisted tree branches, newspapers, plastic trash bags, tires, a child's Big Bird doll with one foot torn away.

He started up the trail from the house, his lungs aching from the cold. A couple of hundred feet beyond the house was another fence, this one in better repair. Its gate was open as well, but hadn't been rammed. It was folded back against the fence, held in place by an ancient, rusting plow.

The ground sloped upward toward the barn. It was plain wood, no paint, the roof shaped like a trapezoid, with a high point sloping down to two outer wings. Behind it, the brush thickened and trees ruled the landscape.

An orange-and-white U-Haul truck was parked in front of the barn, its nose pointed toward Ryan.

The barn door was open.

Ryan stepped closer, his heart in his throat. The door had been padlocked, but the chain was cut through. It dangled from the door, the broken lock itself on the ground like so much litter.

Ryan took Art Dorian's pistol out of his coat pocket and stepped in. The barn itself was dark, but the bright sunlight shafted through the door like a blade. He spotted dark rectangles to the right: bales of hay bound with wire. Surprisingly, it did not smell musty or old, as he'd expected.

The hayloft seemed empty. There was no ladder up to it. Farther, just outside the shaft of sunlight, was one large lumpy shape.

He edged closer. Where was the man? He was here. He *is* here.

Ryan touched the lumpy shape. A tarpaulin. Other

shapes, long and slender, took form under the tarp. Ryan pulled up one end of the tarp and reached out a hand.

Smooth, cold metal.

Lead, he thought. Lead cases, heavy.

His hearing, always his best sense, betrayed him for once. He heard nothing, but caught a sudden odor. An odor he associated with his boyhood. Then he thought of the picture of Ross Mobley and he turned around in time to see the heavy block of wood come down on his head.

47

PAIN.

His head, his neck, his back, and then absurdly disconnected from the rest, his foot.

Ryan stirred against the cold floor of the barn, letting his senses return a little at a time. Vision came first, blurry but all right. Shapes: bales of hay, a few odd pieces of old lumber, the huge canvas tarp. Then came the hearing, a whispering sound on the floor, close to him. Someone moving around quietly.

The smell—the aroma he'd sensed just before he was struck.

Pipe tobacco.

A unique blend, which he'd smelled in one place in his life.

The same place where a huge photo of Ross Mobley sat squarely in the center of a dark paneled wall, surrounded by photos, commendations, plaques.

Ryan sat up and felt along his head. A good-size bump, but he didn't seem to be seriously hurt. He could see part of the piece of lumber with which he'd been hit. It was old and rotten and had split apart. Thank God for small favors.

Bracing himself, he slowly turned around and got to his feet, blinking his eyes against the pain. His head throbbed, the barn tilted a little.

He looked the man in the face, noticed the gun—his gun, Art Dorian's gun—tucked into his waistband.

Ryan blinked.

He swallowed, licked his lips. His mouth felt dry, cracked.

"I'll bet the 'T' stands for Terrence," he finally said.

The man looked at him quizzically.

"T. Jackson Coleridge, attorney at law," Ryan said. "Terrence Jackson Coleridge. You got Terrence from your real name, Ross from your father's name. I always thought that picture behind the desk in your office was some big-shot client of yours, some millionaire oilman or politician. Shows what I knew, right?"

Coleridge smiled slightly. "My father gave me the name of Coleridge after his favorite poet, Samuel Taylor Coleridge. He used to quote 'The Rime of the Ancient Mariner' all the time, for some reason which escapes me to this day. So you figured it out, after all." He clapped his hands together, mocking applause. "Good work, Ryan. You've done what I needed you to do." He swept a hand toward the tarp. "A few bumps in the road, but that's to be expected."

Ryan shook his head. "I didn't want to believe it. I just put it all together this morning. After this little scheme backfired on you when my parents decided not to go through with it, you didn't know what to do. You'd put time and money into being the Whispering Man and creating The New America, and then all your plans were shot to hell. Your father thought your cover was blown, and you knew your little revolution wasn't going to happen. I'm betting Ross Mobley didn't want to have anything to do with you after that."

Coleridge shrugged, the smile still in place.

"No, I don't think so," Ryan said. "So he disowned you, told you to get away from him, that you weren't good enough to be part of ACE, his master creation. Of course, that suited you just fine. You just had to figure out a different way to bring about your plan. You got Clarke to go along with it and somehow you found out the new identities Department Thirty had given to Adam and Eve."

"All Clarke had to give me was the name of their case officer. Once I knew who Dorian was, the rest was relatively easy." The eyes stared straight through Ryan, just as they had always done. "Dorian was new at the job. Department Thirty had just been created, so none of them really knew what they were doing. I followed Dorian everywhere, looking for an opening. One day he evidently forgot something in his office, left his car running, and went back in to get it. He was only gone two minutes and in that time I got in his car, opened his files, and had the names and the city: Edmond, Oklahoma. Within a few months, I took my law degree and set up shop. I got into the same circles as your father, made appropriately flattering noises about you, and a friendship was born. He and your mother told me their fake backgrounds and I played the game with them: you know, the dead young wife, coming west to work on oil contracts, and so on."

"And they never recognized your voice."

"I used a filter when I was Terrence Ross. I placed it on the phone, and it not only gave the whispering effect, but lowered the voice register slightly. Just enough to make it different from my regular voice."

Ryan rubbed his neck. "And you waited and waited. Waiting for your father to die. Just waiting for him to die so you could move. So you could start your war."

"My father spent his entire life in service to a corrupt, immoral system. The Revolution will cleanse this land, will let us start again."

Ryan thought it sounded like a recitation, something Coleridge had said so many times that it had lost meaning. "But you still couldn't do it while he was alive. After he kicked you out of ACE in 1975, you couldn't do it. Even though your whole precious revolution is about standing up to Ross Mobley, you couldn't do it. You were still too intimidated by him."

Coleridge shrugged, the slight smile still in place, as if nothing Ryan said was of consequence.

"And then, seven years ago, he died and you were free. What did you do, call my parents up on the phone as Ross?"

"It was quite easy. I dragged out the old filter, called them, and your mother answered. 'I know who you are,' I said, and I told her it was time to finish what we'd started. Then I hung up, thinking I'd let them simmer for a while, see if they went running to Dorian. But then. . . ." Coleridge's face darkened. "I never expected—"

"That they would commit suicide."

"Damn them!" Coleridge's hand twitched. "I would never have expected that kind of weakness from them." The eyes finally settled on Ryan. "Would you?"

A slow, painful shaking of the head. "No. They waited until I came home. You snapped them into pieces. Whatever thread they'd been hanging onto for twenty years, it all fell apart when you called."

"I thought my plans were over. They were the only ones who knew where the uranium was. I'd lived this strange, surreal existence for twenty years, becoming respected in the community, a legislator, for God's sake! My favorite irony. A distinguished state representative for five terms. And now, the entire reason for my being in this community was gone in a ball of flames."

Coleridge shifted his weight around, his feet shuffling against some of the old straw on the floor. He pulled the gun out of his waistband and his hand twitched again.

"And then the letter came," Ryan said.

Coleridge swiveled his head around to meet Ryan's gaze dead-on. The gun came up. "You know—"

"Oh, yes, I know. The last call I made this morning was to the U.S. Postal Service. It occurred to me that I received this certified letter, forwarded several times, *but I didn't have to sign for it.* You always have to sign for certified mail. So I asked what would happen if you sent a certified letter to someone, but that person had left with no forwarding address. See, I left UCLA and never went back, never told anyone what I was doing. I just had to get away after the funeral. The man at the Postal Service said that, of course, it would be returned to the sender. What if the sender is deceased, I asked him? He told me how they would make every effort to find the recipient, gave me all kinds of anecdotes about mail lost for forty years that eventually found its way home. But I pressed him. He asked about the estate of the deceased. The estate! And then I knew. He said if the recipient could absolutely not be located—remember, I've moved around a lot—and the sender was deceased, the letter would be given to someone with a power of attorney over the estate."

The gun wavered, but Coleridge's eyes were cast iron.

Ryan shuffled his feet, gaining a couple of steps on Coleridge. "So you tried to send it to me in Dayton, but by then I'd mouthed off to my boss and lost my job there. You finally caught up to me in Pensacola. You paid Earl Penders three hundred thousand dollars to trump up some story so I could be fired from WPSC, and then a week ago Tuesday, the day it all happened, you slipped the letter in with the rest of my mail so it would be there when I got home."

Coleridge nodded. "I needed you to be in a position to drop everything. And so you did."

Ryan's voice rose. "So I did. Did you read it? Did you read the letter?"

"Of course I did. When I saw your mother had given you the Department Thirty phone number to call, then I knew there was a message hidden somewhere in that damn orchestra review that would tell you about this place. But try as I might, I couldn't figure it out. That's why I needed you."

"Betrayals all around," Ryan said, the words like ashes in his mouth. "My parents didn't follow through on starting your little war and then they vanished into Department Thirty. So for the next twenty years, you deceived them. You, their friend, attorney, executor of their estate. I remember you on the day they died. Crying there at the police station with your arm around my shoulders. Now I know you were crying because of your precious plan."

"So?" Coleridge said, and made a vague motion with the gun. "You think I really cared about your parents? They were tools of the Revolution, nothing more. You know what they were. They were tools to be used and discarded afterward."

"What I still haven't figured out, though, is why you waited seven years to get to me."

"Planning, Ryan. Planning. I'd been so successful at building a life in Oklahoma as an attorney, legislator, community activist, I had to be equally successful at letting that life fade away. After I received the letter, I set about slowly retiring from public life. I put out word of a mild heart attack, I decided to leave the legislature, I wrapped up my business dealings. I appeared to be the semiretired prominent statesman and lawyer, playing golf and taking naps. When everything was in place, I began searching for you. All those jobs, all those cities—you didn't make it easy for me."

"So sorry," Ryan said.

"I can tell." Coleridge smiled again. "I used your new friend Deputy Kelly to get to you. She conducted her investigation and I followed her. I gave her the name of Terrence Ross. I even made up a wonderful story about how your father whispered the name to me a couple of days before he died. And she bought the whole thing. As for Clarke, aside from making sure Kelly was at the desk when my little package from Cheyenne was dropped off, the idiot wasn't much help until this morning when he got this location out of Kelly. I got a plane, rented a truck to carry the cases out of here, and arrived here an hour ago."

"So all you wanted was to live up to Ross Mobley's expectations. Do something on a grand scale, make Daddy apologize for sending you away to boarding school. The man didn't even give you his name, for God's sake."

"Psychoanalyzing me won't help you." He gestured with the gun. "Enough talk. You're going to load the cases for me. Just as your parents did. Provides a certain continuity, wouldn't you say?"

"No, I wouldn't say."

"Don't mock me! You're the son of killers and you're no different than they were. You have no respect for the things that matter."

Ryan heard a tiny crunch, footsteps on straw, the step of someone used to walking without making noise.

"I don't think so, Jack," said a voice Ryan recognized.

Ryan whipped around so fast he nearly lost his balance.

Standing in the doorway, a shotgun cradled in his hands, was his father.

48

A TRICK OF THE LIGHT.

Stress-induced hallucination, perhaps. Ryan stood motionless, unable to think, unable to speak, almost unable to breathe.

"First of all, Jack, put the gun down," the apparition said.

Coleridge was standing much as Ryan was, rooted to his spot in the barn. The murky eyes were open wide, staring at the man in the doorway.

The man pumped the action of the shotgun and leveled it at Coleridge. "This weapon is so powerful that if you just aim in the general direction you want it to go, it'll blow a hole through anything in its path."

"Frank—" Coleridge said.

"Drop it, Jack. Right now."

Coleridge dropped the automatic on the barn floor.

"Good man. Now kick it away from you."

Coleridge did.

"Very nice. Ryan, son, come over here by me."

Son.

Ryan looked. The barn was spinning and rocking at the same time, a crazed carnival ride, an insane Tilt-a-Whirl.

The man in the doorway.

A little older, a little grayer, more lines on the face. A little more emotion on the face than the quiet passivity that had always lived there before. A little more sadness.

Assassin? Ryan thought.

"Dad?" he said.

Frank Elder nodded. "You were supposed to know right

after . . . well, right after it happened. You weren't supposed to have to live with seven years of pain and thinking that we had . . . oh, well, your mom was always going to be the one to explain it to you. You know I was never good at speeches."

Ryan caught a movement out of the corner of his eye: Coleridge, shuffling on the straw.

"Just stand right there, Jack," Frank Elder said. "You make me nervous when you dance around like that." He looked at Ryan again. "Come on, Ryan."

"Dad?" Ryan said. "I—" His throat tightened. He felt as if he were being strangled.

"Your eyes don't lie, son."

Ryan walked, one foot then the other, slowly, deliberately, away from Coleridge, until he was beside his father.

"I just don't—" Ryan said. He swallowed. "Mom. Where's Mom?"

The sadness in the face intensified. "She died. For real this time. Two summers ago, of a heart attack. You know how she always had to watch her blood pressure. We have a little house north of Blue Eye and she had her flower garden there. She even won awards from the Ozark Garden Club. She had her roses, you know how much she loved roses. I had gone into Springfield to run some errands one Saturday morning, and she was working with her roses, and at some point her heart just gave out. I came home and found her between the red roses and the yellow ones."

"Dad, I—" I can't speak, dammit! Numb, absolutely numb.

Frank hefted the shotgun. "Well, Jack. Or I guess I ought to say Terrence, or maybe Whispering Man, huh? You had quite a little plan, didn't you? Just couldn't give it up, couldn't see that it wouldn't work."

"It will work," Coleridge said, his eyes darting around the barn. "Just because you didn't have the strength to follow through on it doesn't mean anything. I already have another explosives man lined up—"

"Uranium degrades, Jack," Frank said. "Pretty soon it's not even uranium anymore. It becomes thorium as it breaks down. Twenty-seven years is a long time for anything to just sit."

"Do you think I'm a fool?" Coleridge snapped. "I know that and I've already researched it. It will be active enough to build the device I need. It will work."

"No, it won't. When you hired us, it was just another job. Then when we got into it and found out what you really wanted to do . . ." A shake of the head. "See, that's terrorism, not professionalism, and there's always been an important difference between the two. It was a bad idea then and it's a worse idea now. I still can't believe you had us convinced for twenty years. And it took Ryan to put it all together."

"Dad, what happened?" Ryan finally said. He thought of himself, standing by his father's car, watching it burn, watching the stretchers carrying them away, his mother's hand protruding, the ruby ring dragging the ground.

"Well, like I said, your mom was always going to be the one to explain this. She had the idea to send the letter. She thought it might take you a little while, but that you'd figure it out." Frank gave a bitter smile. "Guess she was right, huh? We just didn't think it would take this long. These years have been hell, Ryan, not knowing about you, where you were, what you were doing. But we couldn't risk looking for you, not with Ross still out there. It would have been death for all of us. So we waited for you to figure out the letter and come to us."

Ryan stared at him, at the man he'd thought he once knew. The brown eyes were almost pleading. Adam the assassin; Frank Elder, the gentle, quiet father. Ryan had a vision of himself as a very young child, maybe three or four years old, at the Oklahoma City Zoo. He'd suddenly been terrified of the tigers and had literally clawed his way up his father's back to get away from the exhibit. Frank hadn't said a single word, but had patted his back. Just patted his back and held him. Nothing more or less than that, and he'd been safe, protected.

Protected by a man who once killed people for a living.

Ryan put both hands to his head.

"Ryan—" Frank said softly.

"You faked your suicide," Ryan said.

"Had to," Frank said. "It was the only way to be sure that Ross wouldn't be hanging over us forever. Just like you said a few minutes ago, Ross called us out of the blue, after twenty years. The only variable in the whole plan was you, son."

Ryan stood still. The barn had stopped its crazy ride and he now felt the opposite extreme, an absolute stillness.

"You see," Frank said, "we had to make everyone—Ross, Department Thirty, even you—think we were dead, then we could escape up here and start over yet again. We already had new identities in place." Again, the slight smile. "Everyone up here knows us as the Ryans, Jim and Eva."

Ryan stared at him. Utter stillness.

"Anyway, everyone had to be convinced. Ryan, you have to understand. We knew how much pain it would cause you, but the letter was supposed to bring you up here within a few days. That's why your mom mailed it the day before you came into town, so it would be waiting for you when you went back to school, after our 'funeral.' Dorian would explain most of it to you, then you could come here and we could be together again."

"But the letter got lost in the system when I didn't go back to UCLA," Ryan said.

"Looks that way. Then, like you said, it wound up in Jack's hands." Frank lowered his voice, aiming his eyes as well as the gun at Coleridge. "And he started again with his damned revolution."

"I don't understand," Coleridge said. "The bodies in the car—"

"We had to make it as spectacular as we could, you know," Frank said. "So that everyone believed Frank and Anna Elder were dead. And for all practical purposes, they were. They ceased to exist, not that they ever really existed in the first place, and Jim and Eva Ryan were born. Remember that bad cold snap we had the week before Thanksgiving seven years ago? Down in single digits at night, made big news being so cold so early in the year. Your mom saw in the paper about the four homeless people who froze to death, out under one of the underpasses. Two of them were a man and a woman, roughly our ages, and we had our opportunity.

"We went to the morgue and claimed the bodies. We told the police we'd heard about what happened and wanted to give them a good Christian burial. The county medical examiner's office was so relieved to not have to deal with it that they released the bodies to us with very few questions asked. We'd given false names, of course. In the middle of the night, we put the bodies into the garage, behind some panels I'd hollowed out. We knew they wouldn't have to be there more than a couple of days, and it was cold, so they were pretty well preserved. Then when you came home, Ryan, we made sure we acted strangely so you'd be sure to pick up on it."

Ryan remembered the airport, his mother's face, her fingers plucking at the air; his father gripping his shoulder; the strange preoccupation his mother had with the grackle in the yard. "It was so bizarre," he said. "You were acting crazy, but neither of you would tell me anything." His emotions were a stew: confusion, relief, anger, revulsion. His face felt hot.

Frank nodded. "That was the idea. Then it was a simple matter of electronics. I'd already checked out the construction site so I knew exactly where to hit that equipment. We sent you to the store in your mom's car, then we put the bodies in the back of my car and drove to that 7-Eleven at Danforth and Santa Fe. We pulled around the back, dressed the bodies in our clothes, even put our jewelry and watches on them, and propped them up in the car. We attached the radio-control box and I took the transmitter and steered the car back out to the intersection. It's the same principle as your little toy radio-controlled cars. It's used all the time by the auto makers when they're testing cars on the crash courses. I used the same kind of setup in Europe back in the sixties. The wiring was easy and the box would be melted in the fire. I aimed it right through the intersection and scored a direct hit on that equipment. The bodies were burned beyond identification, and we bet on the police not pressing it, since it was so public."

Coleridge shook his head. "You had us all fooled. I even used my influence to see that no autopsy was done. For the sake of the boy, I told them. It was clear what had happened, so let's spare Ryan the unnecessary additional grief. If only I'd known . . ." He shook his head again. "A brilliant plan, Frank."

Frank shrugged. "We had another car waiting at the back of the 7-Eleven, Jim and Eva Ryan's car. And we just drove away."

Ryan grabbed his father's arm. "But you didn't—" He looked back to Coleridge, then at his father again. "Why didn't you tell me?"

"What could I say? 'Oh, son, your mother and I used to kill people for a living. By the way, how was school today?' When you came up here, we were going to tell you that we had been under witness protection for a murder we'd witnessed just after you were born, something vague about organized crime. I'm sorry you had to go through this, Ryan."

Ryan felt himself breathing, felt the stillness dissolve. "He killed Jeff. He cut Jeff's throat."

"I'm sorry it came to that," Coleridge said. "You weren't on the right track. You weren't paying attention, Ryan. I had to—"

"Not paying attention!" Ryan spun a half turn away from his father, now facing both men. For a moment his anger paralyzed him and he wasn't sure he knew where to direct it. "Christ Almighty, the way you people play God! You slit Jeff Majors's throat just because he was going to meet me."

"It was—"

"And you!" Ryan faced his father again. "An assassin! A professional killer. My God, Dad. All that talk when I was a kid about respecting your fellow man, those lectures about ethics and integrity and tolerance. You . . . hypocrite!"

"I'm not going to defend or explain what your mother

and I did before you were born," Frank said, his voice very soft. "I'm just not. It wouldn't help either of us. But when we found out your mom was pregnant, we had a long discussion about it, and we knew it had to end. We had more money than we could ever spend, so we fulfilled the existing contracts we had, made it known we were retiring, and went to Department Thirty. It was the best we could do. We raised you well. You can't deny that."

Ryan backed away from both of them, until he came in contact with the tarp covering the lead cases. His hand fell on it.

"And this," he said wildly. "A sudden attack of conscience, so you couldn't follow through, is that it?"

"It's part of what cemented our decision to retire. We always agreed we wouldn't do terrorist activities, just highly directed jobs with no outside people hurt. And that's what we did, for the whole time we were in the field."

" 'In the field!' Listen to yourself. In the field! You talk like you were doing door-to-door sales! Why don't you just say that you were out there murdering people, all over the world? And now . . . you never could talk to me when I was growing up, and all of a sudden you're explaining everything? Once you were a professional hit man and now you're a great guy. Explain that!"

"Explain it yourself, Ryan. These last seven years . . . not knowing where you were, what you were doing . . . it's been a strange existence. Sort of a half-life, just like that uranium." He hunched his shoulders. "If it's changed me, then so be it. It didn't happen overnight, but this seven years . . . it's been hard. As for the rest of it, I'm not going to get into that, son. It was complicated, and it's even more complicated now." The nose of the shotgun drooped a couple of inches.

Ryan pulled back a corner of the tarp, exposing the smooth coldness of the lead cases. His eyes were burning and tears were streaking his smooth face. His father's face, he thought. "There's enough nuclear material in this barn to destroy cities, to give radiation sickness to God only knows how many people, and you're not going to get into that?"

His father was shaking his head, now holding the shotgun loosely. His father, who had gone to all his ball games, had let him major in broadcasting even though he didn't like the idea, who'd taught him to fish and canoe and had never raised his voice in anger at him. His father, who didn't or couldn't have feelings . . . until now.

Ryan put his hands to his head again. His father, alive. His mother, dead in her rose bushes of a heart attack, on a summer day in the beautiful Ozarks. So much rage, so much confusion.

"The Revolution will work," Coleridge said. "It will cleanse the nation. Those left standing will be the ones truly fit to govern, and—"

"Oh, stop it, Jack," Ryan said, the thoughts and words hard and hot. "It's just so much sixties-radical bullshit and it won't work. That's just it! Timothy McVeigh's bomb didn't make people rise up against the government and September eleventh didn't change anyone's ideas about the Muslim world and American foreign policy. It doesn't work, all of this has been for nothing! My whole life, everything I thought I was was created because of this, and it was all for nothing!"

"Ryan," his father said.

"No. Don't 'Ryan' me. Since Art Dorian named me, maybe I should have called *him* my father."

Frank flinched. Ignoring Coleridge, he dropped the shotgun on the straw and took a few steps toward Ryan, his hands out. "Don't do this. I know you've been through a lot to get here—"

"And to think," Coleridge said, "that you were once the world's leading assassin."

Ryan and Frank turned to look at him. He was holding another gun, a large automatic.

"You should have searched me while you had the tactical advantage, Frank," Coleridge said.

Frank sighed. "My wife was always better with guns than I

was. It doesn't have to be like this, Jack. You know that, don't you?"

Coleridge smiled, a ghostlike stretching of his facial muscles. "Of course it does. I've known it had to be like this since I was a little boy." He raised the automatic, swinging it from Frank to Ryan and back again. "And here we are. The father and the son. The son and the father. Who dies, then? This is perfect, so beautifully perfect. Because, gentlemen, it's all about fathers and sons."

The barrel of the pistol stopped in front of Ryan.

Nina Reeves put down the phone in Faith Kelly's hospital room and said, "That was Scott. He's met up with the HRT crew from Quantico. SOG is a few minutes ahead of them, already in the air. ETA is twenty minutes from Blue Eye."

Kelly nodded, the bruises on her face throbbing. She picked up her pen and wrote, *I hope we have twenty minutes.*

"It was a father who started all this," Coleridge said. "Maybe it ends with the son." He raised the pistol to Ryan's eye level. "What do you think of that, Frank?"

Frank's voice was eerily calm. "It still won't work, not even if you shoot both of us. You can't get those cases out of here yourself. They're more than forty pounds each and there are ninety-seven of them. Ninety-seven, Jack, and you're an old man."

A shadow crossed Coleridge's face.

Frank put a hand in his pocket, jingling keys and coins. He seemed almost folksy, Ryan thought. "Didn't think of that, did you? See, we used a crew of twelve when we brought them up here. Dug them up from the underground, paid them off, and sent them back under. You'll have a heart attack before you get even half of them loaded."

Coleridge was as silent-faced as stone.

"Dad—" Ryan said.

"You're right," Coleridge said suddenly.

They both looked at him.

"You're right, Frank. I didn't consider that possibility.

That's why I hired you and your wife, to do the legwork for me. That was the whole idea. And now I suppose your healthy young son will have to do the work instead."

Coleridge swung the pistol around to Frank Elder.

Ryan saw the change in his father's eyes, saw his face go slack.

"No!" Ryan screamed.

The gun roared and bucked and Ryan saw his father double over as if he'd been punched in the stomach.

"Dad!" he screamed, and his anger at his father was gone. His only thought: I saw my father die once. Not again, I have so much to ask. . . .

Coleridge fired again, bellowing incoherently, this time close to Ryan. Ryan dove to the ground, rolling under a corner of the tarp.

"Come now, Ryan!" Coleridge shouted. "You have work to do! You'll be part of history!" His voice changed, and the well-educated aristocratic attorney was back, the wild-eyed radical gone. How quickly he shifts between the two, Ryan thought. "But you can take your time to grieve for your father, and perhaps for your own life."

Insane, Ryan thought. Whatever that means, he's insane.

"I'm not going to kill you, Ryan," Coleridge called.

Ryan shuddered under the tarp, the lead cases against his back.

"It was never in my plan to kill you. You couldn't help the circumstances of your birth. I used you, yes, but never with the intent of killing you. I'd often thought you might want to kill your father when you found out what he was, but alas, I've had to do that for you. Perhaps you'd like to stay here while he dies. After all, you have nowhere else to go."

Ryan breathed quietly through his mouth. His brain began to fog. He peered around one edge of the tarp. Coleridge was standing over Frank with a disgusted look on his face. Then he simply shrugged and walked to the door of the barn.

"I'll give you some time," Coleridge called. "When your father is dead, we will proceed. Sit with him if you like. I won't stop you." He took a few steps into the bright sunlight. "I'll be waiting in the truck. I hate the smell of barns."

He walked to the U-Haul and climbed into the cab, closing the door quietly.

Ryan rolled out from under the tarp and crawled to his father. Frank Elder was still in a sitting position, holding his belly.

Blood was streaming from the older man's stomach and he was bracing himself against the floor with one hand.

"Dad—"

Frank shook his head. "No. Just a belly wound." He squeezed his eyes open and closed rapidly. "Stop him. I'll . . . be okay." He pointed to the shotgun a few feet away.

"Dad, I—"

"One thing." He started to wheeze. "Your mom and I were thinking of you. We screwed up, but we knew we couldn't help him start his war. Should have . . . told you a long time ago."

"Dad, why did you—"

Another head shake. "Stop . . . him. I may be an old killer, but he's a . . . lunatic." He closed one hand on Ryan's arm. "I'm sorry."

Ryan picked up the shotgun with both hands. "Are you sure—"

"Go," Frank Elder said. "After all . . . this . . . don't let him . . ."

"All right." Ryan felt strangely disconnected, as if he were watching the whole scene from underwater. "I'll . . . I'll be back, Dad."

Frank Elder tried to say something else—Ryan thought he caught a *d* sound, but it was thick and wet and he couldn't finish it. He nodded and waved a hand toward Ryan—*Go on, do what you have to do.*

Ryan looked back once and ran out of the barn.

49

COLERIDGE WATCHED IN THE TRUCK'S BIG SIDEVIEW mirror and saw Frank Elder wave Ryan away. Oh, how noble, he thought. Then, a thread of anger wormed its way into his consciousness: I gave him a chance, an opportunity to be with his father when he died, this time a real death. He watched as the boy moved slowly toward the back of the truck, holding the shotgun. And this is how he repays me, by creeping toward me with that ridiculous gun.

So the game's not over after all.

"All right, Ryan," he said aloud, in a very even voice. Then his tone dropped and he was the Whispering Man again: "I guess I'll have to load the uranium myself after all."

He reached for the truck's ignition.

When the U-Haul's big engine roared to life, Ryan jumped, losing his grip on the shotgun. When the white taillights came on, he stood riveted for a moment, then leaped to the side as the truck lurched backward, its open rear doors rattling back and forth.

Ryan screamed wordlessly, tumbling to the side and rolling into a stump. The truck had stopped just inches away from the wall of the barn.

The white lights went off and he heard the gears grind. It lurched forward a few feet, then stopped. The white lights came on again and the wheels began to angle in a different direction.

When Coleridge stepped on the gas, the truck lumbered back again, and this time it crunched into the wall as Ryan dove out of the way again.

"You're crazy, Jack!" Ryan shouted, then thought: For

someone who wasn't going to kill me, you're trying awfully hard to do it . . .

The truck lurched forward again. The door swung out and Ryan reached out and gripped it, the metal cutting into his hands.

"What a wonderful game, Ryan!" Coleridge shouted through the open window. "I could have used your help a little longer, but since you seem to want to play instead of work. . . ."

The U-Haul plowed forward and bounded down the trail, Ryan hanging from the door. As he swung out, he caught a glimpse of his father, lying down now, his head turned toward Ryan.

The truck rolled through the interior gate, moving toward the house and the road below, zigging and zagging from side to side, Coleridge doing his best to shake Ryan off. On one of the door's inward swings, Ryan got one hand, then both, around the lower edge of the top of the truck.

Think, think! Coleridge would have to slow down at the foot of the driveway to get onto the road. If he didn't, the truck would go in the ditch.

Okay, Jack, I'll play. But my rules this time.

Scott Hendler sat in the rear of the helicopter as it barreled southward from Springfield. One of the flak-jacketed Special Operations Group members handed him a note from the pilot. Hendler read it twice, then said to the SOG members, "We have a report of shots fired in the area, right along the state line, west of Blue Eye. A concerned citizen, worried that someone was hunting out of season." He looked up. "What's our ETA?"

"Five minutes!" the pilot shouted.

"We may have civilians down," Hendler said. "Be ready for anything."

Frank Elder didn't really expect Ryan to catch Coleridge. But more than anything, he didn't want his son to watch him die. He knew the wound was much worse than he'd let on to Ryan. He already felt light-headed and wondered how much blood he'd lost.

Ryan didn't deserve the life he'd inherited, Frank thought. He deserved real people for parents, not phantoms. But still and all, we raised him well.

Frank began to see faces: his wife, his own parents, men he'd killed when he was Adam. A strange gray mist hovered at the edge of his vision and he felt the weariness settle in on his shoulders.

So this is what it feels like. He'd dealt it to so many others, and this is what it feels like.

He still had one regret, one last thing he'd wanted to say to the boy, but the words wouldn't come.

A good boy, Frank thought, then corrected himself: A good man.

He lay back on the cold floor of the barn and let the gray mist steal over him.

As Coleridge braked at the bottom of the driveway, Ryan hoisted himself up with both arms.

Just like chin-ups back in school. God, I hated doing chin-ups, he thought.

Then he was flat on the roof of the truck and it was turning.

Left. Why the hell was he going left? Blue Eye was the other direction. There was nothing down this road except the cemetery, and a little farther—

He remembered his father's voice, behind the wheel—*End of the line, troops!*

But Coleridge had never been here before. He didn't know what lay down this little mountain road.

"Oh my God," Ryan muttered.

He inched forward on his belly, raising his head into the bright, sunny cold. The hills rose around him, pastoral, silent, mocking the violence and blood that had come here.

Then, sound. Another engine. A car, behind, coming from

the direction of Blue Eye. Ryan looked back: a dark sedan, a single person in the front seat. He couldn't tell anything else. The vision was never as good as the hearing.

The truck hurtled west along the state line, picking up speed. They passed the cemetery. Ryan saw the flowers there, even in January. The best-kept cemetery he'd ever seen. He remembered what he'd thought as a teenager: The town takes care of its dead.

He inched forward, approaching the front of the truck, the "cab-over," which was directly above Coleridge's head.

He looked up. Coleridge was going faster.

A dog barked up ahead. A shape loomed, coming toward them now like a missile.

End of the line, troops!

The truck was too large, and was going too fast to stop, or even to turn onto the gravel path when the road dead-ended.

Ryan remembered the huge elm tree that towered at the end of the road. He remembered wanting to climb it as a child, but it was so old and so massive, there were no branches near the ground for him to grab onto. It was dead center at the point where the road ended.

His mother had said, more than once, *I hope no one ever comes down this road going too fast and doesn't see the turn.*

Ryan gripped the front of the cab-over. Below, he heard Coleridge screaming again. He imagined him throwing his hands in front of his face.

Ryan felt the leafless branch of the tree brush his back.

End of the line, troops!

His father was lying back in the barn, bleeding. Dad. Oh God, Dad, why did it have to be this way?

When the truck slammed into the huge old tree, Ryan slid forward as if the top of the truck were greased. Then he was airborne, pinwheeling his arms through some of the lower branches of the tree. He felt the flesh of his arms shredding.

He twisted his body around, saw the truck with its nose crumpled into the tree, the windshield shattered, the hood smoking, one headlight loose like an eyeball popped out of its socket.

He heard something else, something above and beyond the crash. His name. Someone was calling his name.

Surreal. Impossible.

Ryan covered his head as he landed, some distance beyond the tree. He landed on his left side and he felt something crack. His already twice-injured foot seemed to come down at a different angle than the rest of his body and it sent flames up his leg, all the way to his neck.

Then everything was still. The dog barked again, this time closer, somewhere near the house that stood just south of the tree. And there again was the voice, calling his name.

His eyes fluttered and then everything was black.

Coleridge never saw the tree. One moment the road was there, then it was gone. His head had slammed against the steering wheel, but the wheel was padded with a foam rubber cover, and other than a small cut above his eye, he seemed remarkably unhurt.

He looked around, letting his eyes come back into focus, listening to the hissing of the radiator before him. Ryan Elder!

Curse the boy! He had turned out to be far more trouble than he was worth! He came from bad seed, and look what had happened now!

Why, Daddy, why? he heard clearly.

Coleridge whipped around, as if expecting to see the boy—himself, expecting to see himself at age seven, pleading with his father to explain the cruelty, the isolation, why he couldn't even have his name.

Whisper! You must always whisper! The enemy is everywhere!

Coleridge flinched. Now it was as if the boy was talking to him, the seven-year-old version of himself talking to the adult.

Coleridge screamed and put his hands over his ears.

Out there somewhere, in the field before him, was another "boy."

Coleridge finally understood. He could make the boy-Jack be quiet, stop his pleading, give him some justice, by destroying the boy in the field, by putting an end to all these betrayals.

The boy-Jack was silent for a moment, as if waiting.

Coleridge found his gun on the floorboard and gripped it tightly. He opened the door and climbed down. A little more blood ran into his eye, and his neck seemed to hurt, but he was still intact, further proof that he had a destiny yet to fulfill.

From somewhere behind, he heard a voice calling: "Ryan!"

A woman's voice.

Not now. Leave me alone. I have business to finish. First the father, then the son.

Another sound, this time above him. Blades whipping through the air, coming quickly.

Not now, damn you all!

Coleridge stepped around the smoking hulk of the U-Haul. He'd seen the boy's body go flying through the air when the truck hit the tree. Ryan was probably dead already, but . . .

There he was, curled up in a ball, just on the other side of the tree. Coleridge squared his shoulders and stood erect with military precision as blood ran into his eye.

He stood over Ryan's motionless body.

Why, Daddy, why?

He aimed the pistol.

Footsteps crunched the dead grass near Ryan, closer than the voice that kept insistently calling to him.

Ryan's eyes were still closed. He felt as if they were gummed shut. But the smell—there was the pipe tobacco again, that special blend. Very near him, right over him.

"Well, Ryan," Coleridge said. "The game didn't work out the way we expected it to and play time is over. I have work to do. Important work."

"No, you don't," said Cass Chambers.

Ryan managed to open one eye. Just that simple action

hurt, the pain like innumerable tiny screws tightening slowly in his body. He saw Coleridge standing over him, the gun pointing somewhere below his neck. But the man wasn't looking at him. Ryan opened the other eye.

It wasn't an apparition. He wasn't hallucinating. Cass stood a few feet away, wearing her heavy black coat, both her hands in her pockets.

How? Ryan tried to form the thought.

"Go away, young woman," Coleridge said. "I thought I made it clear you had no business being a part of this."

"I don't like knives," Cass said.

"Excuse me?"

"Knives. I don't like them. You used one to slit my clothes back in Oklahoma City. I've seen enough knives to last several lifetimes."

"Well, I'm so sorry. You're making me nervous, standing there with your hands in your pockets. Please take them out."

Cass inclined her head skyward and raised her voice. "Hear that? There are two helicopters. One's a Hostage Rescue Unit from the FBI. One is Special Operations Group from the Marshals Service. I talked to Deputy Kelly on the phone just a couple of hours ago. Your goon Clarke didn't kill her." She cocked her head. "Getting louder. They'll be dropping a little ladder off the side of one of those helicopters in about two minutes, and they'll be all over you. You don't have a way out of this."

Coleridge waved the gun. Ryan opened his eyes wider. The muzzle was no longer pointed directly at him.

"Nonsense," Coleridge said. "Even if that is the FBI, which I doubt, they will listen to me."

"Oh, you think so?"

"Yes, I do. Please take your hands out of your pockets. Slowly."

Cass sighed. "I suppose you have me."

"I do. Let's stop this little game. I have important work to do."

Ryan watched as Cass very slowly began to take her left hand out of the coat pocket.

"That's right," Coleridge said.

Cass nodded.

She extended her hand palm out toward Coleridge.

Coleridge's eyes strayed, drawn by the stumps, by the thumb and little finger at their strange angle. His grip on the gun loosened.

"Your fingers—" Coleridge said.

Sound and light exploded in Ryan's being, and with all his strength, he clasped his hands together and swung them at the back of Coleridge's knee.

Coleridge let out a gasp and pitched forward, the pistol flying into the brown grass.

"Ryan!" Cass yelled.

Ryan launched himself on top of Coleridge, trying to get his hands around the older man's throat. But Coleridge was strong and in less pain than Ryan and he threw Ryan off.

Ryan rolled, bouncing on his buttocks, and Coleridge stomped on his injured foot.

Ryan howled into the bright cloudless sky, rolling away. Coleridge was instantly beside him, scrabbling in the grass.

"The gun," Coleridge muttered.

Ryan skittered away from him, raising himself onto his hands and knees. Coleridge saw him getting up and his face twisted into an animal snarl. Coleridge stopped rummaging in the grass and came at Ryan.

"Stop!" Cass yelled.

Coleridge got hold of Ryan's damaged foot and began beating it against the ground. Every blow sent superheated needles from toes to neck. Ryan extended his hands, clawing for purchase on the hard ground.

His fingers brushed against something hard and cold. Not natural.

He pulled at the gun, trying to get a firm grip. He twisted his head and saw Cass with a pistol in her right hand. Where did she get a gun? Wait, she grew up on a farm. Her father—

But she couldn't shoot, not with the two of them locked together like this.

Ryan clawed the ground and felt his fingernails splitting. The gun was slippery and Coleridge was still holding him.

He gained an inch. He wrapped his hand around the butt of the gun, and with his foot screaming, he twisted around and kicked Coleridge in the face.

His foot seemed to explode then, but he was free from Coleridge's grip. He scrambled away a few feet and toppled onto his side in the grass.

Coleridge bellowed, holding the side of his head, blood streaming into his eye.

He straightened to his full height, coming for Ryan again.

Ryan saw Cass out of the corner of one eye. She was raising the pistol. He raised his.

"I have—" Coleridge snarled.

Ryan and Cass fired at the same time.

Ryan saw nothing else. The hand holding the gun was now very heavy and his ears were filled with the helicopter, men yelling, the dog barking ceaselessly, Cass running, screaming.

Coleridge, falling to the ground. Not moving.

For a pure second, all the sound stopped. Then Cass's arms were around him. "You—" he croaked. "But your father—"

"Shh," she said. "Later."

A man's voice, almost lost in the helicopter noise, said, "He's dead."

"They're not talking about me, are they?" Ryan said thickly.

Cass put his head in her lap. The pain was everywhere, and Ryan couldn't tell where the pain ended and he began.

"Not this time," Cass said. "Nope, not this time."

EPILOGUE

CONSCIOUSNESS CAME AND WENT LIKE THE CYCLING OF the seasons, little bits here and there. Mainly Ryan remembered sounds—people talking in hushed voices, the swish of plastic on metal as IV bottles were changed, the hum of the automated blood pressure cuff—and he remembered not being able to move his foot.

He also remembered Cass. Every time he came awake for a little while, she was sitting by his bed, usually reading a newspaper or magazine. Then, somehow, she would know he was awake and she would put down what she was reading and look over at him with those huge eyes. He would try to talk, and sometimes he actually did, but then he would drift away again, into the blackness.

Once, when he awoke, another woman was in the room and he knew he should remember who she was. She was tall, taller than Cass, with red hair. There was a large bandage around her neck and her face seemed to be cut and bruised. She looked at him and spoke to him and he said something back and that was all, and then the woman was gone.

Three and a half days after being airlifted from the field near Blue Eye to the hospital in Springfield, Ryan regained a real consciousness.

He knew he was awake because he was in pain. Not his foot—he still couldn't feel it—but his ribs, his back, his neck, his head, his arms.

He looked over at Cass, which hurt his neck.

"Hi," she said.

Ryan swallowed. His throat felt like someone had been scrubbing the inside of it with steel wool.

"Take it slowly," Cass said.

He nodded and that hurt too.

"Hi," he said, and it was a rasp.

She smiled at him and he thought he had never seen anything so beautiful.

"You've been here," he said.

"Yes, the whole time."

"But your father—the accident."

Cass smiled. "He's fine. Sprained an ankle is all. I got to the house and he was sitting in his chair flirting with the home health nurse. He was lucid most of the time I was there, and before I could get a single word out, he said, 'Cassandra, it's not fair for you to be shut up in this house with a sick old man and not have a life of your own.' We made some compromises. It'll work."

"Did you tell your father about all this?"

"No. All I told him was that there was someone who might need me and that I needed to be there for them. When he's with himself, Daddy's a very smart man. He said, 'Then what are you doing around here?' and went back to flirting with his nurse. My friend in Elk City who teaches special ed is married to a man who has a pilot's license. I convinced him it was an emergency and had him fly me to Springfield. I rented a car there and drove to Blue Eye."

"Gun?" Ryan was suddenly very tired.

"My dad's old forty-four. I grew up with guns. My brothers and I could shoot before we could drive. I don't necessarily like them, but I know my way around them."

Ryan shook his head painfully. "My dad?"

Cass leaned in close to him. "He died on Saturday."

"What's today?"

"It's Monday night, about eight o'clock."

Ryan closed his eyes.

Tuesday morning, he woke up at a few minutes after 7:00, and there was Cass, reading the newspaper. A nurse was in the room, checking his IV lines.

"Good morning, Mr. Elder," she said.

He nodded.

"How's the pain this morning?" the nurse asked.

"Hurts like hell."

She smiled, a warm smile. "Welcome back to the land of the living."

A few minutes later, Faith Kelly came into the room and stood at the foot of his bed.

"Well," Kelly said, her voice still raspy, but growing stronger. "Glad to have you back with us."

"You look terrible."

"Flatterer." They smiled at each other.

"What happened to you?"

She explained, then said, "Clarke's under indictment for more charges than you can possibly imagine. Murder, conspiracy to commit murder, conspiracy to commit an act of terrorism, even a bunch of national security things for revealing classified information to Ross . . . um, Coleridge. Then there's attempted murder of a federal law enforcement officer, namely me. His lawyer's trying to arrange a plea bargain that would keep him in isolation when he gets to prison, away from the general prison population."

"Heard you got him where it hurts."

Kelly smiled, the bruise on the left side of her face knitting into a starlike shape.

"Remind me not to get you mad at me," Ryan said. "How bad am I?"

"Better let the doctors tell you. I will say this, though: lots of broken bones, though no internal damage. And your foot? Every single bone in your foot was broken, some of them in more than one place. Don't plan on running any marathons."

"My dad died." A statement, not a question.

Kelly nodded. "He'd lost a lot of blood and was already unconscious when SOG got to him. The bullet did a lot of damage, tore up his insides. They airlifted him here, but he never regained consciousness. He died the next morning." Kelly shuffled from one foot to the other. "Ryan, I want you to understand something. We didn't know your parents had aked the suicide. They fooled Department Thirty as well as everyone else."

"I know," Ryan said. "That's exactly what they wanted, and I guess they were pretty good at what they did. Where's Dad now?"

"He was taken to the county morgue, pending your decision on what you want to do."

"Where's my mother buried?"

"In the Blue Eye cemetery, the one just down the road from—"

"I know where it is." Ryan thought of all the flowers. His mother would like that. "I have one request."

"What?"

"I want their stones to have their real names on them. Whatever name my mother is buried under, I want it changed to the real one."

"That's fair." Kelly held up a file folder. "I have something here for you."

Ryan looked at her.

"Those two things you asked me to get for you." She patted the file and handed it to Cass. "Oh, by the way, I mentioned the lawn-mowing incident to Yorkton. He said he still has the note, and he's as impressed with you now as he was then. Those were his exact words. Also, about the information in there. . . ." She pointed to the folder.

"I know, I know, it's classified."

"No, that's not what I was going to say." She looked thoughtful for a moment, touching the bandage around her throat. "Maybe you should let them rest in peace." She looked as if she was going to say something else, then stopped. "I guess that's all I have to say."

"Thanks. I'll think about it. About Coleridge—"

"You both shot him at the same time, at almost exactly the same spot. One bullet from the front, one from the rear. It's impossible to tell which one killed him." She waited a moment, took a breath. "What will you do now?"

Ryan thought, Good question. Then he caught sight of Cass beside him. He swallowed.

"I think . . ." he said, stopped, started again. "There's a sick man in Cheyenne who needs someone to help take care of him. I've heard that it's easier being a caregiver if there are two people to split up the responsibilities." He looked at Cass. "Didn't I hear that somewhere?"

Cass nodded, her eyes glistening, unable to speak.

"Yeah, I thought I heard that somewhere. And maybe I could find some kids that I could treat sort of like honorary nieces and nephews."

"Maybe so," Cass whispered.

"And there's a classroom full of kids who need music on Friday mornings. I don't know much about Chopin, but maybe I could learn about that too."

Kelly smiled, and she thought she'd better get out of this room or she was going to cry too. "Sounds like you have it all planned out."

"Not really," Ryan said. "I'm making it up as I go. What about you, Deputy Kelly?"

"I still have a job, even though the U.S. Attorney's not sure whether to be glad we exposed Clarke or angry at the scandal and bad publicity. But I have a job. I think I'm going to take a few days off, though, and drive up to see my parents. I need to talk to my own father and maybe this time he'll talk to me too."

Ryan nodded. "Good idea. Talking to your father, I mean." He reached out and took Cass's hand.

Three weeks later, Cass drove the rented car through Blue Eye, turning at the store with the purple awning.

"The man who runs the store called your father after you stopped there," Cass said. "He and your dad had gotten to be friends, and when the old man saw someone who looked exactly like his friend Jim Ryan, he just had to let him know."

Ryan nodded without speaking and went back to the file. On the cover was stamped CLASSIFIED with the printed title: TRANSCRIPT OF INTERVIEW BETWEEN ARTHUR DORIAN, DEPT. 30, USDOJ, JAMES ALEXANDER BRICKENS, AND NATALIA ANASTASIA FERENCIK BRICKENS, JULY 27, 1976.

Ryan opened the file, then closed it again. Let them rest in peace, he thought.

Cass turned in at the gate to the Blue Eye cemetery and drove the car along the tiny gravel path toward the back. All around, the mountains seemed to shelter them. She stopped and helped Ryan out of the car.

Arms around each other, they buddy-walked to the graves. The markers were new and simple, no dates or phrases like "Beloved Mother and Father" carved into them. They were rose-colored, with only the names—James Alexander Brickens and Natalia Anastasia Brickens—carved in medium-size letters. Simple, like the cemetery itself.

Ryan looked around, feeling the quiet. A dog barked somewhere down the road. Cass put her arm around him, supporting him.

"Do you want me to start calling you David?" she asked.

Ryan thought of the birth certificate Kelly had brought him, the faded paper showing that one David James Brickens had been born in Bloomington, Indiana.

David James Brickens.

He thought of his father, bleeding in the barn just down the road, and the last thing he'd tried to say. Ryan thought he'd been trying to call him David, to call him just once by the name his parents had given him.

Who am I? he'd asked Kelly on the phone.

Who am I?

David Brickens. But David Brickens was a stranger. Now he knew the name, but he didn't know that person, could never know that person. David Brickens was just a baby boy who'd been born in Bloomington, Indiana, probably while his parents were on their way to somewhere else.

Ryan wiped his eyes with the back of his hand. The anger, his old companion, didn't seem to be anywhere he could find. Oh, it was still there, all right, like leftovers at the bottom of a pot. But when he'd awakened in the hospital with Cass sitting beside him, he'd felt something else. He had yet to figure out what it was, but he'd decided it was all right. Whatever it was, it was all right, after all.

Even though Ryan Elder didn't really exist, that was all he could be. Ryan Elder, a product of James and Natalia Brickens's guilt and Art Dorian's imagination.

He heard the dog barking and thought of Coleridge, coming for him. Thought of killing Coleridge, of the life he'd taken to save his own. He knew Cass dreamed about it. She thrashed and talked in her sleep, reaching toward him.

He looked at the stones again: JAMES ALEXANDER BRICKENS. NATALIA ANASTASIA BRICKENS.

David James Brickens.

Maybe David should have his own marker here, Ryan thought. The boy who never was.

He turned back to Cass. "No," he finally said. "Just stay with me."

"I will."

"I promise not to call you Alicia, if you promise not to call me David."

"Deal."

The dog barked again, way down the road, and a solitary bird—Ryan thought it might have been a grackle, but he wasn't sure—called from a tree somewhere nearby. His foot began to pain him again and his chest heaved. Breathing was still occasionally difficult. He leaned against Cass, and together they began to make their way back toward the car.